THE

CLUES

THE MAZE OF BONES

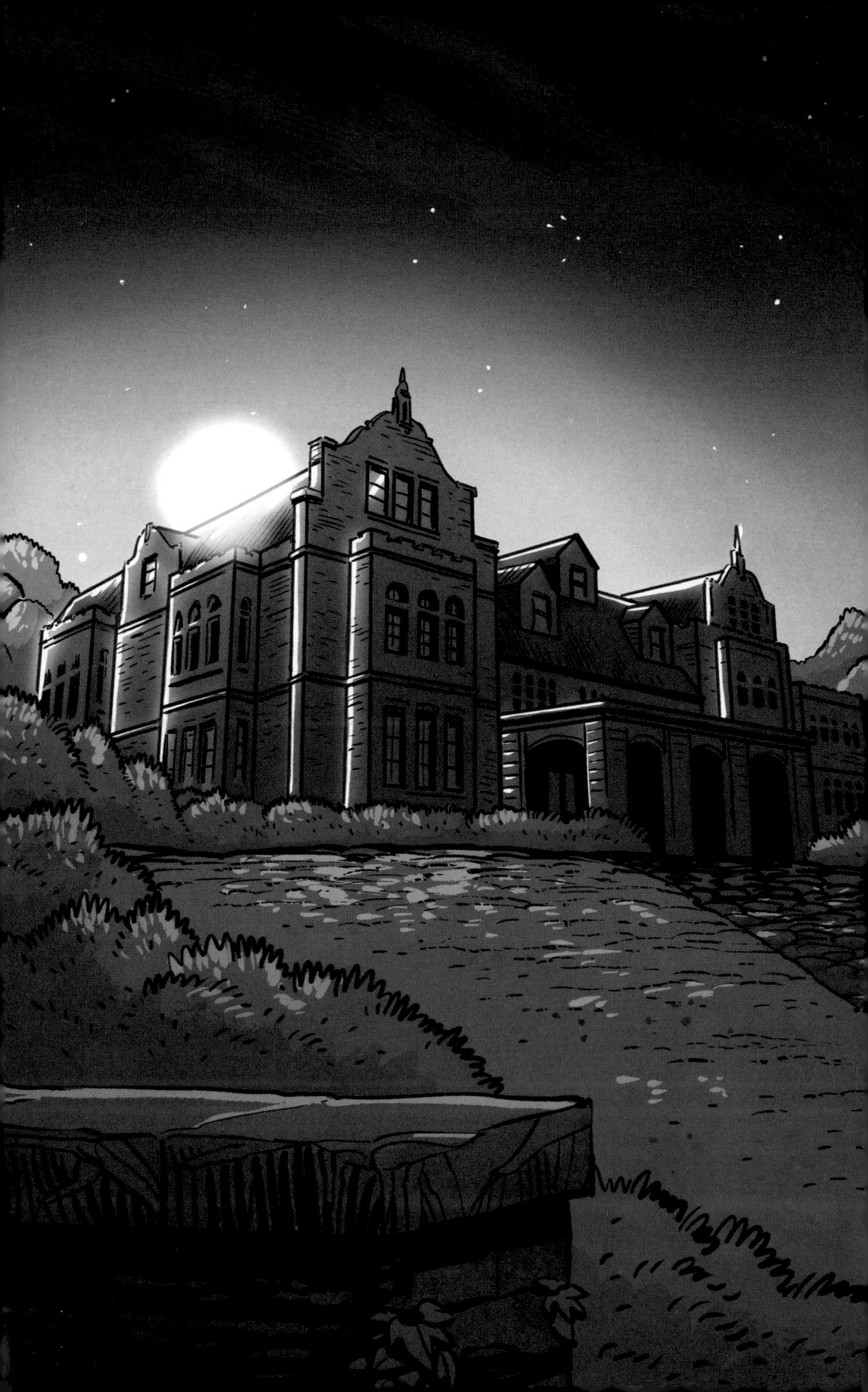

THE 39 CLUES

THE MAZE OF BONES
BY RICK RIORDAN

A GRAPHIC NOVEL BY
ETHAN YOUNG

WITH COLOR BY GEORGE WILLAMS

graphix

AN IMPRINT OF

■SCHOLASTIC

All rights reserved. Published by Graphix, an imprint of
Scholastic Inc., **Publishers since 1920**. SCHOLASTIC, GRAPHIX,
and associated logos are trademarks and/or registered
trademarks of Scholastic Inc.

The publisher does not have any control over and does not assume any
responsibility for author or third-party websites or their content.

Library of Congress Control Number: 2022944706

ISBN 978-1-338-80337-2 (hardcover)
ISBN 978-1-338-80336-5 (paperback)

10 9 8 7 6 5 4 3 2   23 24 25 26 27

Printed in China   62
First edition, April 2023

Edited by Mallory Kass
Lettering by Sara Linsley
Book design by Carina Taylor
Creative Director: Phil Falco
Publisher: David Saylor

For Haley and Patrick,
who accepted the challenge.
—RR

For all the adventure seekers out there.
—EY

ONE

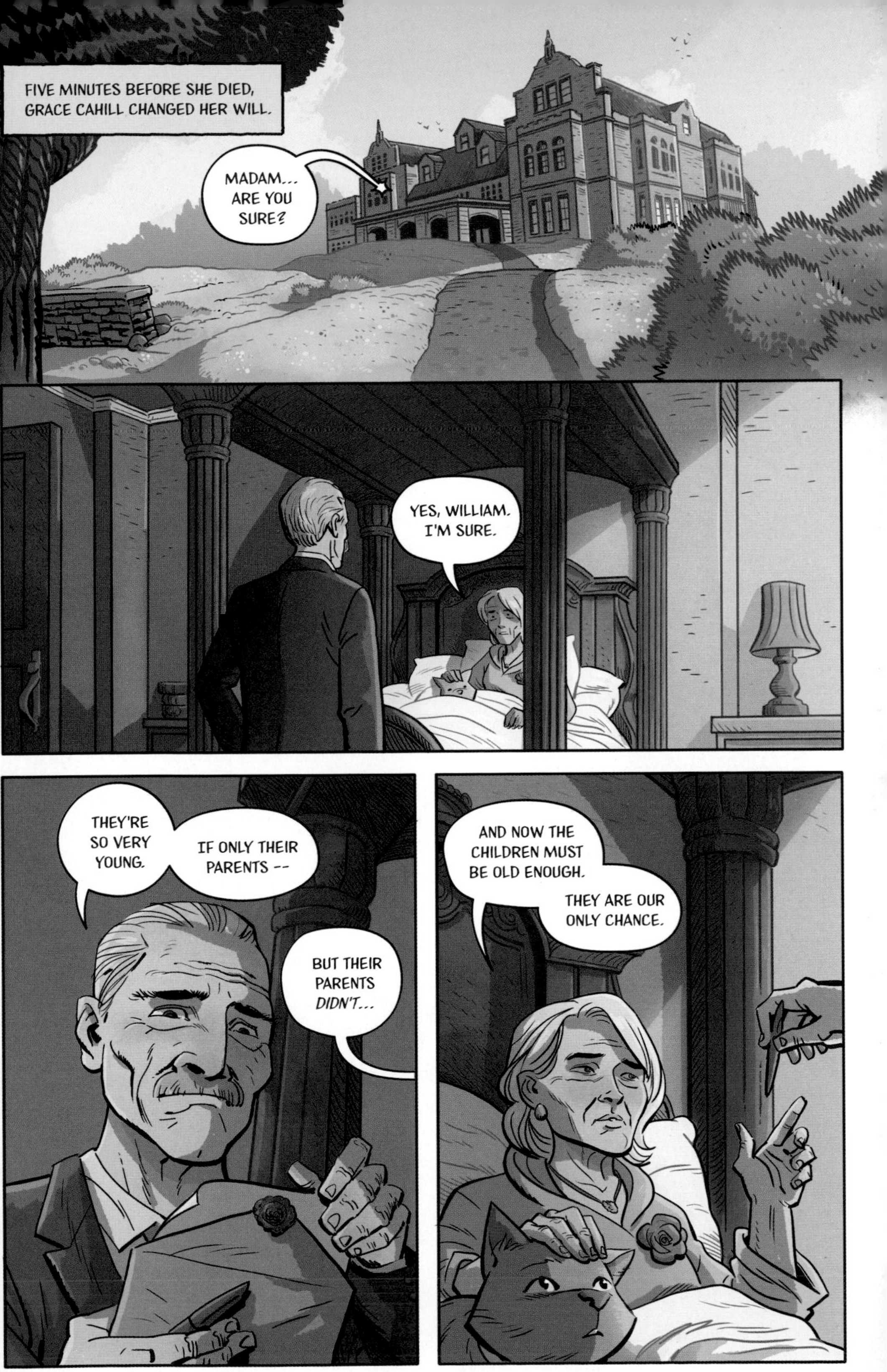
FIVE MINUTES BEFORE SHE DIED, GRACE CAHILL CHANGED HER WILL.
MADAM... ARE YOU SURE?
YES, WILLIAM. I'M SURE.
THEY'RE SO VERY YOUNG.
IF ONLY THEIR PARENTS --
BUT THEIR PARENTS *DIDN'T*...
AND NOW THE CHILDREN MUST BE OLD ENOUGH.
THEY ARE OUR ONLY CHANCE.

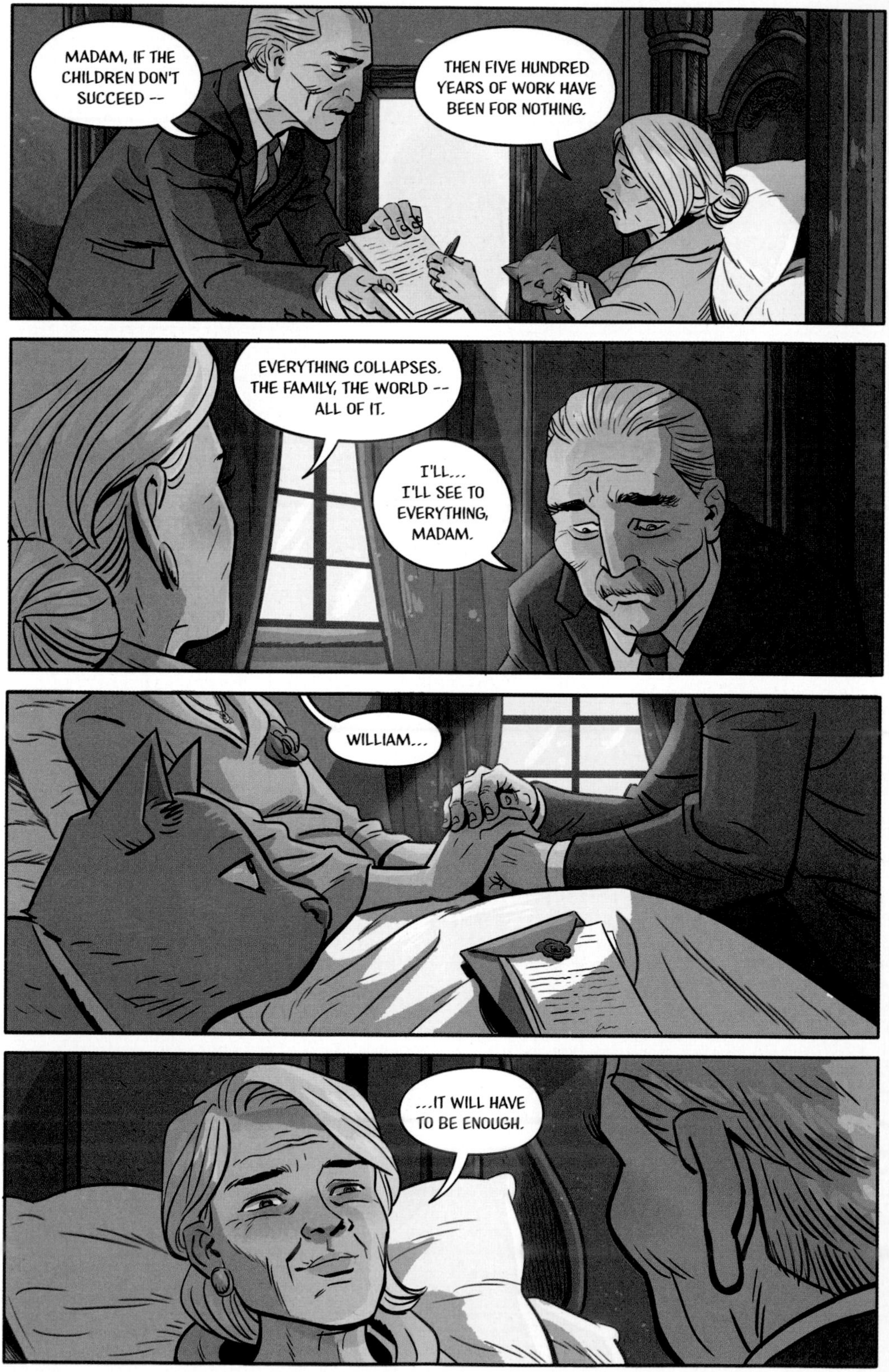
MADAM, IF THE CHILDREN DON'T SUCCEED --
THEN FIVE HUNDRED YEARS OF WORK HAVE BEEN FOR NOTHING.
EVERYTHING COLLAPSES. THE FAMILY, THE WORLD -- ALL OF IT.
I'LL... I'LL SEE TO EVERYTHING, MADAM.
WILLIAM...
...IT WILL HAVE TO BE ENOUGH.

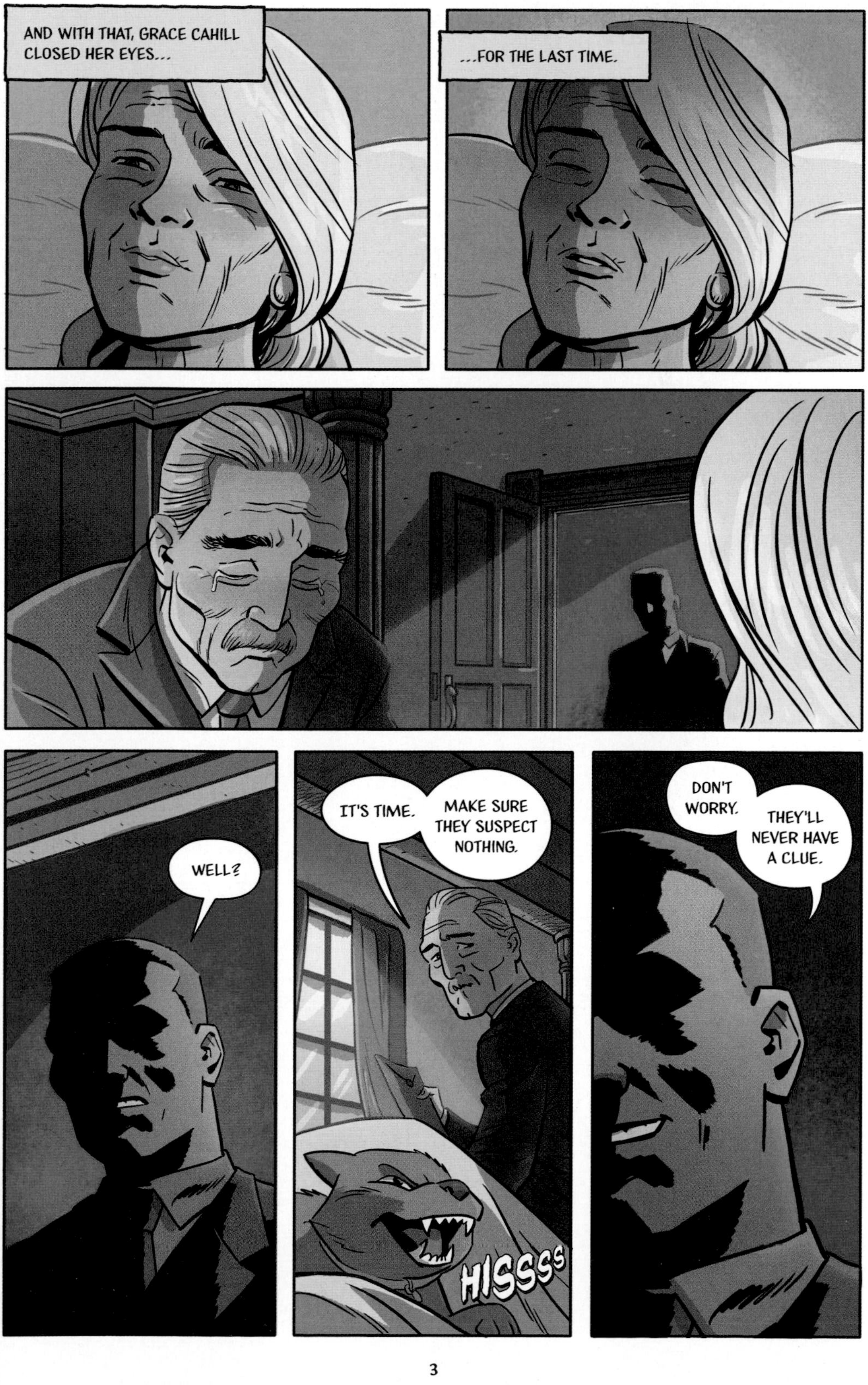
AND WITH THAT, GRACE CAHILL CLOSED HER EYES...
...FOR THE LAST TIME.
WELL?
IT'S TIME.
MAKE SURE THEY SUSPECT NOTHING.
HISSSS
DON'T WORRY.
THEY'LL NEVER HAVE A CLUE.

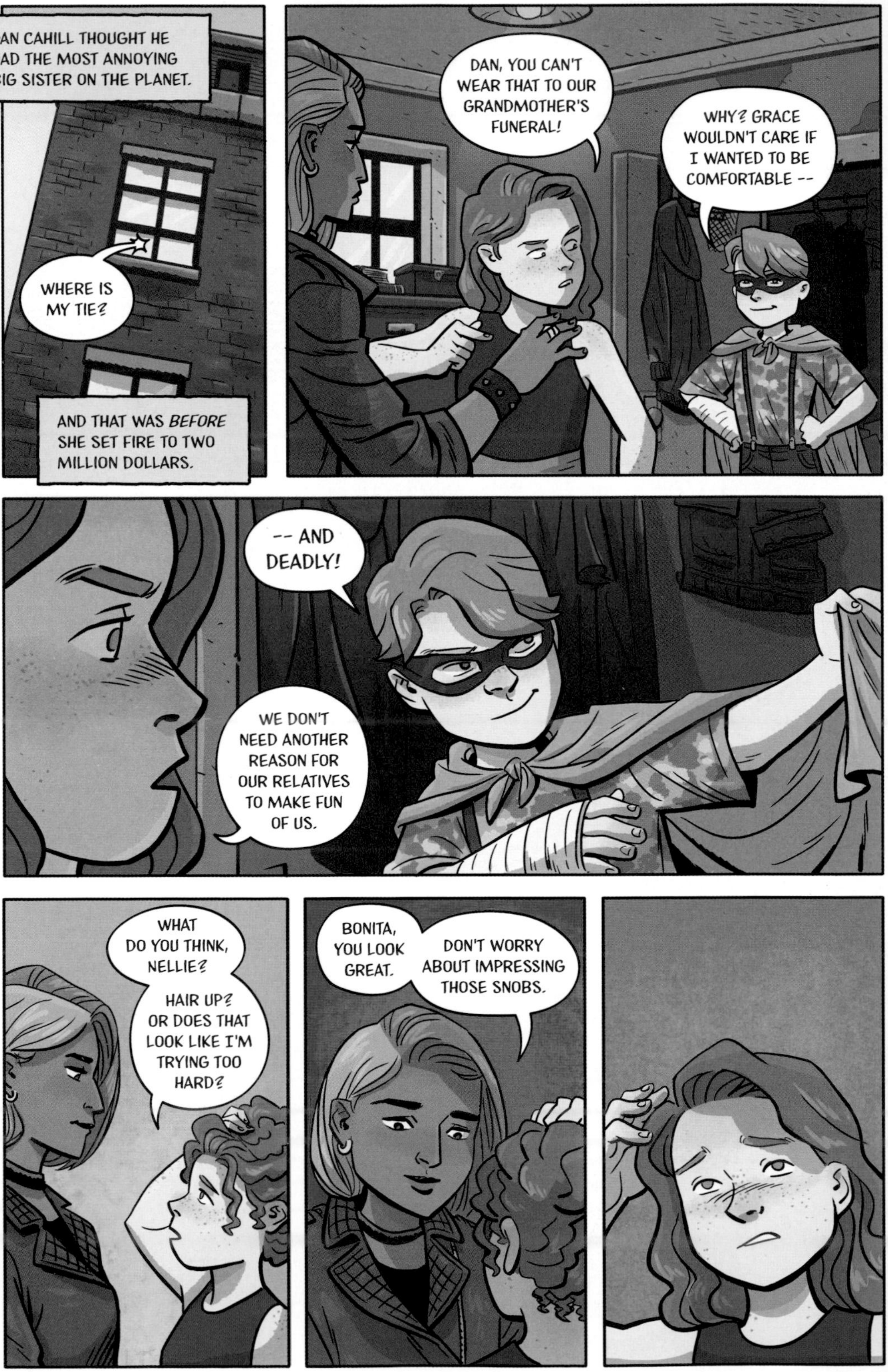
DAN CAHILL THOUGHT HE HAD THE MOST ANNOYING BIG SISTER ON THE PLANET.
WHERE IS MY TIE?
AND THAT WAS *BEFORE* SHE SET FIRE TO TWO MILLION DOLLARS.
DAN, YOU CAN'T WEAR THAT TO OUR GRANDMOTHER'S FUNERAL!
WHY? GRACE WOULDN'T CARE IF I WANTED TO BE COMFORTABLE --
-- AND DEADLY!
WE DON'T NEED ANOTHER REASON FOR OUR RELATIVES TO MAKE FUN OF US.
WHAT DO YOU THINK, NELLIE?
HAIR UP? OR DOES THAT LOOK LIKE I'M TRYING TOO HARD?
BONITA, YOU LOOK GREAT.
DON'T WORRY ABOUT IMPRESSING THOSE SNOBS.

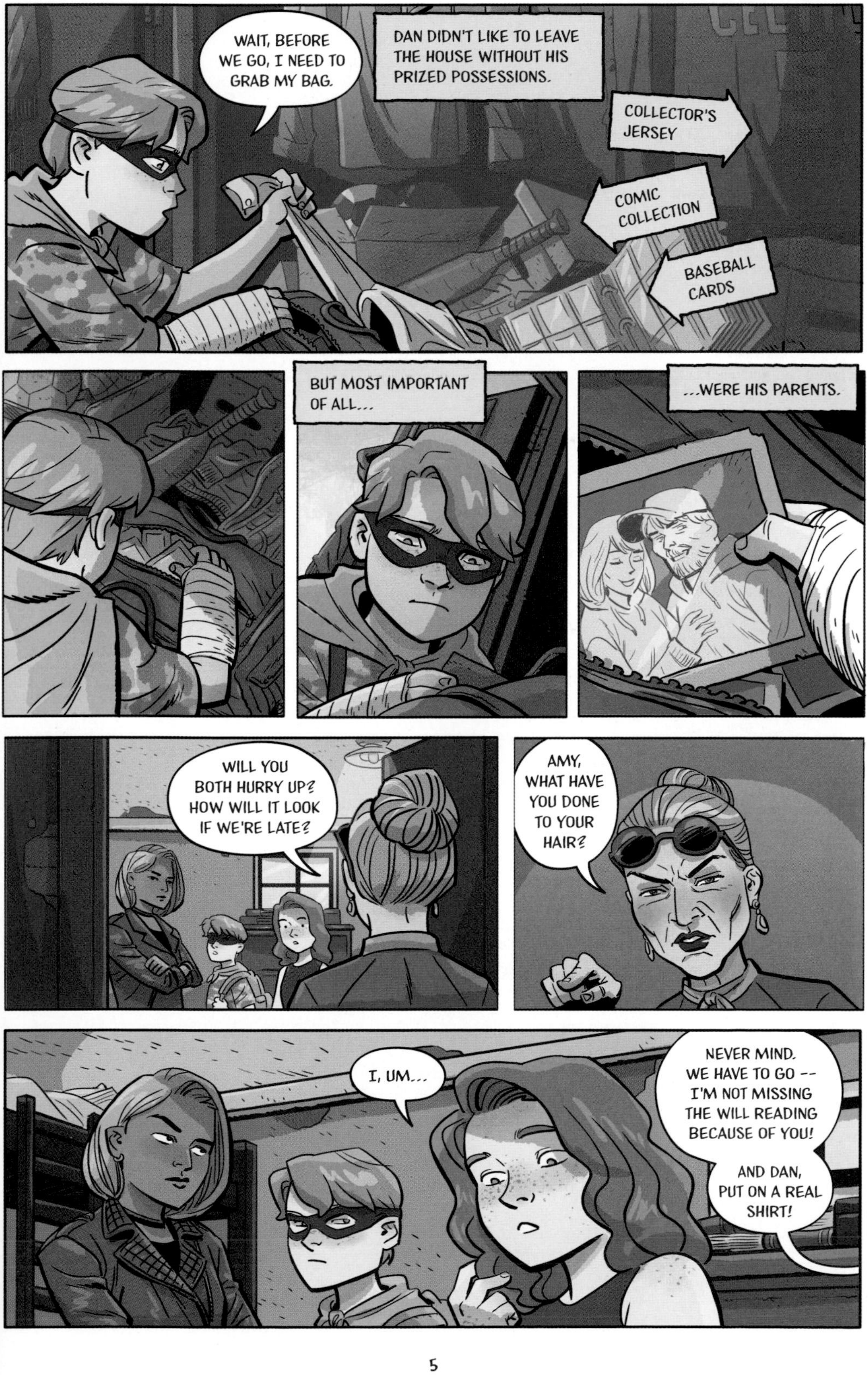

WAIT, BEFORE WE GO, I NEED TO GRAB MY BAG.
DAN DIDN'T LIKE TO LEAVE THE HOUSE WITHOUT HIS PRIZED POSSESSIONS.
COLLECTOR'S JERSEY
COMIC COLLECTION
BASEBALL CARDS
BUT MOST IMPORTANT OF ALL...
...WERE HIS PARENTS.
WILL YOU BOTH HURRY UP? HOW WILL IT LOOK IF WE'RE LATE?
AMY, WHAT HAVE YOU DONE TO YOUR HAIR?
I, UM...
NEVER MIND. WE HAVE TO GO -- I'M NOT MISSING THE WILL READING BECAUSE OF YOU!
AND DAN, PUT ON A REAL SHIRT!

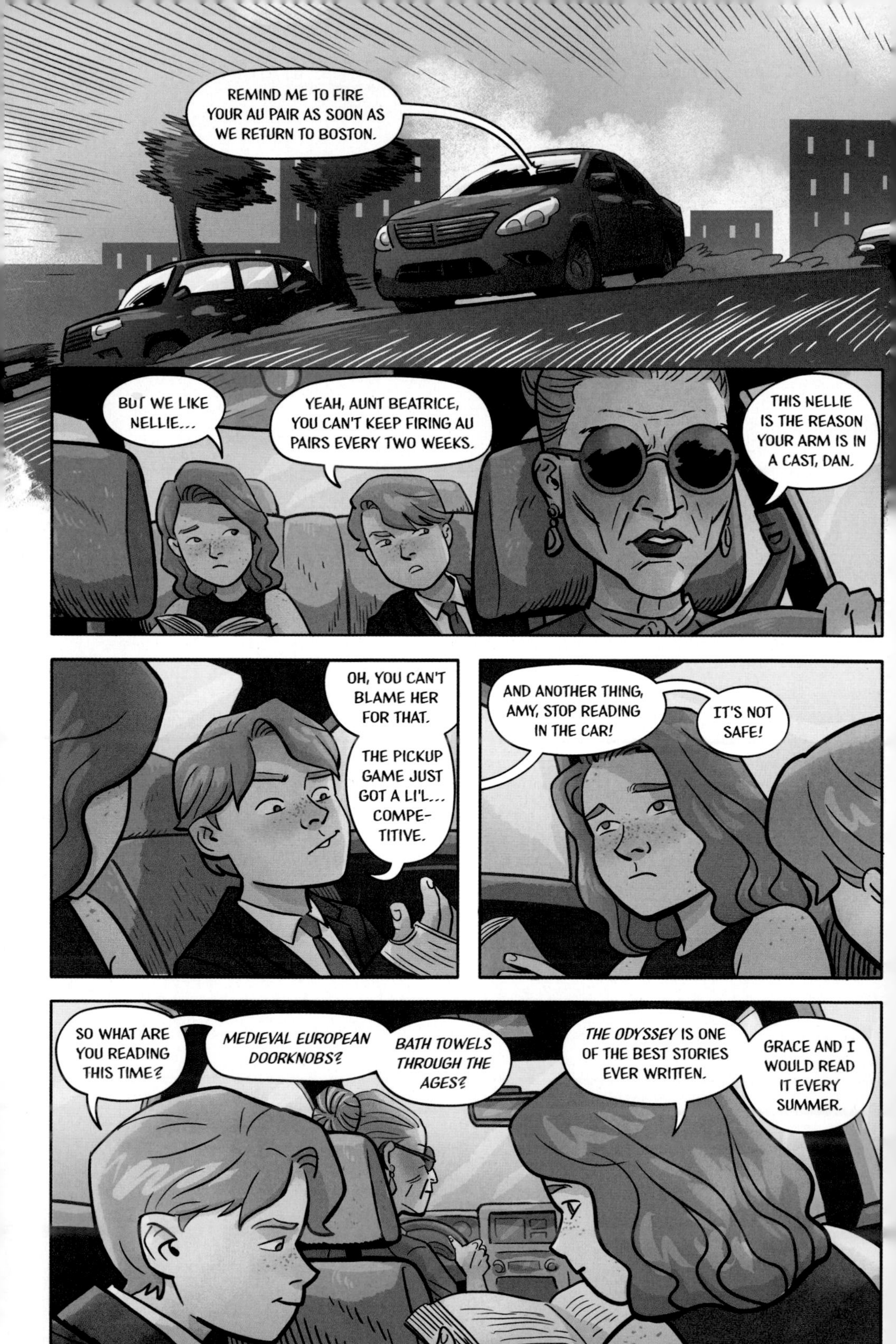
REMIND ME TO FIRE YOUR AU PAIR AS SOON AS WE RETURN TO BOSTON.
BUT WE LIKE NELLIE...
YEAH, AUNT BEATRICE, YOU CAN'T KEEP FIRING AU PAIRS EVERY TWO WEEKS.
THIS NELLIE IS THE REASON YOUR ARM IS IN A CAST, DAN.
OH, YOU CAN'T BLAME HER FOR THAT.
THE PICKUP GAME JUST GOT A LI'L... COMPETITIVE.
AND ANOTHER THING, AMY, STOP READING IN THE CAR!
IT'S NOT SAFE!
SO WHAT ARE YOU READING THIS TIME?
MEDIEVAL EUROPEAN DOORKNOBS?
BATH TOWELS THROUGH THE AGES?
THE ODYSSEY IS ONE OF THE BEST STORIES EVER WRITTEN.
GRACE AND I WOULD READ IT EVERY SUMMER.

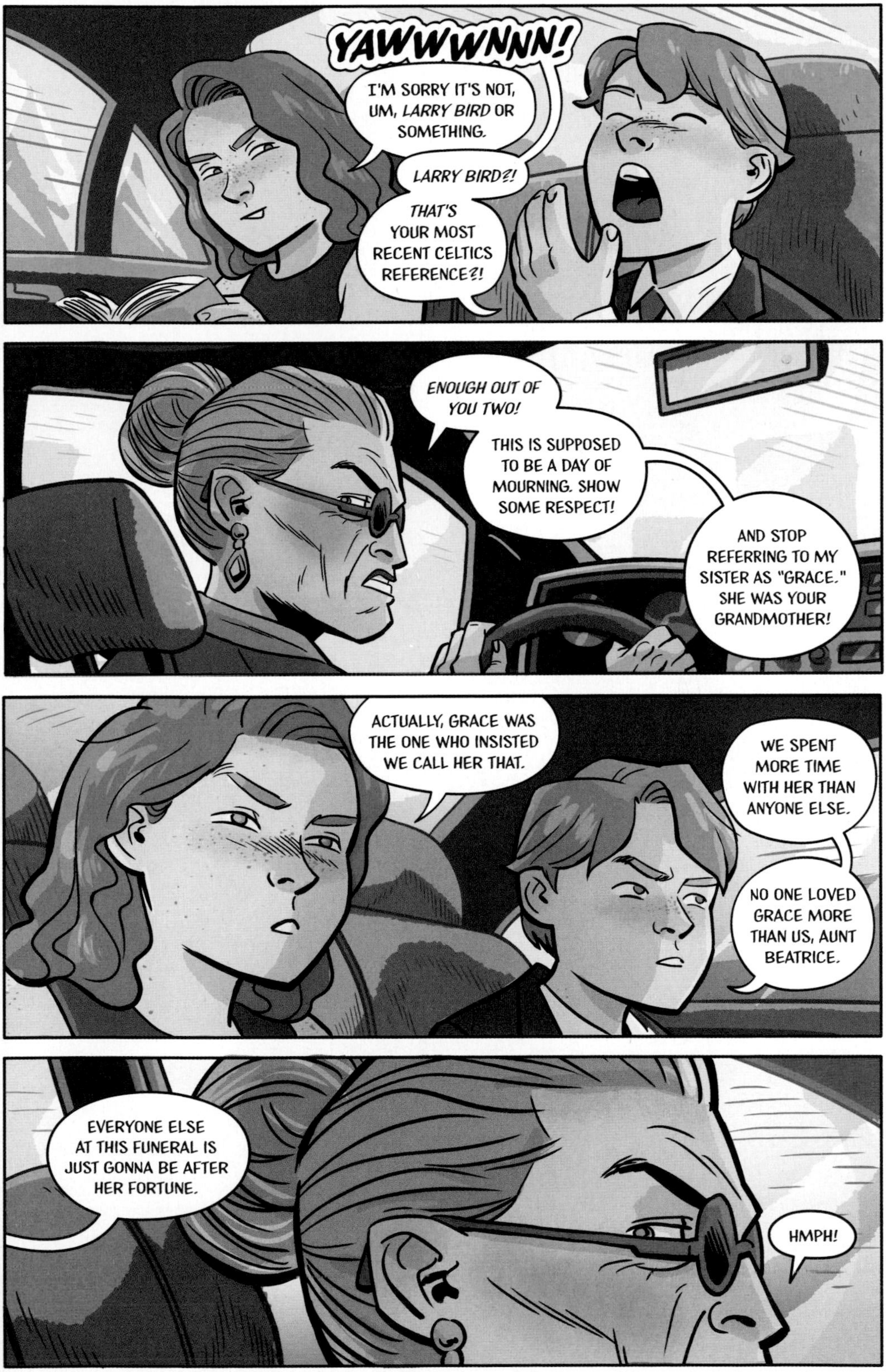
YAWWWNNN!
I'M SORRY IT'S NOT, UM, *LARRY BIRD* OR SOMETHING.
LARRY BIRD?!
THAT'S YOUR MOST RECENT CELTICS REFERENCE?!
ENOUGH OUT OF YOU TWO!
THIS IS SUPPOSED TO BE A DAY OF MOURNING. SHOW SOME RESPECT!
AND STOP REFERRING TO MY SISTER AS "GRACE." SHE WAS YOUR GRANDMOTHER!
ACTUALLY, GRACE WAS THE ONE WHO INSISTED WE CALL HER THAT.
WE SPENT MORE TIME WITH HER THAN ANYONE ELSE.
NO ONE LOVED GRACE MORE THAN US, AUNT BEATRICE.
EVERYONE ELSE AT THIS FUNERAL IS JUST GONNA BE AFTER HER FORTUNE.
HMPH!

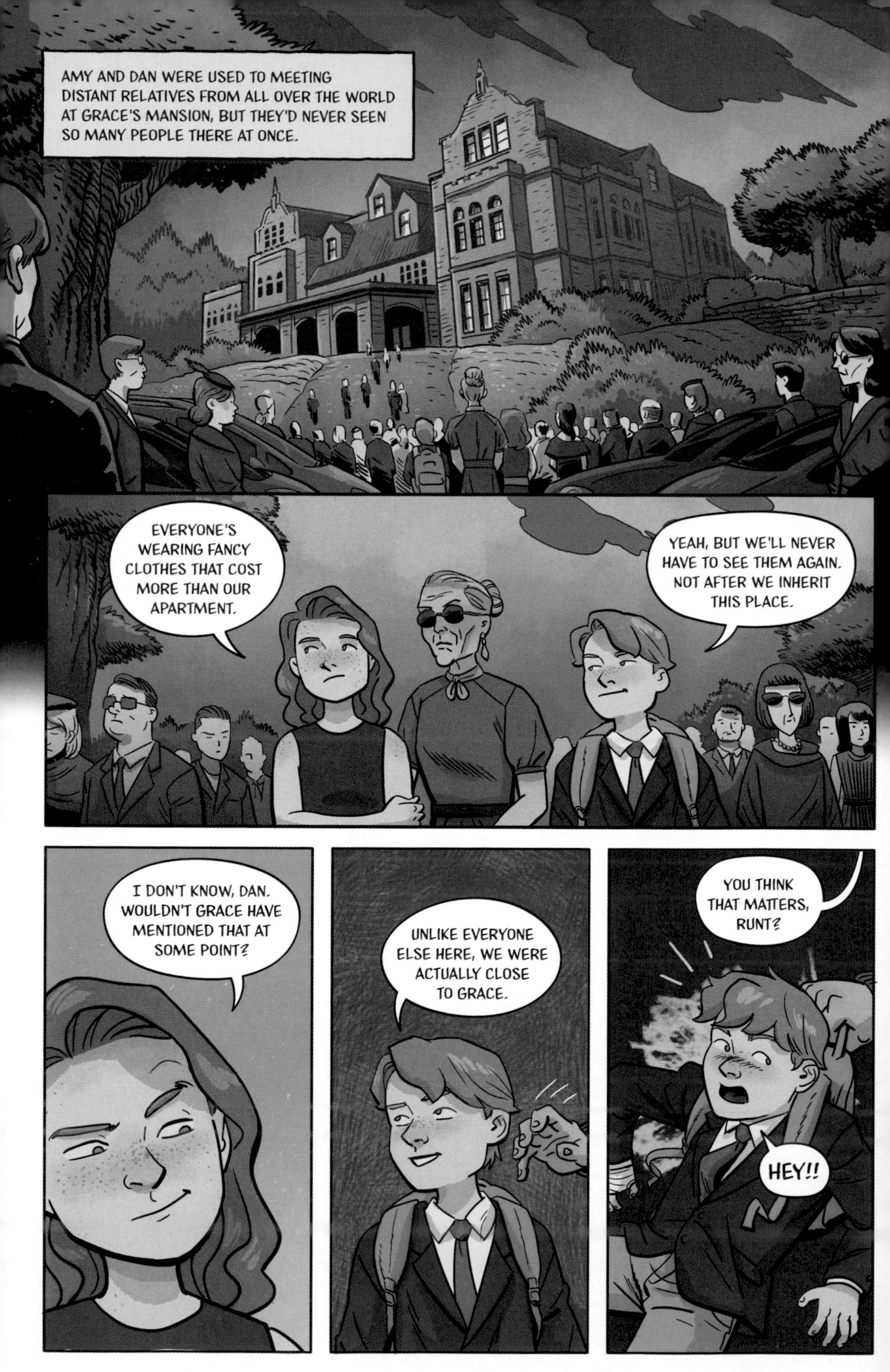
AMY AND DAN WERE USED TO MEETING DISTANT RELATIVES FROM ALL OVER THE WORLD AT GRACE'S MANSION, BUT THEY'D NEVER SEEN SO MANY PEOPLE THERE AT ONCE.
EVERYONE'S WEARING FANCY CLOTHES THAT COST MORE THAN OUR APARTMENT.
YEAH, BUT WE'LL NEVER HAVE TO SEE THEM AGAIN. NOT AFTER WE INHERIT THIS PLACE.
I DON'T KNOW, DAN. WOULDN'T GRACE HAVE MENTIONED THAT AT SOME POINT?
UNLIKE EVERYONE ELSE HERE, WE WERE ACTUALLY CLOSE TO GRACE.
YOU THINK THAT MATTERS, RUNT?
HEY!!

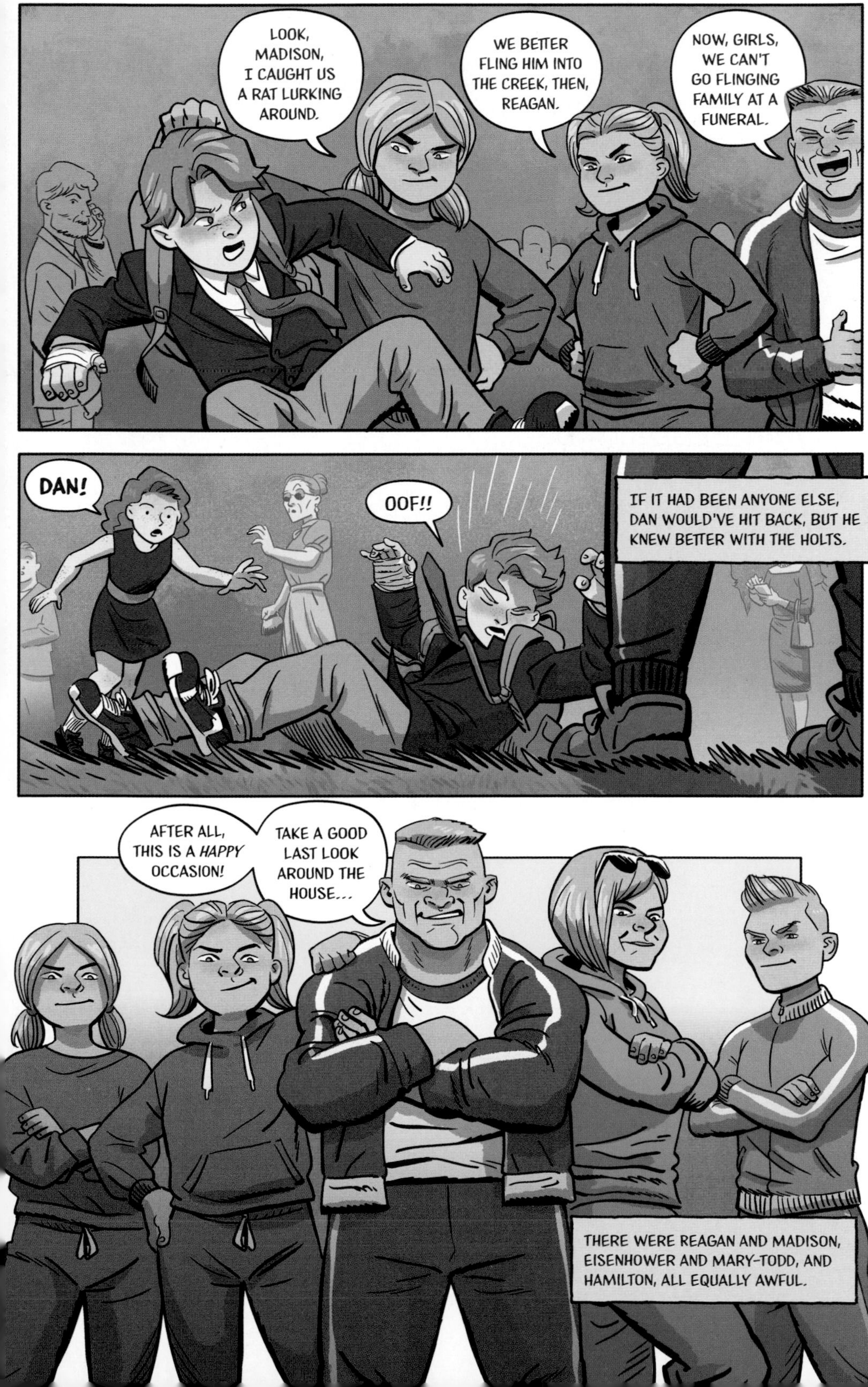
LOOK, MADISON, I CAUGHT US A RAT LURKING AROUND.
WE BETTER FLING HIM INTO THE CREEK, THEN, REAGAN.
NOW, GIRLS, WE CAN'T GO FLINGING FAMILY AT A FUNERAL.
DAN!
OOF!!
IF IT HAD BEEN ANYONE ELSE, DAN WOULD'VE HIT BACK, BUT HE KNEW BETTER WITH THE HOLTS.
AFTER ALL, THIS IS A *HAPPY* OCCASION!
TAKE A GOOD LAST LOOK AROUND THE HOUSE...
THERE WERE REAGAN AND MADISON, EISENHOWER AND MARY-TODD, AND HAMILTON, ALL EQUALLY AWFUL.

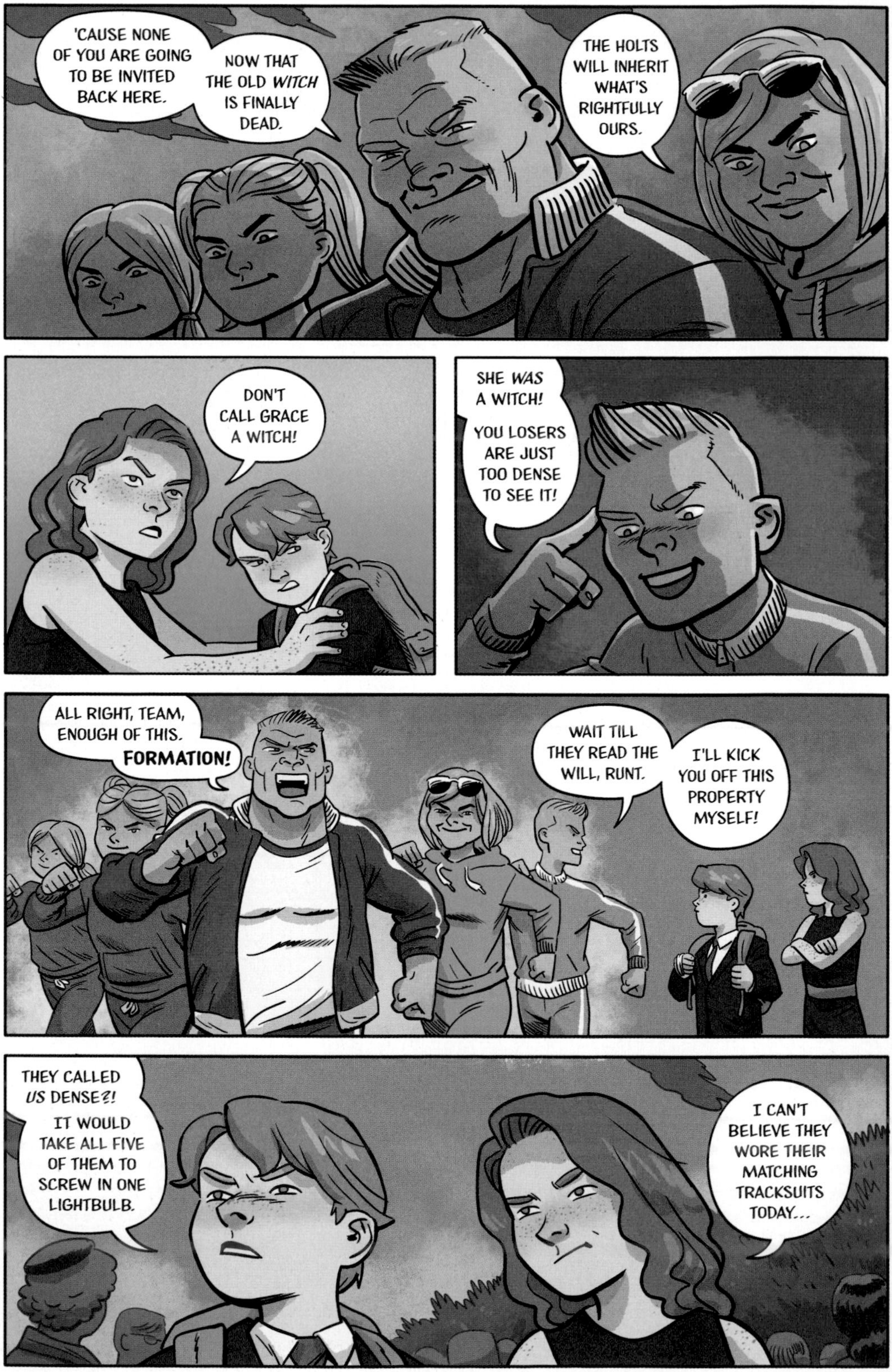
'CAUSE NONE OF YOU ARE GOING TO BE INVITED BACK HERE.
NOW THAT THE OLD *WITCH* IS FINALLY DEAD.
THE HOLTS WILL INHERIT WHAT'S RIGHTFULLY OURS.
DON'T CALL GRACE A WITCH!
SHE *WAS* A WITCH!
YOU LOSERS ARE JUST TOO DENSE TO SEE IT!
ALL RIGHT, TEAM, ENOUGH OF THIS. **FORMATION!**
WAIT TILL THEY READ THE WILL, RUNT.
I'LL KICK YOU OFF THIS PROPERTY MYSELF!
THEY CALLED *US* DENSE?!
IT WOULD TAKE ALL FIVE OF THEM TO SCREW IN ONE LIGHTBULB.
I CAN'T BELIEVE THEY WORE THEIR MATCHING TRACKSUITS TODAY...

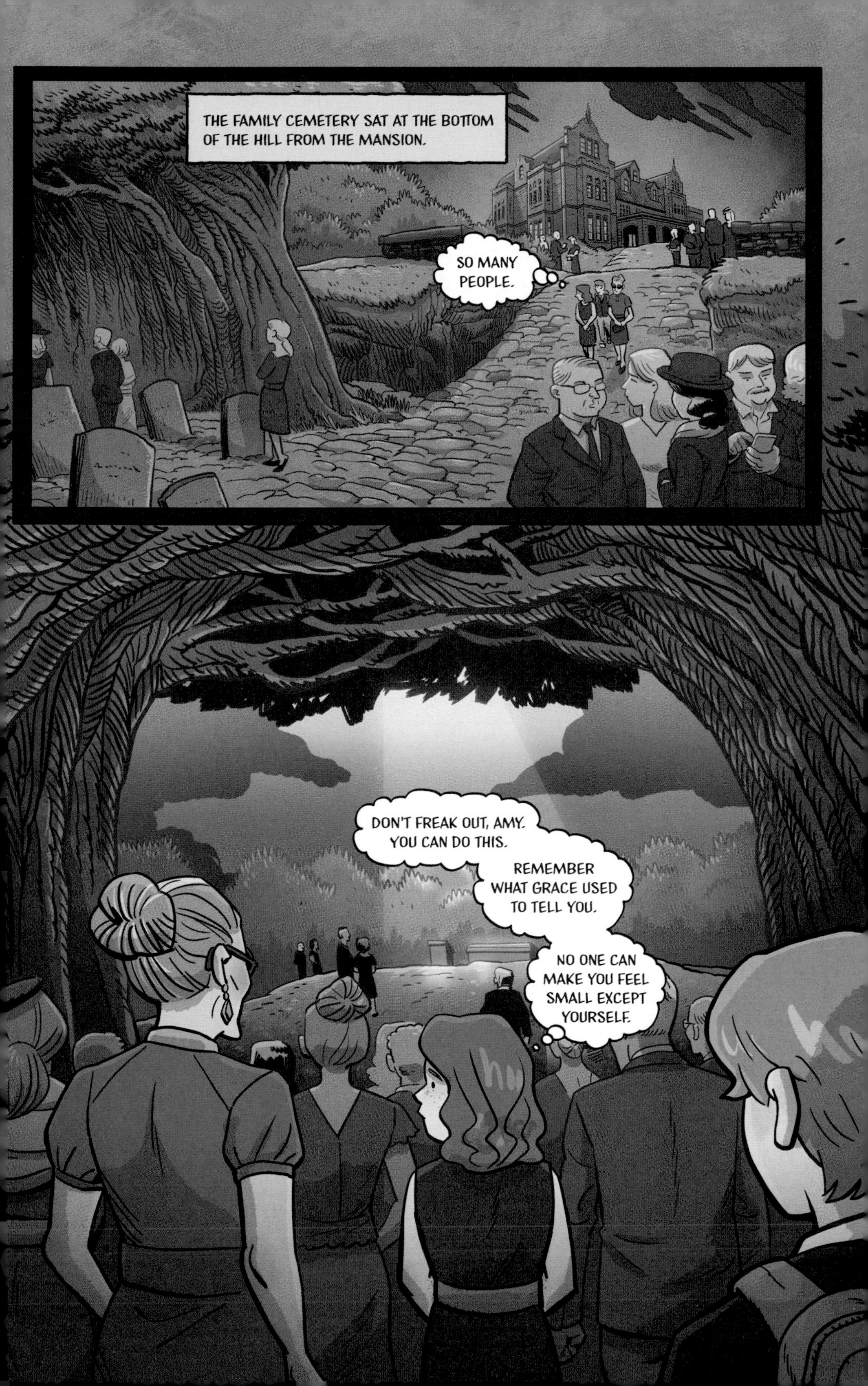
THE FAMILY CEMETERY SAT AT THE BOTTOM OF THE HILL FROM THE MANSION.
SO MANY PEOPLE.
DON'T FREAK OUT, AMY. YOU CAN DO THIS.
REMEMBER WHAT GRACE USED TO TELL YOU.
NO ONE CAN MAKE YOU FEEL SMALL EXCEPT YOURSELF.

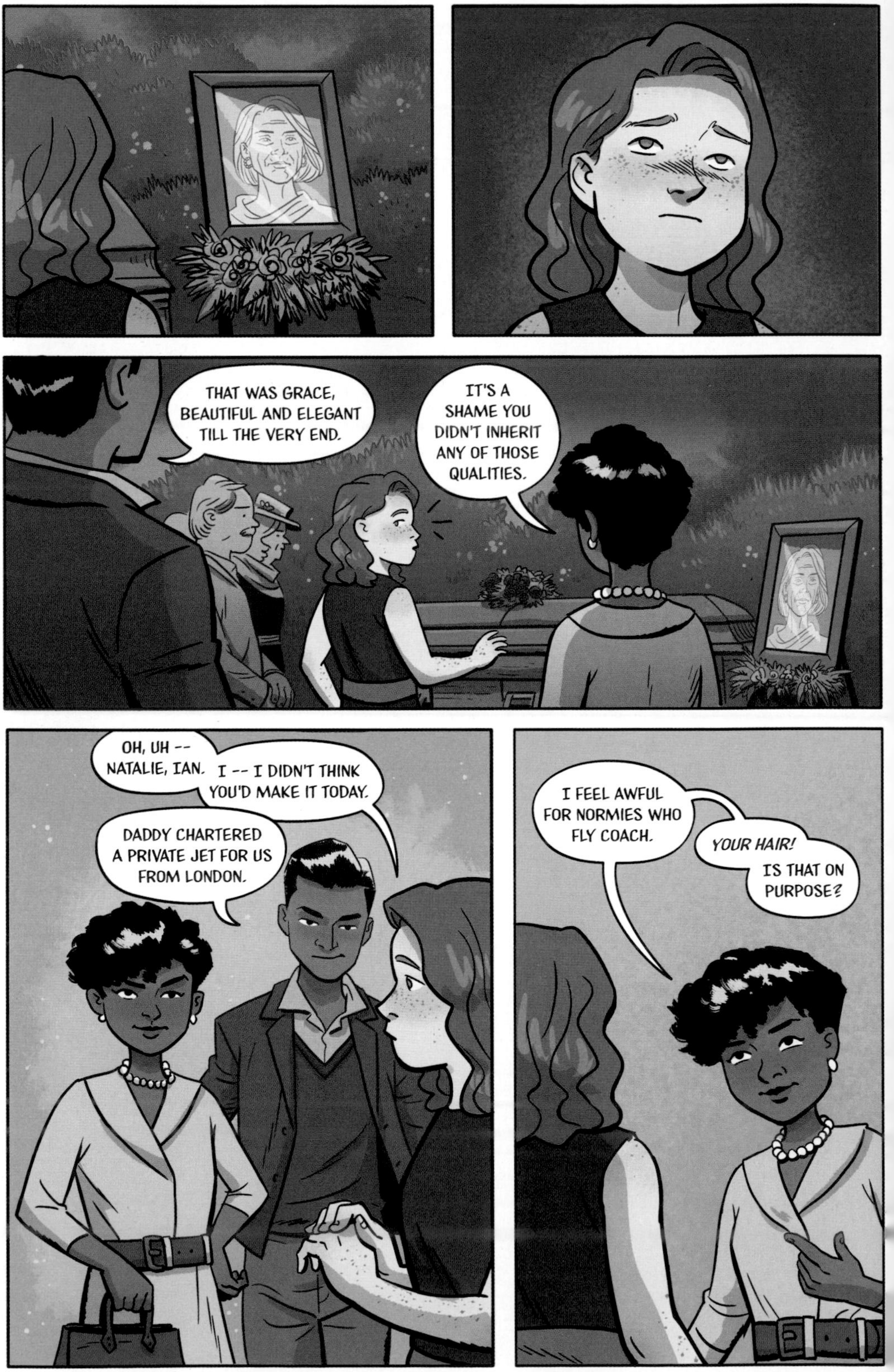
THAT WAS GRACE, BEAUTIFUL AND ELEGANT TILL THE VERY END.
IT'S A SHAME YOU DIDN'T INHERIT ANY OF THOSE QUALITIES.
OH, UH -- NATALIE, IAN.
I -- I DIDN'T THINK YOU'D MAKE IT TODAY.
DADDY CHARTERED A PRIVATE JET FOR US FROM LONDON.
I FEEL AWFUL FOR NORMIES WHO FLY COACH.
YOUR HAIR!
IS THAT ON PURPOSE?

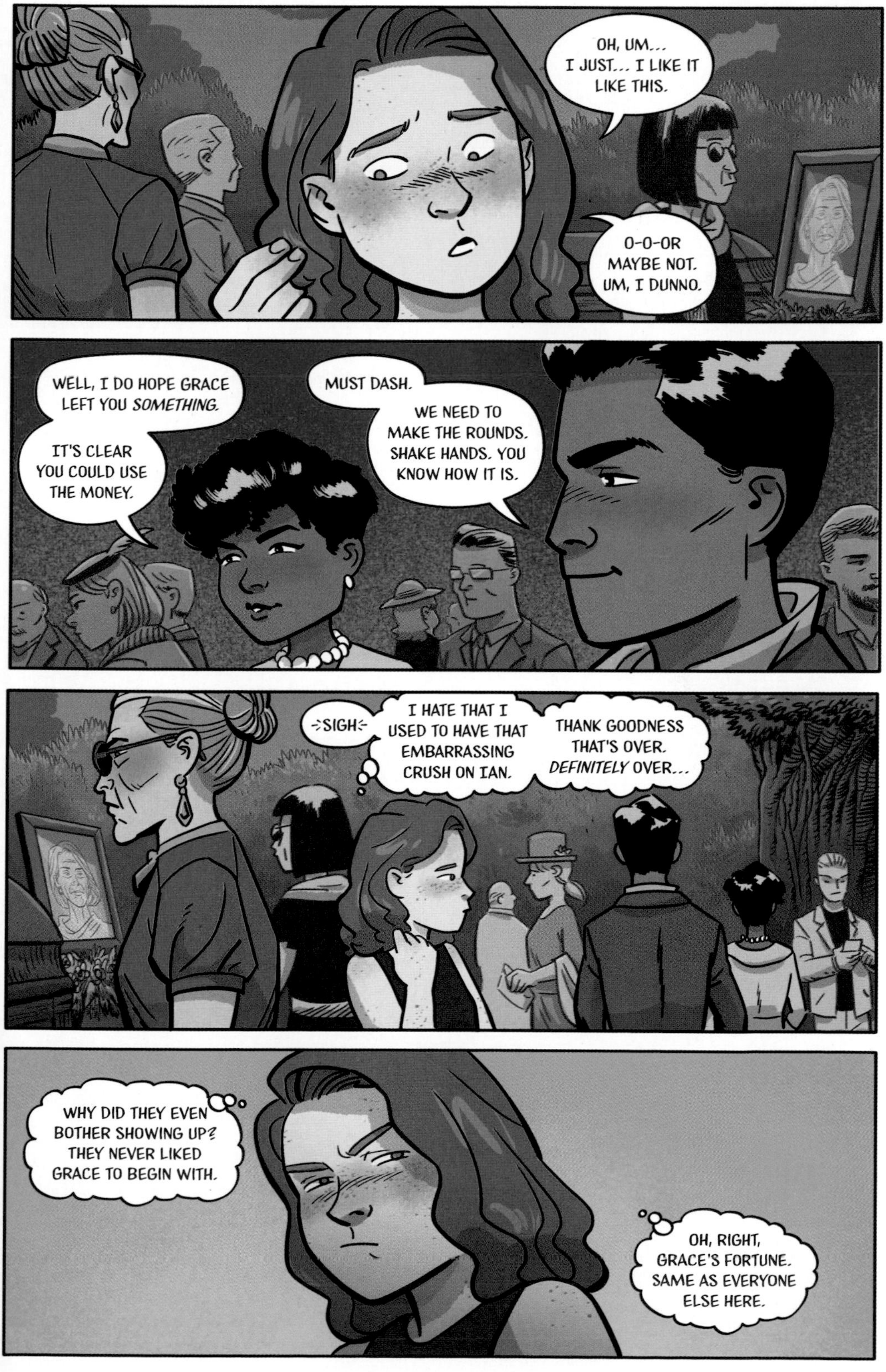
OH, UM... I JUST... I LIKE IT LIKE THIS.
O-O-OR MAYBE NOT. UM, I DUNNO.
WELL, I DO HOPE GRACE LEFT YOU *SOMETHING.*
IT'S CLEAR YOU COULD USE THE MONEY.
MUST DASH.
WE NEED TO MAKE THE ROUNDS. SHAKE HANDS. YOU KNOW HOW IT IS.
SIGH
I HATE THAT I USED TO HAVE THAT EMBARRASSING CRUSH ON IAN.
THANK GOODNESS THAT'S OVER. *DEFINITELY* OVER...
WHY DID THEY EVEN BOTHER SHOWING UP? THEY NEVER LIKED GRACE TO BEGIN WITH.
OH, RIGHT, GRACE'S FORTUNE. SAME AS EVERYONE ELSE HERE.

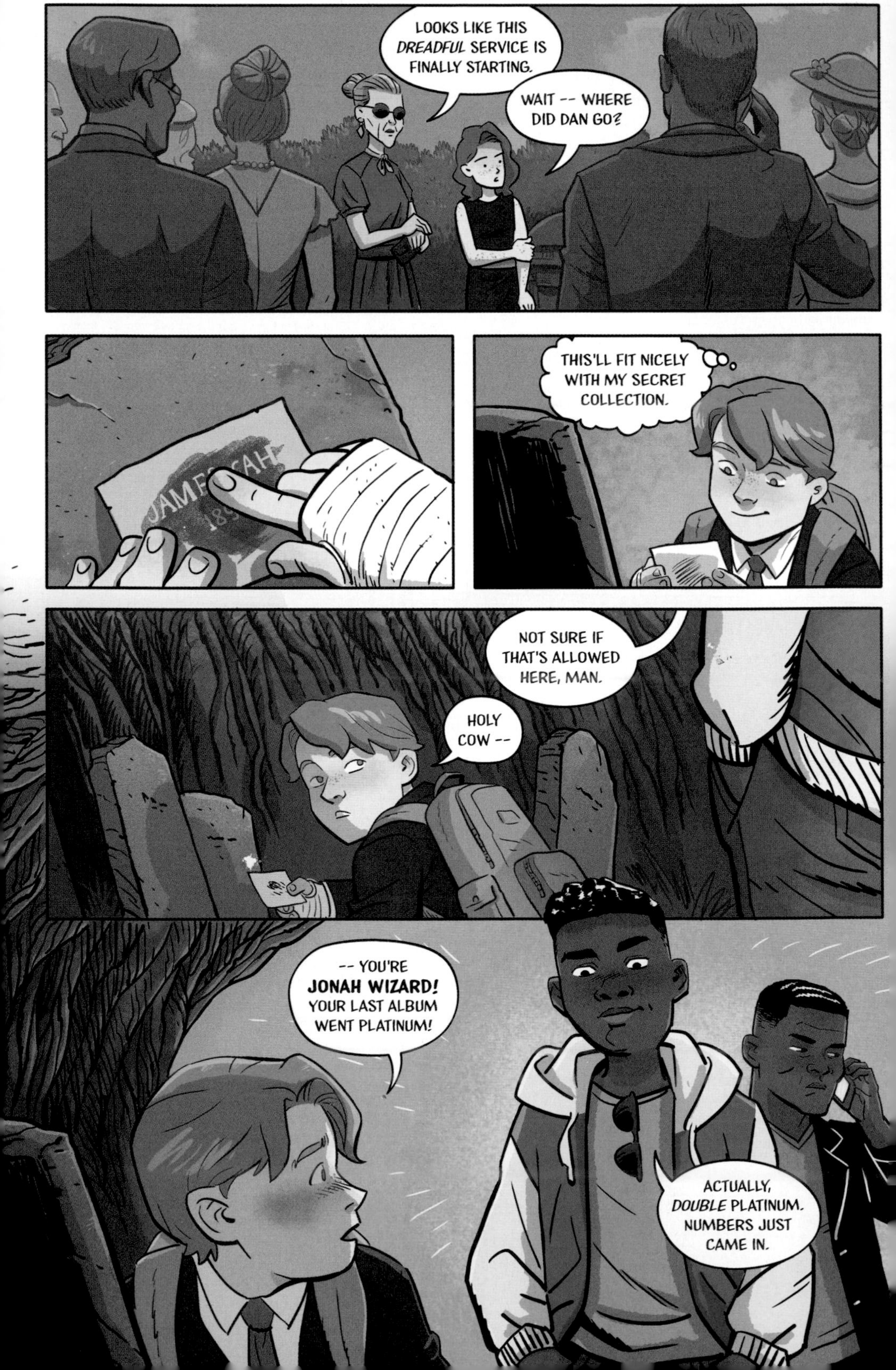
LOOKS LIKE THIS *DREADFUL* SERVICE IS FINALLY STARTING.
WAIT -- WHERE DID DAN GO?
THIS'LL FIT NICELY WITH MY SECRET COLLECTION.
NOT SURE IF THAT'S ALLOWED HERE, MAN.
HOLY COW --
-- YOU'RE **JONAH WIZARD!** YOUR LAST ALBUM WENT PLATINUM!
ACTUALLY, *DOUBLE* PLATINUM. NUMBERS JUST CAME IN.

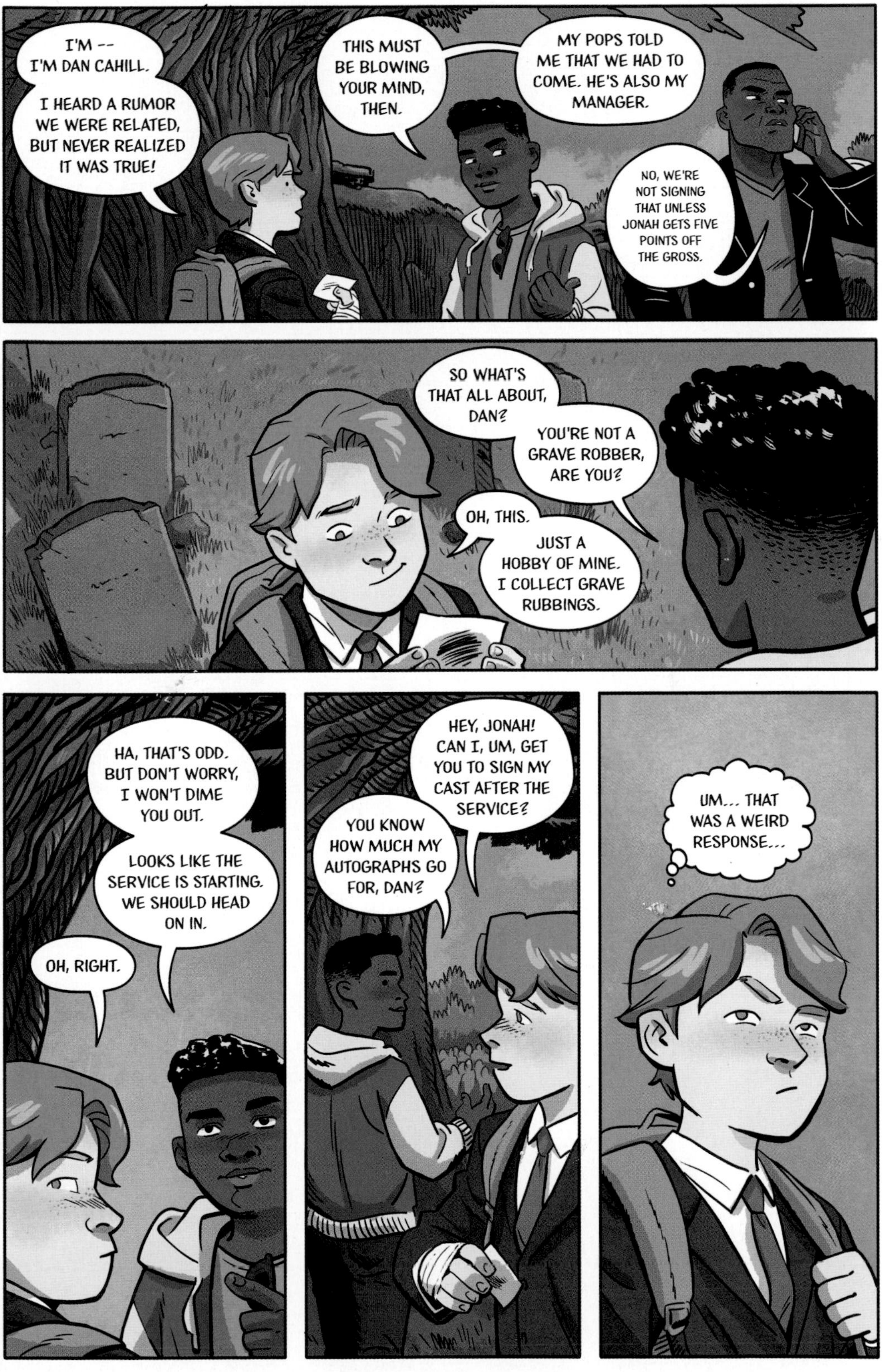
I'M -- I'M DAN CAHILL.
I HEARD A RUMOR WE WERE RELATED, BUT NEVER REALIZED IT WAS TRUE!
THIS MUST BE BLOWING YOUR MIND, THEN.
MY POPS TOLD ME THAT WE HAD TO COME. HE'S ALSO MY MANAGER.
NO, WE'RE NOT SIGNING THAT UNLESS JONAH GETS FIVE POINTS OFF THE GROSS.
SO WHAT'S THAT ALL ABOUT, DAN?
YOU'RE NOT A GRAVE ROBBER, ARE YOU?
OH, THIS.
JUST A HOBBY OF MINE. I COLLECT GRAVE RUBBINGS.
HA, THAT'S ODD. BUT DON'T WORRY, I WON'T DIME YOU OUT.
LOOKS LIKE THE SERVICE IS STARTING. WE SHOULD HEAD ON IN.
OH, RIGHT.
HEY, JONAH! CAN I, UM, GET YOU TO SIGN MY CAST AFTER THE SERVICE?
YOU KNOW HOW MUCH MY AUTOGRAPHS GO FOR, DAN?
UM... THAT WAS A WEIRD RESPONSE...

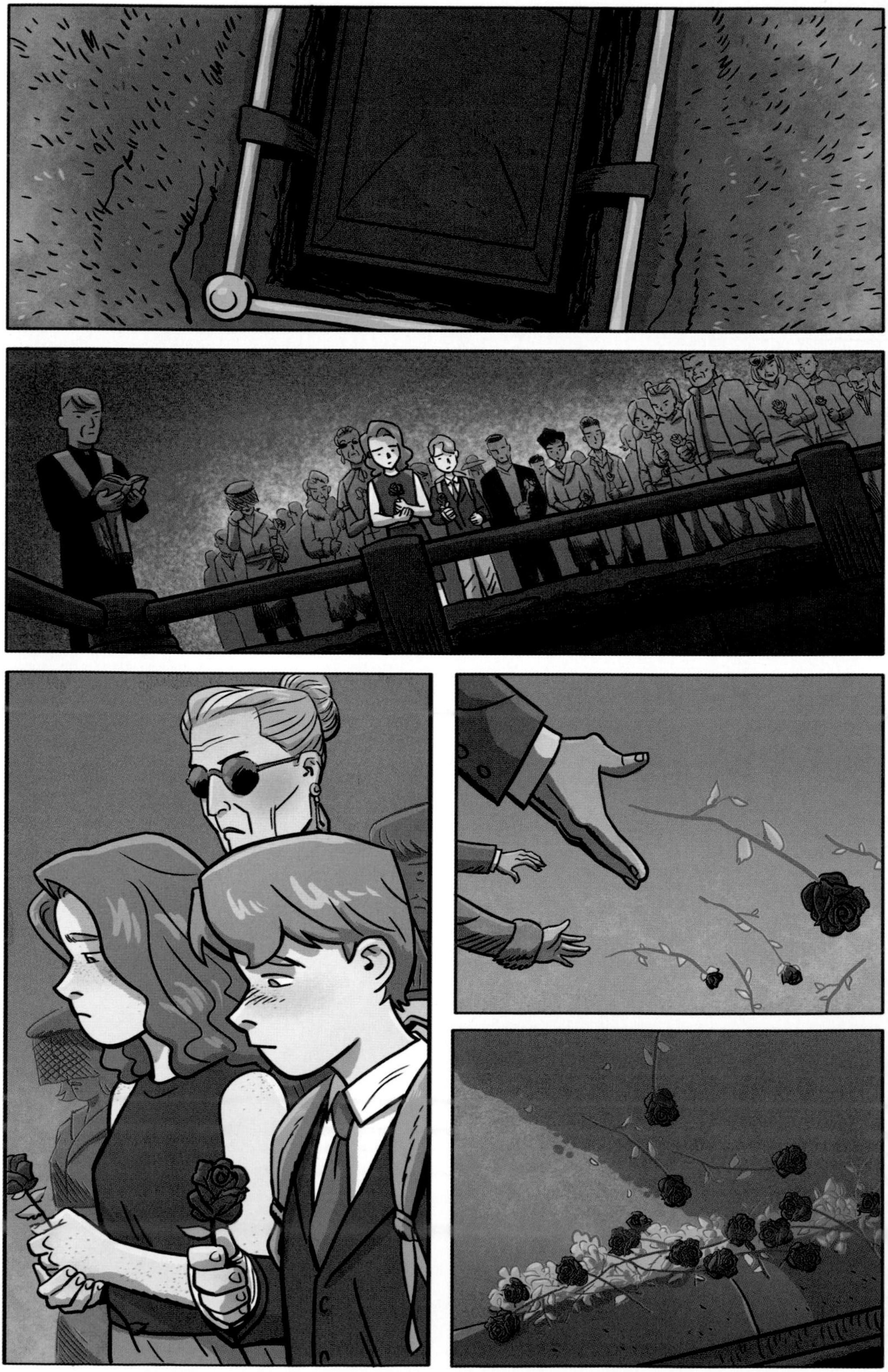

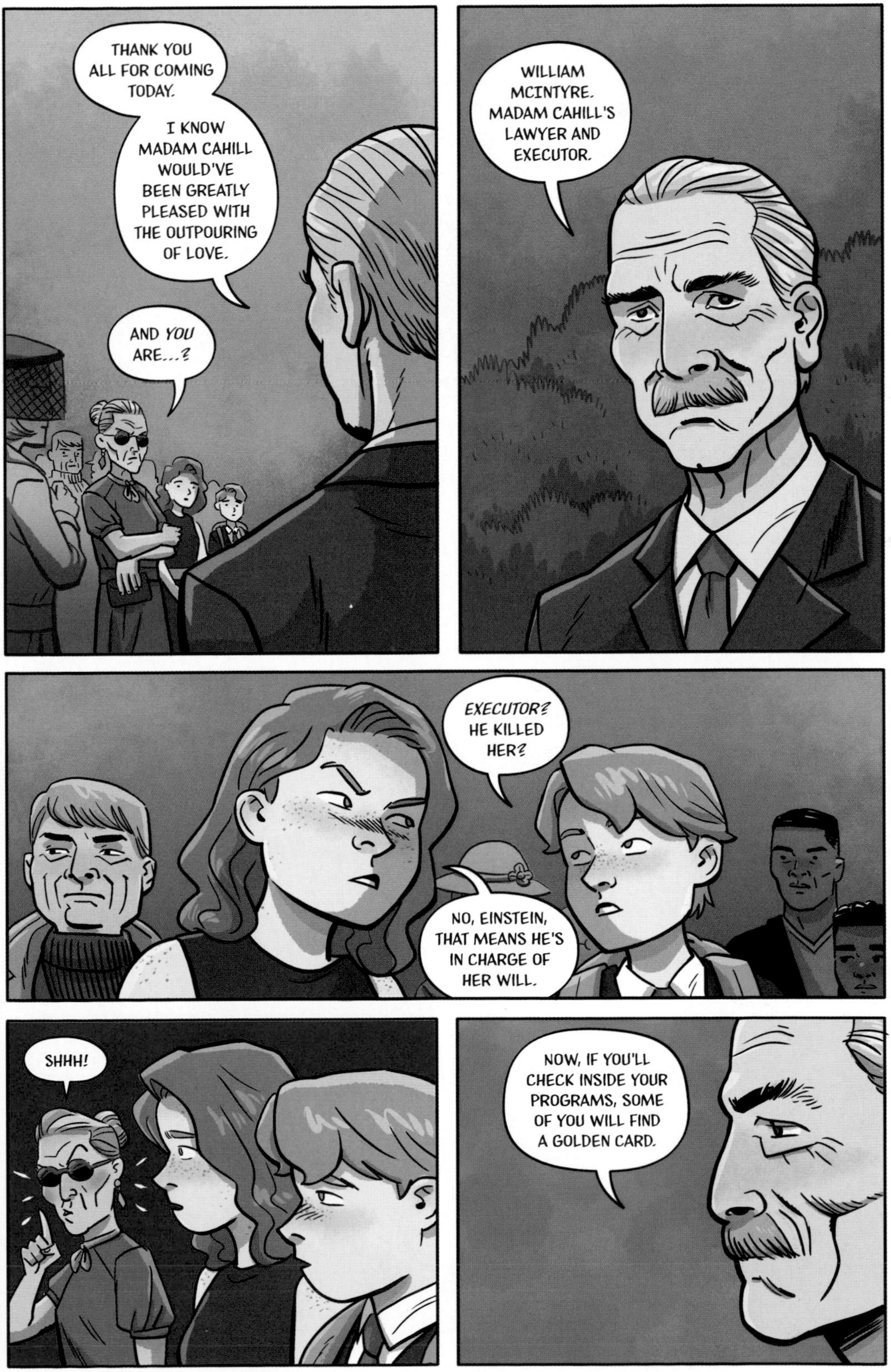
THANK YOU ALL FOR COMING TODAY.
I KNOW MADAM CAHILL WOULD'VE BEEN GREATLY PLEASED WITH THE OUTPOURING OF LOVE.
AND *YOU* ARE...?
WILLIAM MCINTYRE. MADAM CAHILL'S LAWYER AND EXECUTOR.
EXECUTOR? HE KILLED HER?
NO, EINSTEIN, THAT MEANS HE'S IN CHARGE OF HER WILL.
SHHH!
NOW, IF YOU'LL CHECK INSIDE YOUR PROGRAMS, SOME OF YOU WILL FIND A GOLDEN CARD.

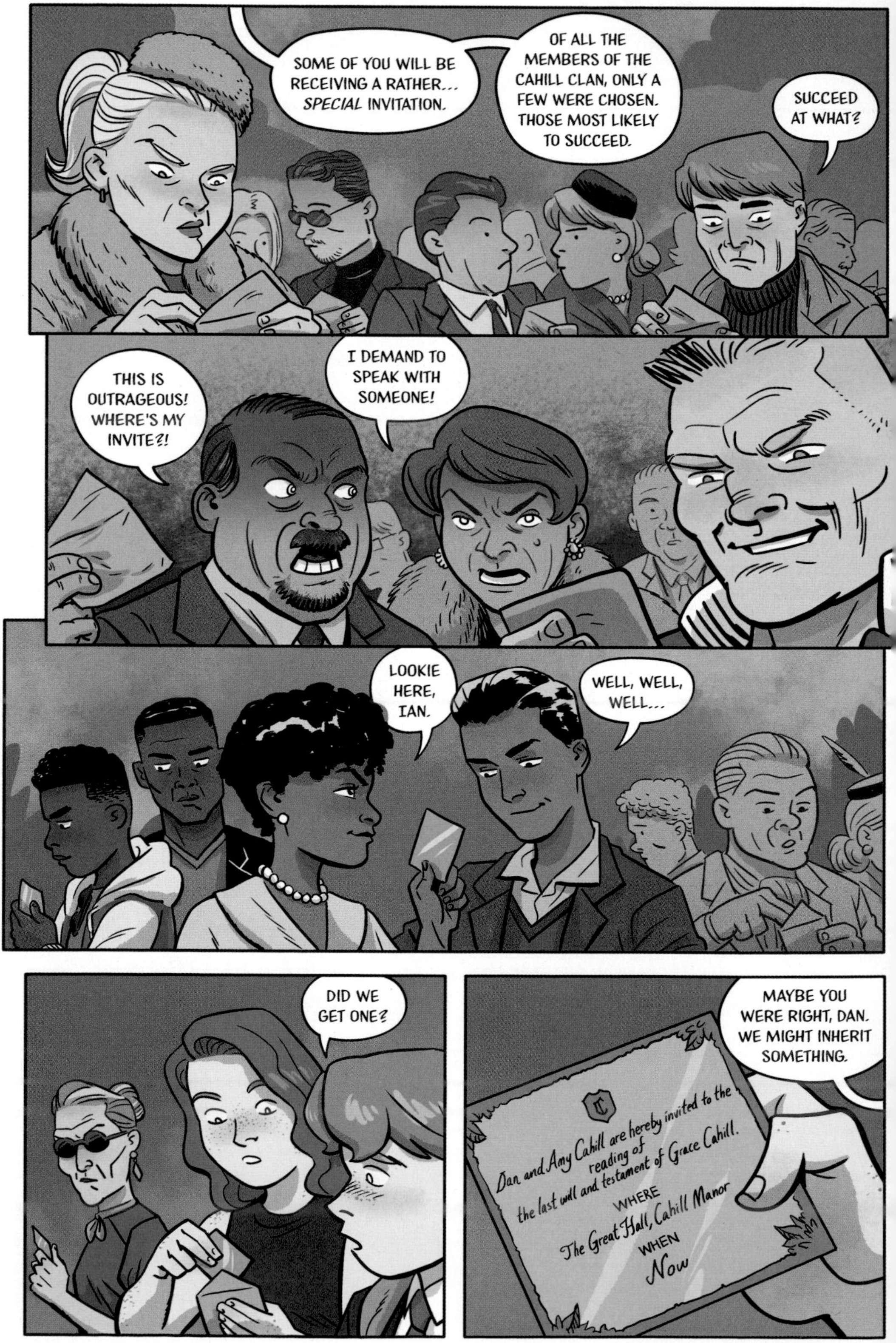
SOME OF YOU WILL BE RECEIVING A RATHER... *SPECIAL* INVITATION.
OF ALL THE MEMBERS OF THE CAHILL CLAN, ONLY A FEW WERE CHOSEN. THOSE MOST LIKELY TO SUCCEED.
SUCCEED AT WHAT?
THIS IS OUTRAGEOUS! WHERE'S MY INVITE?!
I DEMAND TO SPEAK WITH SOMEONE!
LOOKIE HERE, IAN.
WELL, WELL, WELL...
DID WE GET ONE?
MAYBE YOU WERE RIGHT, DAN. WE MIGHT INHERIT SOMETHING.
Dan and Amy Cahill are hereby invited to the reading of the last will and testament of Grace Cahill.
WHERE
The Great Hall, Cahill Manor
WHEN
Now

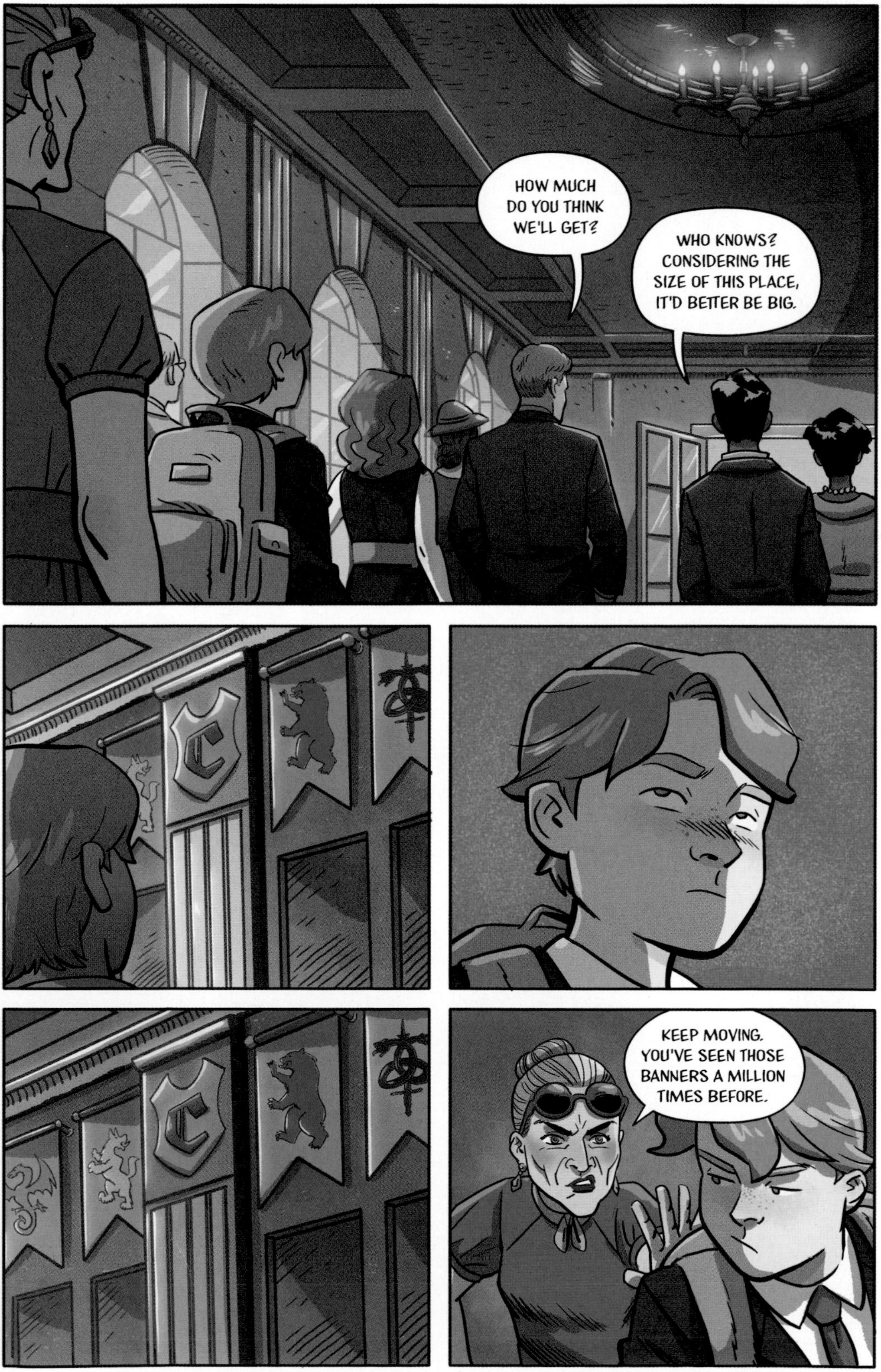
HOW MUCH DO YOU THINK WE'LL GET?
WHO KNOWS? CONSIDERING THE SIZE OF THIS PLACE, IT'D BETTER BE BIG.
KEEP MOVING. YOU'VE SEEN THOSE BANNERS A MILLION TIMES BEFORE.

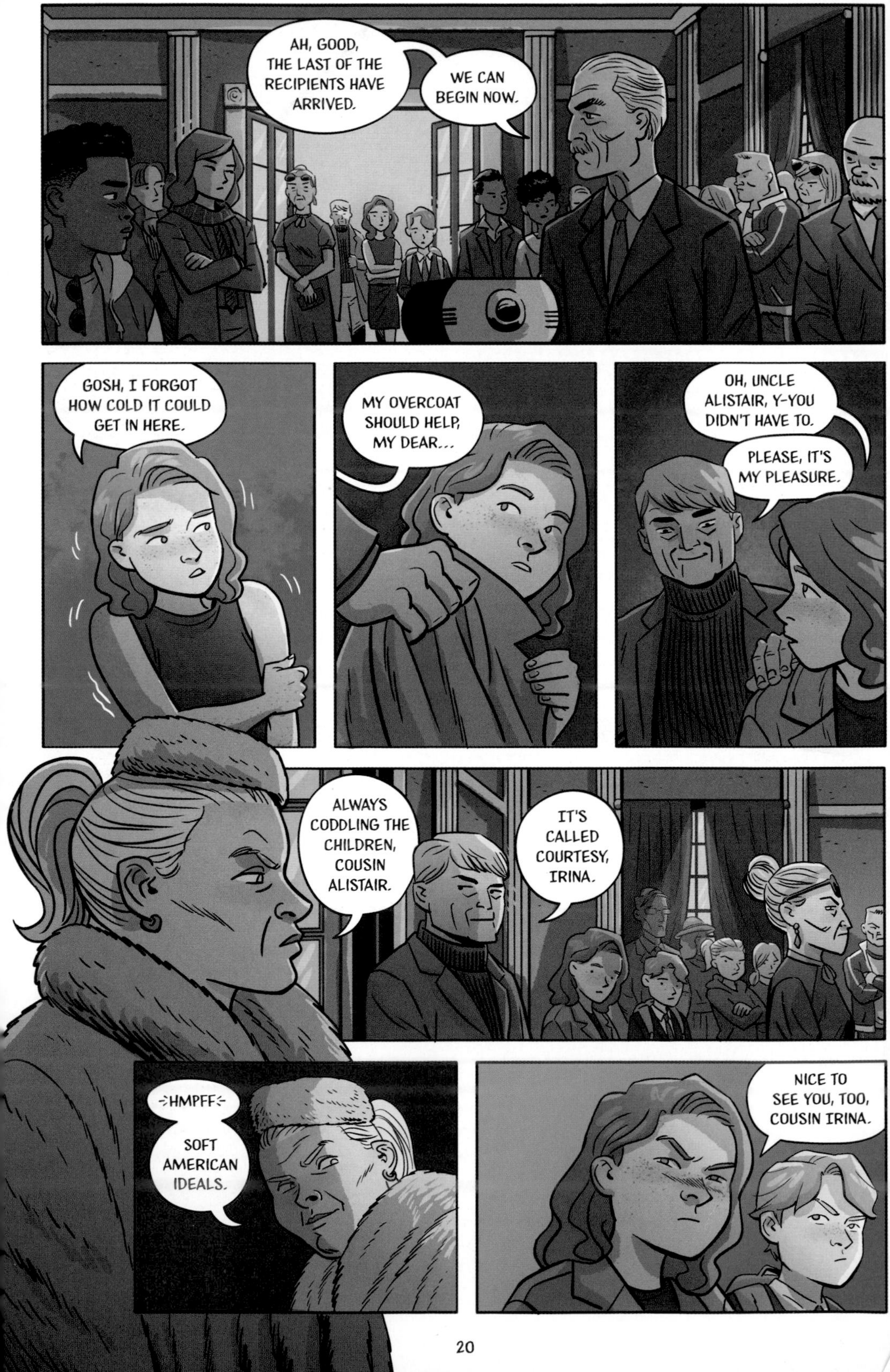
AH, GOOD, THE LAST OF THE RECIPIENTS HAVE ARRIVED.
WE CAN BEGIN NOW.
GOSH, I FORGOT HOW COLD IT COULD GET IN HERE.
MY OVERCOAT SHOULD HELP, MY DEAR...
OH, UNCLE ALISTAIR, Y-YOU DIDN'T HAVE TO.
PLEASE, IT'S MY PLEASURE.
ALWAYS CODDLING THE CHILDREN, COUSIN ALISTAIR.
IT'S CALLED COURTESY, IRINA.
HMPFF
SOFT AMERICAN IDEALS.
NICE TO SEE YOU, TOO, COUSIN IRINA.

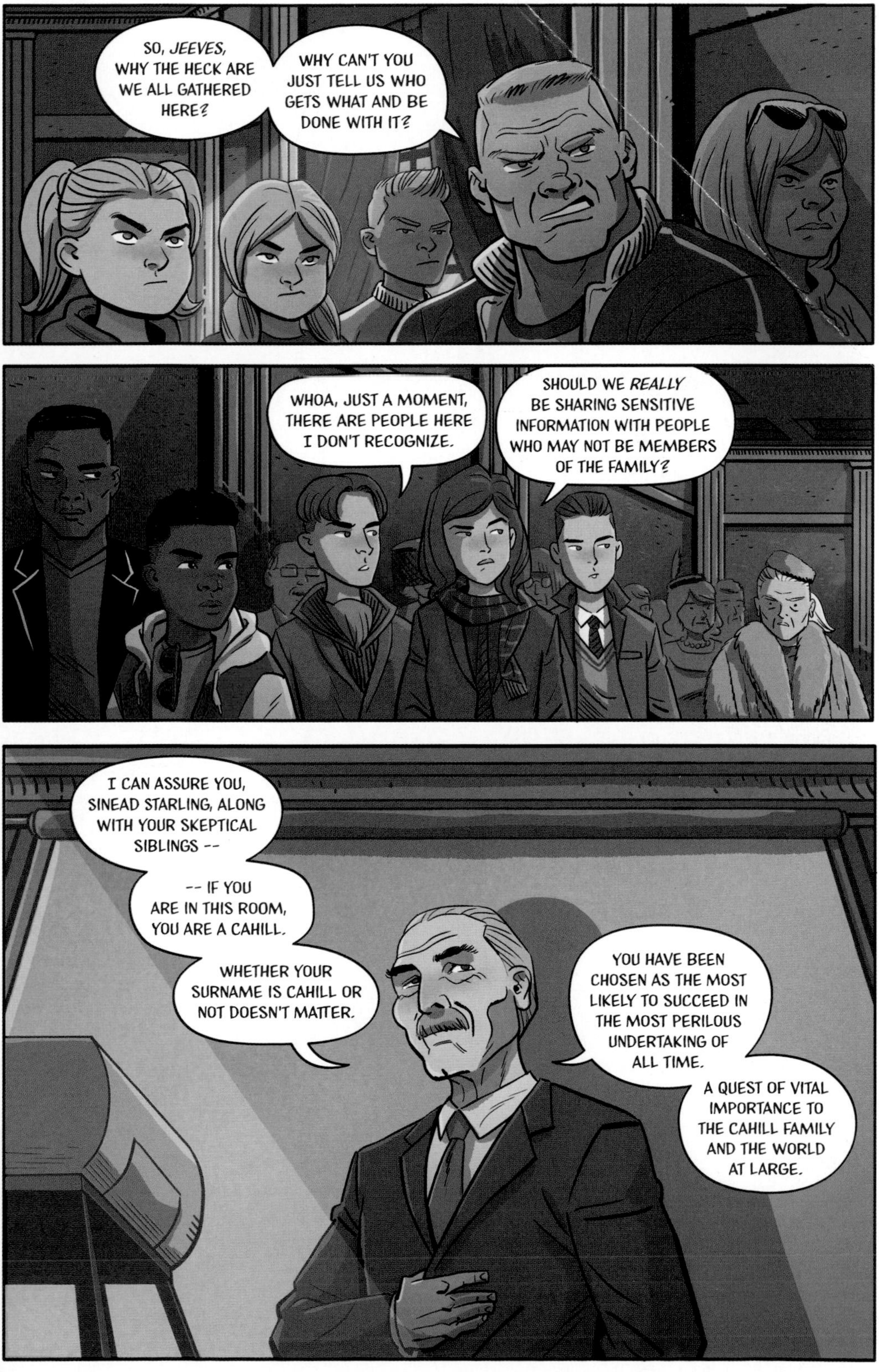
SO, *JEEVES*, WHY THE HECK ARE WE ALL GATHERED HERE?
WHY CAN'T YOU JUST TELL US WHO GETS WHAT AND BE DONE WITH IT?
WHOA, JUST A MOMENT, THERE ARE PEOPLE HERE I DON'T RECOGNIZE.
SHOULD WE *REALLY* BE SHARING SENSITIVE INFORMATION WITH PEOPLE WHO MAY NOT BE MEMBERS OF THE FAMILY?
I CAN ASSURE YOU, SINEAD STARLING, ALONG WITH YOUR SKEPTICAL SIBLINGS --
-- IF YOU ARE IN THIS ROOM, YOU ARE A CAHILL.
WHETHER YOUR SURNAME IS CAHILL OR NOT DOESN'T MATTER.
YOU HAVE BEEN CHOSEN AS THE MOST LIKELY TO SUCCEED IN THE MOST PERILOUS UNDERTAKING OF ALL TIME.
A QUEST OF VITAL IMPORTANCE TO THE CAHILL FAMILY AND THE WORLD AT LARGE.

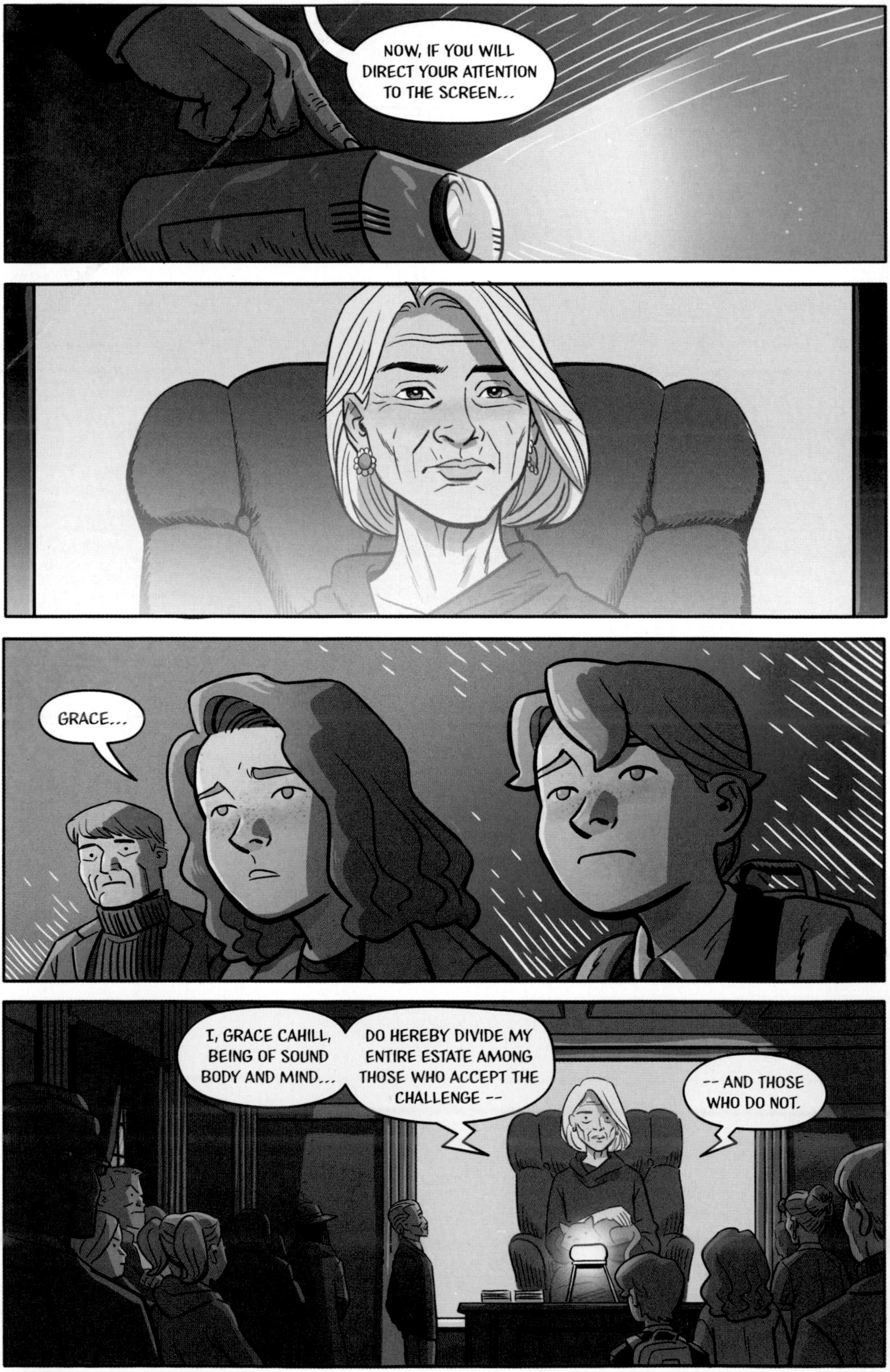
NOW, IF YOU WILL DIRECT YOUR ATTENTION TO THE SCREEN...
GRACE...
I, GRACE CAHILL, BEING OF SOUND BODY AND MIND...
DO HEREBY DIVIDE MY ENTIRE ESTATE AMONG THOSE WHO ACCEPT THE CHALLENGE --
-- AND THOSE WHO DO NOT.

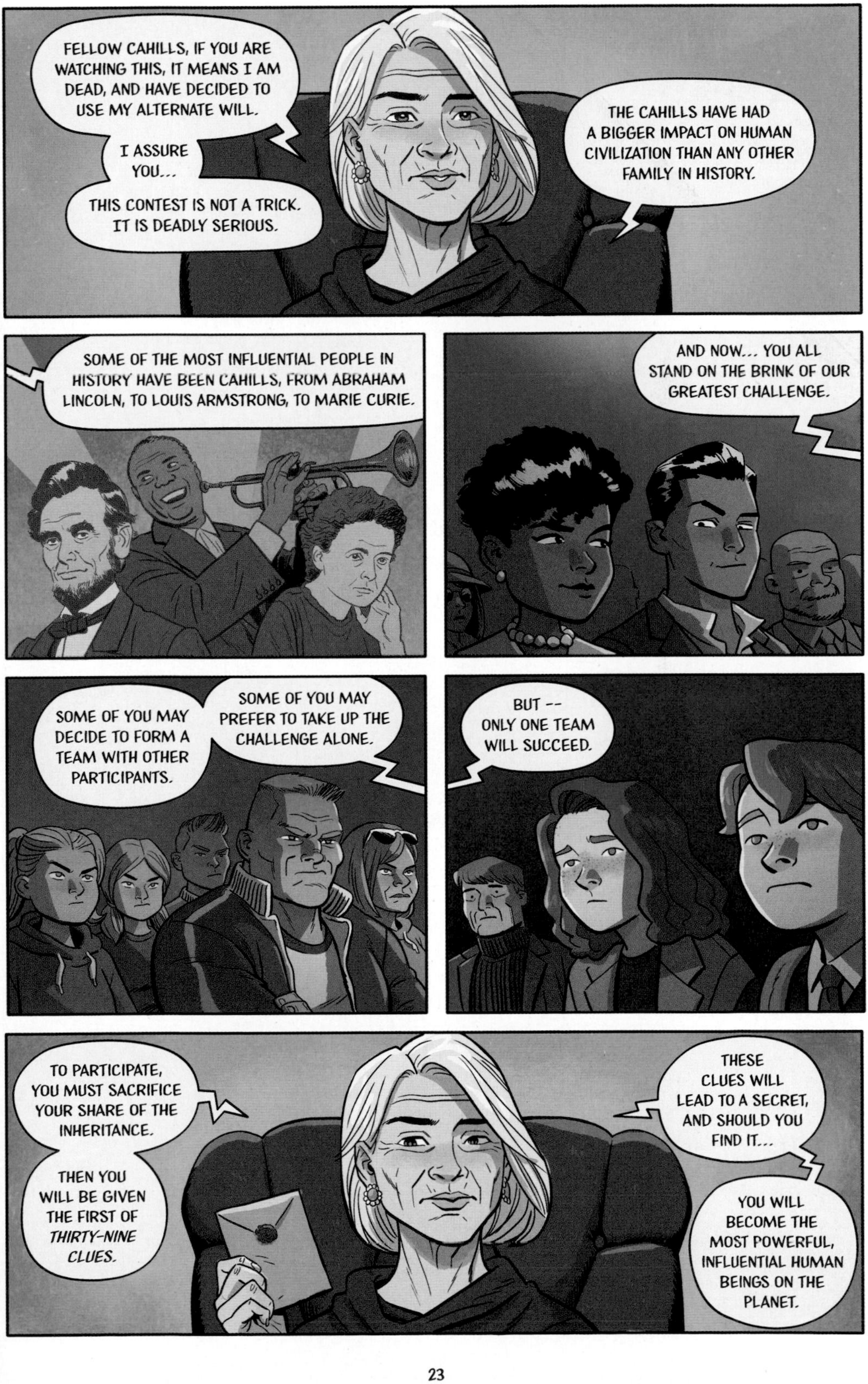
FELLOW CAHILLS, IF YOU ARE WATCHING THIS, IT MEANS I AM DEAD, AND HAVE DECIDED TO USE MY ALTERNATE WILL.
I ASSURE YOU...
THIS CONTEST IS NOT A TRICK. IT IS DEADLY SERIOUS.
THE CAHILLS HAVE HAD A BIGGER IMPACT ON HUMAN CIVILIZATION THAN ANY OTHER FAMILY IN HISTORY.
SOME OF THE MOST INFLUENTIAL PEOPLE IN HISTORY HAVE BEEN CAHILLS, FROM ABRAHAM LINCOLN, TO LOUIS ARMSTRONG, TO MARIE CURIE.
AND NOW... YOU ALL STAND ON THE BRINK OF OUR GREATEST CHALLENGE.
SOME OF YOU MAY DECIDE TO FORM A TEAM WITH OTHER PARTICIPANTS.
SOME OF YOU MAY PREFER TO TAKE UP THE CHALLENGE ALONE.
BUT -- ONLY ONE TEAM WILL SUCCEED.
TO PARTICIPATE, YOU MUST SACRIFICE YOUR SHARE OF THE INHERITANCE.
THEN YOU WILL BE GIVEN THE FIRST OF *THIRTY-NINE CLUES.*
THESE CLUES WILL LEAD TO A SECRET, AND SHOULD YOU FIND IT...
YOU WILL BECOME THE MOST POWERFUL, INFLUENTIAL HUMAN BEINGS ON THE PLANET.

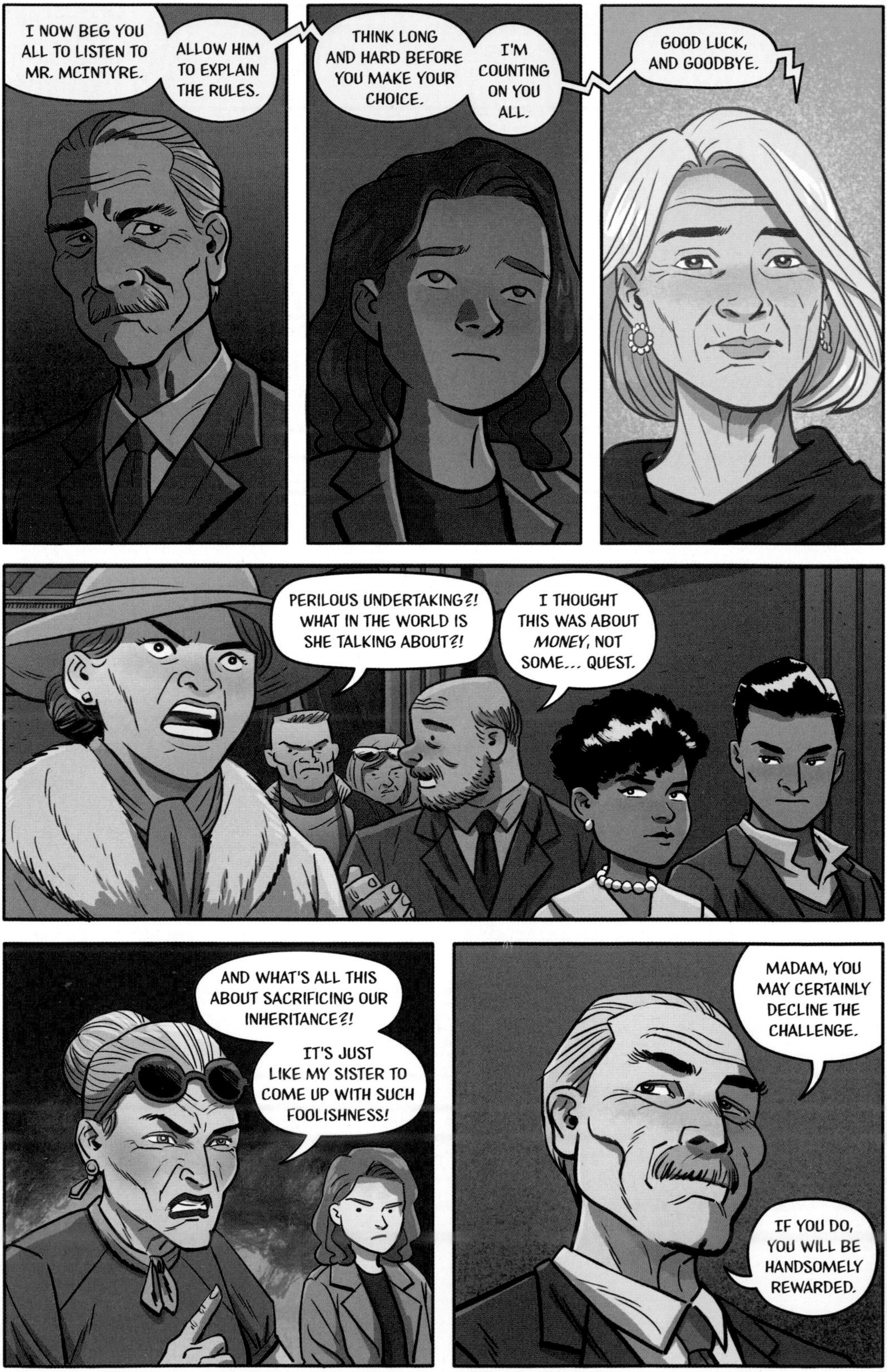
I NOW BEG YOU ALL TO LISTEN TO MR. MCINTYRE.
ALLOW HIM TO EXPLAIN THE RULES.
THINK LONG AND HARD BEFORE YOU MAKE YOUR CHOICE.
I'M COUNTING ON YOU ALL.
GOOD LUCK, AND GOODBYE.
PERILOUS UNDERTAKING?! WHAT IN THE WORLD IS SHE TALKING ABOUT?!
I THOUGHT THIS WAS ABOUT *MONEY*, NOT SOME... QUEST.
AND WHAT'S ALL THIS ABOUT SACRIFICING OUR INHERITANCE?!
IT'S JUST LIKE MY SISTER TO COME UP WITH SUCH FOOLISHNESS!
MADAM, YOU MAY CERTAINLY DECLINE THE CHALLENGE.
IF YOU DO, YOU WILL BE HANDSOMELY REWARDED.

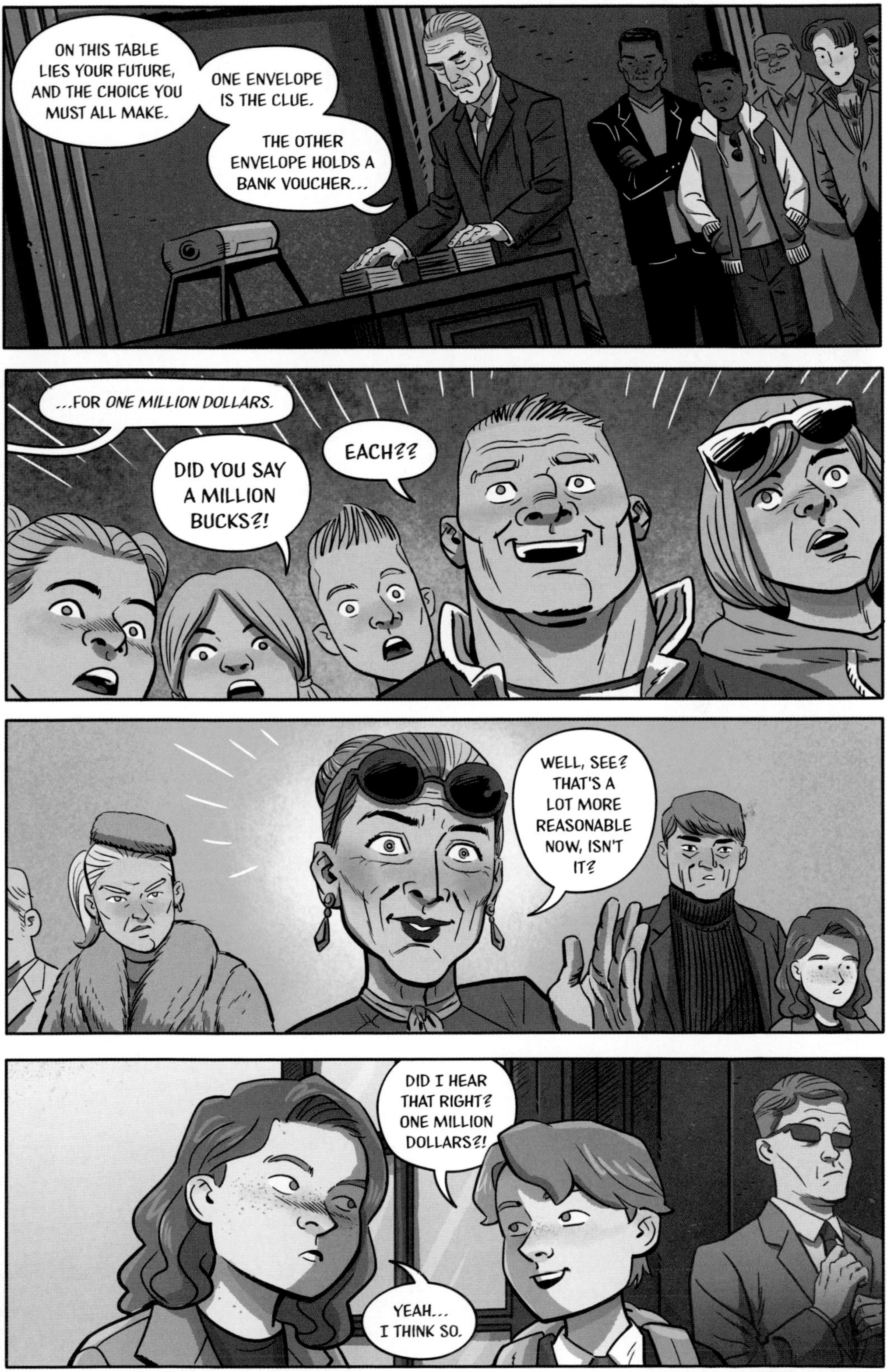
ON THIS TABLE LIES YOUR FUTURE, AND THE CHOICE YOU MUST ALL MAKE.
ONE ENVELOPE IS THE CLUE.
THE OTHER ENVELOPE HOLDS A BANK VOUCHER...
...FOR *ONE MILLION DOLLARS.*
DID YOU SAY A MILLION BUCKS?!
EACH??
WELL, SEE? THAT'S A LOT MORE REASONABLE NOW, ISN'T IT?
DID I HEAR THAT RIGHT? ONE MILLION DOLLARS?!
YEAH... I THINK SO.

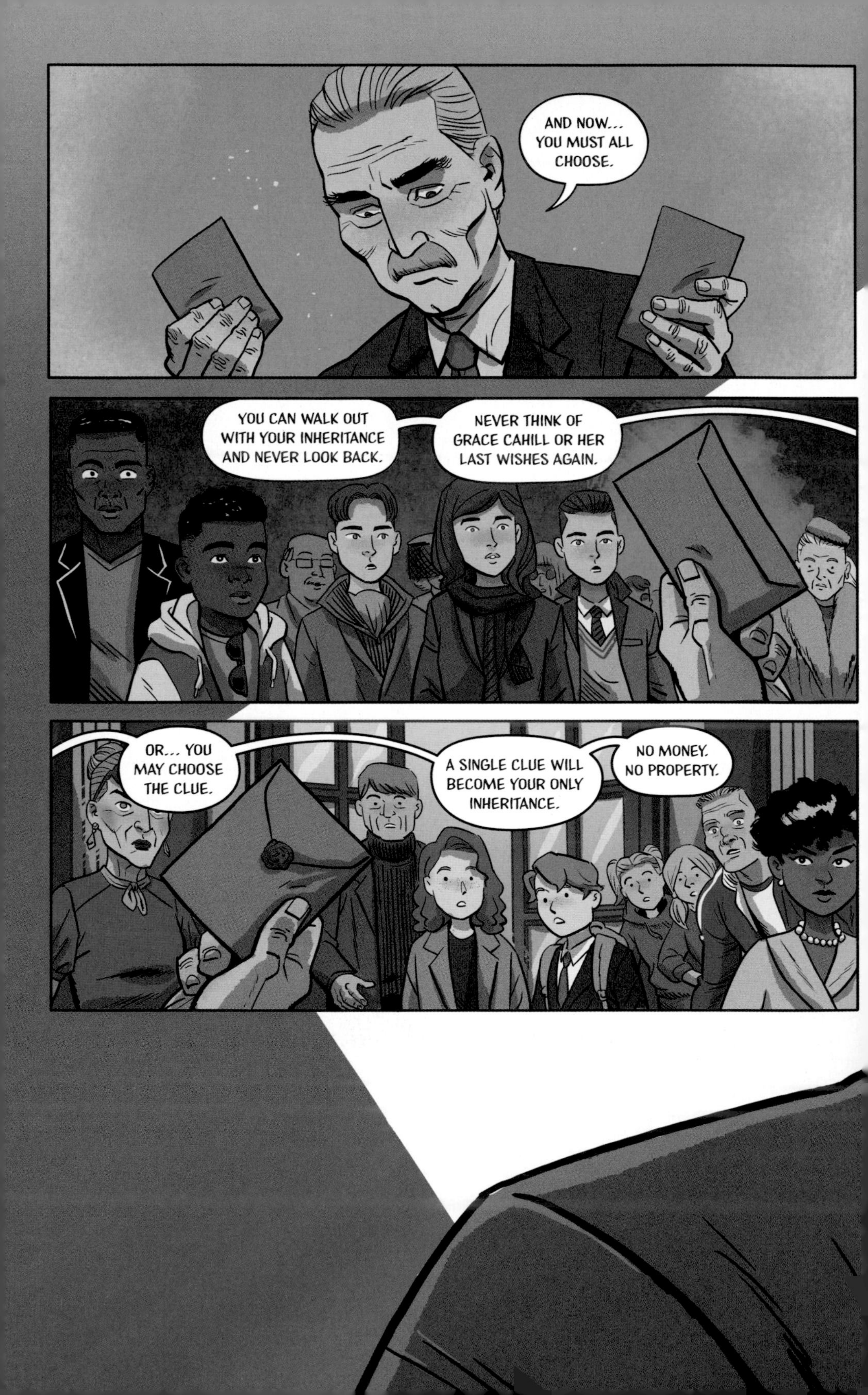
AND NOW... YOU MUST ALL CHOOSE.
YOU CAN WALK OUT WITH YOUR INHERITANCE AND NEVER LOOK BACK.
NEVER THINK OF GRACE CAHILL OR HER LAST WISHES AGAIN.
OR... YOU MAY CHOOSE THE CLUE.
A SINGLE CLUE WILL BECOME YOUR ONLY INHERITANCE.
NO MONEY. NO PROPERTY.

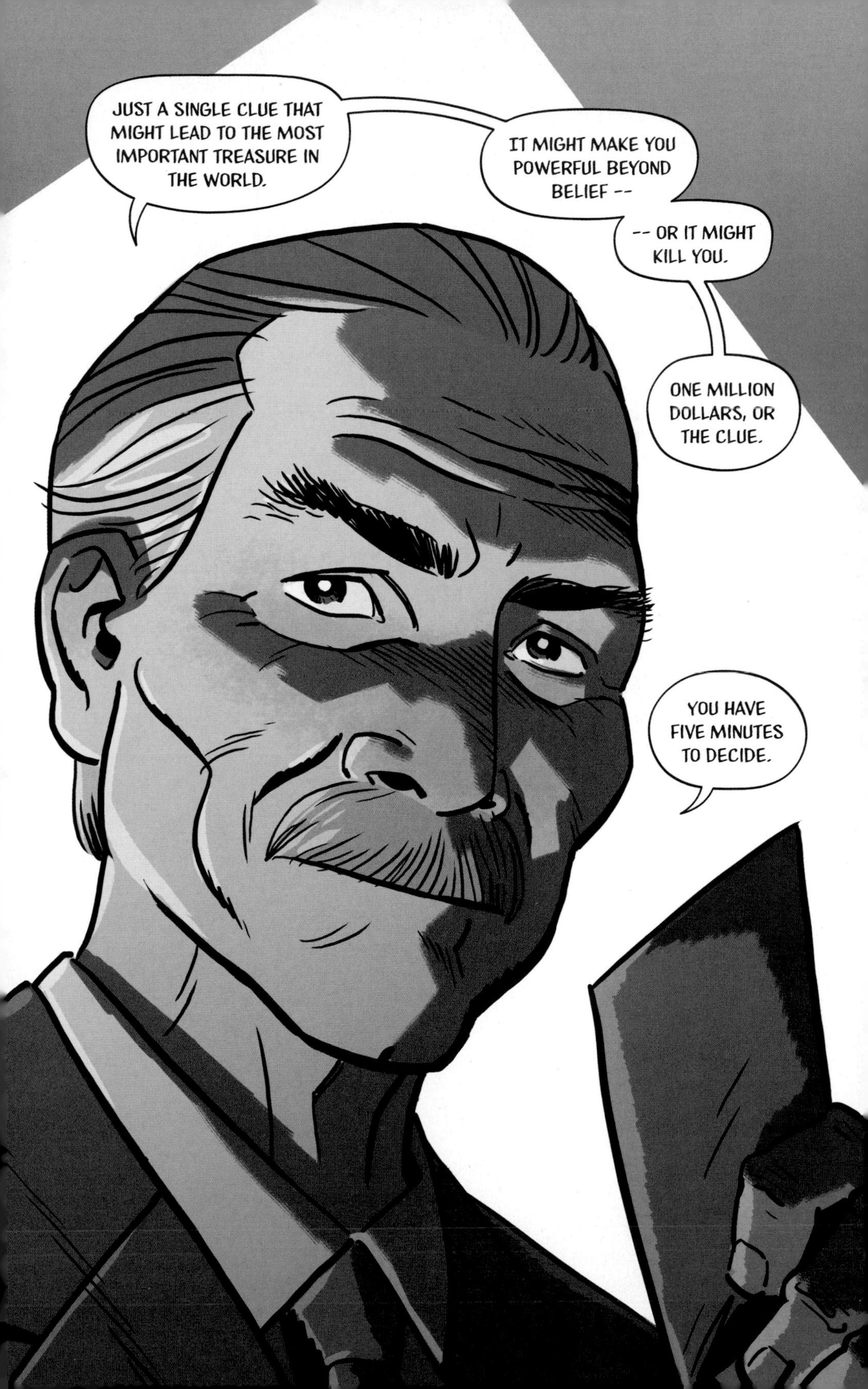
JUST A SINGLE CLUE THAT MIGHT LEAD TO THE MOST IMPORTANT TREASURE IN THE WORLD.
IT MIGHT MAKE YOU POWERFUL BEYOND BELIEF --
-- OR IT MIGHT KILL YOU.
ONE MILLION DOLLARS, OR THE CLUE.
YOU HAVE FIVE MINUTES TO DECIDE.

TWO

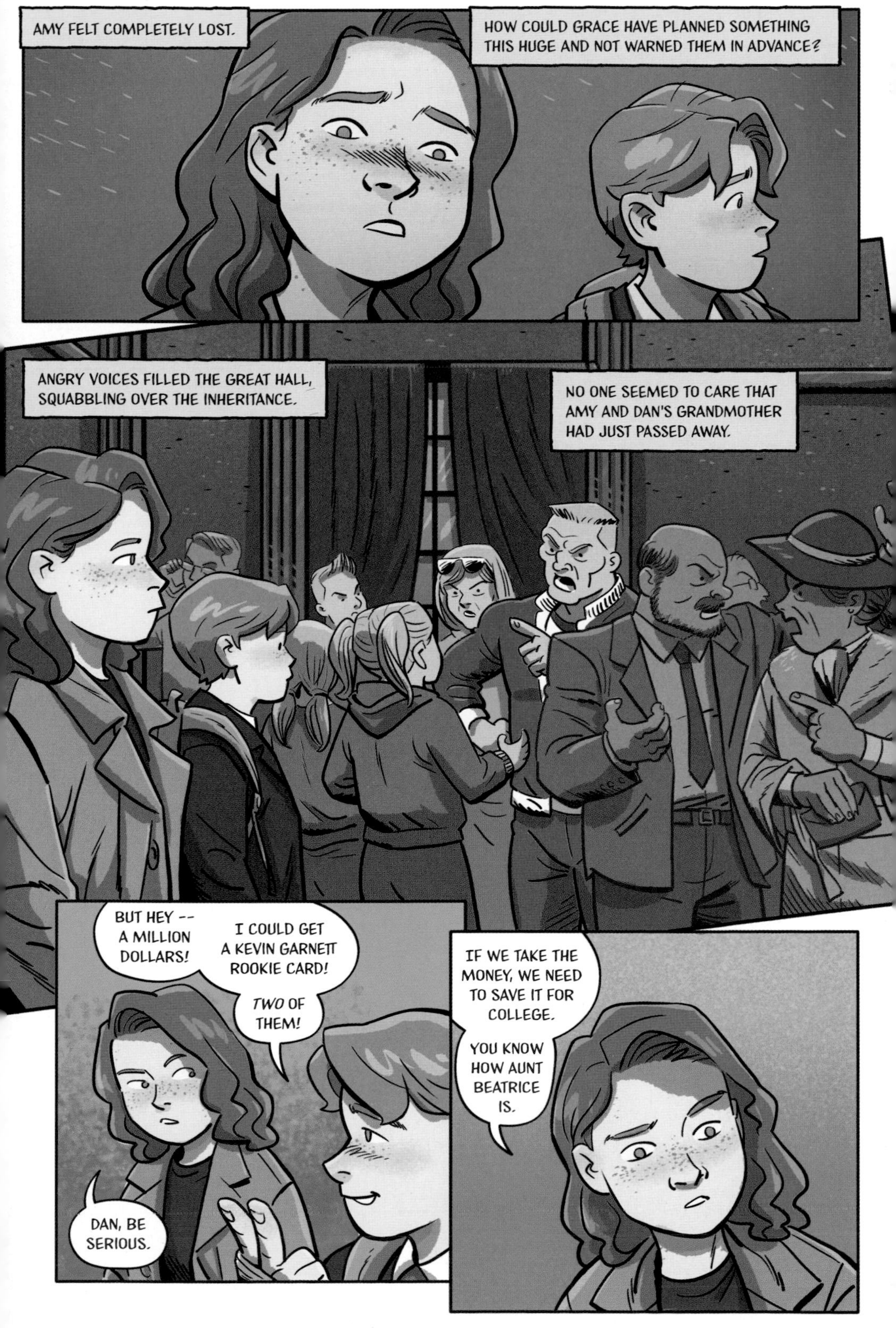
AMY FELT COMPLETELY LOST.
HOW COULD GRACE HAVE PLANNED SOMETHING THIS HUGE AND NOT WARNED THEM IN ADVANCE?
ANGRY VOICES FILLED THE GREAT HALL, SQUABBLING OVER THE INHERITANCE.
NO ONE SEEMED TO CARE THAT AMY AND DAN'S GRANDMOTHER HAD JUST PASSED AWAY.
BUT HEY -- A MILLION DOLLARS!
I COULD GET A KEVIN GARNETT ROOKIE CARD!
TWO OF THEM!
DAN, BE SERIOUS.
IF WE TAKE THE MONEY, WE NEED TO SAVE IT FOR COLLEGE.
YOU KNOW HOW AUNT BEATRICE IS.

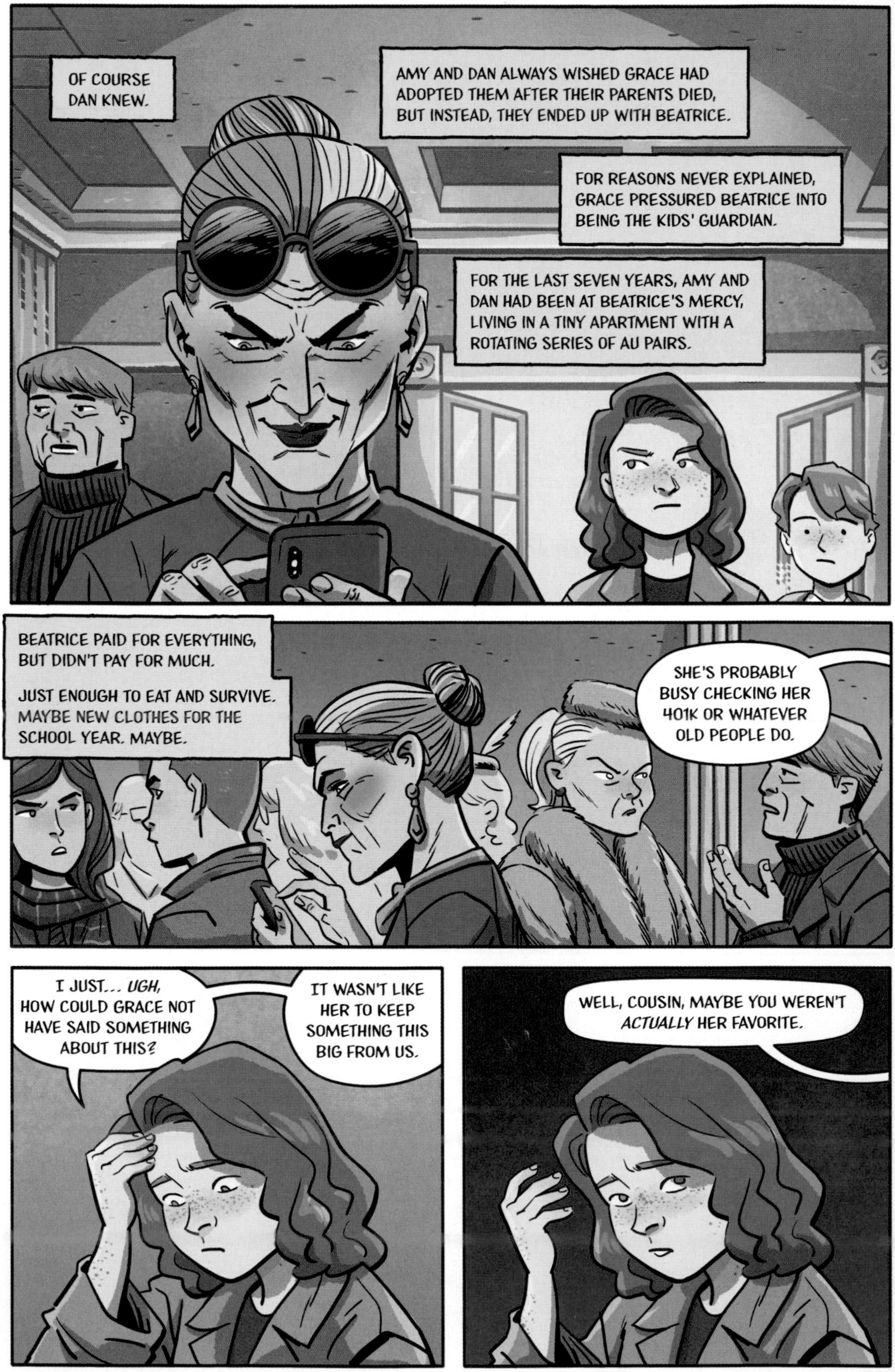
OF COURSE DAN KNEW.
AMY AND DAN ALWAYS WISHED GRACE HAD ADOPTED THEM AFTER THEIR PARENTS DIED, BUT INSTEAD, THEY ENDED UP WITH BEATRICE.
FOR REASONS NEVER EXPLAINED, GRACE PRESSURED BEATRICE INTO BEING THE KIDS' GUARDIAN.
FOR THE LAST SEVEN YEARS, AMY AND DAN HAD BEEN AT BEATRICE'S MERCY, LIVING IN A TINY APARTMENT WITH A ROTATING SERIES OF AU PAIRS.
BEATRICE PAID FOR EVERYTHING, BUT DIDN'T PAY FOR MUCH.
JUST ENOUGH TO EAT AND SURVIVE. MAYBE NEW CLOTHES FOR THE SCHOOL YEAR. MAYBE.
SHE'S PROBABLY BUSY CHECKING HER 401K OR WHATEVER OLD PEOPLE DO.
I JUST... *UGH*, HOW COULD GRACE NOT HAVE SAID SOMETHING ABOUT THIS?
IT WASN'T LIKE HER TO KEEP SOMETHING THIS BIG FROM US.
WELL, COUSIN, MAYBE YOU WEREN'T *ACTUALLY* HER FAVORITE.

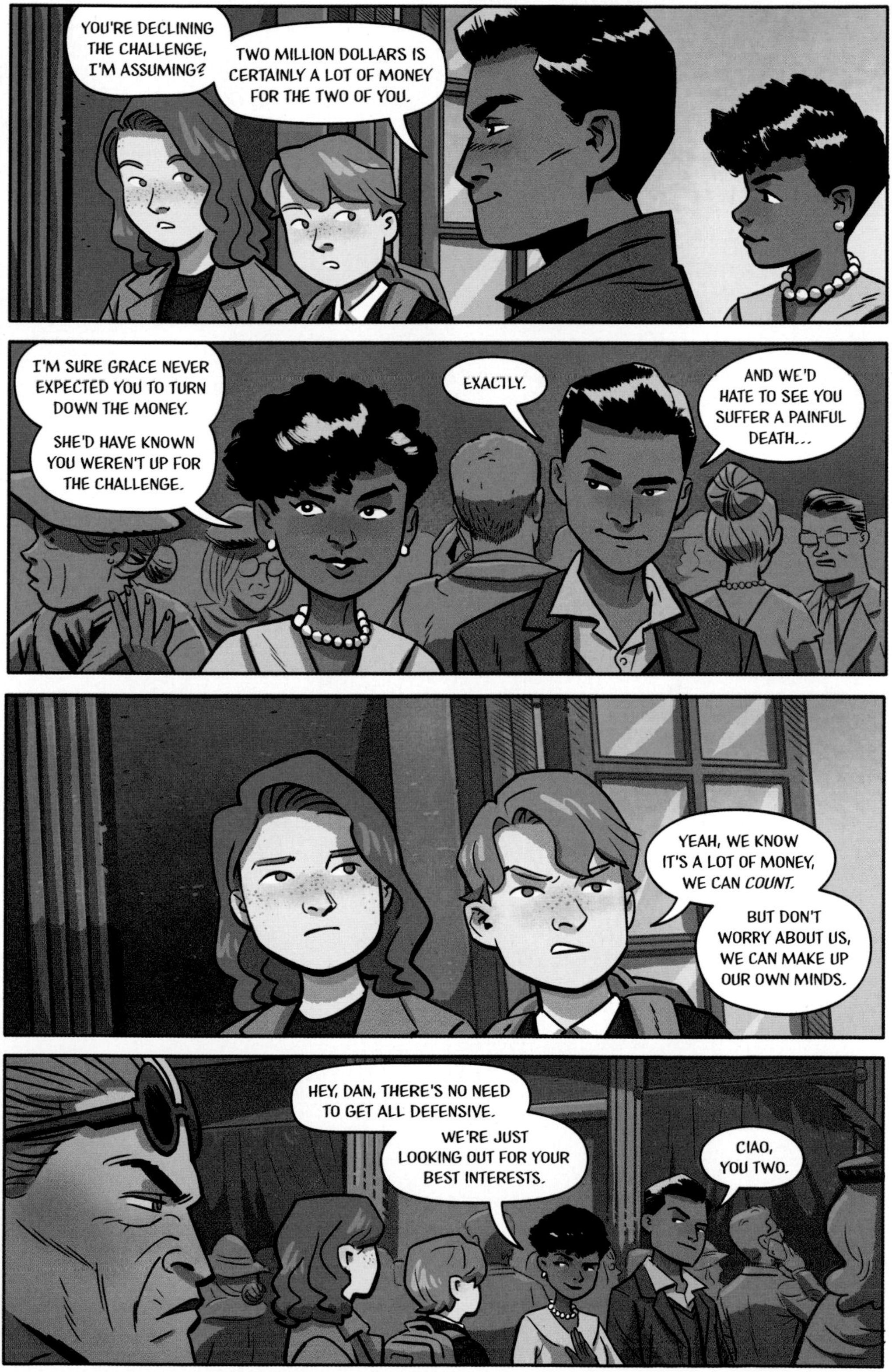
YOU'RE DECLINING THE CHALLENGE, I'M ASSUMING?
TWO MILLION DOLLARS IS CERTAINLY A LOT OF MONEY FOR THE TWO OF YOU.
I'M SURE GRACE NEVER EXPECTED YOU TO TURN DOWN THE MONEY.
SHE'D HAVE KNOWN YOU WEREN'T UP FOR THE CHALLENGE.
EXACTLY.
AND WE'D HATE TO SEE YOU SUFFER A PAINFUL DEATH...
YEAH, WE KNOW IT'S A LOT OF MONEY, WE CAN *COUNT*.
BUT DON'T WORRY ABOUT US, WE CAN MAKE UP OUR OWN MINDS.
HEY, DAN, THERE'S NO NEED TO GET ALL DEFENSIVE.
WE'RE JUST LOOKING OUT FOR YOUR BEST INTERESTS.
CIAO, YOU TWO.

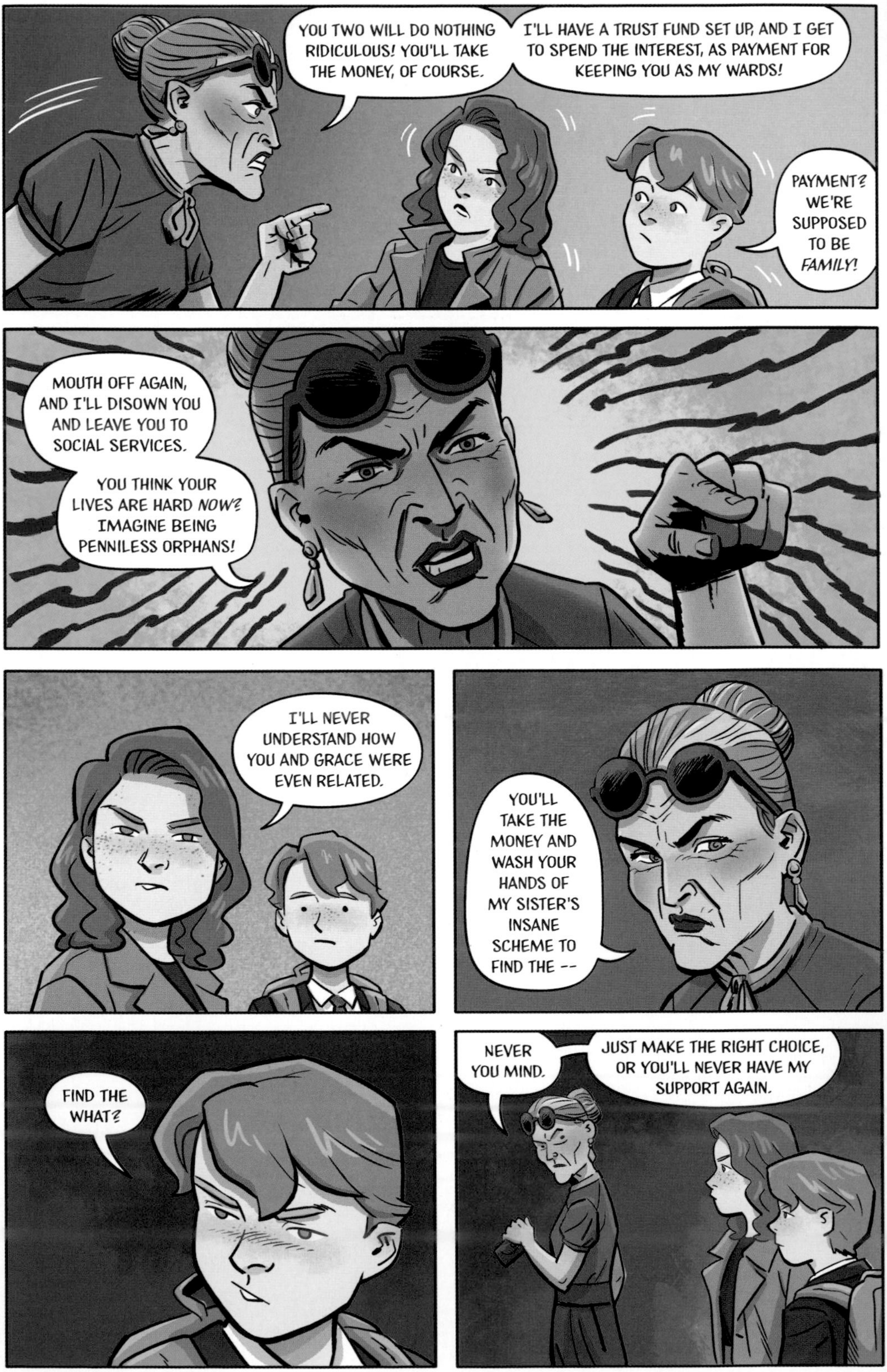
YOU TWO WILL DO NOTHING RIDICULOUS! YOU'LL TAKE THE MONEY, OF COURSE.
I'LL HAVE A TRUST FUND SET UP, AND I GET TO SPEND THE INTEREST, AS PAYMENT FOR KEEPING YOU AS MY WARDS!
PAYMENT? WE'RE SUPPOSED TO BE *FAMILY!*
MOUTH OFF AGAIN, AND I'LL DISOWN YOU AND LEAVE YOU TO SOCIAL SERVICES.
YOU THINK YOUR LIVES ARE HARD *NOW?* IMAGINE BEING PENNILESS ORPHANS!
I'LL NEVER UNDERSTAND HOW YOU AND GRACE WERE EVEN RELATED.
YOU'LL TAKE THE MONEY AND WASH YOUR HANDS OF MY SISTER'S INSANE SCHEME TO FIND THE --
FIND THE WHAT?
NEVER YOU MIND.
JUST MAKE THE RIGHT CHOICE, OR YOU'LL NEVER HAVE MY SUPPORT AGAIN.

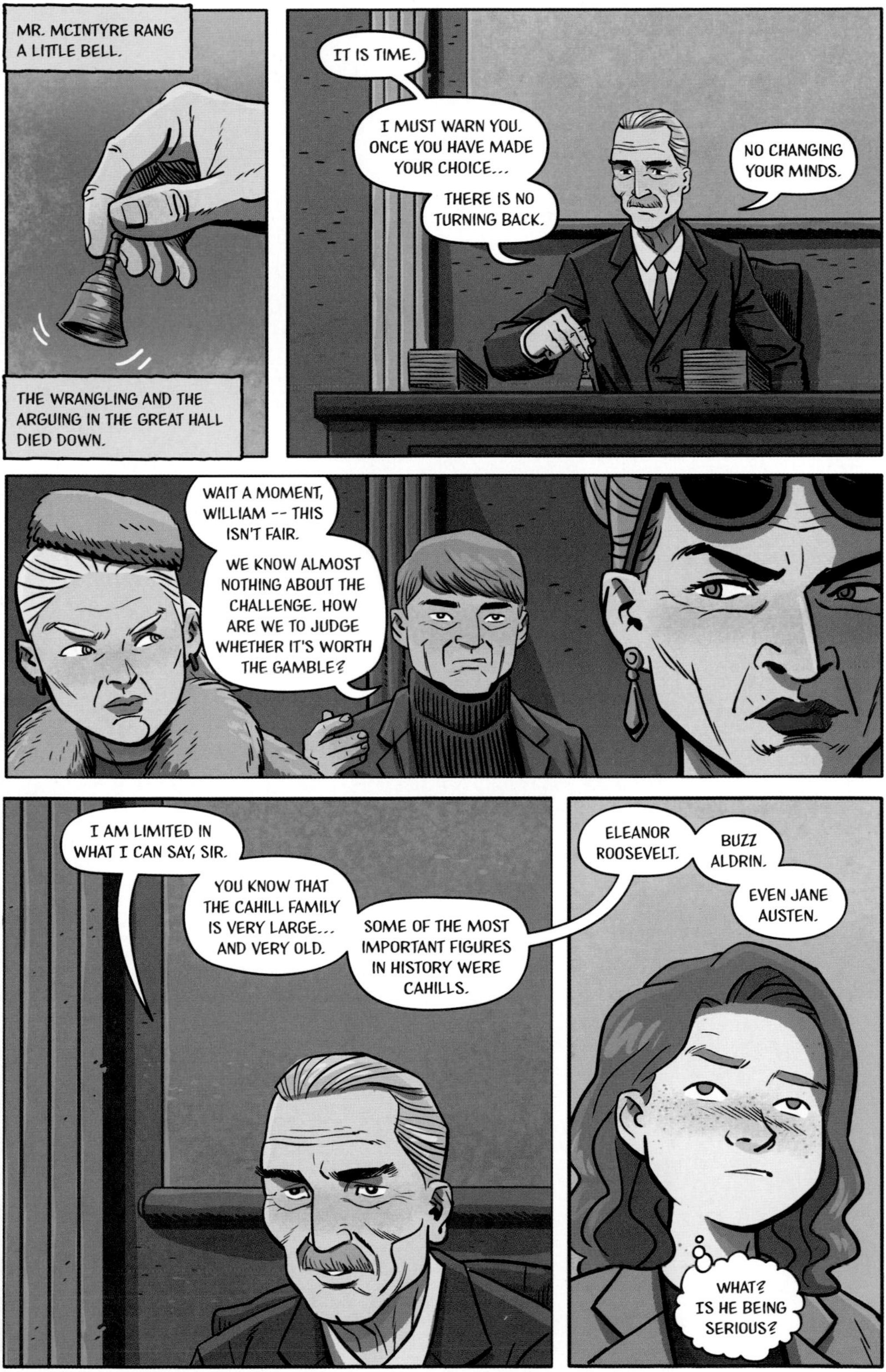
MR. MCINTYRE RANG A LITTLE BELL.
THE WRANGLING AND THE ARGUING IN THE GREAT HALL DIED DOWN.
IT IS TIME.
I MUST WARN YOU. ONCE YOU HAVE MADE YOUR CHOICE...
THERE IS NO TURNING BACK.
NO CHANGING YOUR MINDS.
WAIT A MOMENT, WILLIAM -- THIS ISN'T FAIR.
WE KNOW ALMOST NOTHING ABOUT THE CHALLENGE. HOW ARE WE TO JUDGE WHETHER IT'S WORTH THE GAMBLE?
I AM LIMITED IN WHAT I CAN SAY, SIR.
YOU KNOW THAT THE CAHILL FAMILY IS VERY LARGE... AND VERY OLD.
SOME OF THE MOST IMPORTANT FIGURES IN HISTORY WERE CAHILLS.
ELEANOR ROOSEVELT.
BUZZ ALDRIN.
EVEN JANE AUSTEN.
WHAT? IS HE BEING SERIOUS?

OH, COME ON! THAT'S IMPOSSIBLE! YOU'RE PUTTIN' US ON, JEEVES!

I AM COMPLETELY SERIOUS.

AND YET, ALL THE PREVIOUS ACCOMPLISHMENTS OF THE CAHILL CLAN ARE NOTHING COMPARED TO THE CHALLENGE THAT NOW FACES YOU ALL.

EMBARKING UPON THIS QUEST...

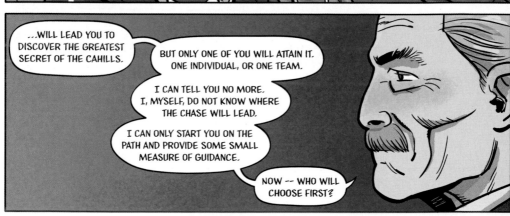

...WILL LEAD YOU TO DISCOVER THE GREATEST SECRET OF THE CAHILLS.

BUT ONLY ONE OF YOU WILL ATTAIN IT. ONE INDIVIDUAL, OR ONE TEAM.

I CAN TELL YOU NO MORE. I, MYSELF, DO NOT KNOW WHERE THE CHASE WILL LEAD.

I CAN ONLY START YOU ON THE PATH AND PROVIDE SOME SMALL MEASURE OF GUIDANCE.

NOW -- WHO WILL CHOOSE FIRST?

THIS IS ABSURD!

ANY OF YOU WHO PLAY THIS SILLY GAME ARE FOOLS!

I'LL TAKE THE MONEY.

AS YOU WISH, MADAM.

AS SOON AS YOU LEAVE THIS ROOM, THE NUMBERS ON THIS VOUCHER WILL BECOME ACTIVE.

YOU MAY WITHDRAW YOUR MONEY FROM THE ROYAL BANK OF SCOTLAND AT YOUR LEISURE.

WHO'S NEXT?

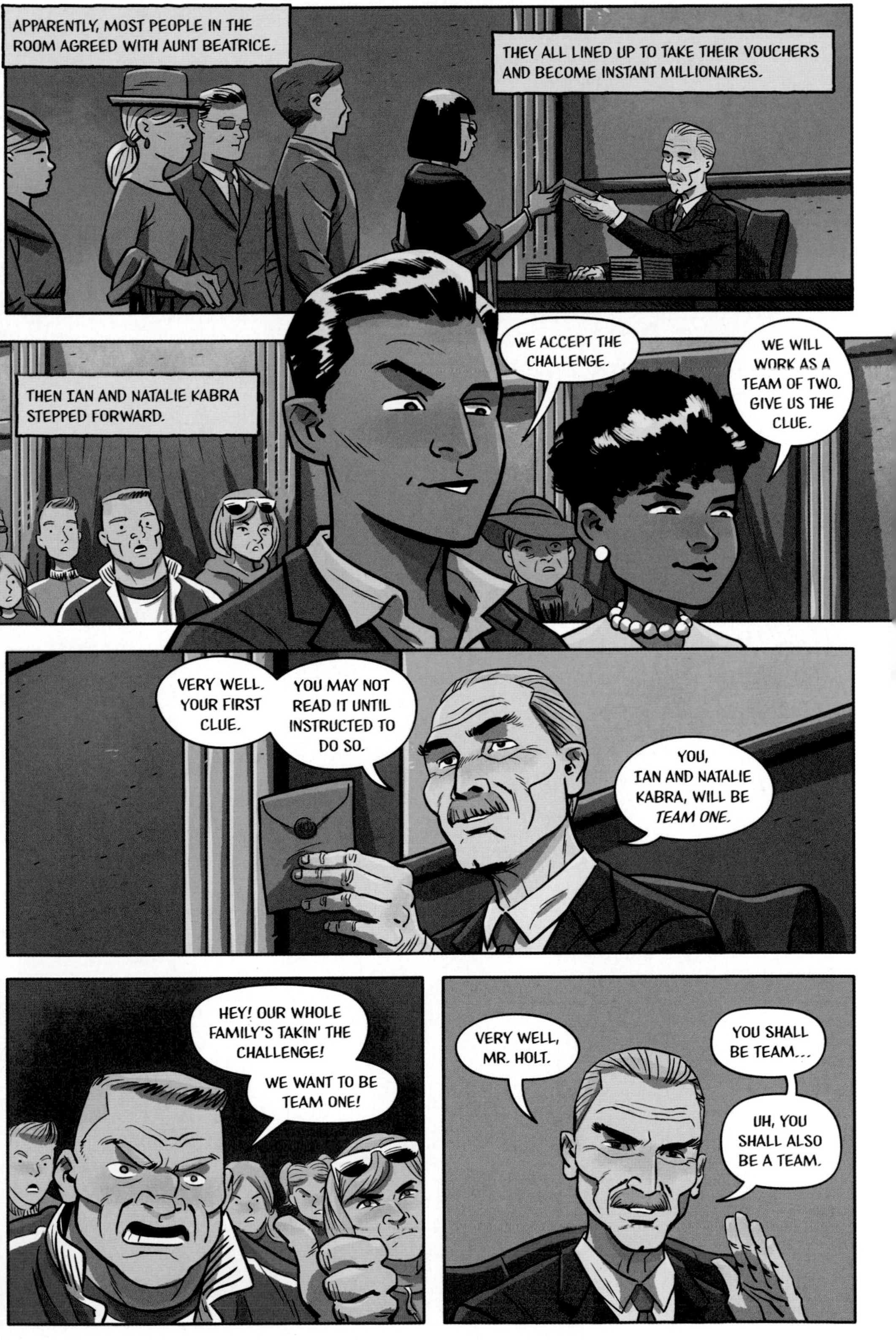
APPARENTLY, MOST PEOPLE IN THE ROOM AGREED WITH AUNT BEATRICE.
THEY ALL LINED UP TO TAKE THEIR VOUCHERS AND BECOME INSTANT MILLIONAIRES.
THEN IAN AND NATALIE KABRA STEPPED FORWARD.
WE ACCEPT THE CHALLENGE.
WE WILL WORK AS A TEAM OF TWO. GIVE US THE CLUE.
VERY WELL. YOUR FIRST CLUE.
YOU MAY NOT READ IT UNTIL INSTRUCTED TO DO SO.
YOU, IAN AND NATALIE KABRA, WILL BE *TEAM ONE.*
HEY! OUR WHOLE FAMILY'S TAKIN' THE CHALLENGE!
WE WANT TO BE TEAM ONE!
VERY WELL, MR. HOLT.
YOU SHALL BE TEAM...
UH, YOU SHALL ALSO BE A TEAM.

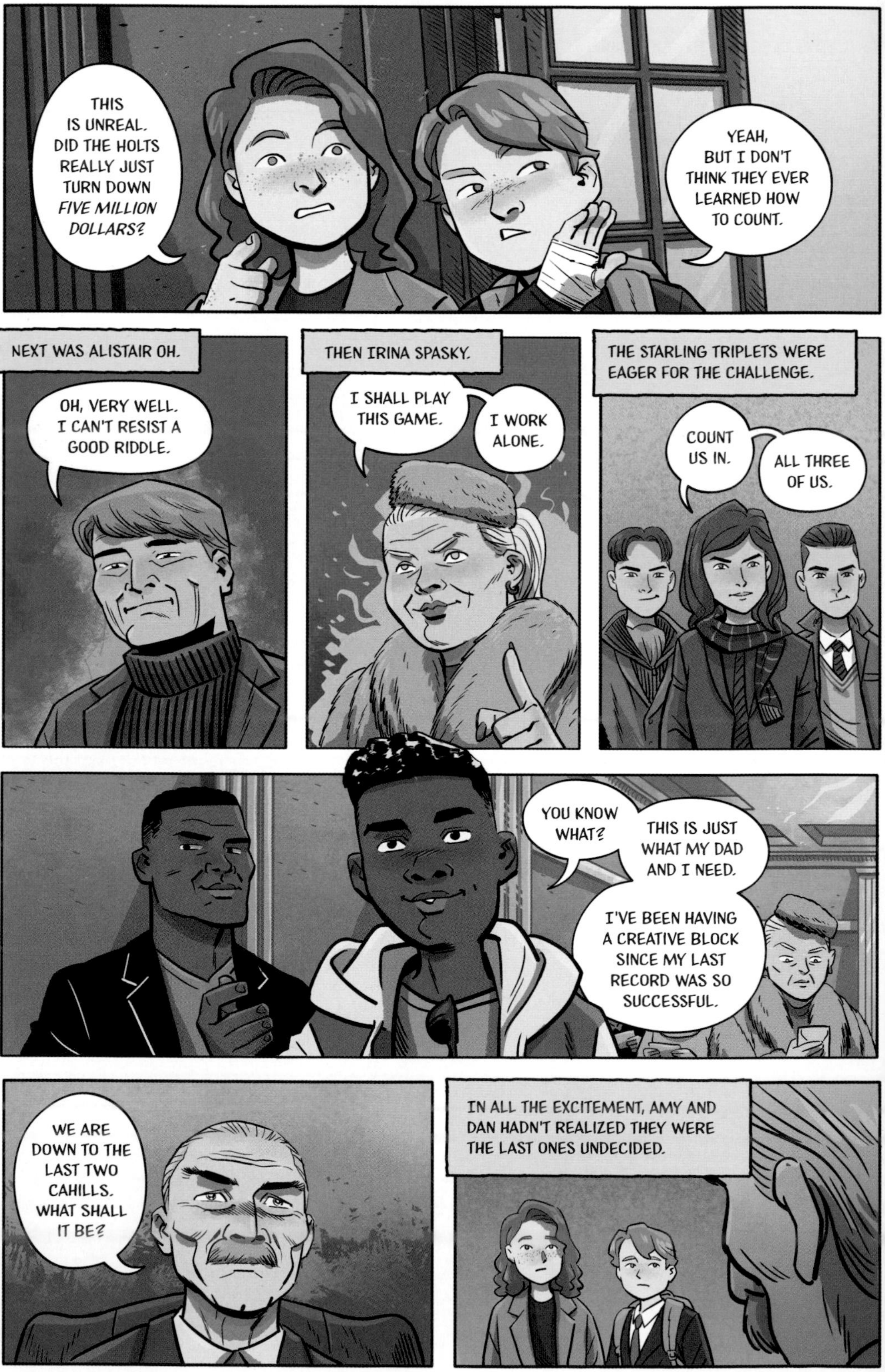
THIS IS UNREAL. DID THE HOLTS REALLY JUST TURN DOWN *FIVE MILLION DOLLARS*?
YEAH, BUT I DON'T THINK THEY EVER LEARNED HOW TO COUNT.
NEXT WAS ALISTAIR OH.
OH, VERY WELL. I CAN'T RESIST A GOOD RIDDLE.
THEN IRINA SPASKY.
I SHALL PLAY THIS GAME.
I WORK ALONE.
THE STARLING TRIPLETS WERE EAGER FOR THE CHALLENGE.
COUNT US IN.
ALL THREE OF US.
YOU KNOW WHAT?
THIS IS JUST WHAT MY DAD AND I NEED.
I'VE BEEN HAVING A CREATIVE BLOCK SINCE MY LAST RECORD WAS SO SUCCESSFUL.
WE ARE DOWN TO THE LAST TWO CAHILLS. WHAT SHALL IT BE?
IN ALL THE EXCITEMENT, AMY AND DAN HADN'T REALIZED THEY WERE THE LAST ONES UNDECIDED.

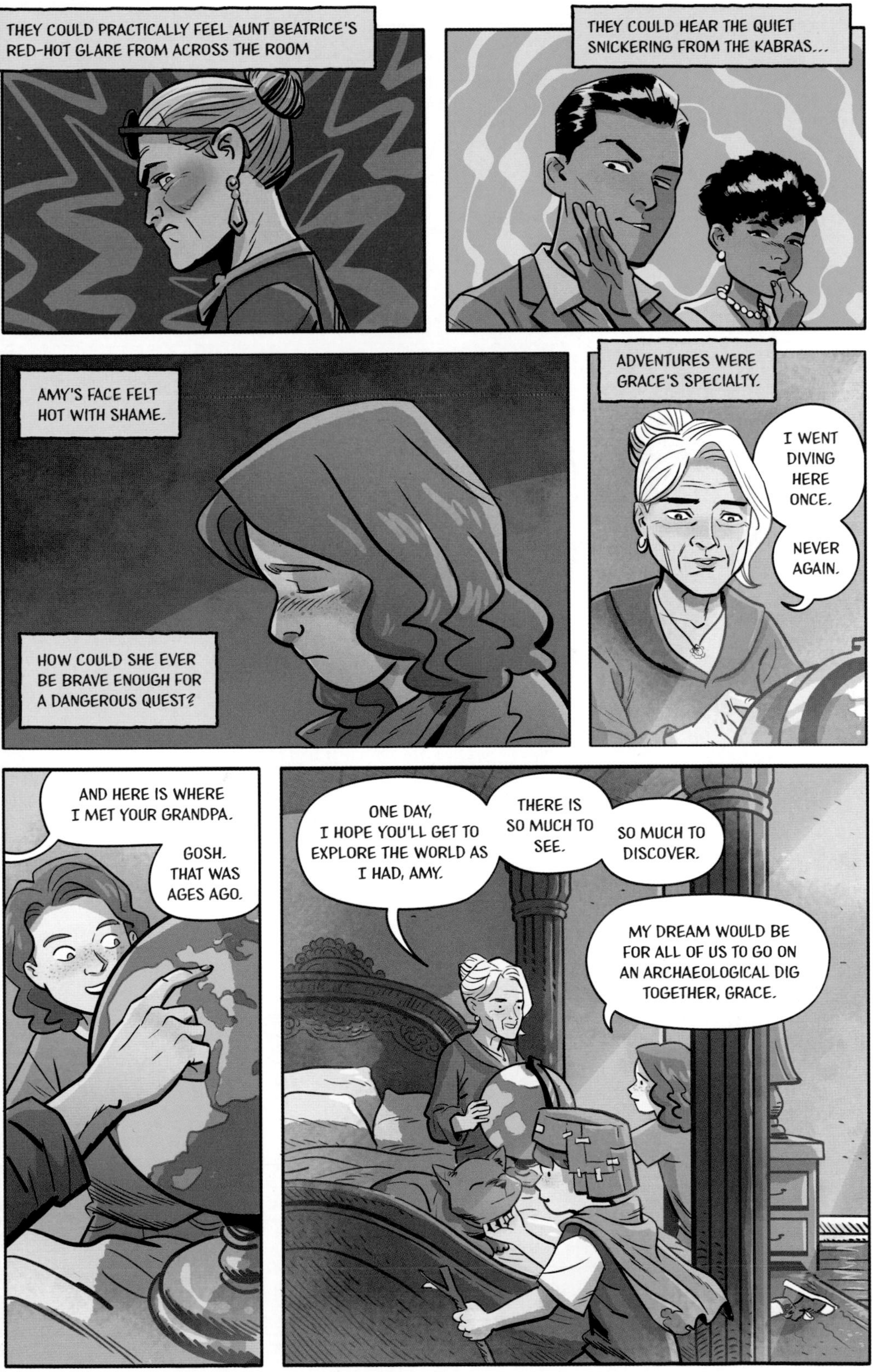
THEY COULD PRACTICALLY FEEL AUNT BEATRICE'S RED-HOT GLARE FROM ACROSS THE ROOM
THEY COULD HEAR THE QUIET SNICKERING FROM THE KABRAS...
AMY'S FACE FELT HOT WITH SHAME.
HOW COULD SHE EVER BE BRAVE ENOUGH FOR A DANGEROUS QUEST?
ADVENTURES WERE GRACE'S SPECIALTY.
I WENT DIVING HERE ONCE.
NEVER AGAIN.
AND HERE IS WHERE I MET YOUR GRANDPA.
GOSH. THAT WAS AGES AGO.
ONE DAY, I HOPE YOU'LL GET TO EXPLORE THE WORLD AS I HAD, AMY.
THERE IS SO MUCH TO SEE.
SO MUCH TO DISCOVER.
MY DREAM WOULD BE FOR ALL OF US TO GO ON AN ARCHAEOLOGICAL DIG TOGETHER, GRACE.

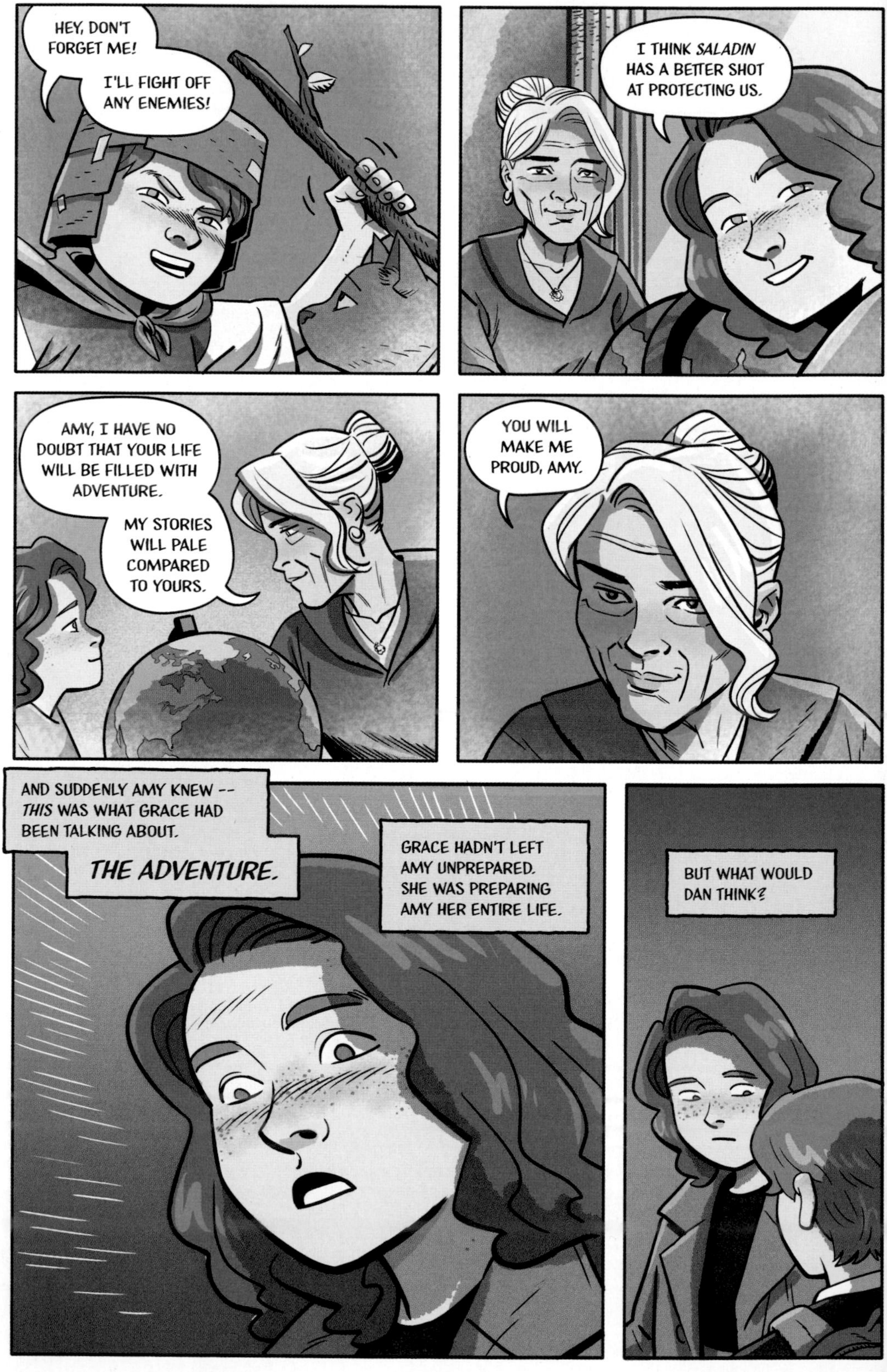
HEY, DON'T FORGET ME!
I'LL FIGHT OFF ANY ENEMIES!
I THINK *SALADIN* HAS A BETTER SHOT AT PROTECTING US.
AMY, I HAVE NO DOUBT THAT YOUR LIFE WILL BE FILLED WITH ADVENTURE.
MY STORIES WILL PALE COMPARED TO YOURS.
YOU WILL MAKE ME PROUD, AMY.
AND SUDDENLY AMY KNEW -- *THIS* WAS WHAT GRACE HAD BEEN TALKING ABOUT.
THE ADVENTURE.
GRACE HADN'T LEFT AMY UNPREPARED. SHE WAS PREPARING AMY HER ENTIRE LIFE.
BUT WHAT WOULD DAN THINK?

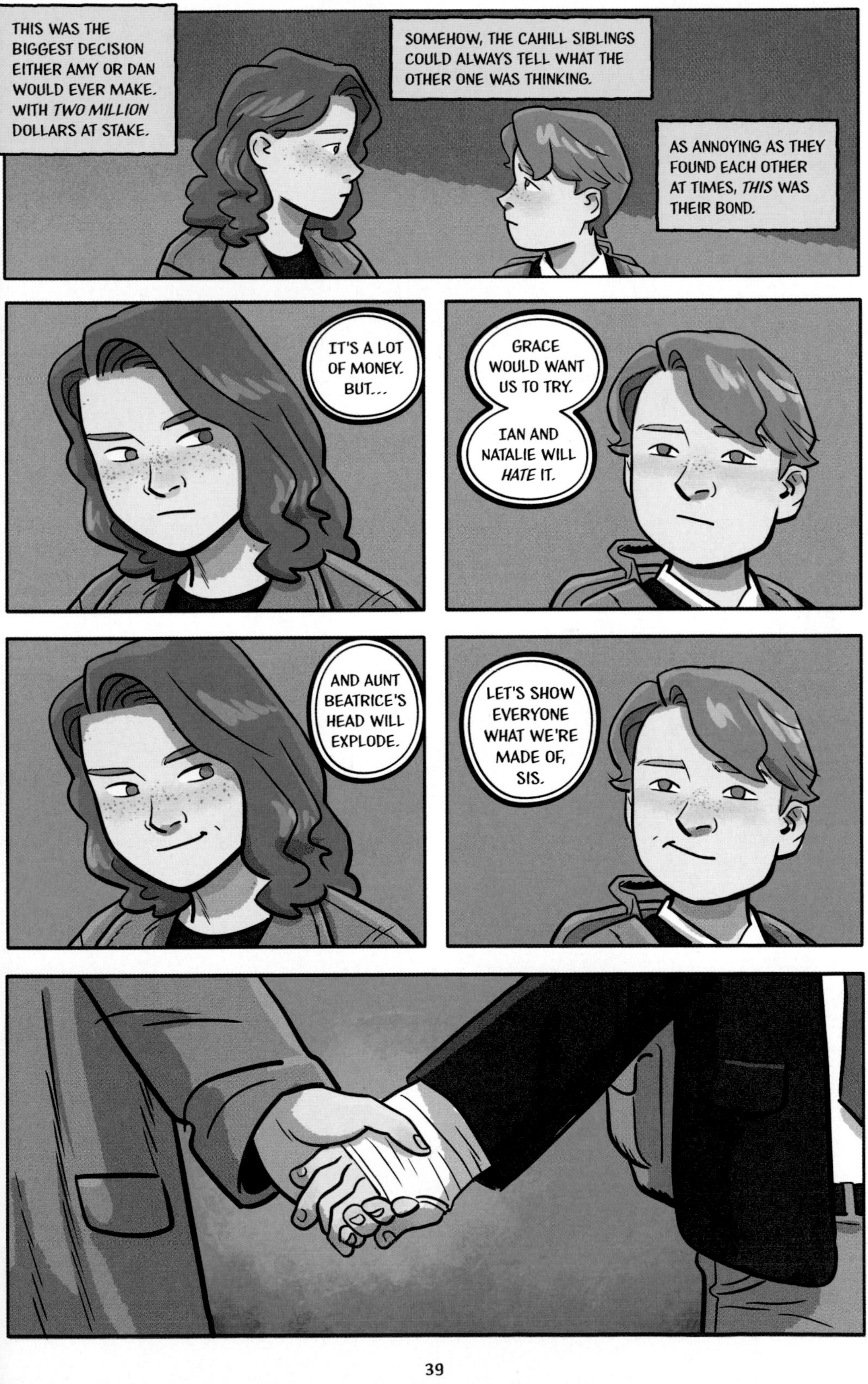

THIS WAS THE BIGGEST DECISION EITHER AMY OR DAN WOULD EVER MAKE. WITH *TWO MILLION* DOLLARS AT STAKE.
SOMEHOW, THE CAHILL SIBLINGS COULD ALWAYS TELL WHAT THE OTHER ONE WAS THINKING.
AS ANNOYING AS THEY FOUND EACH OTHER AT TIMES, *THIS* WAS THEIR BOND.
IT'S A LOT OF MONEY. BUT...
GRACE WOULD WANT US TO TRY.
IAN AND NATALIE WILL *HATE* IT.
AND AUNT BEATRICE'S HEAD WILL EXPLODE.
LET'S SHOW EVERYONE WHAT WE'RE MADE OF, SIS.

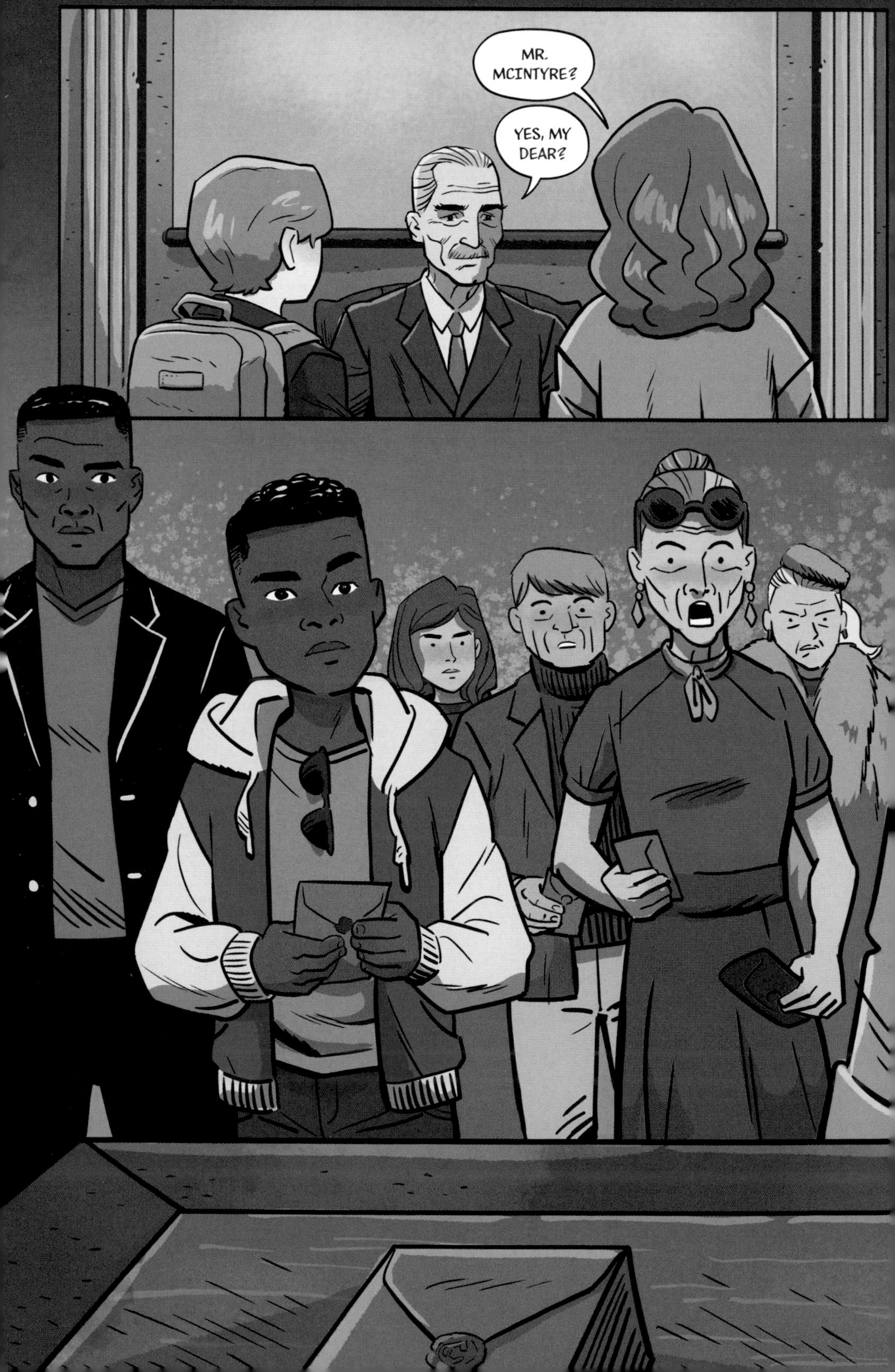
MR. MCINTYRE?
YES, MY DEAR?

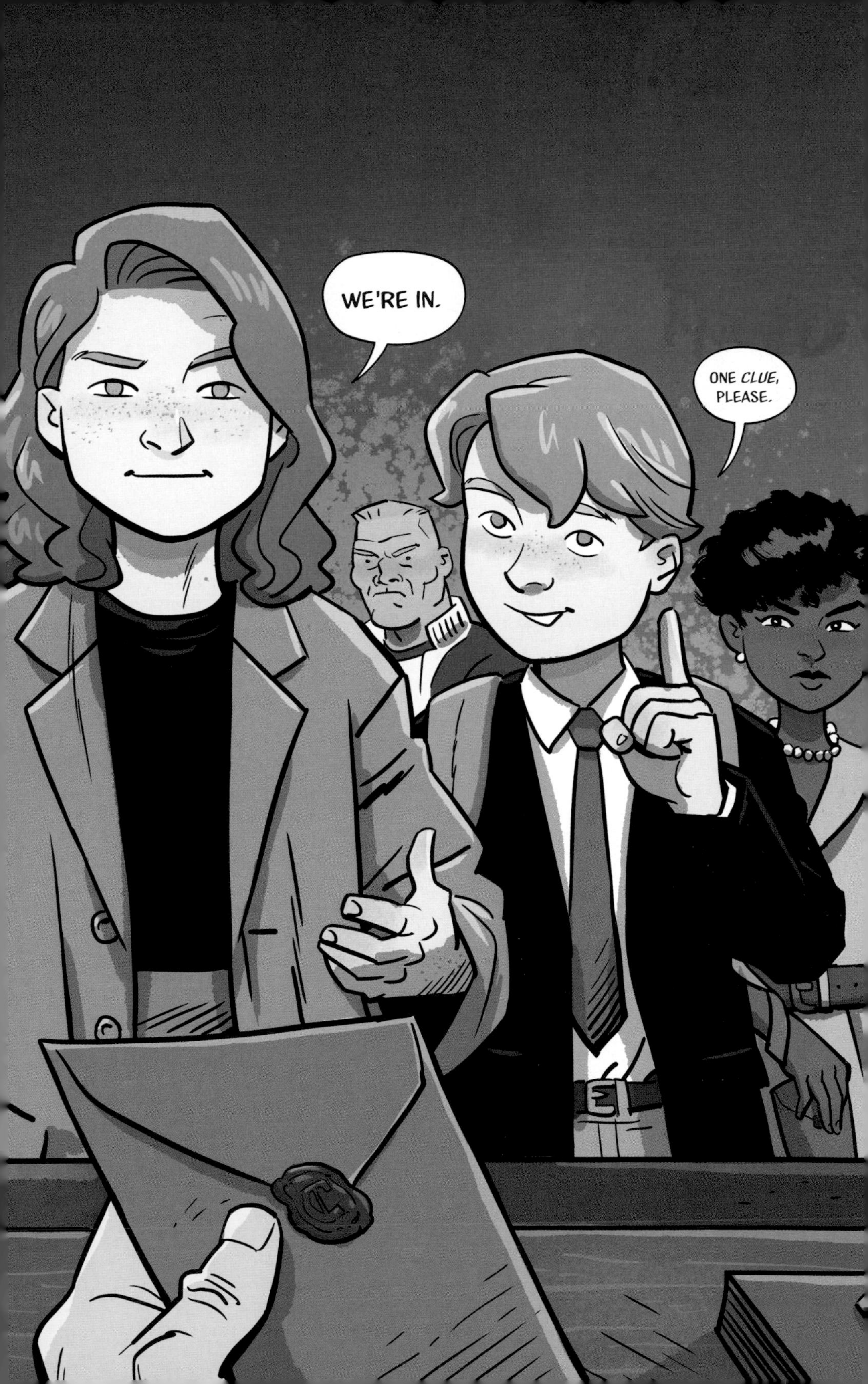
WE'RE IN.
ONE *CLUE*, PLEASE.

THREE

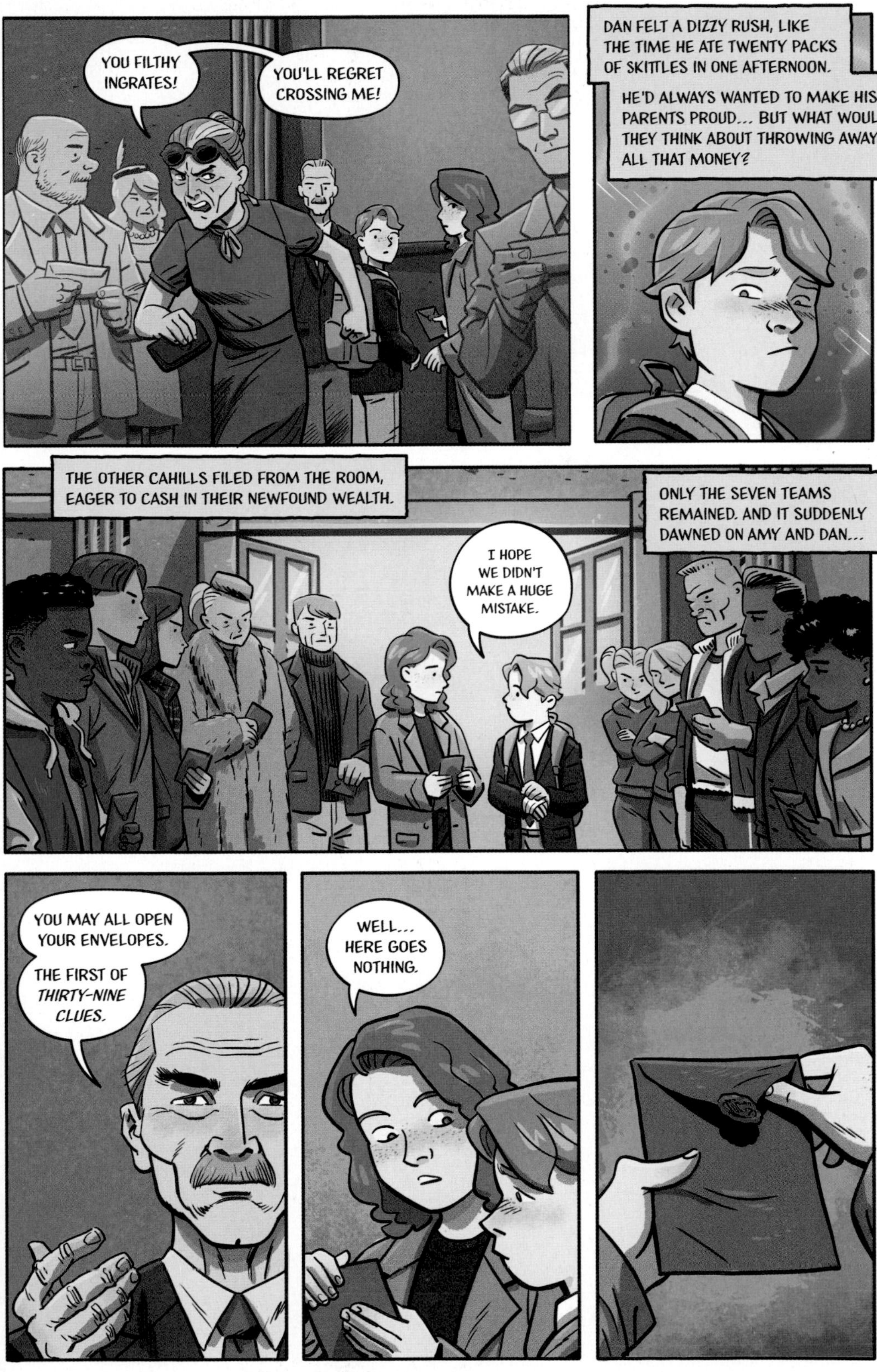
YOU FILTHY INGRATES!
YOU'LL REGRET CROSSING ME!
DAN FELT A DIZZY RUSH, LIKE THE TIME HE ATE TWENTY PACKS OF SKITTLES IN ONE AFTERNOON.
HE'D ALWAYS WANTED TO MAKE HIS PARENTS PROUD... BUT WHAT WOULD THEY THINK ABOUT THROWING AWAY ALL THAT MONEY?
THE OTHER CAHILLS FILED FROM THE ROOM, EAGER TO CASH IN THEIR NEWFOUND WEALTH.
I HOPE WE DIDN'T MAKE A HUGE MISTAKE.
ONLY THE SEVEN TEAMS REMAINED. AND IT SUDDENLY DAWNED ON AMY AND DAN...
YOU MAY ALL OPEN YOUR ENVELOPES.
THE FIRST OF *THIRTY-NINE CLUES.*
WELL... HERE GOES NOTHING.

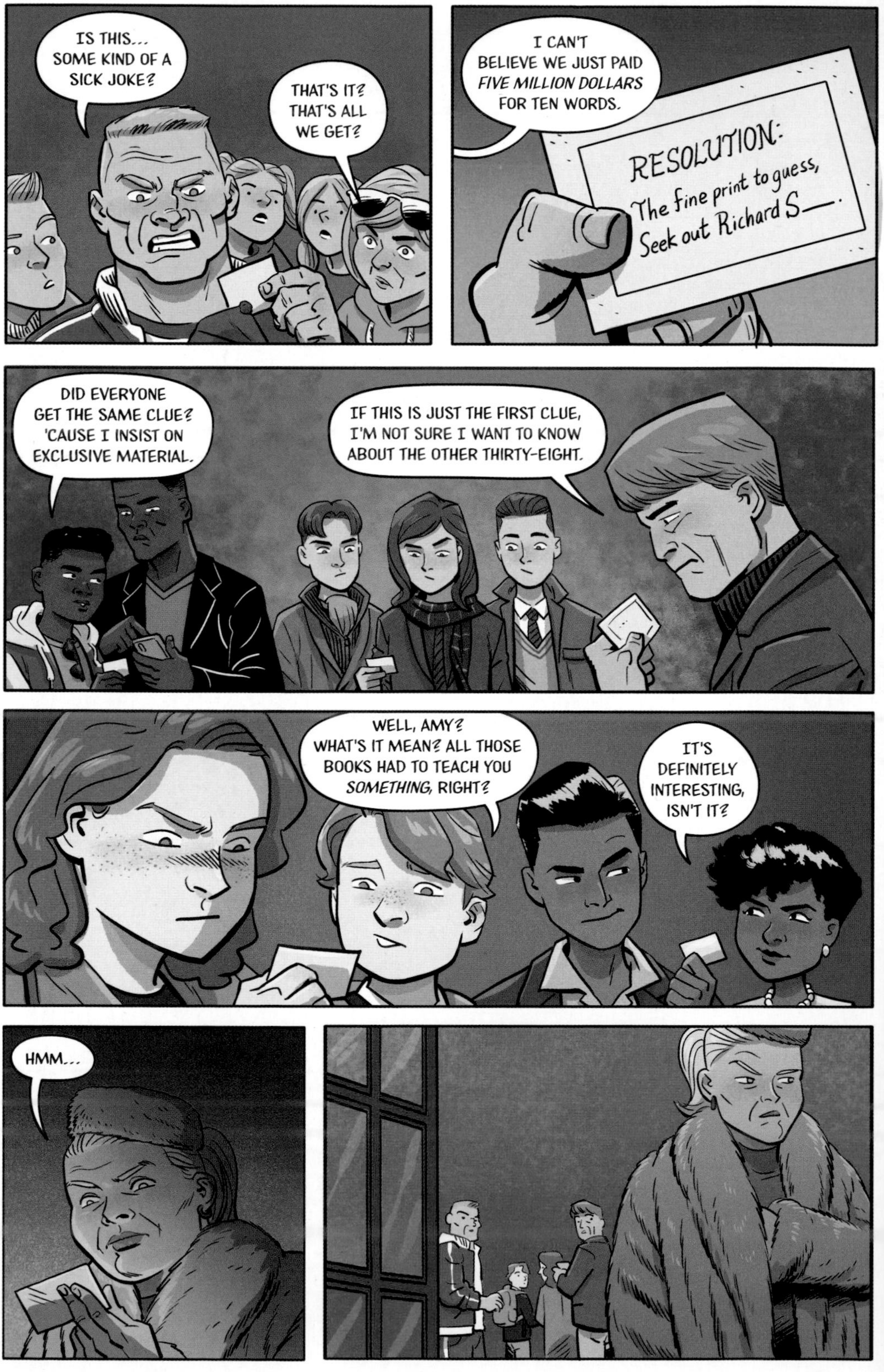
IS THIS... SOME KIND OF A SICK JOKE?
THAT'S IT? THAT'S ALL WE GET?
I CAN'T BELIEVE WE JUST PAID *FIVE MILLION DOLLARS* FOR TEN WORDS.
RESOLUTION:
The fine print to guess,
Seek out Richard S___.
DID EVERYONE GET THE SAME CLUE? 'CAUSE I INSIST ON EXCLUSIVE MATERIAL.
IF THIS IS JUST THE FIRST CLUE, I'M NOT SURE I WANT TO KNOW ABOUT THE OTHER THIRTY-EIGHT.
WELL, AMY? WHAT'S IT MEAN? ALL THOSE BOOKS HAD TO TEACH YOU *SOMETHING*, RIGHT?
IT'S DEFINITELY INTERESTING, ISN'T IT?
HMM...

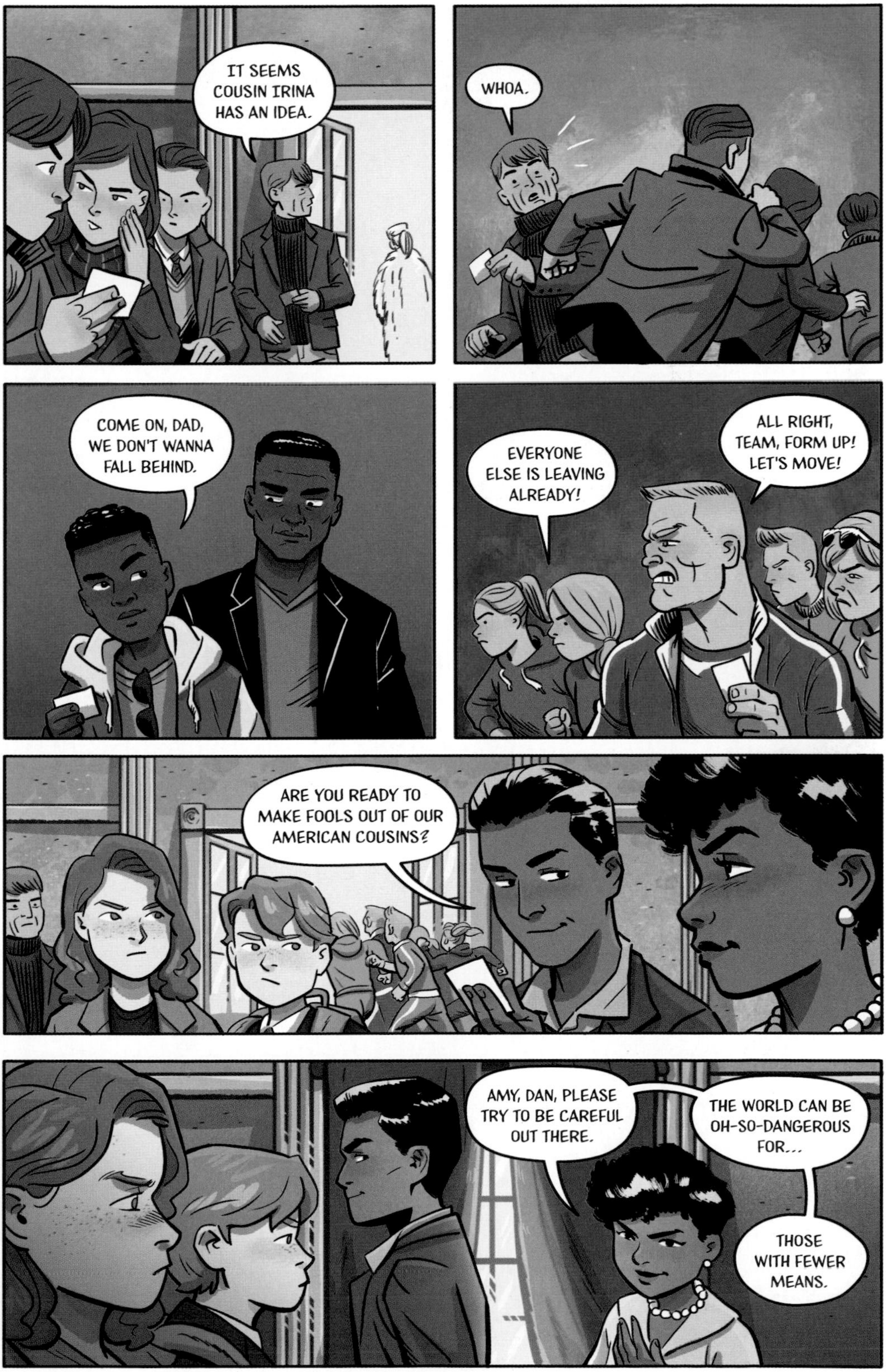
IT SEEMS COUSIN IRINA HAS AN IDEA.
WHOA.
COME ON, DAD, WE DON'T WANNA FALL BEHIND.
EVERYONE ELSE IS LEAVING ALREADY!
ALL RIGHT, TEAM, FORM UP! LET'S MOVE!
ARE YOU READY TO MAKE FOOLS OUT OF OUR AMERICAN COUSINS?
AMY, DAN, PLEASE TRY TO BE CAREFUL OUT THERE.
THE WORLD CAN BE OH-SO-DANGEROUS FOR...
THOSE WITH FEWER MEANS.

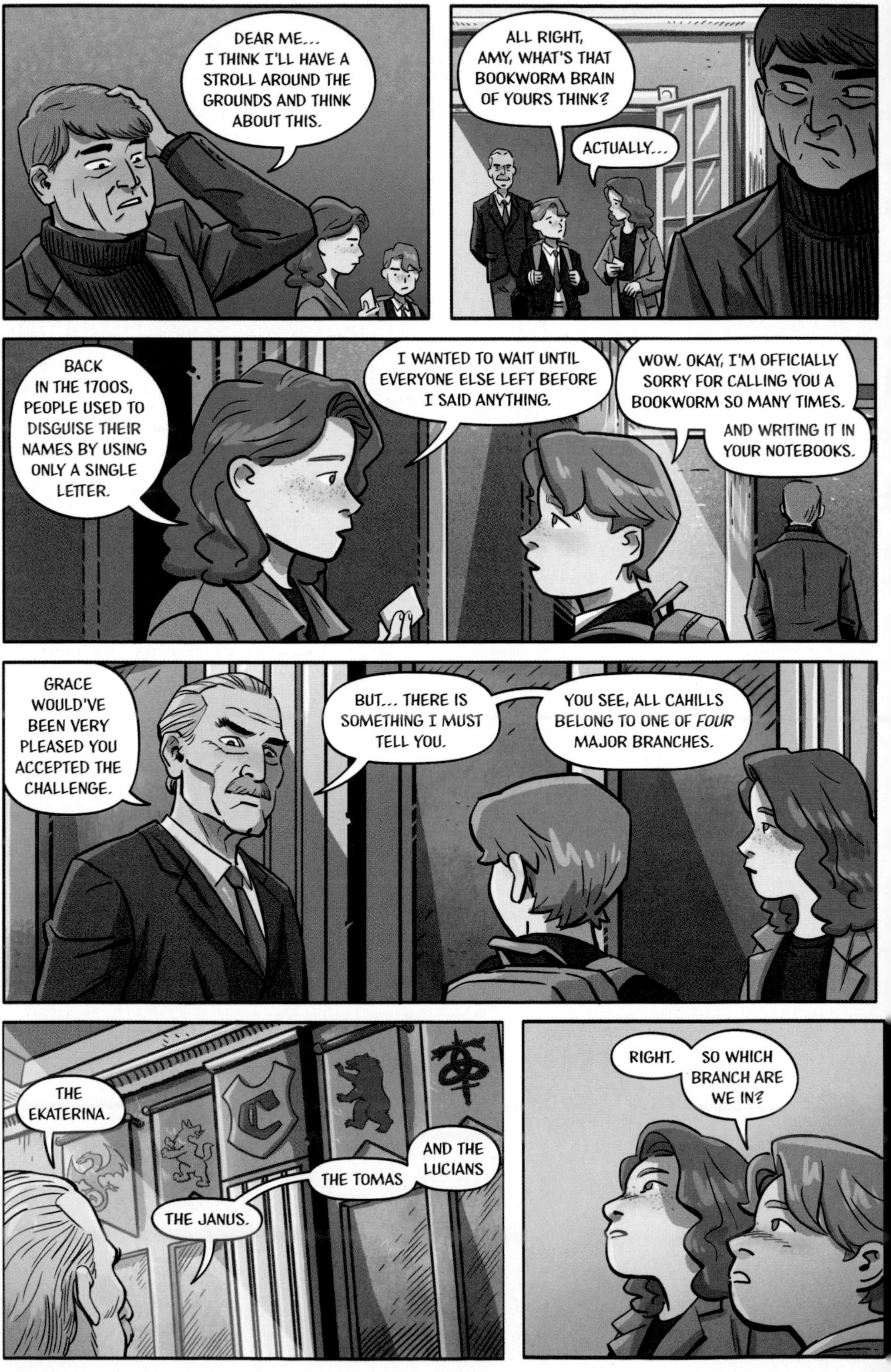
DEAR ME... I THINK I'LL HAVE A STROLL AROUND THE GROUNDS AND THINK ABOUT THIS.
ALL RIGHT, AMY, WHAT'S THAT BOOKWORM BRAIN OF YOURS THINK?
ACTUALLY...
BACK IN THE 1700S, PEOPLE USED TO DISGUISE THEIR NAMES BY USING ONLY A SINGLE LETTER.
I WANTED TO WAIT UNTIL EVERYONE ELSE LEFT BEFORE I SAID ANYTHING.
WOW. OKAY, I'M OFFICIALLY SORRY FOR CALLING YOU A BOOKWORM SO MANY TIMES.
AND WRITING IT IN YOUR NOTEBOOKS.
GRACE WOULD'VE BEEN VERY PLEASED YOU ACCEPTED THE CHALLENGE.
BUT... THERE IS SOMETHING I MUST TELL YOU.
YOU SEE, ALL CAHILLS BELONG TO ONE OF *FOUR* MAJOR BRANCHES.
THE EKATERINA.
THE JANUS.
THE TOMAS
AND THE LUCIANS
RIGHT.
SO WHICH BRANCH ARE WE IN?

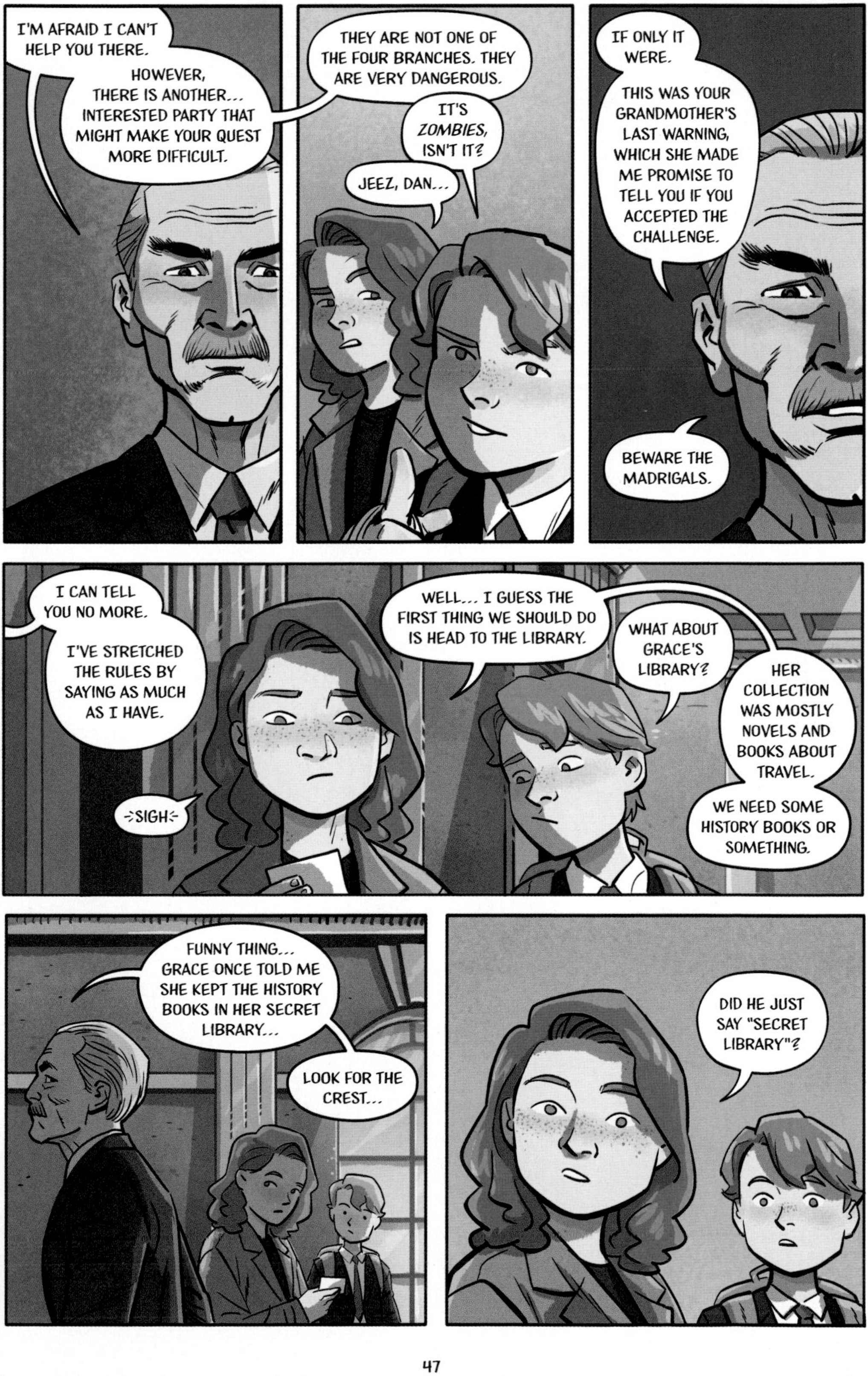
I'M AFRAID I CAN'T HELP YOU THERE.
HOWEVER, THERE IS ANOTHER... INTERESTED PARTY THAT MIGHT MAKE YOUR QUEST MORE DIFFICULT.
THEY ARE NOT ONE OF THE FOUR BRANCHES. THEY ARE VERY DANGEROUS.
IT'S *ZOMBIES*, ISN'T IT?
JEEZ, DAN...
IF ONLY IT WERE.
THIS WAS YOUR GRANDMOTHER'S LAST WARNING, WHICH SHE MADE ME PROMISE TO TELL YOU IF YOU ACCEPTED THE CHALLENGE.
BEWARE THE MADRIGALS.
I CAN TELL YOU NO MORE.
I'VE STRETCHED THE RULES BY SAYING AS MUCH AS I HAVE.
SIGH
WELL... I GUESS THE FIRST THING WE SHOULD DO IS HEAD TO THE LIBRARY.
WHAT ABOUT GRACE'S LIBRARY?
HER COLLECTION WAS MOSTLY NOVELS AND BOOKS ABOUT TRAVEL.
WE NEED SOME HISTORY BOOKS OR SOMETHING.
FUNNY THING... GRACE ONCE TOLD ME SHE KEPT THE HISTORY BOOKS IN HER SECRET LIBRARY...
LOOK FOR THE CREST...
DID HE JUST SAY "SECRET LIBRARY"?

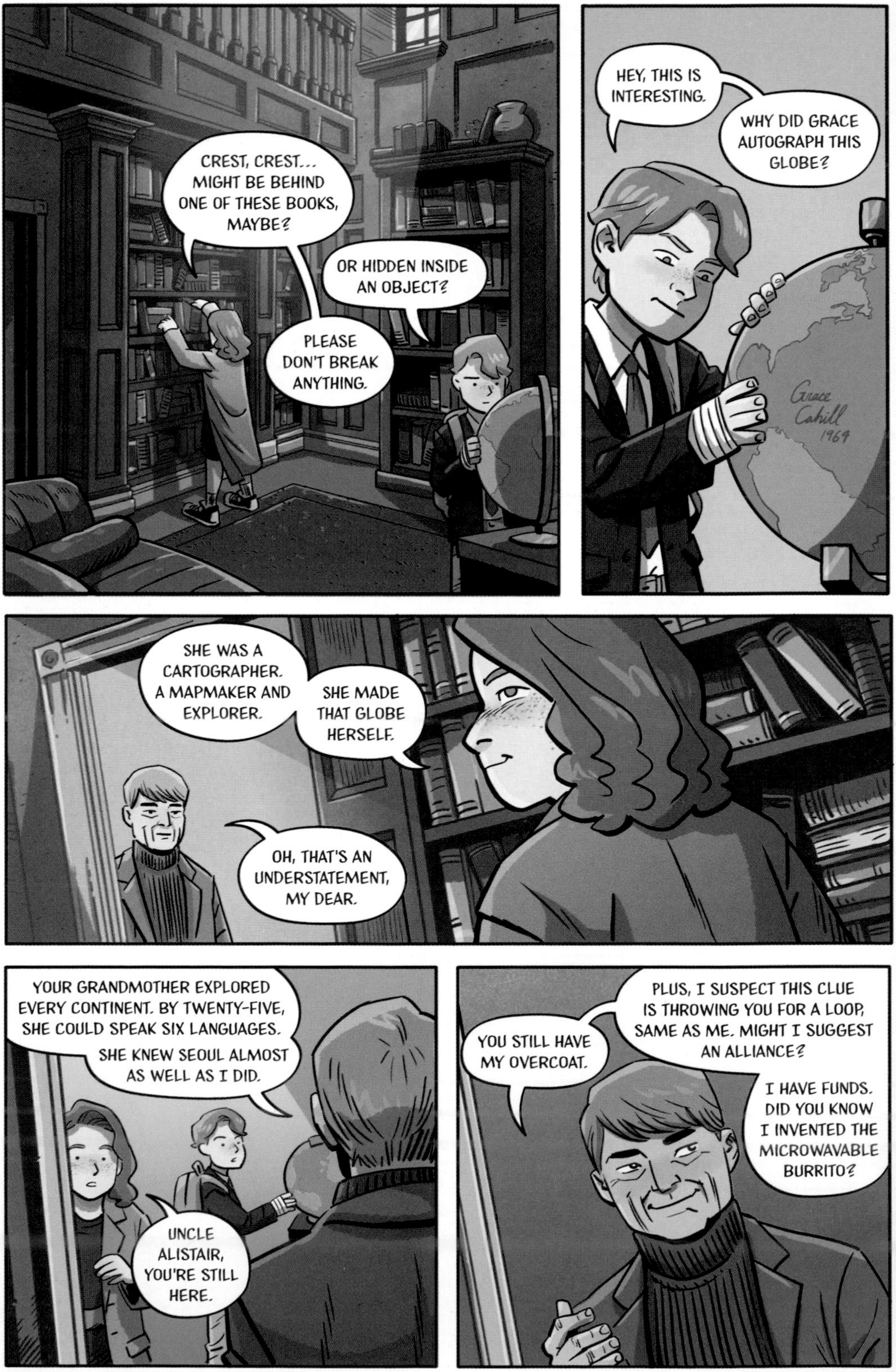
CREST, CREST... MIGHT BE BEHIND ONE OF THESE BOOKS, MAYBE?
OR HIDDEN INSIDE AN OBJECT?
PLEASE DON'T BREAK ANYTHING.
HEY, THIS IS INTERESTING.
WHY DID GRACE AUTOGRAPH THIS GLOBE?
Grace Cahill 1964
SHE WAS A CARTOGRAPHER. A MAPMAKER AND EXPLORER.
SHE MADE THAT GLOBE HERSELF.
OH, THAT'S AN UNDERSTATEMENT, MY DEAR.
YOUR GRANDMOTHER EXPLORED EVERY CONTINENT. BY TWENTY-FIVE, SHE COULD SPEAK SIX LANGUAGES.
SHE KNEW SEOUL ALMOST AS WELL AS I DID.
UNCLE ALISTAIR, YOU'RE STILL HERE.
YOU STILL HAVE MY OVERCOAT.
PLUS, I SUSPECT THIS CLUE IS THROWING YOU FOR A LOOP, SAME AS ME. MIGHT I SUGGEST AN ALLIANCE?
I HAVE FUNDS. DID YOU KNOW I INVENTED THE MICROWAVABLE BURRITO?

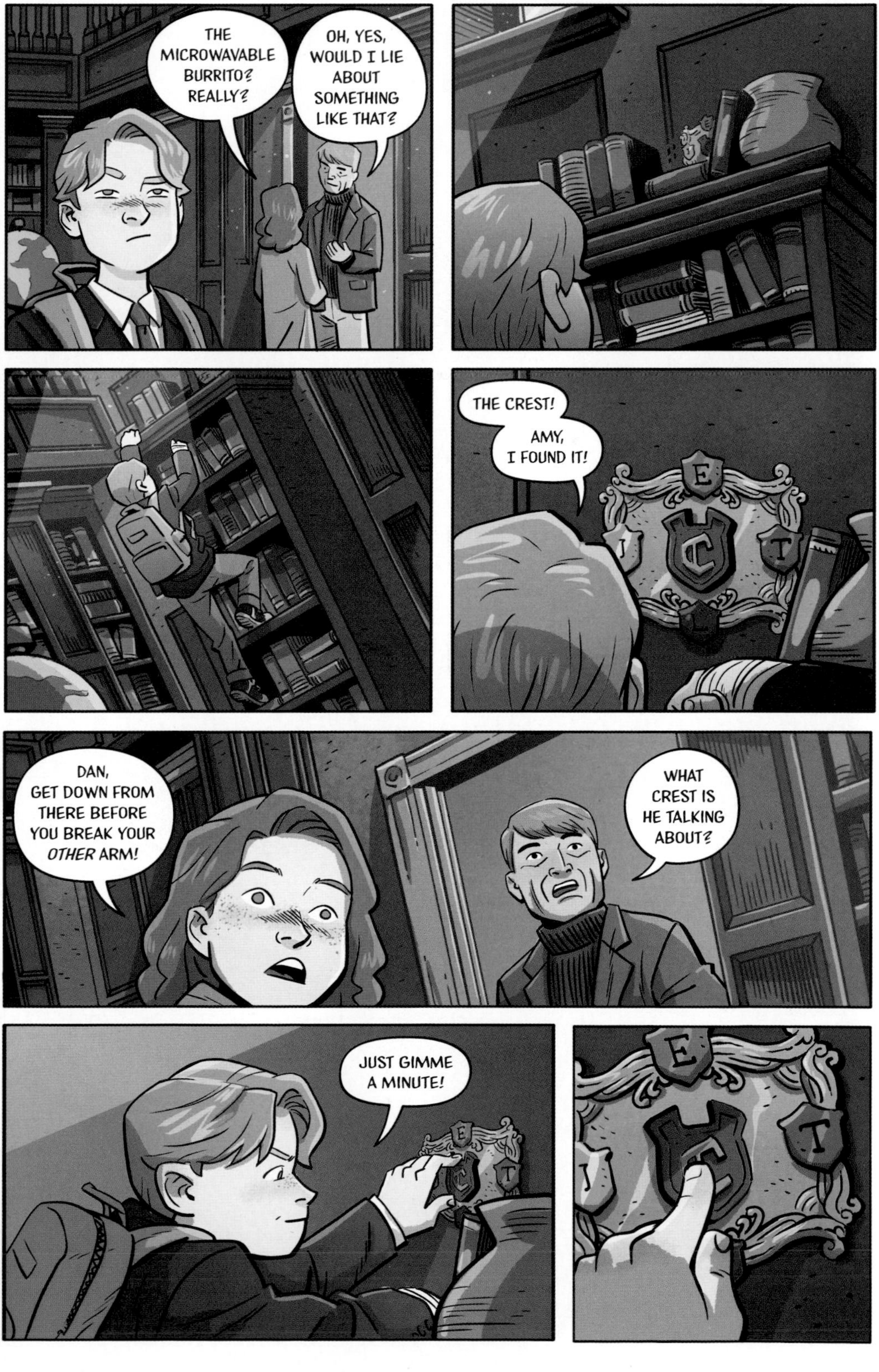
THE MICROWAVABLE BURRITO? REALLY?
OH, YES, WOULD I LIE ABOUT SOMETHING LIKE THAT?
THE CREST!
AMY, I FOUND IT!
E
I
C
T
DAN, GET DOWN FROM THERE BEFORE YOU BREAK YOUR *OTHER* ARM!
WHAT CREST IS HE TALKING ABOUT?
JUST GIMME A MINUTE!
E
T
E
T

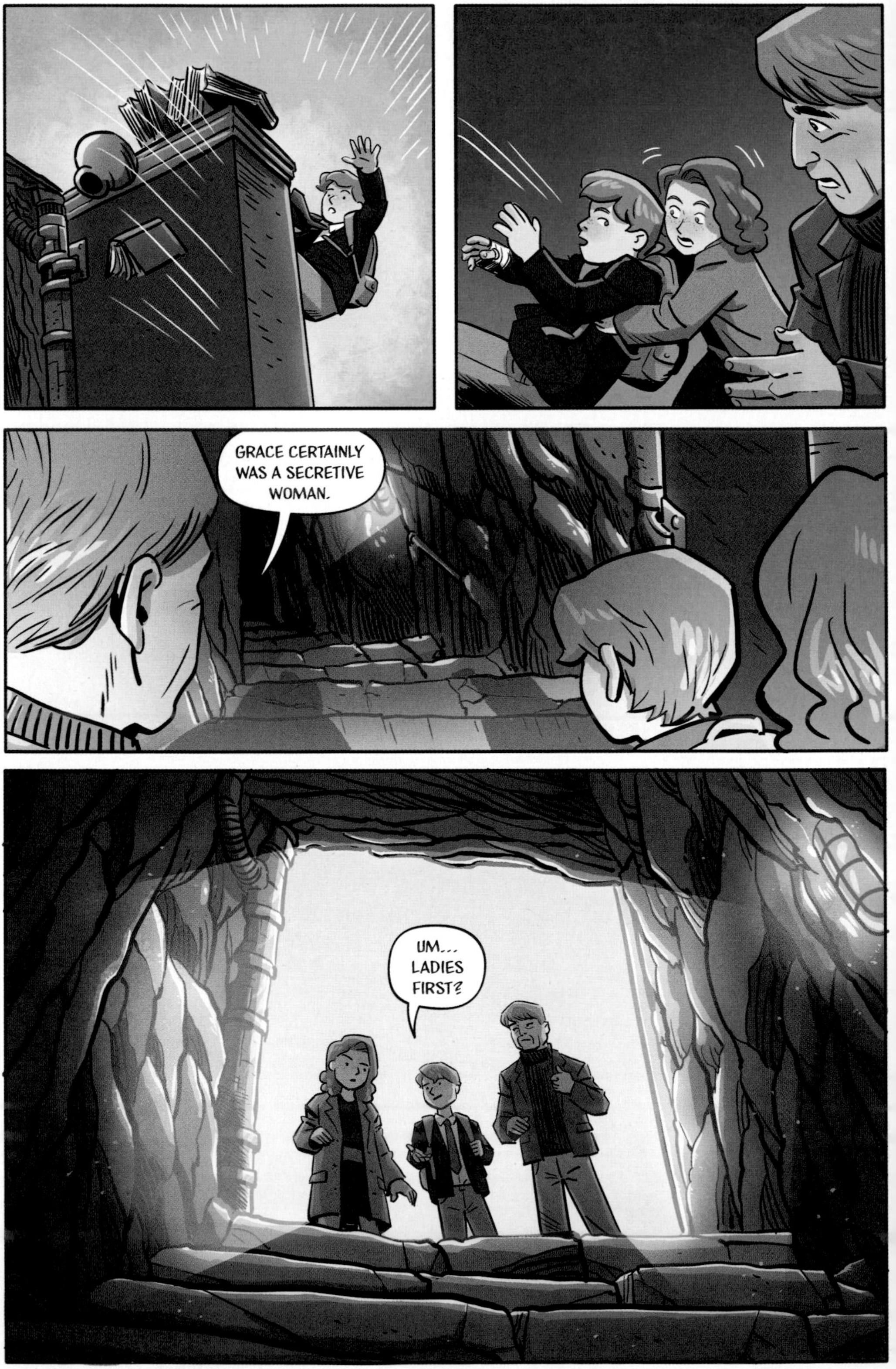
GRACE CERTAINLY WAS A SECRETIVE WOMAN.
UM... LADIES FIRST?

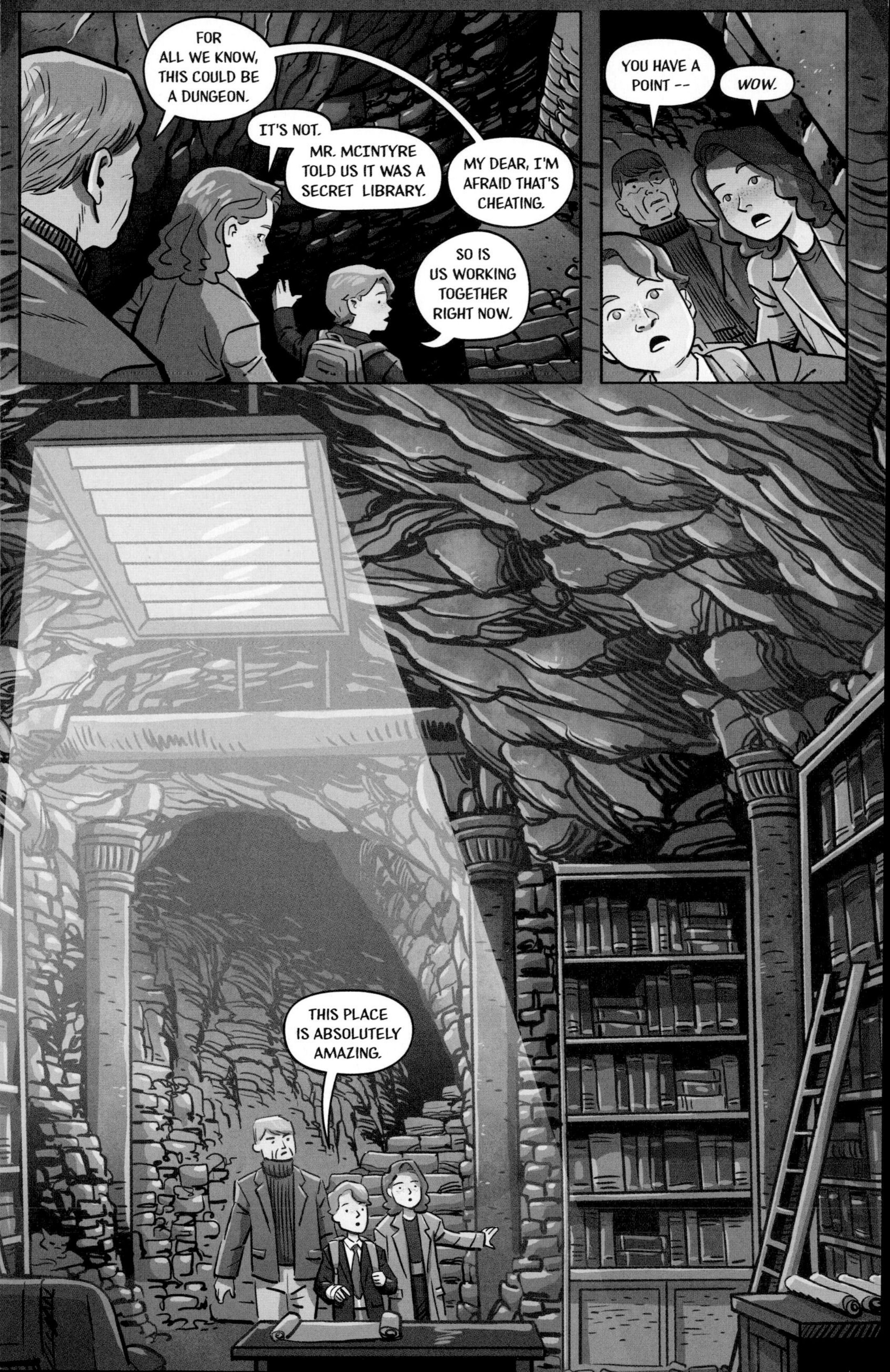
FOR ALL WE KNOW, THIS COULD BE A DUNGEON.
IT'S NOT.
MR. MCINTYRE TOLD US IT WAS A SECRET LIBRARY.
MY DEAR, I'M AFRAID THAT'S CHEATING.
SO IS US WORKING TOGETHER RIGHT NOW.
YOU HAVE A POINT --
WOW.
THIS PLACE IS ABSOLUTELY AMAZING.

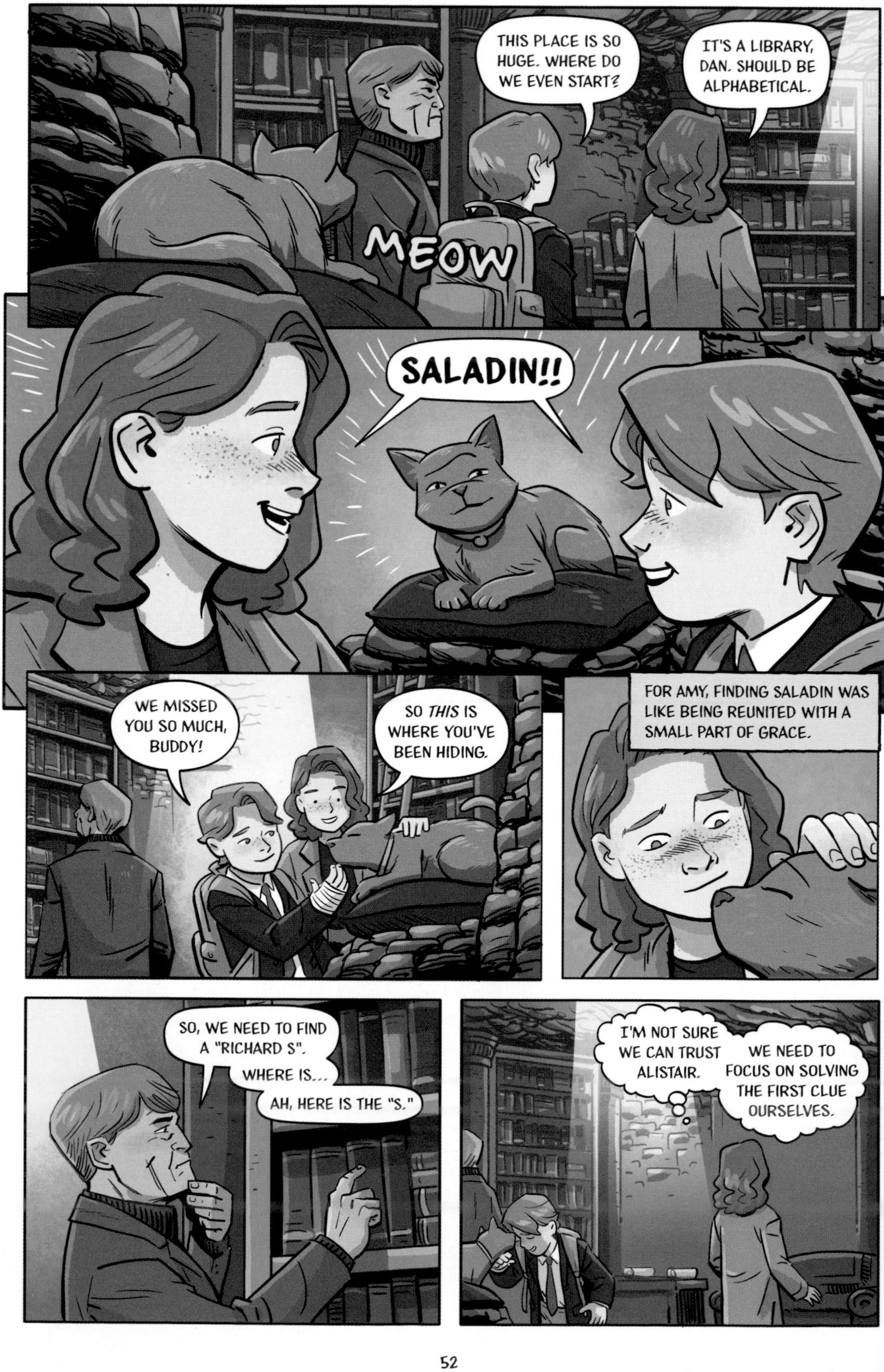
THIS PLACE IS SO HUGE. WHERE DO WE EVEN START?
IT'S A LIBRARY, DAN. SHOULD BE ALPHABETICAL.
MEOW
SALADIN!!
WE MISSED YOU SO MUCH, BUDDY!
SO *THIS* IS WHERE YOU'VE BEEN HIDING.
FOR AMY, FINDING SALADIN WAS LIKE BEING REUNITED WITH A SMALL PART OF GRACE.
SO, WE NEED TO FIND A "RICHARD S".
WHERE IS...
AH, HERE IS THE "S."
I'M NOT SURE WE CAN TRUST ALISTAIR.
WE NEED TO FOCUS ON SOLVING THE FIRST CLUE OURSELVES.

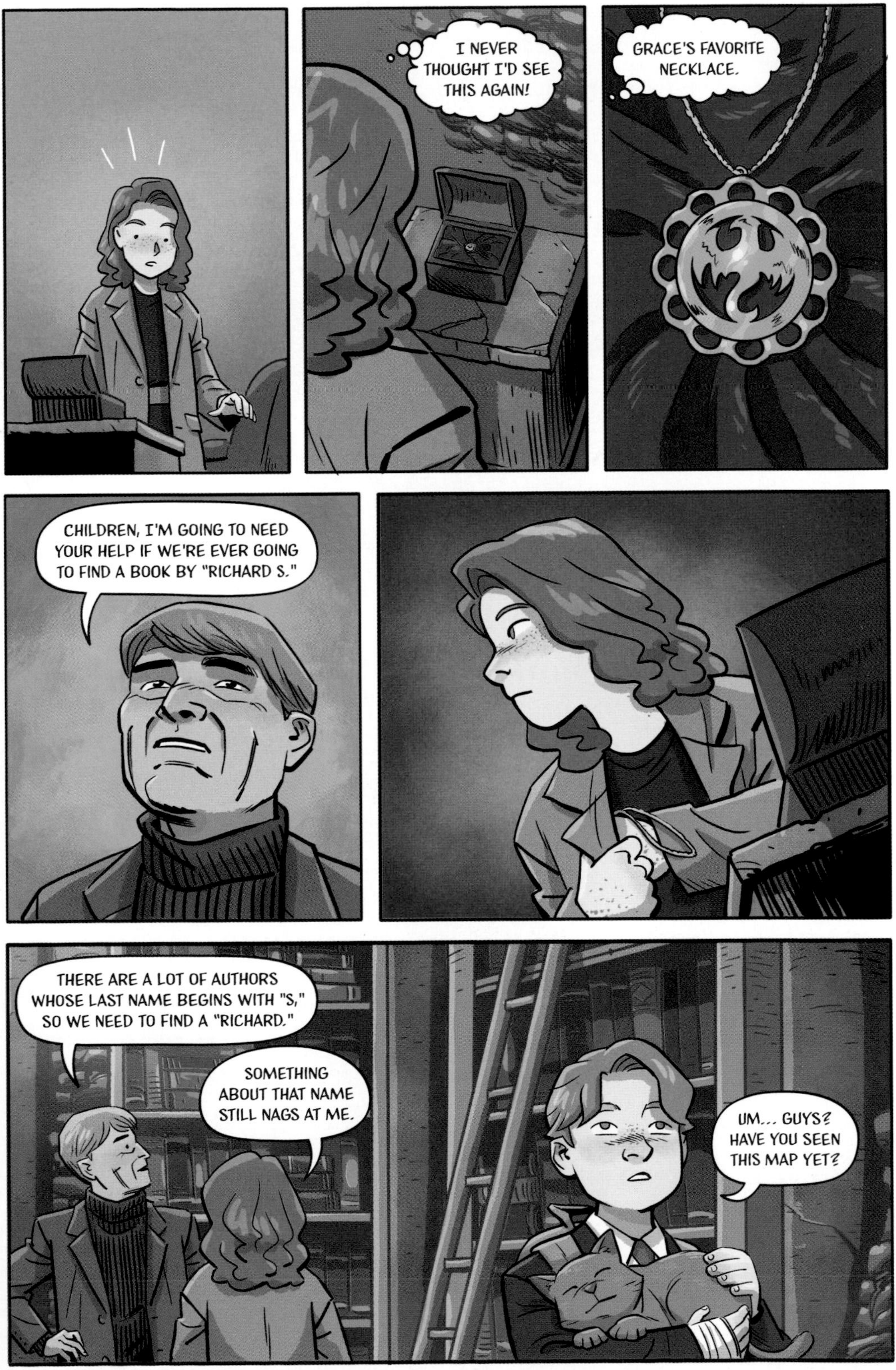
I NEVER THOUGHT I'D SEE THIS AGAIN!
GRACE'S FAVORITE NECKLACE.
CHILDREN, I'M GOING TO NEED YOUR HELP IF WE'RE EVER GOING TO FIND A BOOK BY "RICHARD S."
THERE ARE A LOT OF AUTHORS WHOSE LAST NAME BEGINS WITH "S," SO WE NEED TO FIND A "RICHARD."
SOMETHING ABOUT THAT NAME STILL NAGS AT ME.
UM... GUYS? HAVE YOU SEEN THIS MAP YET?

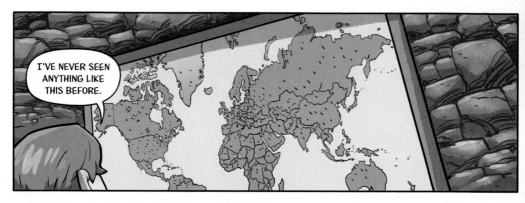

I'VE NEVER SEEN ANYTHING LIKE THIS BEFORE.

ALL THESE MARKERS... MOST CURIOUS.

MAYBE SOMETHING ABOUT THE CAHILLS?

IF THOSE PINS ARE CAHILLS, THEN WE STARTED IN EUROPE AND SPREAD ACROSS THE WORLD...

WAIT, THAT'S IT!

EUROPE, COLONIES, NORTH AMERICA...

WE'RE NOT SUPPOSED TO LOOK IN THE "S" SECTION--

WE NEED TO LOOK IN THE "F"!

COME ON, IT'S GOTTA BE HERE...

YES! FOUND IT!

POOR RICHARD'S ALMANACK, FOR THE YEAR 1739, BY RICHARD SAUNDERS.

OF COURSE! VERY GOOD, MY DEAR!

WAIT, SO THIS IS THE BOOK WE'RE LOOKING FOR?

WHY WAS IT UNDER "F"?

BECAUSE "RICHARD SAUNDERS" WAS A PSEUDONYM FOR *BENJAMIN FRANKLIN*, DAN!

I DID A REPORT ON HIM LAST YEAR.

THIS ALMANACK HAD FACTS FOR FARMERS. IT'S LIKE A YEARBOOK WITH USEFUL TIPS AND STUFF.

FRANKLIN PUT HIS FAMOUS QUOTATIONS IN HERE.

Poor Richard's ALMANACK

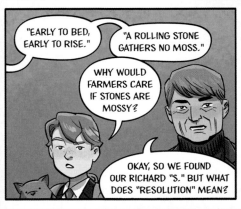

"EARLY TO BED, EARLY TO RISE."

"A ROLLING STONE GATHERS NO MOSS."

WHY WOULD FARMERS CARE IF STONES ARE MOSSY?

OKAY, SO WE FOUND OUR RICHARD "S." BUT WHAT DOES "RESOLUTION" MEAN?

FRANKLIN WOULD WRITE RESOLUTIONS FOR HIMSELF ALL YEAR ROUND TO IMPROVE HIMSELF.

BUT THOSE ARE FOUND IN A DIFFERENT BOOK. HIS AUTOBIOGRAPHY, I THINK.

MAYBE THE WORD "RESOLUTION" WAS JUST THERE TO HELP US *THINK* ABOUT FRANKLIN --

-- OH MY GOD.

WHAT IS IT?

THIS... THIS IS *MOM'S* HANDWRITING IN HERE.

WHAT?!

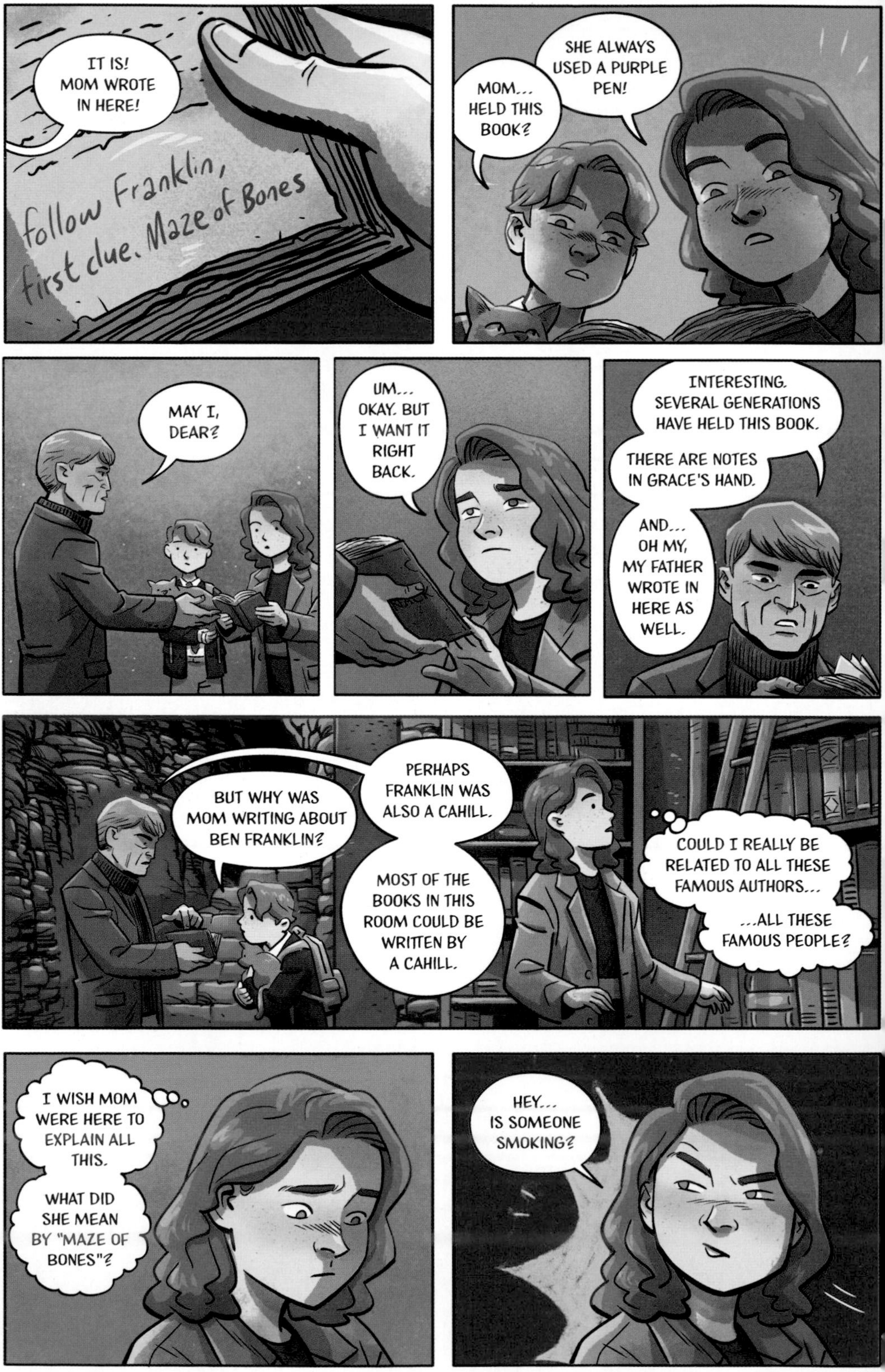
IT IS! MOM WROTE IN HERE!
follow Franklin, first clue. Maze of Bones
MOM... HELD THIS BOOK?
SHE ALWAYS USED A PURPLE PEN!
MAY I, DEAR?
UM... OKAY. BUT I WANT IT RIGHT BACK.
INTERESTING. SEVERAL GENERATIONS HAVE HELD THIS BOOK.
THERE ARE NOTES IN GRACE'S HAND.
AND... OH MY, MY FATHER WROTE IN HERE AS WELL.
BUT WHY WAS MOM WRITING ABOUT BEN FRANKLIN?
PERHAPS FRANKLIN WAS ALSO A CAHILL.
MOST OF THE BOOKS IN THIS ROOM COULD BE WRITTEN BY A CAHILL.
COULD I REALLY BE RELATED TO ALL THESE FAMOUS AUTHORS...
...ALL THESE FAMOUS PEOPLE?
I WISH MOM WERE HERE TO EXPLAIN ALL THIS.
WHAT DID SHE MEAN BY "MAZE OF BONES"?
HEY... IS SOMEONE SMOKING?

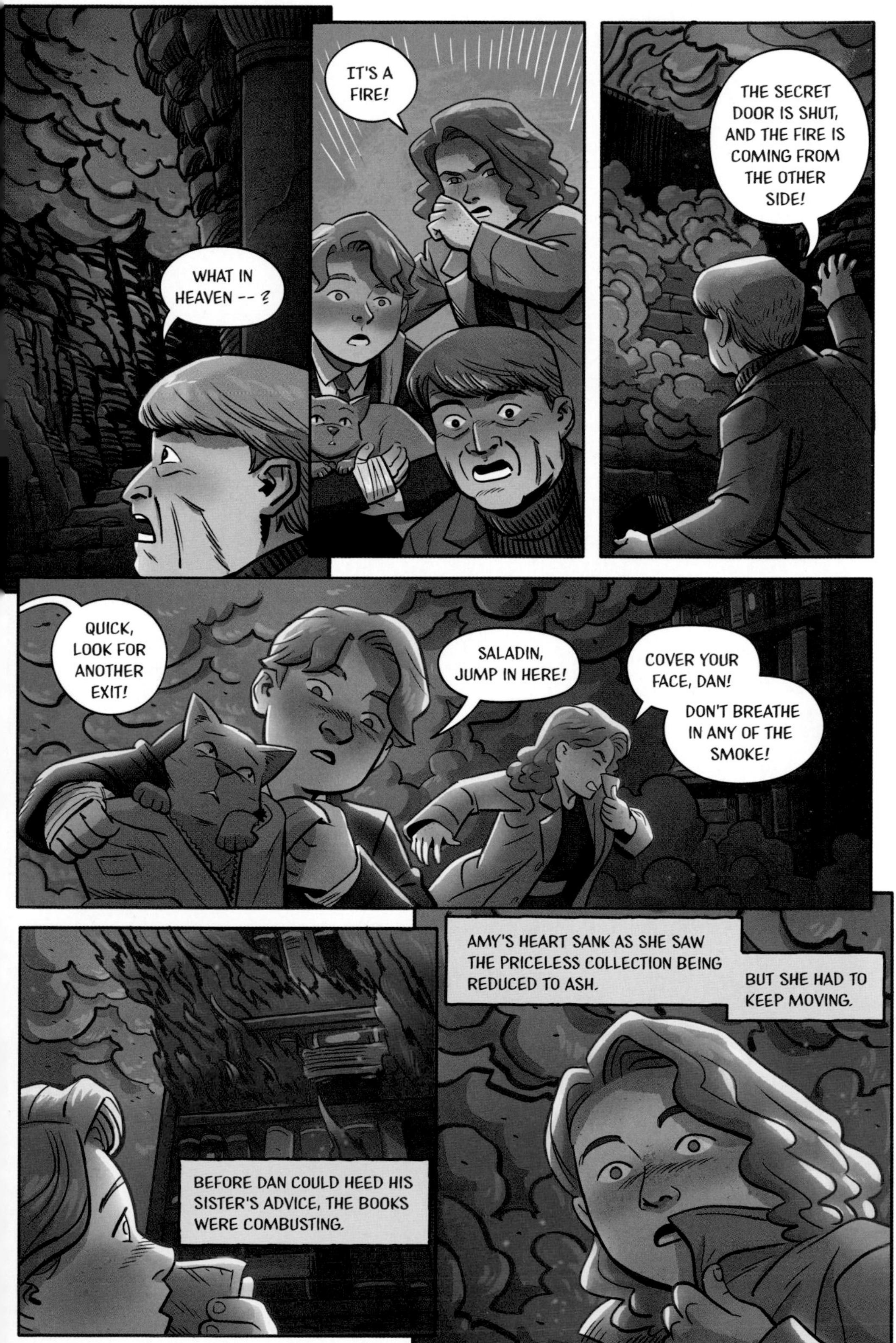
WHAT IN HEAVEN -- ?
IT'S A FIRE!
THE SECRET DOOR IS SHUT, AND THE FIRE IS COMING FROM THE OTHER SIDE!
QUICK, LOOK FOR ANOTHER EXIT!
SALADIN, JUMP IN HERE!
COVER YOUR FACE, DAN!
DON'T BREATHE IN ANY OF THE SMOKE!
BEFORE DAN COULD HEED HIS SISTER'S ADVICE, THE BOOKS WERE COMBUSTING.
AMY'S HEART SANK AS SHE SAW THE PRICELESS COLLECTION BEING REDUCED TO ASH.
BUT SHE HAD TO KEEP MOVING.

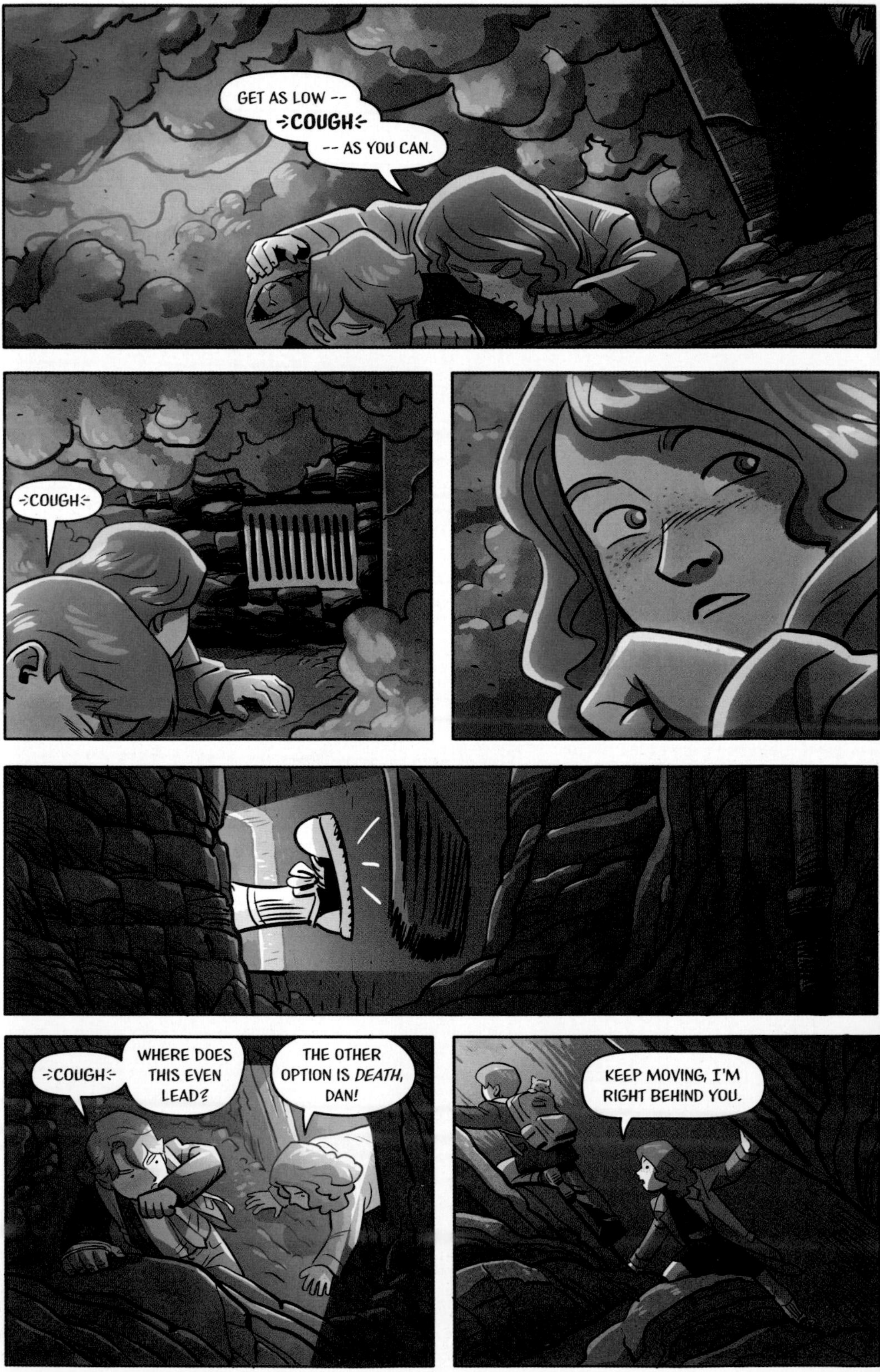
GET AS LOW --
COUGH
-- AS YOU CAN.
COUGH
COUGH
WHERE DOES THIS EVEN LEAD?
THE OTHER OPTION IS *DEATH*, DAN!
KEEP MOVING, I'M RIGHT BEHIND YOU.

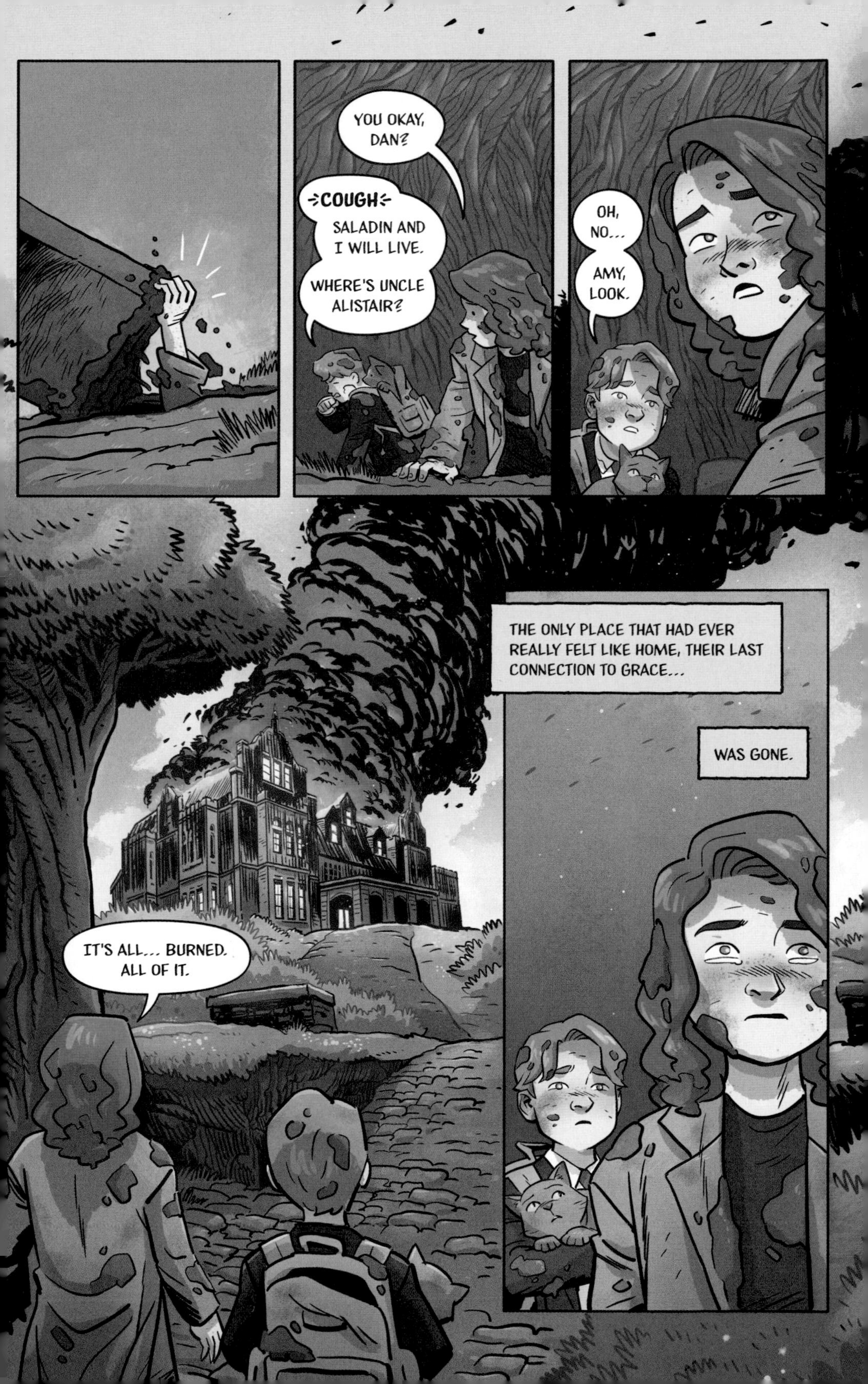
YOU OKAY, DAN?
COUGH
SALADIN AND I WILL LIVE.
WHERE'S UNCLE ALISTAIR?
OH, NO...
AMY, LOOK.
THE ONLY PLACE THAT HAD EVER REALLY FELT LIKE HOME, THEIR LAST CONNECTION TO GRACE...
IT'S ALL... BURNED. ALL OF IT.
WAS GONE.

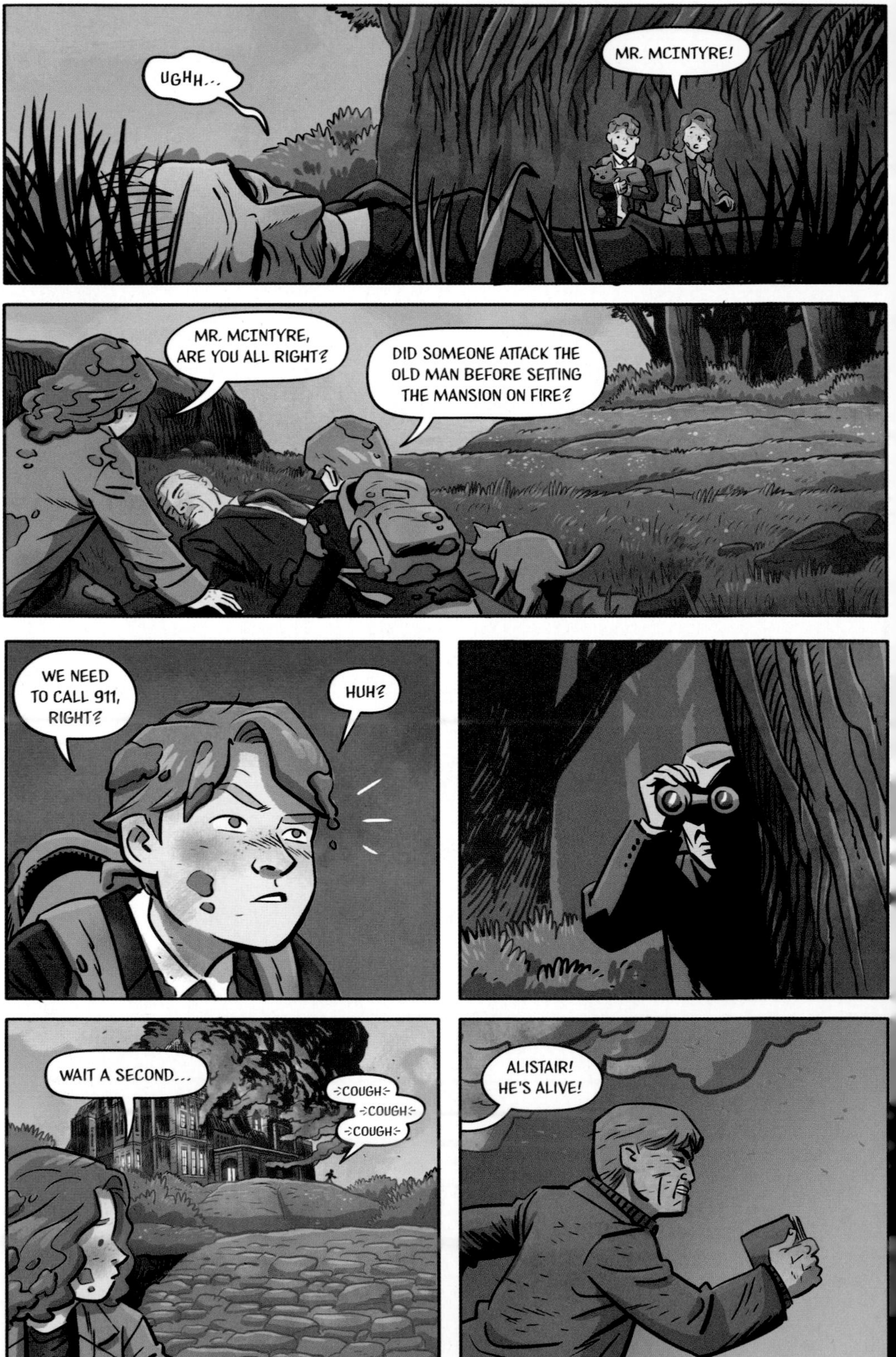
UGHH...
MR. MCINTYRE!
MR. MCINTYRE, ARE YOU ALL RIGHT?
DID SOMEONE ATTACK THE OLD MAN BEFORE SETTING THE MANSION ON FIRE?
WE NEED TO CALL 911, RIGHT?
HUH?
WAIT A SECOND...
COUGH
COUGH
COUGH
ALISTAIR! HE'S ALIVE!

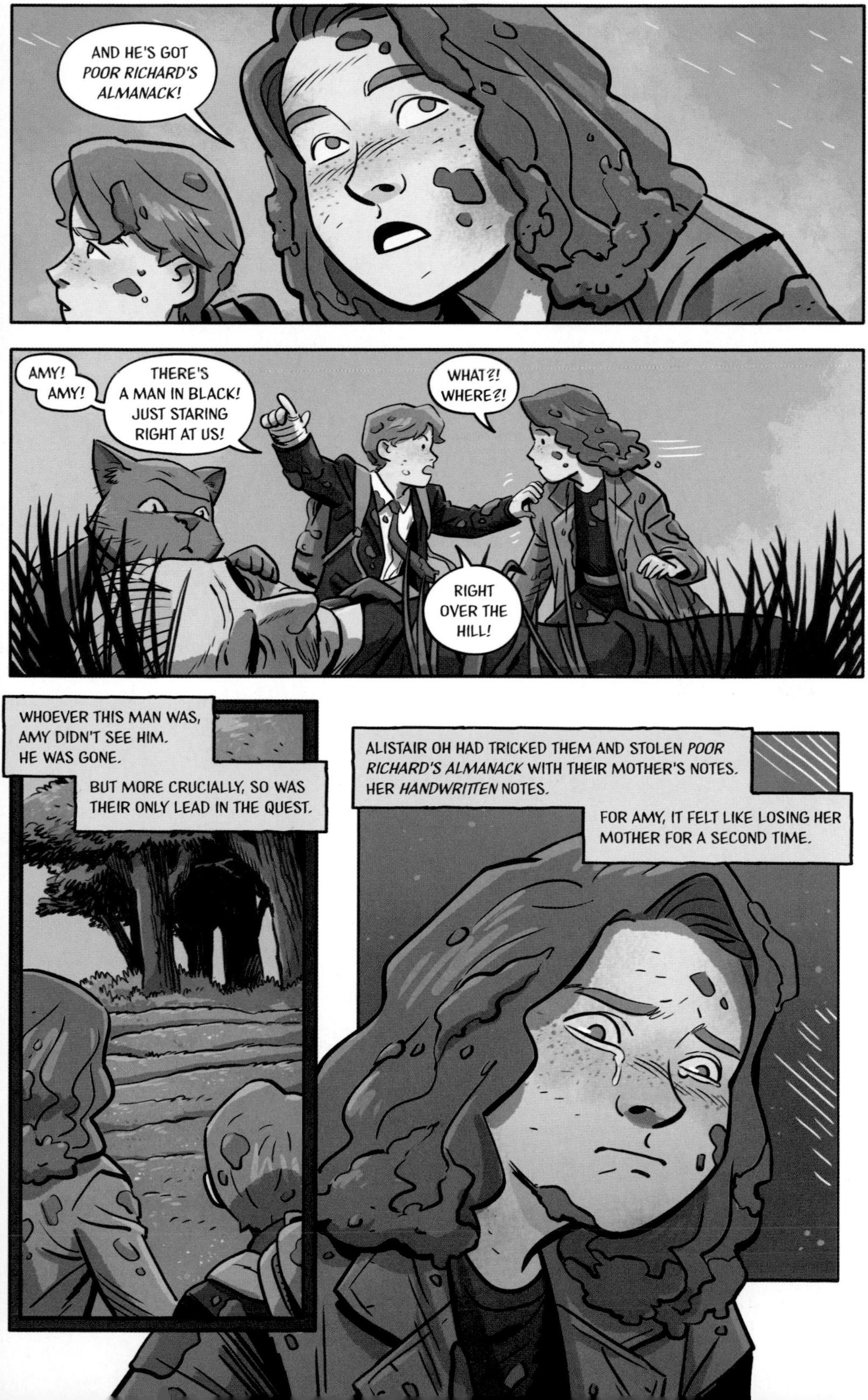
AND HE'S GOT *POOR RICHARD'S ALMANACK!*
AMY! AMY!
THERE'S A MAN IN BLACK! JUST STARING RIGHT AT US!
WHAT?! WHERE?!
RIGHT OVER THE HILL!
WHOEVER THIS MAN WAS, AMY DIDN'T SEE HIM. HE WAS GONE.
BUT MORE CRUCIALLY, SO WAS THEIR ONLY LEAD IN THE QUEST.
ALISTAIR OH HAD TRICKED THEM AND STOLEN *POOR RICHARD'S ALMANACK* WITH THEIR MOTHER'S NOTES. HER *HANDWRITTEN* NOTES.
FOR AMY, IT FELT LIKE LOSING HER MOTHER FOR A SECOND TIME.

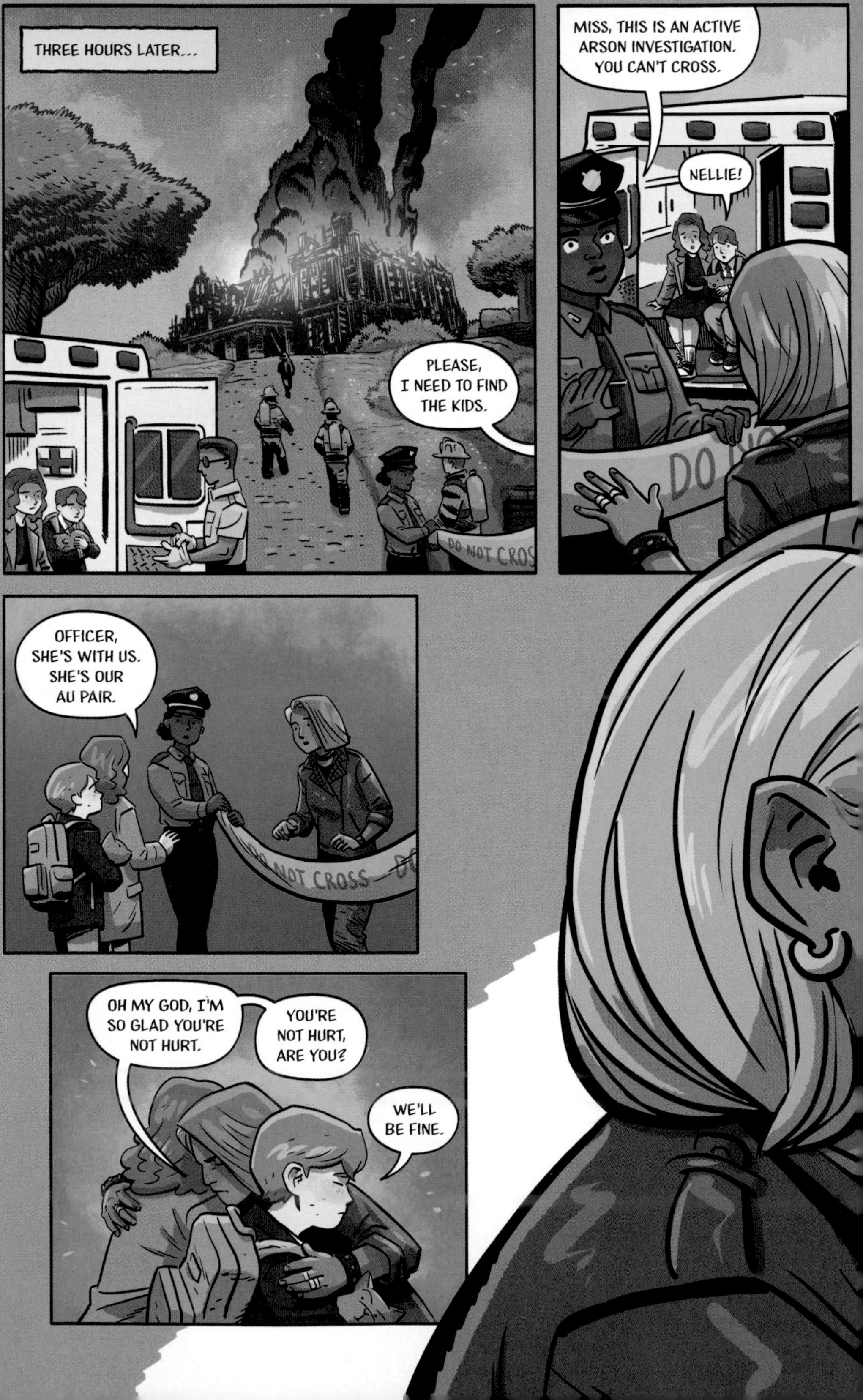
THREE HOURS LATER...
PLEASE, I NEED TO FIND THE KIDS.
DO NOT CROS
MISS, THIS IS AN ACTIVE ARSON INVESTIGATION. YOU CAN'T CROSS.
NELLIE!
DO
OFFICER, SHE'S WITH US. SHE'S OUR AU PAIR.
DO NOT CROSS
OH MY GOD, I'M SO GLAD YOU'RE NOT HURT.
YOU'RE NOT HURT, ARE YOU?
WE'LL BE FINE.

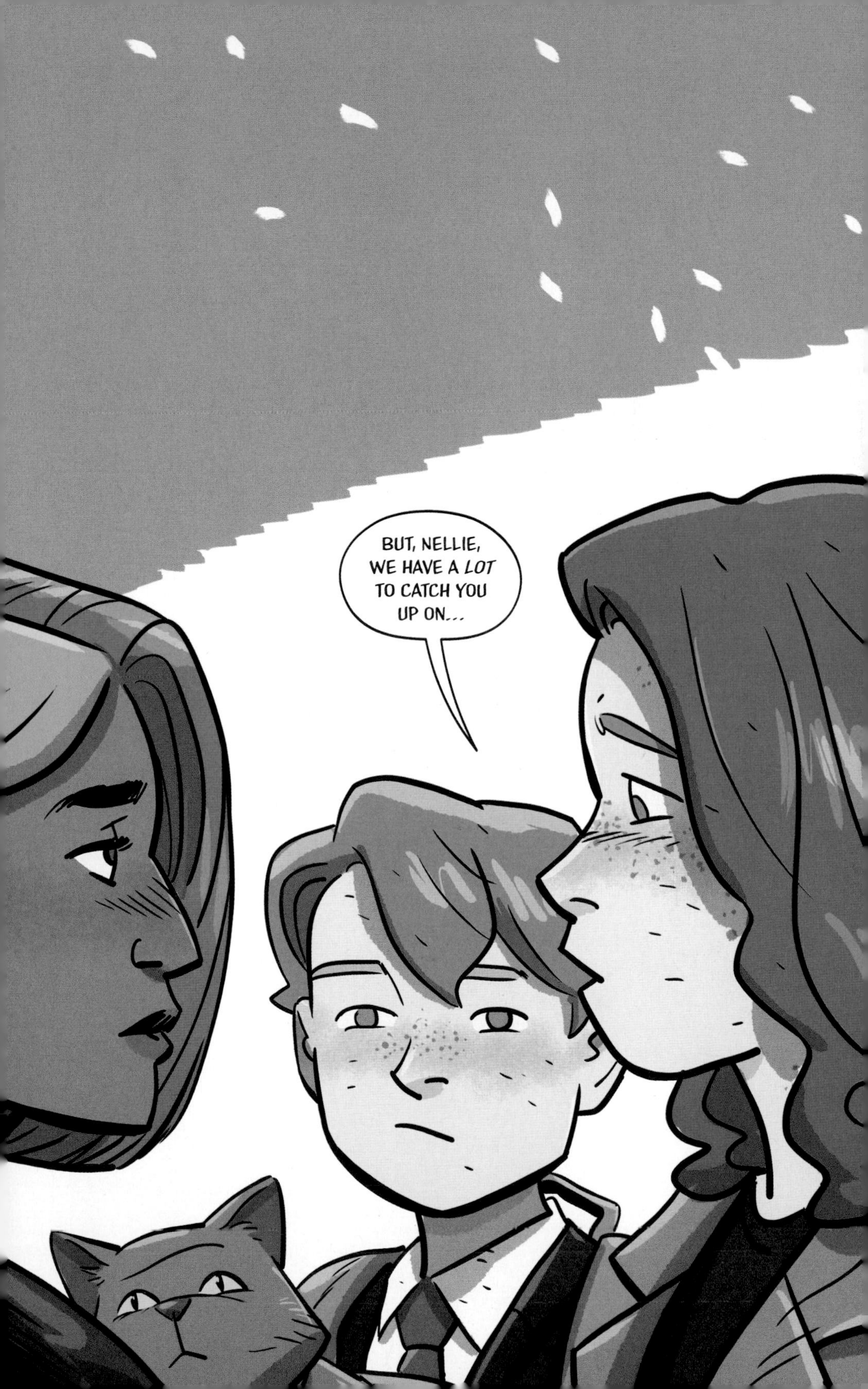
BUT, NELLIE, WE HAVE A *LOT* TO CATCH YOU UP ON...

FOUR

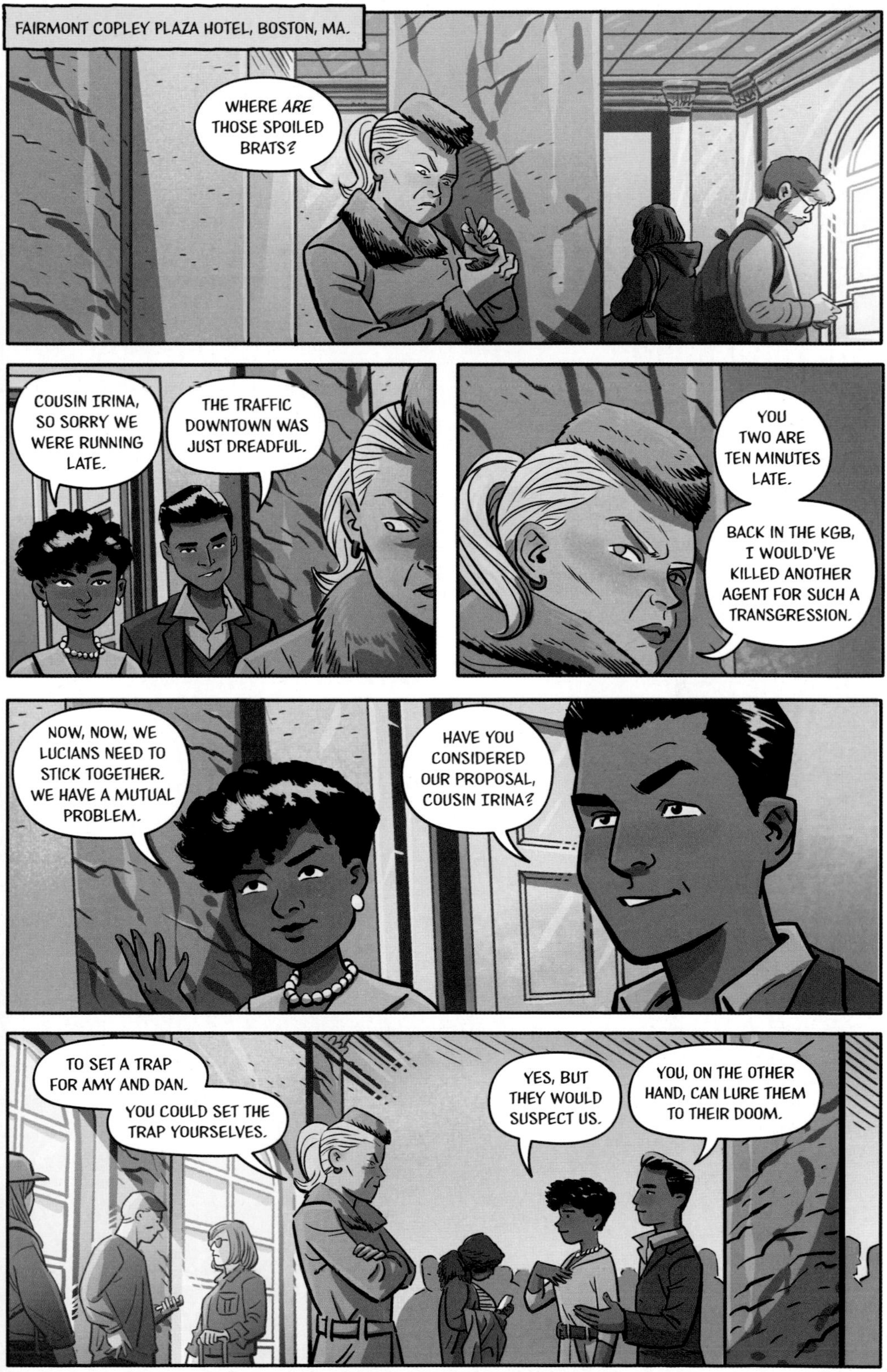
FAIRMONT COPLEY PLAZA HOTEL, BOSTON, MA.
WHERE *ARE* THOSE SPOILED BRATS?
COUSIN IRINA, SO SORRY WE WERE RUNNING LATE.
THE TRAFFIC DOWNTOWN WAS JUST DREADFUL.
YOU TWO ARE TEN MINUTES LATE.
BACK IN THE KGB, I WOULD'VE KILLED ANOTHER AGENT FOR SUCH A TRANSGRESSION.
NOW, NOW, WE LUCIANS NEED TO STICK TOGETHER. WE HAVE A MUTUAL PROBLEM.
HAVE YOU CONSIDERED OUR PROPOSAL, COUSIN IRINA?
TO SET A TRAP FOR AMY AND DAN.
YOU COULD SET THE TRAP YOURSELVES.
YES, BUT THEY WOULD SUSPECT US.
YOU, ON THE OTHER HAND, CAN LURE THEM TO THEIR DOOM.

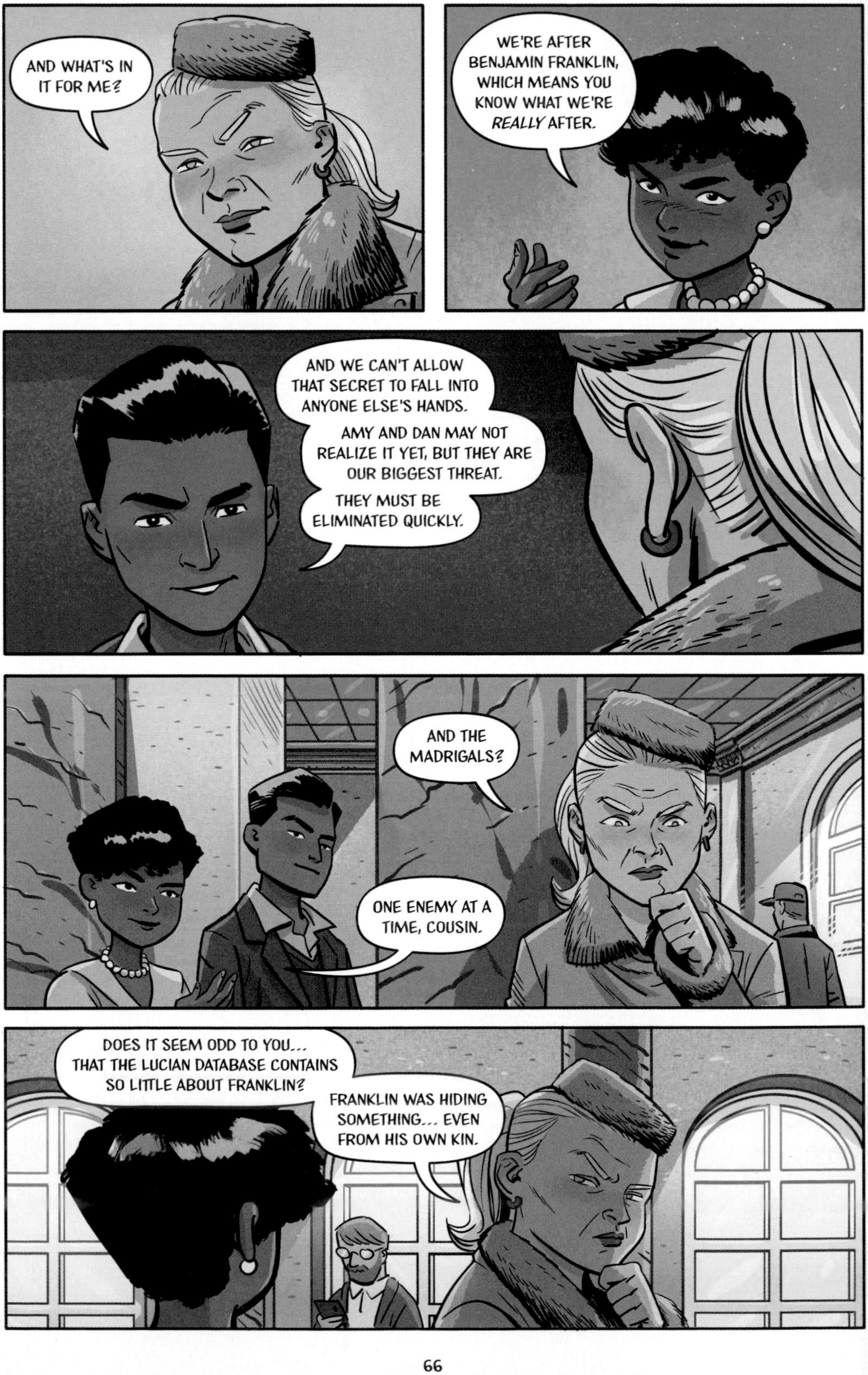
AND WHAT'S IN IT FOR ME?
WE'RE AFTER BENJAMIN FRANKLIN, WHICH MEANS YOU KNOW WHAT WE'RE *REALLY* AFTER.
AND WE CAN'T ALLOW THAT SECRET TO FALL INTO ANYONE ELSE'S HANDS.
AMY AND DAN MAY NOT REALIZE IT YET, BUT THEY ARE OUR BIGGEST THREAT.
THEY MUST BE ELIMINATED QUICKLY.
AND THE MADRIGALS?
ONE ENEMY AT A TIME, COUSIN.
DOES IT SEEM ODD TO YOU... THAT THE LUCIAN DATABASE CONTAINS SO LITTLE ABOUT FRANKLIN?
FRANKLIN WAS HIDING SOMETHING... EVEN FROM HIS OWN KIN.

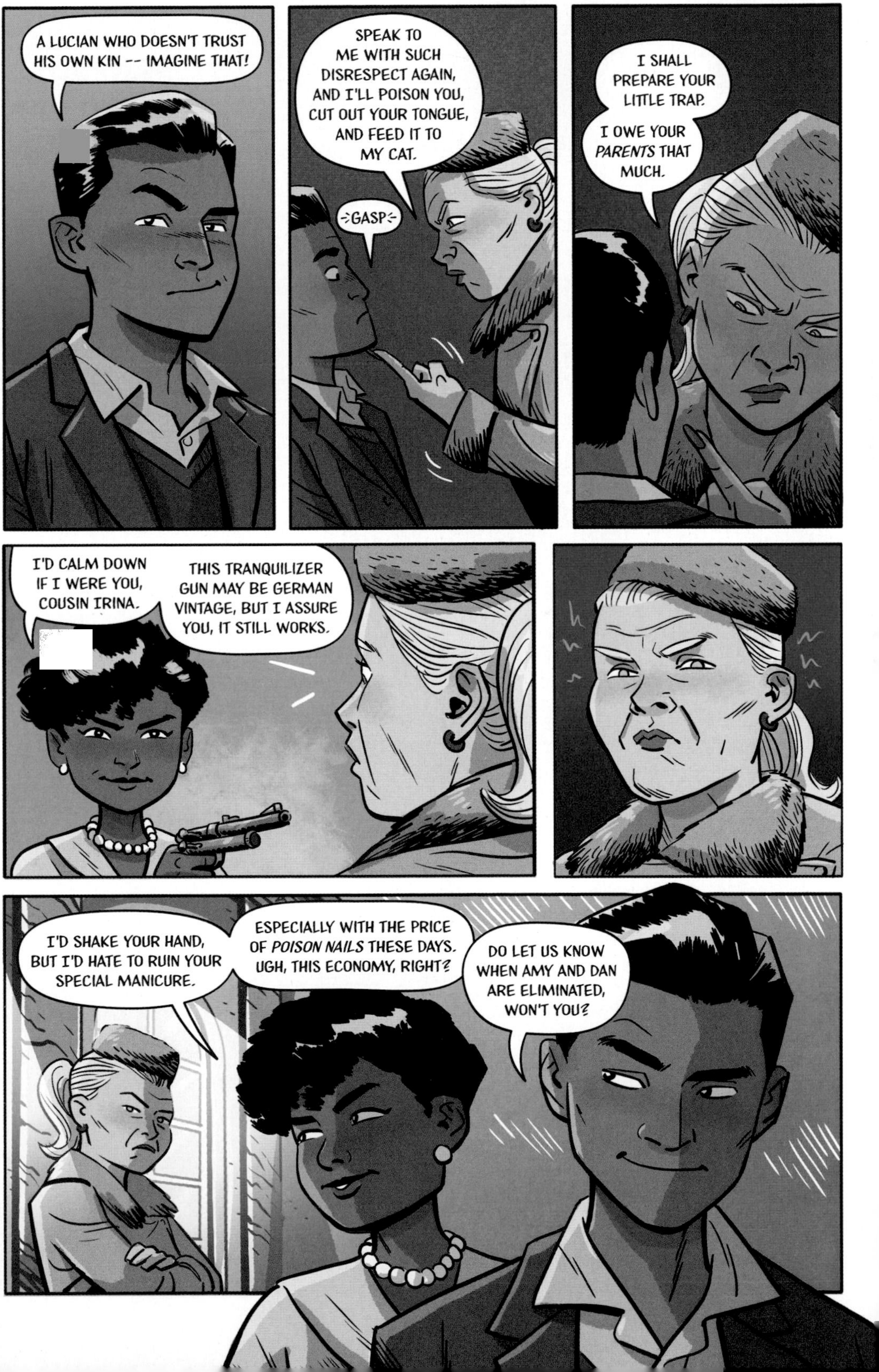
A LUCIAN WHO DOESN'T TRUST HIS OWN KIN -- IMAGINE THAT!
SPEAK TO ME WITH SUCH DISRESPECT AGAIN, AND I'LL POISON YOU, CUT OUT YOUR TONGUE, AND FEED IT TO MY CAT.
GASP
I SHALL PREPARE YOUR LITTLE TRAP.
I OWE YOUR *PARENTS* THAT MUCH.
I'D CALM DOWN IF I WERE YOU, COUSIN IRINA.
THIS TRANQUILIZER GUN MAY BE GERMAN VINTAGE, BUT I ASSURE YOU, IT STILL WORKS.
I'D SHAKE YOUR HAND, BUT I'D HATE TO RUIN YOUR SPECIAL MANICURE.
ESPECIALLY WITH THE PRICE OF *POISON NAILS* THESE DAYS. UGH, THIS ECONOMY, RIGHT?
DO LET US KNOW WHEN AMY AND DAN ARE ELIMINATED, WON'T YOU?

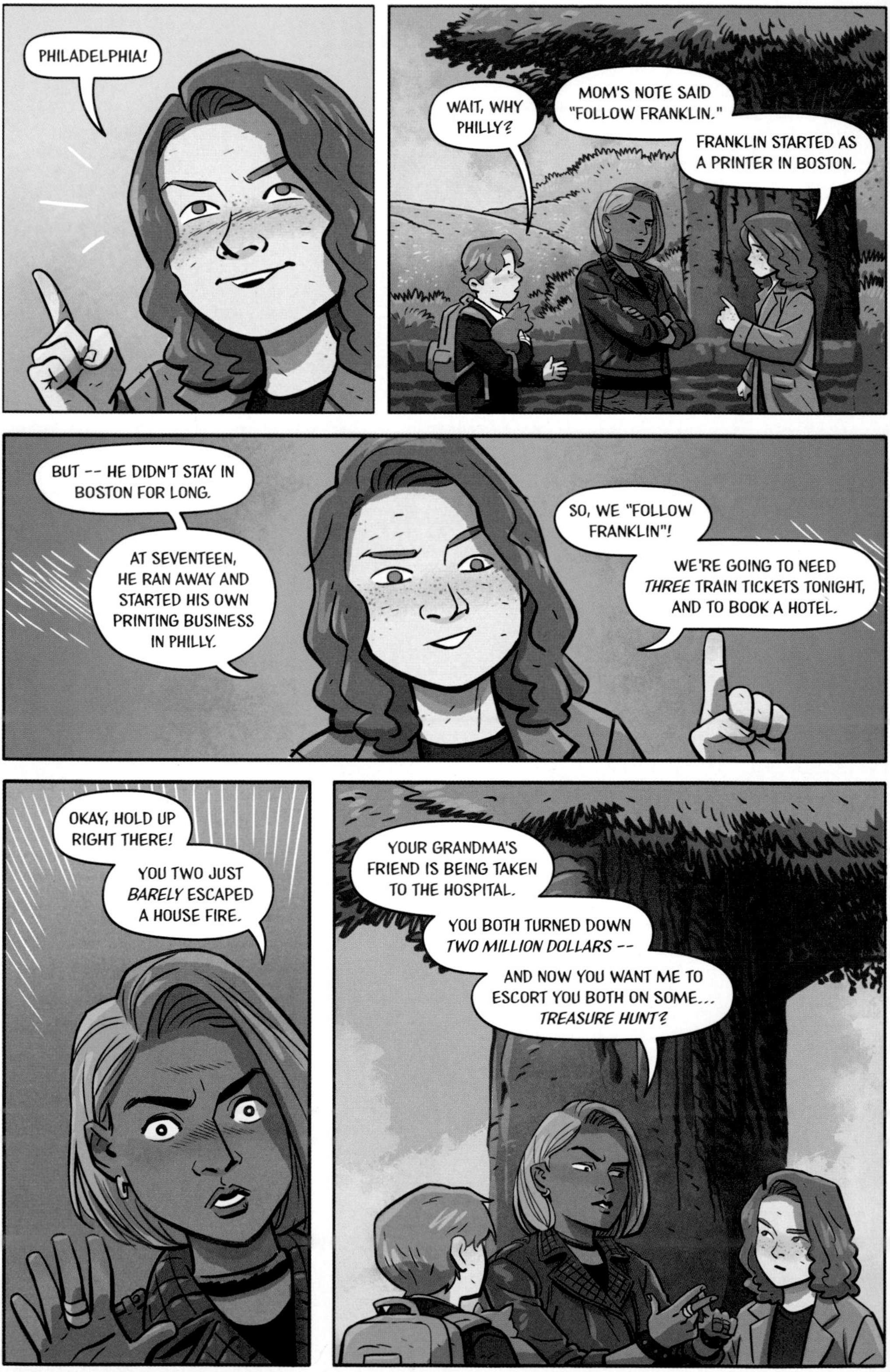
PHILADELPHIA!
WAIT, WHY PHILLY?
MOM'S NOTE SAID "FOLLOW FRANKLIN."
FRANKLIN STARTED AS A PRINTER IN BOSTON.
BUT -- HE DIDN'T STAY IN BOSTON FOR LONG.
AT SEVENTEEN, HE RAN AWAY AND STARTED HIS OWN PRINTING BUSINESS IN PHILLY.
SO, WE "FOLLOW FRANKLIN"!
WE'RE GOING TO NEED *THREE* TRAIN TICKETS TONIGHT, AND TO BOOK A HOTEL.
OKAY, HOLD UP RIGHT THERE!
YOU TWO JUST *BARELY* ESCAPED A HOUSE FIRE.
YOUR GRANDMA'S FRIEND IS BEING TAKEN TO THE HOSPITAL.
YOU BOTH TURNED DOWN *TWO MILLION DOLLARS* --
AND NOW YOU WANT ME TO ESCORT YOU BOTH ON SOME... *TREASURE HUNT?*

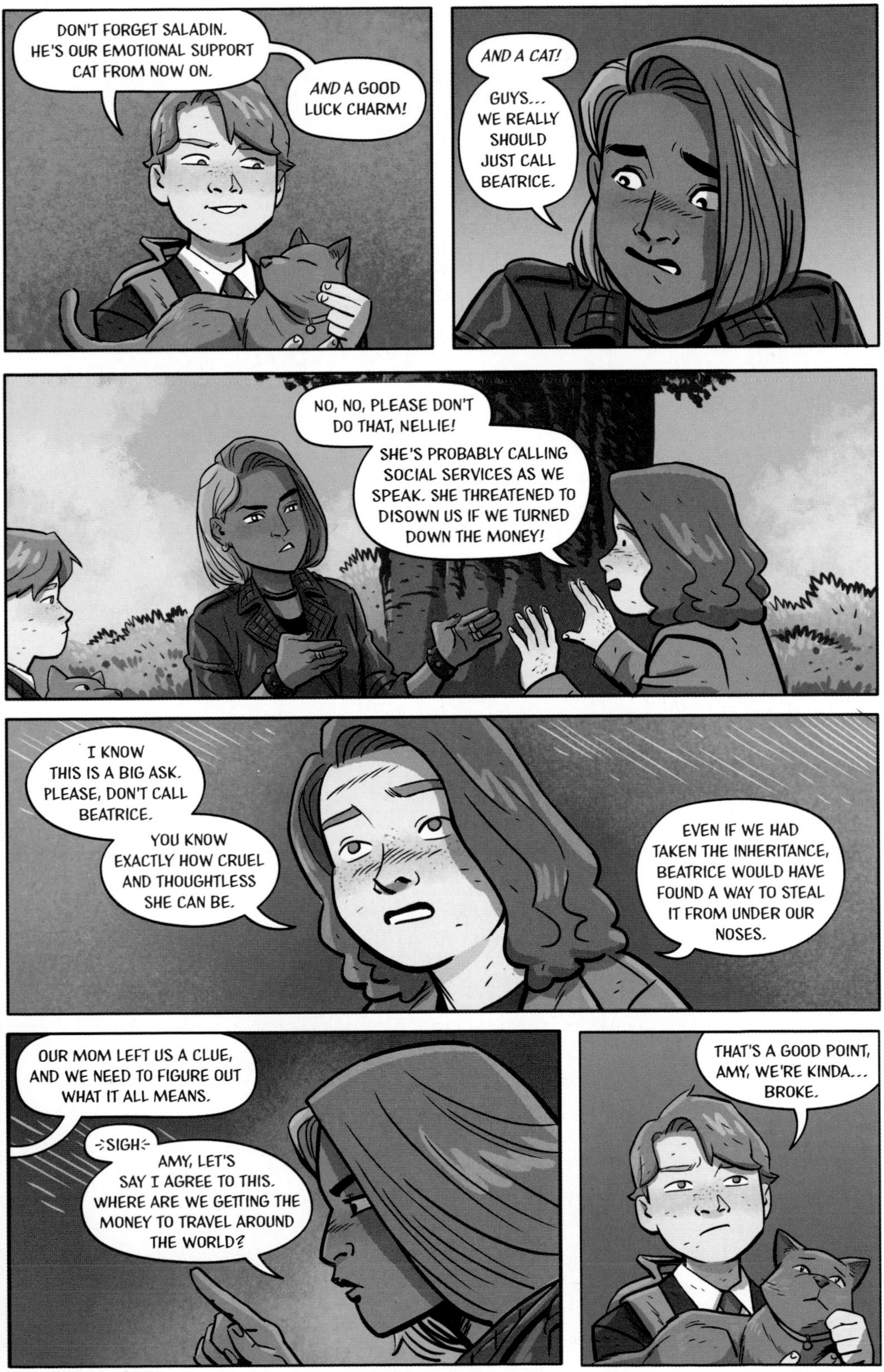
DON'T FORGET SALADIN. HE'S OUR EMOTIONAL SUPPORT CAT FROM NOW ON.
AND A GOOD LUCK CHARM!
AND A CAT!
GUYS... WE REALLY SHOULD JUST CALL BEATRICE.
NO, NO, PLEASE DON'T DO THAT, NELLIE!
SHE'S PROBABLY CALLING SOCIAL SERVICES AS WE SPEAK. SHE THREATENED TO DISOWN US IF WE TURNED DOWN THE MONEY!
I KNOW THIS IS A BIG ASK. PLEASE, DON'T CALL BEATRICE.
YOU KNOW EXACTLY HOW CRUEL AND THOUGHTLESS SHE CAN BE.
EVEN IF WE HAD TAKEN THE INHERITANCE, BEATRICE WOULD HAVE FOUND A WAY TO STEAL IT FROM UNDER OUR NOSES.
OUR MOM LEFT US A CLUE, AND WE NEED TO FIGURE OUT WHAT IT ALL MEANS.
SIGH
AMY, LET'S SAY I AGREE TO THIS. WHERE ARE WE GETTING THE MONEY TO TRAVEL AROUND THE WORLD?
THAT'S A GOOD POINT, AMY. WE'RE KINDA... BROKE.

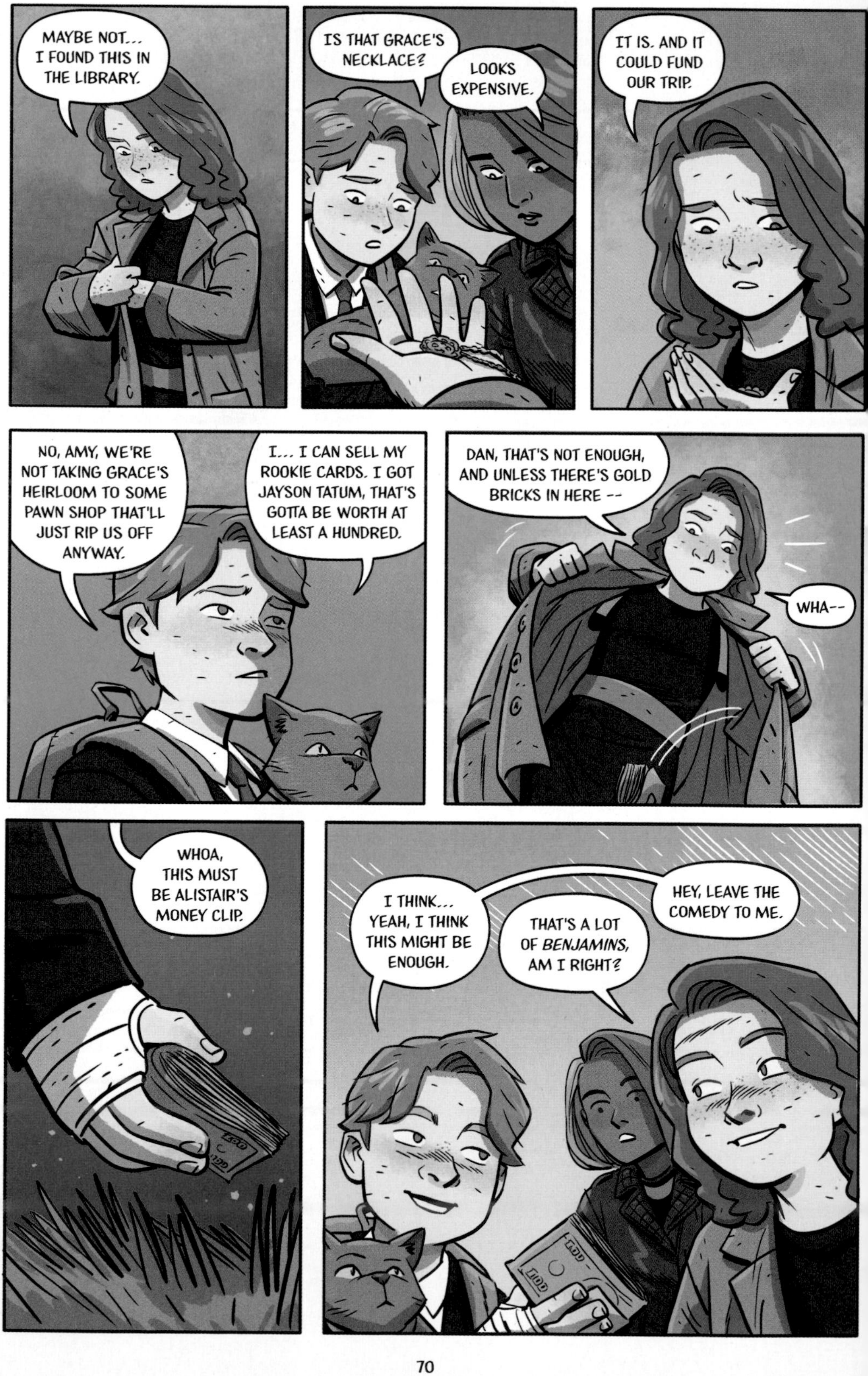
MAYBE NOT... I FOUND THIS IN THE LIBRARY.
IS THAT GRACE'S NECKLACE?
LOOKS EXPENSIVE.
IT IS. AND IT COULD FUND OUR TRIP.
NO, AMY, WE'RE NOT TAKING GRACE'S HEIRLOOM TO SOME PAWN SHOP THAT'LL JUST RIP US OFF ANYWAY.
I... I CAN SELL MY ROOKIE CARDS. I GOT JAYSON TATUM, THAT'S GOTTA BE WORTH AT LEAST A HUNDRED.
DAN, THAT'S NOT ENOUGH, AND UNLESS THERE'S GOLD BRICKS IN HERE --
WHA--
WHOA, THIS MUST BE ALISTAIR'S MONEY CLIP.
I THINK... YEAH, I THINK THIS MIGHT BE ENOUGH.
THAT'S A LOT OF *BENJAMINS*, AM I RIGHT?
HEY, LEAVE THE COMEDY TO ME.

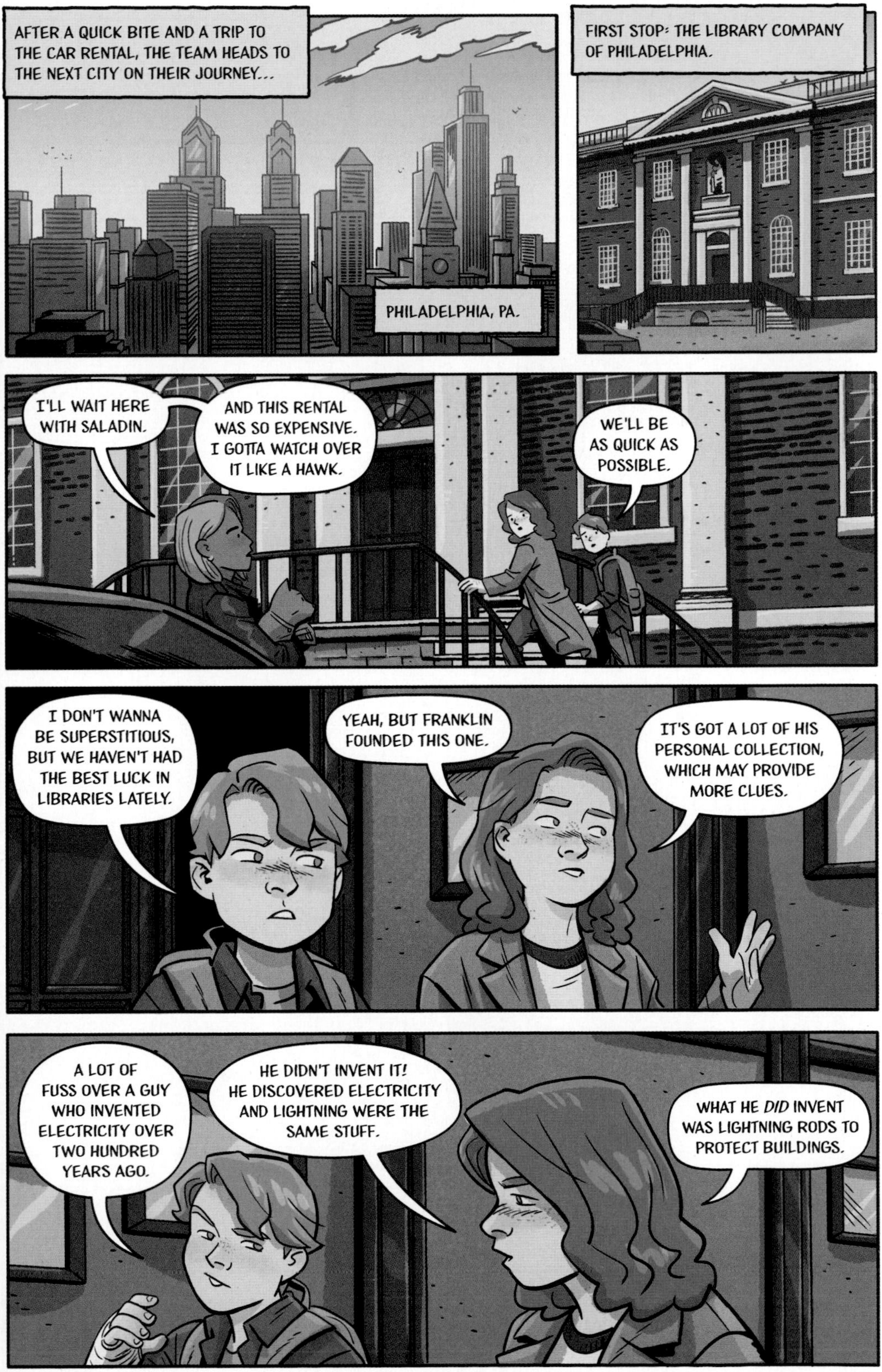
AFTER A QUICK BITE AND A TRIP TO THE CAR RENTAL, THE TEAM HEADS TO THE NEXT CITY ON THEIR JOURNEY...
PHILADELPHIA, PA.
FIRST STOP: THE LIBRARY COMPANY OF PHILADELPHIA.
I'LL WAIT HERE WITH SALADIN.
AND THIS RENTAL WAS SO EXPENSIVE. I GOTTA WATCH OVER IT LIKE A HAWK.
WE'LL BE AS QUICK AS POSSIBLE.
I DON'T WANNA BE SUPERSTITIOUS, BUT WE HAVEN'T HAD THE BEST LUCK IN LIBRARIES LATELY.
YEAH, BUT FRANKLIN FOUNDED THIS ONE.
IT'S GOT A LOT OF HIS PERSONAL COLLECTION, WHICH MAY PROVIDE MORE CLUES.
A LOT OF FUSS OVER A GUY WHO INVENTED ELECTRICITY OVER TWO HUNDRED YEARS AGO.
HE DIDN'T INVENT IT! HE DISCOVERED ELECTRICITY AND LIGHTNING WERE THE SAME STUFF.
WHAT HE *DID* INVENT WAS LIGHTNING RODS TO PROTECT BUILDINGS.

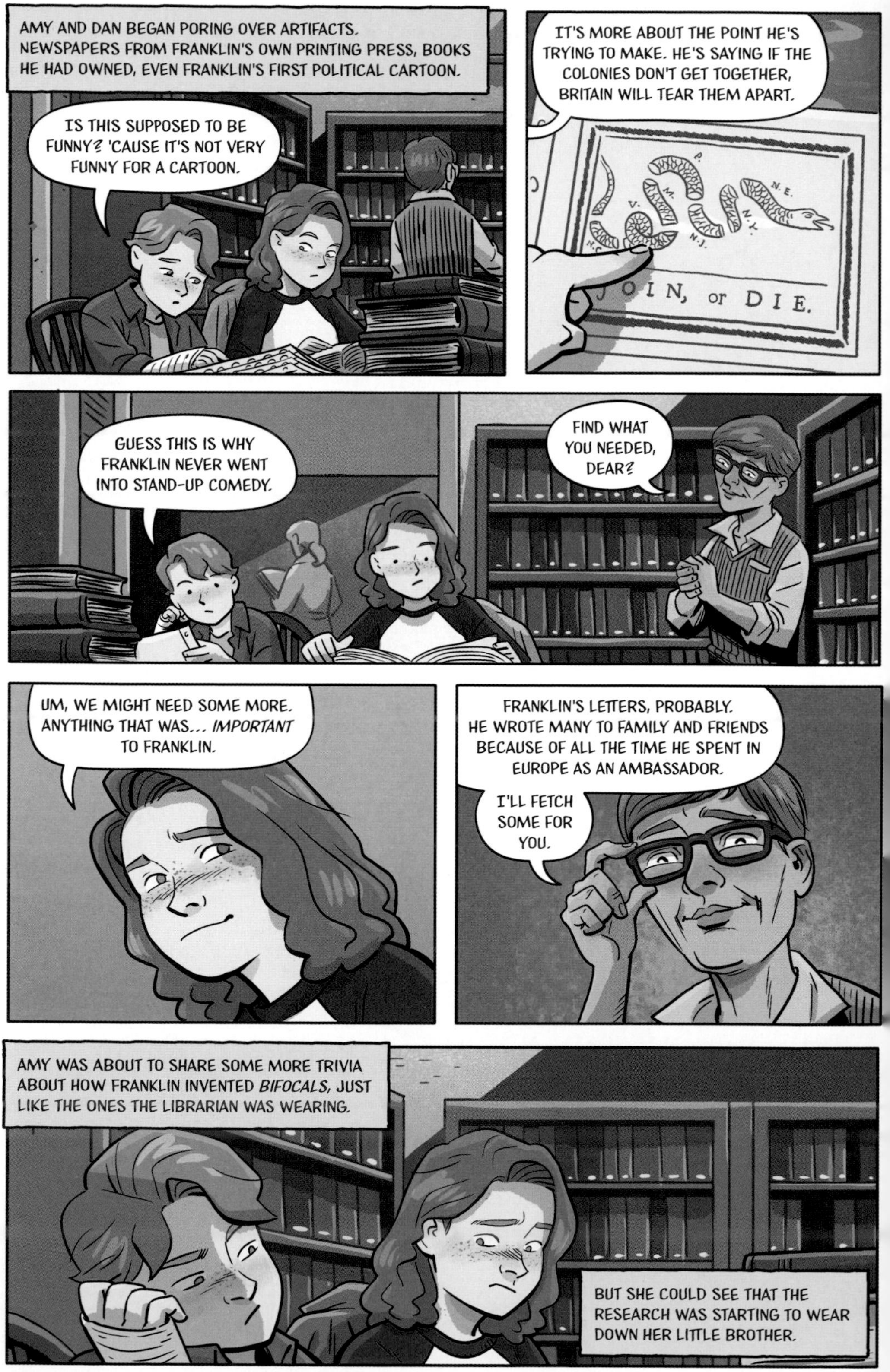
AMY AND DAN BEGAN PORING OVER ARTIFACTS. NEWSPAPERS FROM FRANKLIN'S OWN PRINTING PRESS, BOOKS HE HAD OWNED, EVEN FRANKLIN'S FIRST POLITICAL CARTOON.
IS THIS SUPPOSED TO BE FUNNY? 'CAUSE IT'S NOT VERY FUNNY FOR A CARTOON.
IT'S MORE ABOUT THE POINT HE'S TRYING TO MAKE. HE'S SAYING IF THE COLONIES DON'T GET TOGETHER, BRITAIN WILL TEAR THEM APART.
JOIN, or DIE.
GUESS THIS IS WHY FRANKLIN NEVER WENT INTO STAND-UP COMEDY.
FIND WHAT YOU NEEDED, DEAR?
UM, WE MIGHT NEED SOME MORE. ANYTHING THAT WAS... *IMPORTANT* TO FRANKLIN.
FRANKLIN'S LETTERS, PROBABLY. HE WROTE MANY TO FAMILY AND FRIENDS BECAUSE OF ALL THE TIME HE SPENT IN EUROPE AS AN AMBASSADOR.
I'LL FETCH SOME FOR YOU.
AMY WAS ABOUT TO SHARE SOME MORE TRIVIA ABOUT HOW FRANKLIN INVENTED *BIFOCALS*, JUST LIKE THE ONES THE LIBRARIAN WAS WEARING.
BUT SHE COULD SEE THAT THE RESEARCH WAS STARTING TO WEAR DOWN HER LITTLE BROTHER.

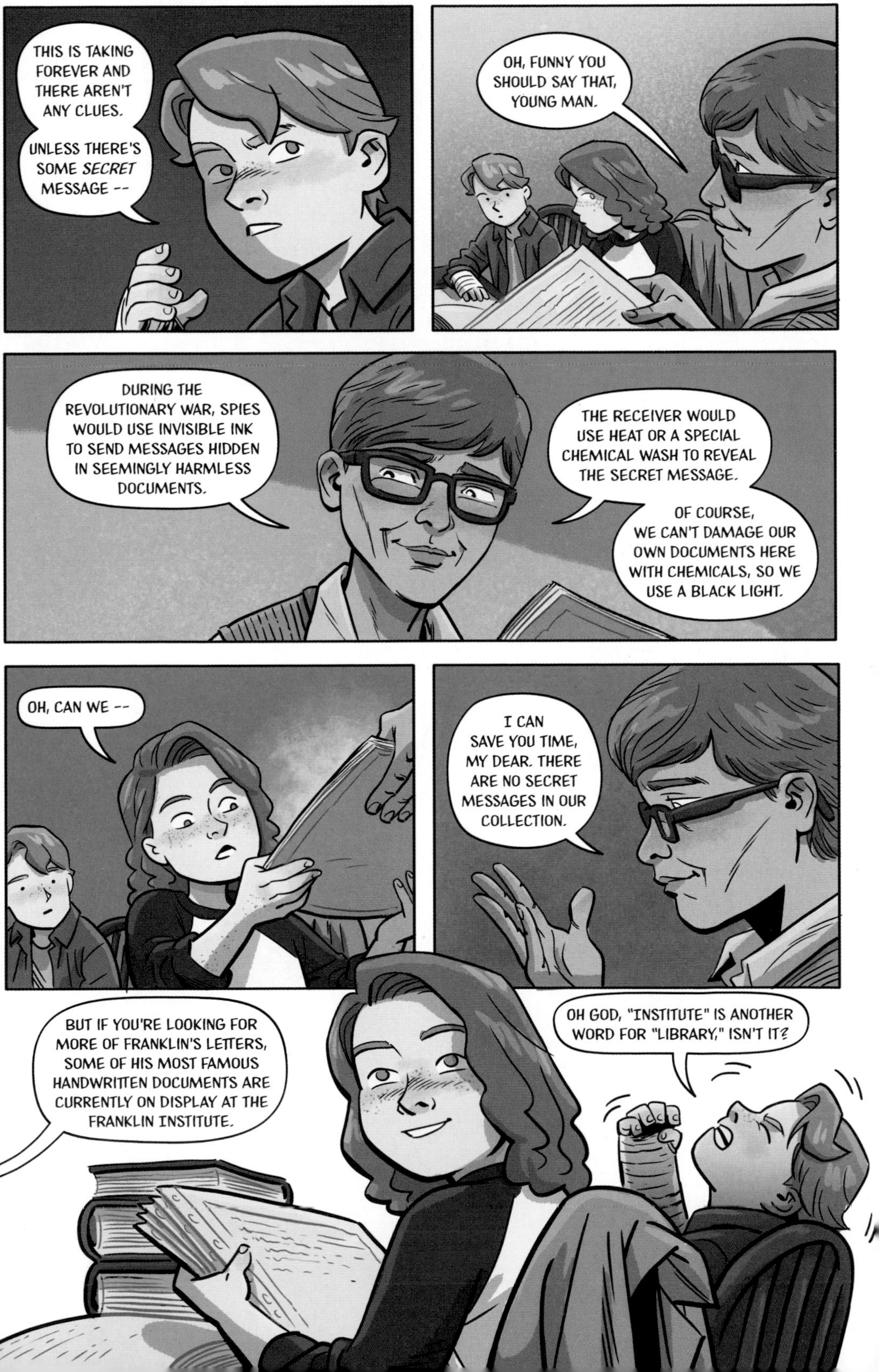
THIS IS TAKING FOREVER AND THERE AREN'T ANY CLUES.
UNLESS THERE'S SOME *SECRET* MESSAGE --
OH, FUNNY YOU SHOULD SAY THAT, YOUNG MAN.
DURING THE REVOLUTIONARY WAR, SPIES WOULD USE INVISIBLE INK TO SEND MESSAGES HIDDEN IN SEEMINGLY HARMLESS DOCUMENTS.
THE RECEIVER WOULD USE HEAT OR A SPECIAL CHEMICAL WASH TO REVEAL THE SECRET MESSAGE.
OF COURSE, WE CAN'T DAMAGE OUR OWN DOCUMENTS HERE WITH CHEMICALS, SO WE USE A BLACK LIGHT.
OH, CAN WE --
I CAN SAVE YOU TIME, MY DEAR. THERE ARE NO SECRET MESSAGES IN OUR COLLECTION.
BUT IF YOU'RE LOOKING FOR MORE OF FRANKLIN'S LETTERS, SOME OF HIS MOST FAMOUS HANDWRITTEN DOCUMENTS ARE CURRENTLY ON DISPLAY AT THE FRANKLIN INSTITUTE.
OH GOD, "INSTITUTE" IS ANOTHER WORD FOR "LIBRARY," ISN'T IT?

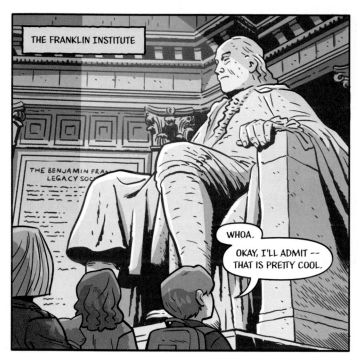

THE FRANKLIN INSTITUTE

THE BENJAMIN FRA[N]
LEGACY SOC[...]

WHOA.

OKAY, I'LL ADMIT -- THAT IS PRETTY COOL.

LET'S GET MOVING -- WE HAVE TO FIND THOSE DOCUMENTS.

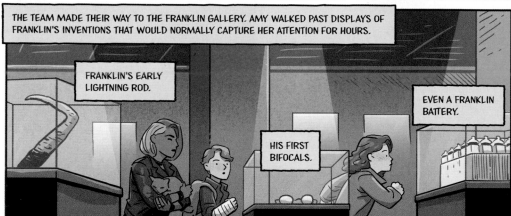

THE TEAM MADE THEIR WAY TO THE FRANKLIN GALLERY. AMY WALKED PAST DISPLAYS OF FRANKLIN'S INVENTIONS THAT WOULD NORMALLY CAPTURE HER ATTENTION FOR HOURS.

FRANKLIN'S EARLY LIGHTNING ROD.

HIS FIRST BIFOCALS.

EVEN A FRANKLIN BATTERY.

BUT TIME WAS OF THE ESSENCE.

THIS SURE IS A LOT OF PARCHMENT.

THIS IS IT. FRANKLIN'S LETTERS.

DAN, DID YOU DOWNLOAD THAT BLACK LIGHT APP YET?

YEAH, GIMME ONE SECOND TO OPEN IT.

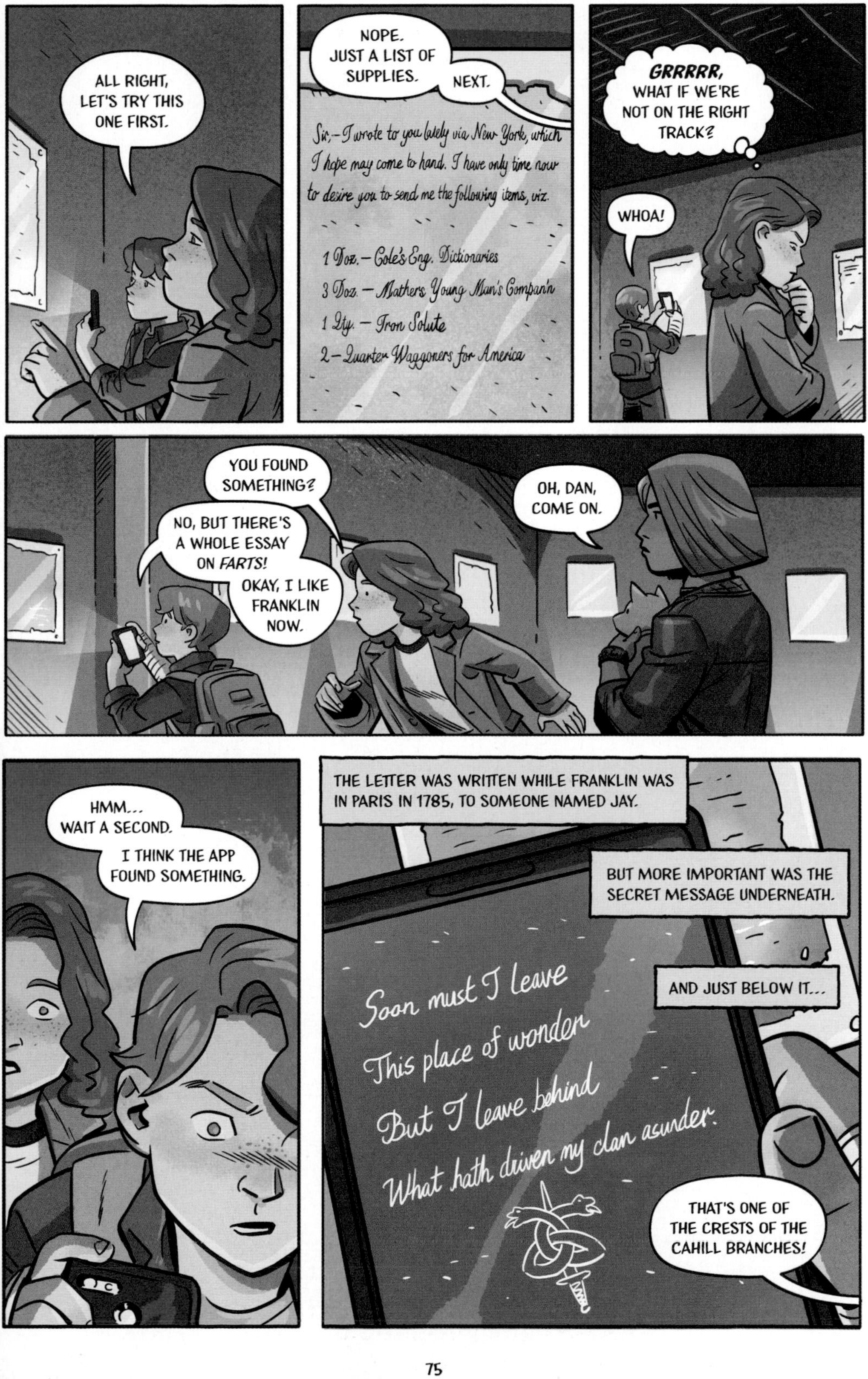
ALL RIGHT, LET'S TRY THIS ONE FIRST.
NOPE. JUST A LIST OF SUPPLIES.
NEXT.
Sir,—I wrote to you lately via New York, which I hope may come to hand. I have only time now to desire you to send me the following items, viz.
1 Doz.—Cole's Eng. Dictionaries
3 Doz.—Mathers Young Man's Compan'n
1 Qty.—Iron Solute
2—Quarter Waggoners for America
GRRRRR, WHAT IF WE'RE NOT ON THE RIGHT TRACK?
WHOA!
YOU FOUND SOMETHING?
NO, BUT THERE'S A WHOLE ESSAY ON FARTS!
OKAY, I LIKE FRANKLIN NOW.
OH, DAN, COME ON.
HMM... WAIT A SECOND.
I THINK THE APP FOUND SOMETHING.
THE LETTER WAS WRITTEN WHILE FRANKLIN WAS IN PARIS IN 1785, TO SOMEONE NAMED JAY.
BUT MORE IMPORTANT WAS THE SECRET MESSAGE UNDERNEATH.
AND JUST BELOW IT...
Soon must I leave
This place of wonder
But I leave behind
What hath driven my clan asunder.
THAT'S ONE OF THE CRESTS OF THE CAHILL BRANCHES!

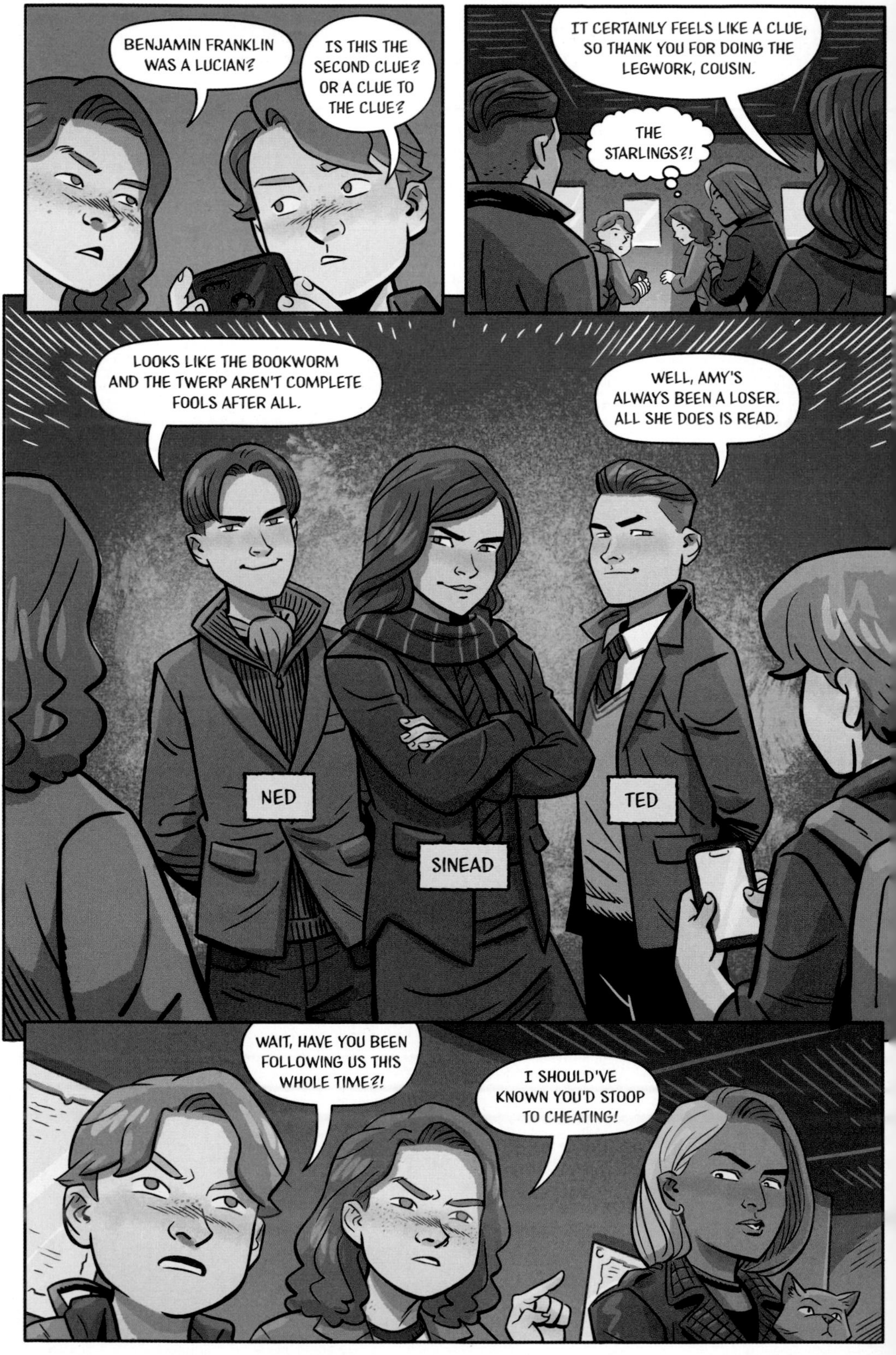
BENJAMIN FRANKLIN WAS A LUCIAN?
IS THIS THE SECOND CLUE? OR A CLUE TO THE CLUE?
IT CERTAINLY FEELS LIKE A CLUE, SO THANK YOU FOR DOING THE LEGWORK, COUSIN.
THE STARLINGS?!
LOOKS LIKE THE BOOKWORM AND THE TWERP AREN'T COMPLETE FOOLS AFTER ALL.
WELL, AMY'S ALWAYS BEEN A LOSER. ALL SHE DOES IS READ.
NED
SINEAD
TED
WAIT, HAVE YOU BEEN FOLLOWING US THIS WHOLE TIME?!
I SHOULD'VE KNOWN YOU'D STOOP TO CHEATING!

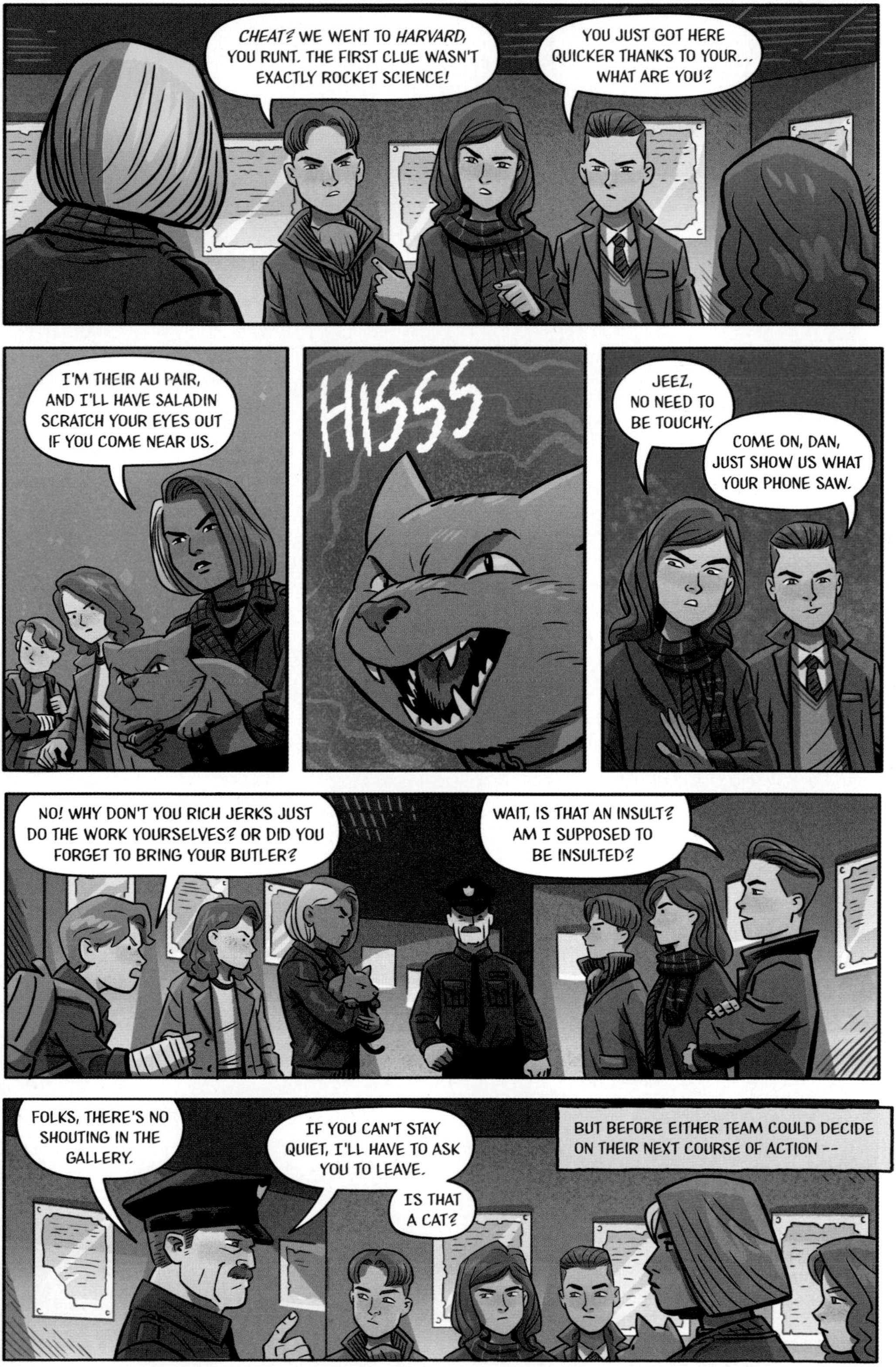
CHEAT? WE WENT TO HARVARD, YOU RUNT. THE FIRST CLUE WASN'T EXACTLY ROCKET SCIENCE!
YOU JUST GOT HERE QUICKER THANKS TO YOUR... WHAT ARE YOU?
I'M THEIR AU PAIR, AND I'LL HAVE SALADIN SCRATCH YOUR EYES OUT IF YOU COME NEAR US.
HISSS
JEEZ, NO NEED TO BE TOUCHY.
COME ON, DAN, JUST SHOW US WHAT YOUR PHONE SAW.
NO! WHY DON'T YOU RICH JERKS JUST DO THE WORK YOURSELVES? OR DID YOU FORGET TO BRING YOUR BUTLER?
WAIT, IS THAT AN INSULT? AM I SUPPOSED TO BE INSULTED?
FOLKS, THERE'S NO SHOUTING IN THE GALLERY.
IF YOU CAN'T STAY QUIET, I'LL HAVE TO ASK YOU TO LEAVE.
IS THAT A CAT?
BUT BEFORE EITHER TEAM COULD DECIDE ON THEIR NEXT COURSE OF ACTION --

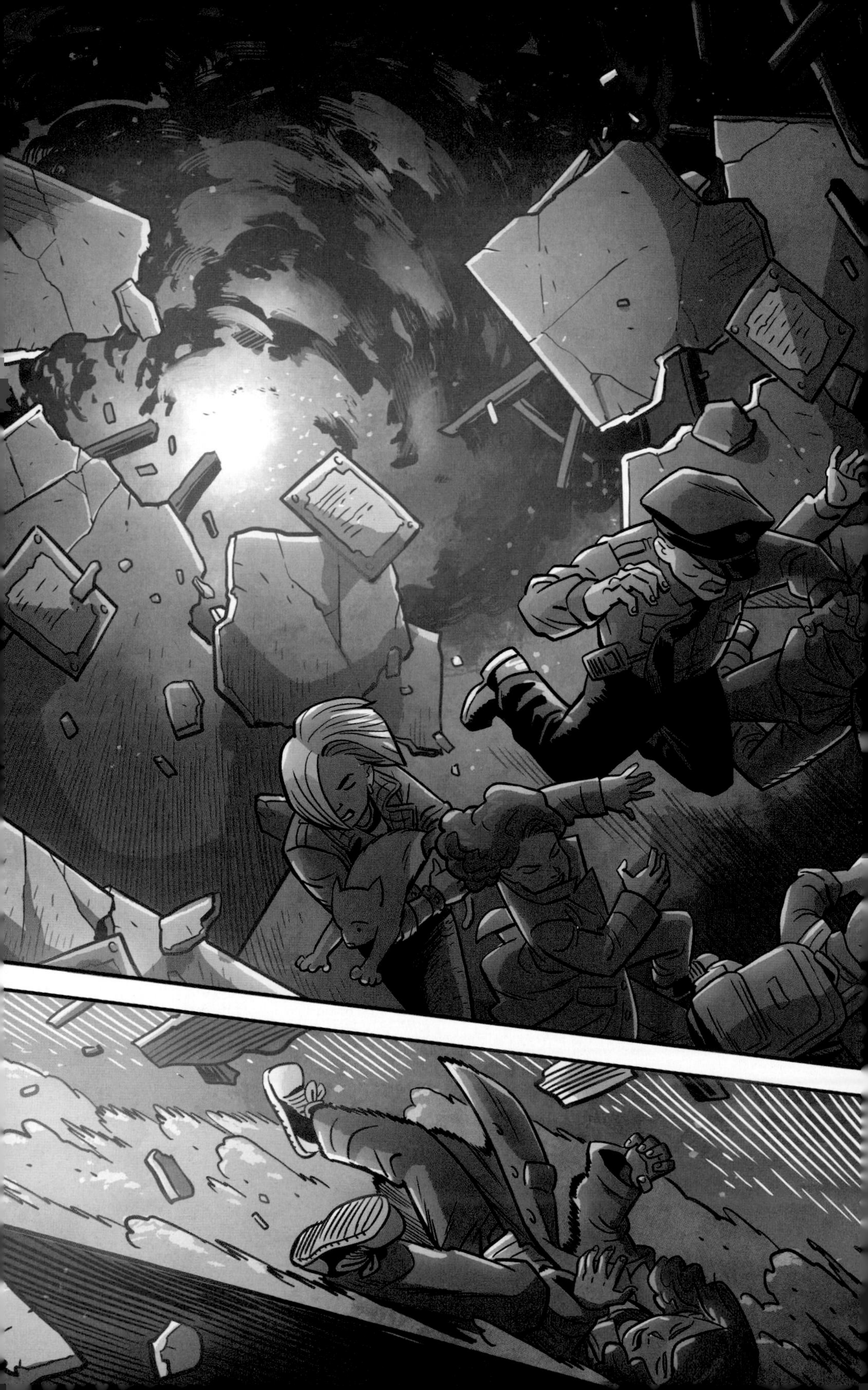

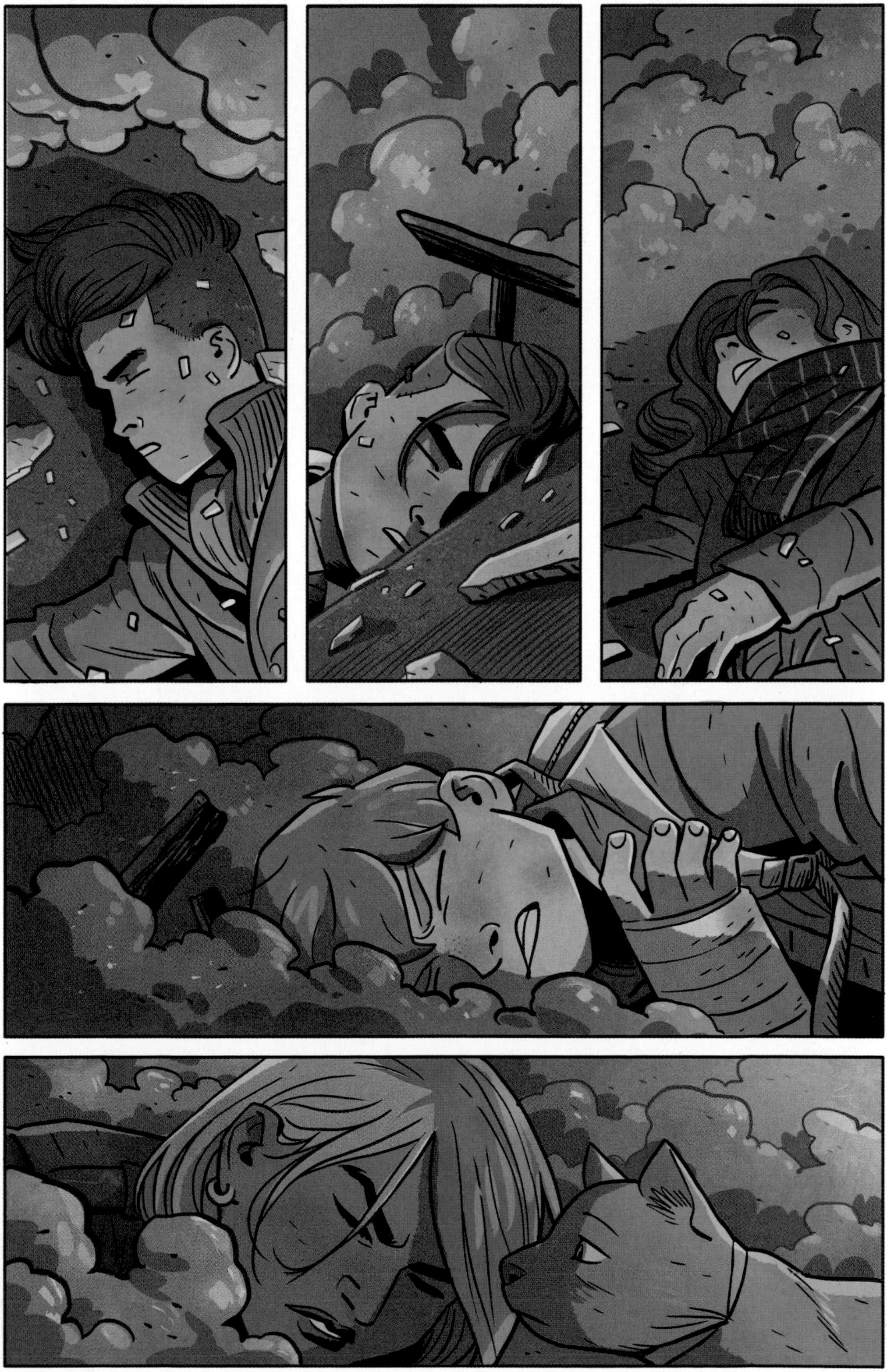

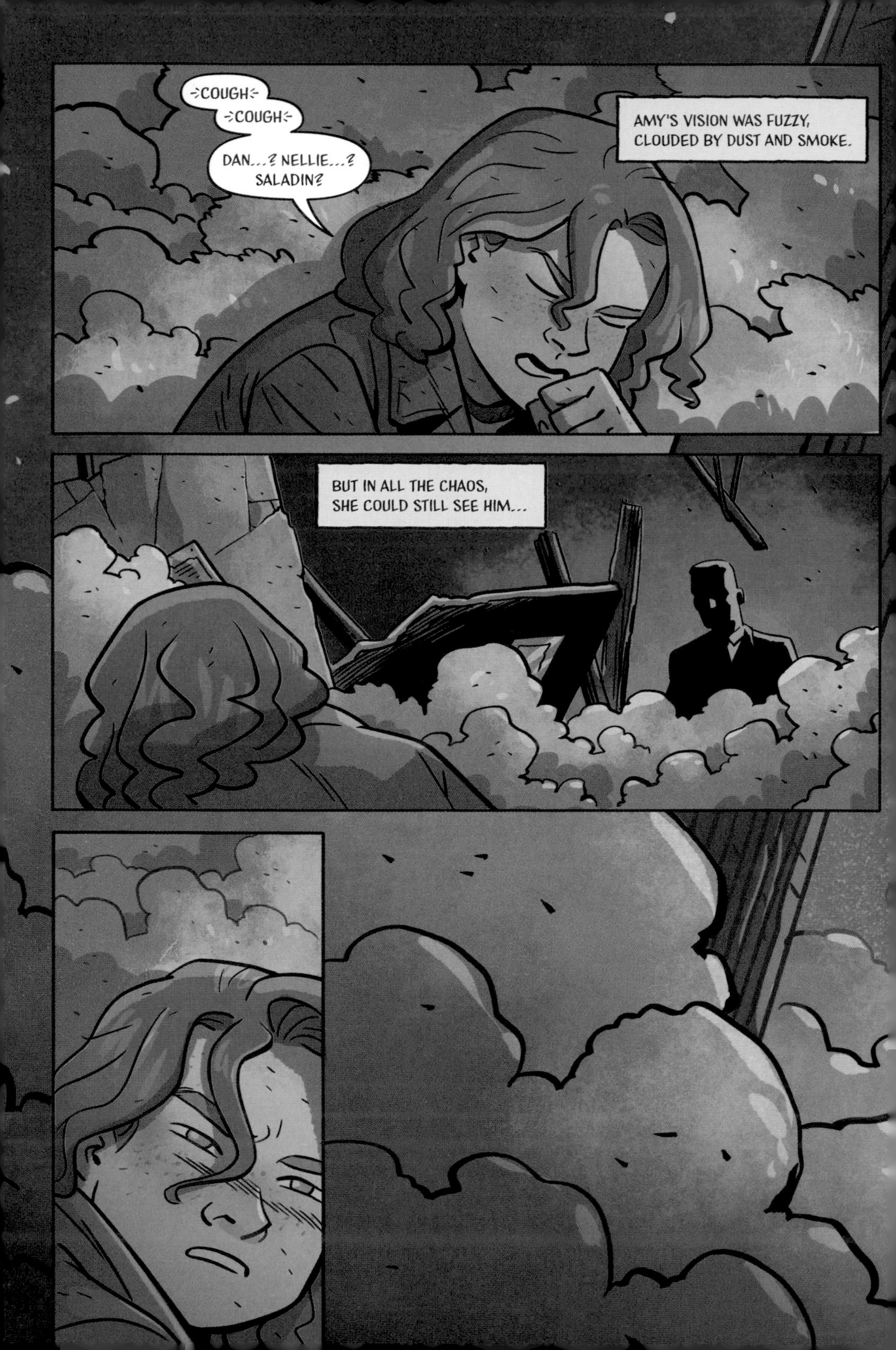

COUGH
COUGH
DAN...? NELLIE...? SALADIN?
AMY'S VISION WAS FUZZY, CLOUDED BY DUST AND SMOKE.
BUT IN ALL THE CHAOS, SHE COULD STILL SEE HIM...

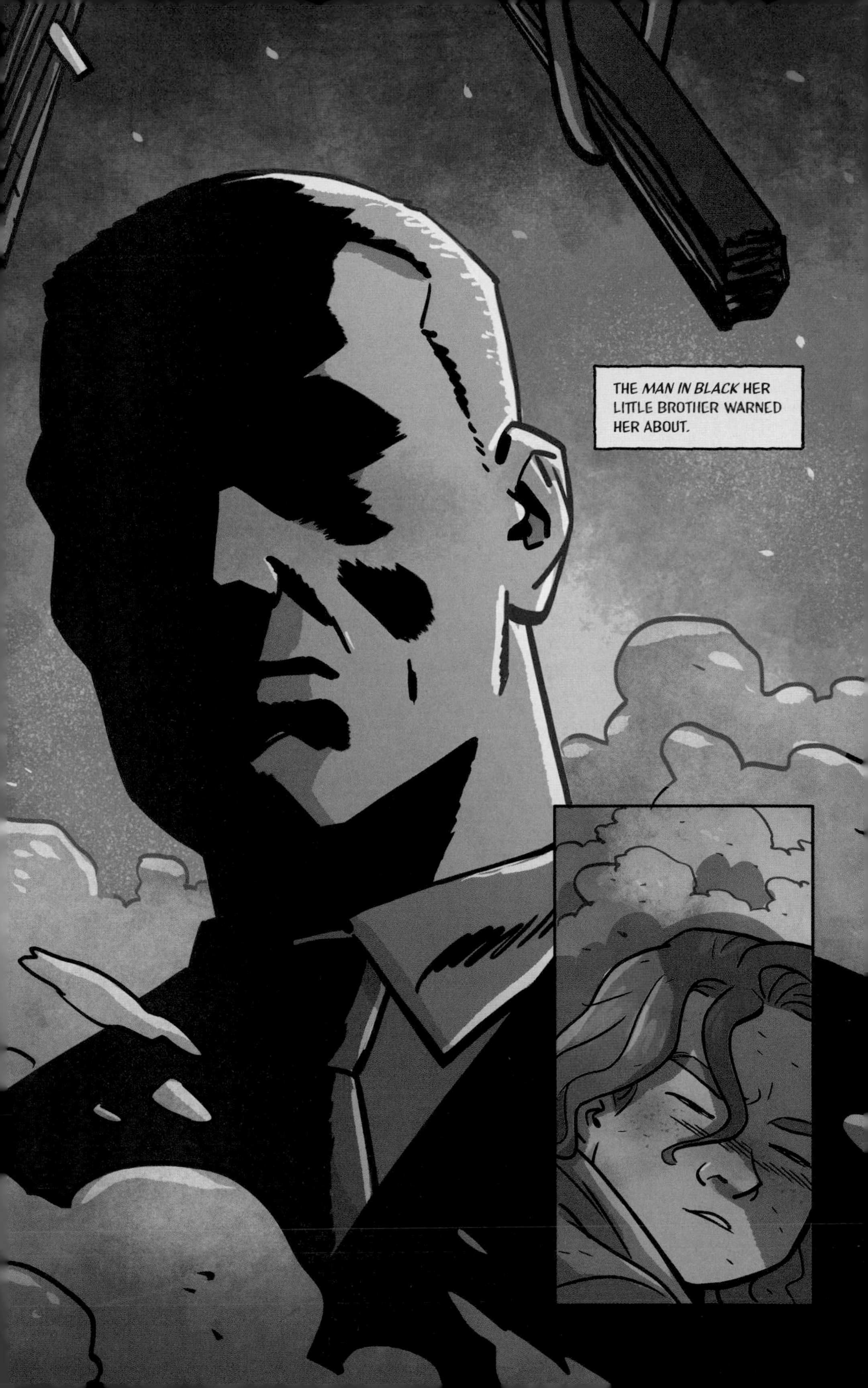
THE *MAN IN BLACK* HER LITTLE BROTHER WARNED HER ABOUT.

FIVE

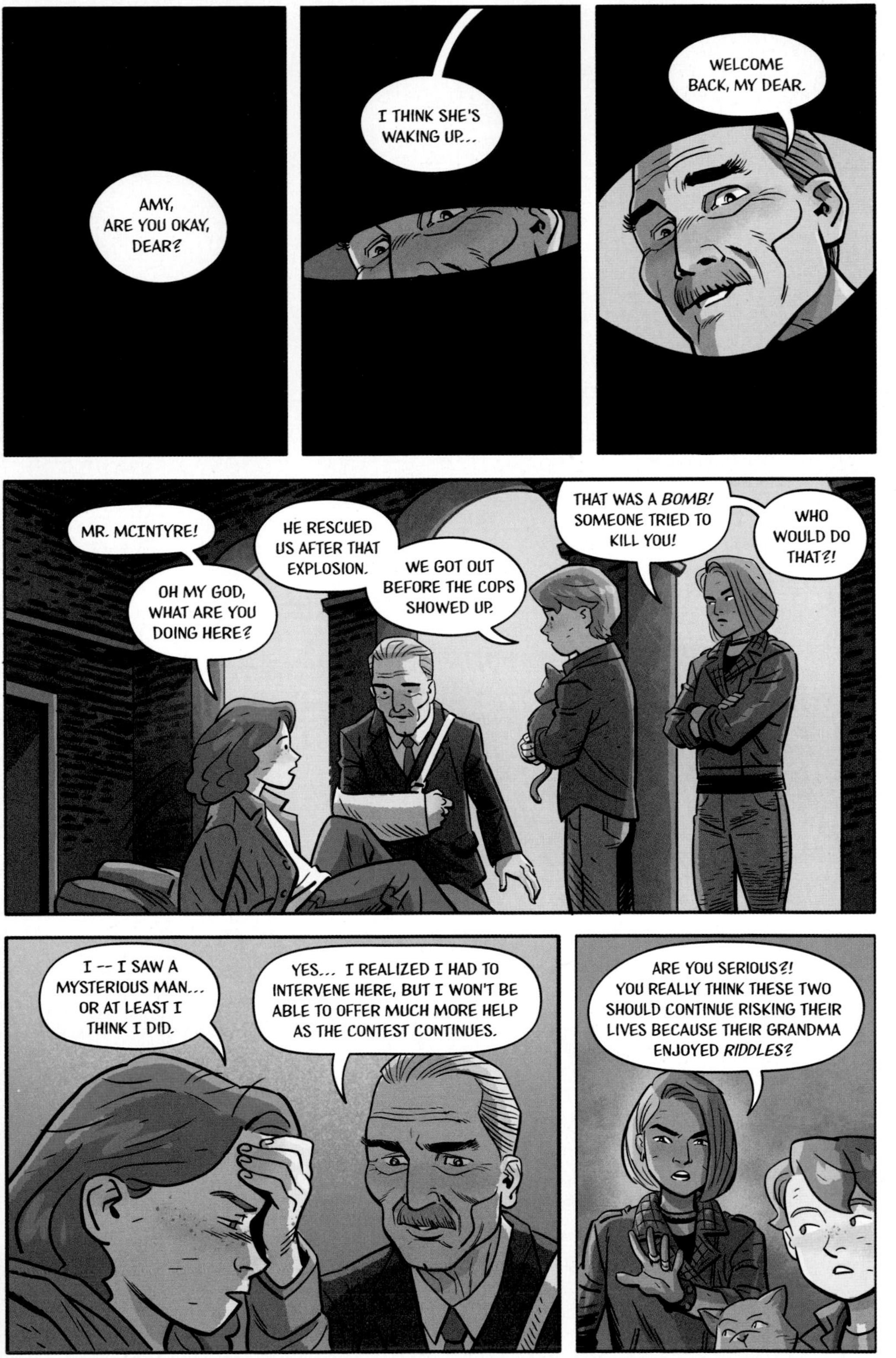

AMY, ARE YOU OKAY, DEAR?
I THINK SHE'S WAKING UP...
WELCOME BACK, MY DEAR.
MR. MCINTYRE!
OH MY GOD, WHAT ARE YOU DOING HERE?
HE RESCUED US AFTER THAT EXPLOSION.
WE GOT OUT BEFORE THE COPS SHOWED UP.
THAT WAS A *BOMB!* SOMEONE TRIED TO KILL YOU!
WHO WOULD DO THAT?!
I -- I SAW A MYSTERIOUS MAN... OR AT LEAST I THINK I DID.
YES... I REALIZED I HAD TO INTERVENE HERE, BUT I WON'T BE ABLE TO OFFER MUCH MORE HELP AS THE CONTEST CONTINUES.
ARE YOU SERIOUS?! YOU REALLY THINK THESE TWO SHOULD CONTINUE RISKING THEIR LIVES BECAUSE THEIR GRANDMA ENJOYED *RIDDLES*?

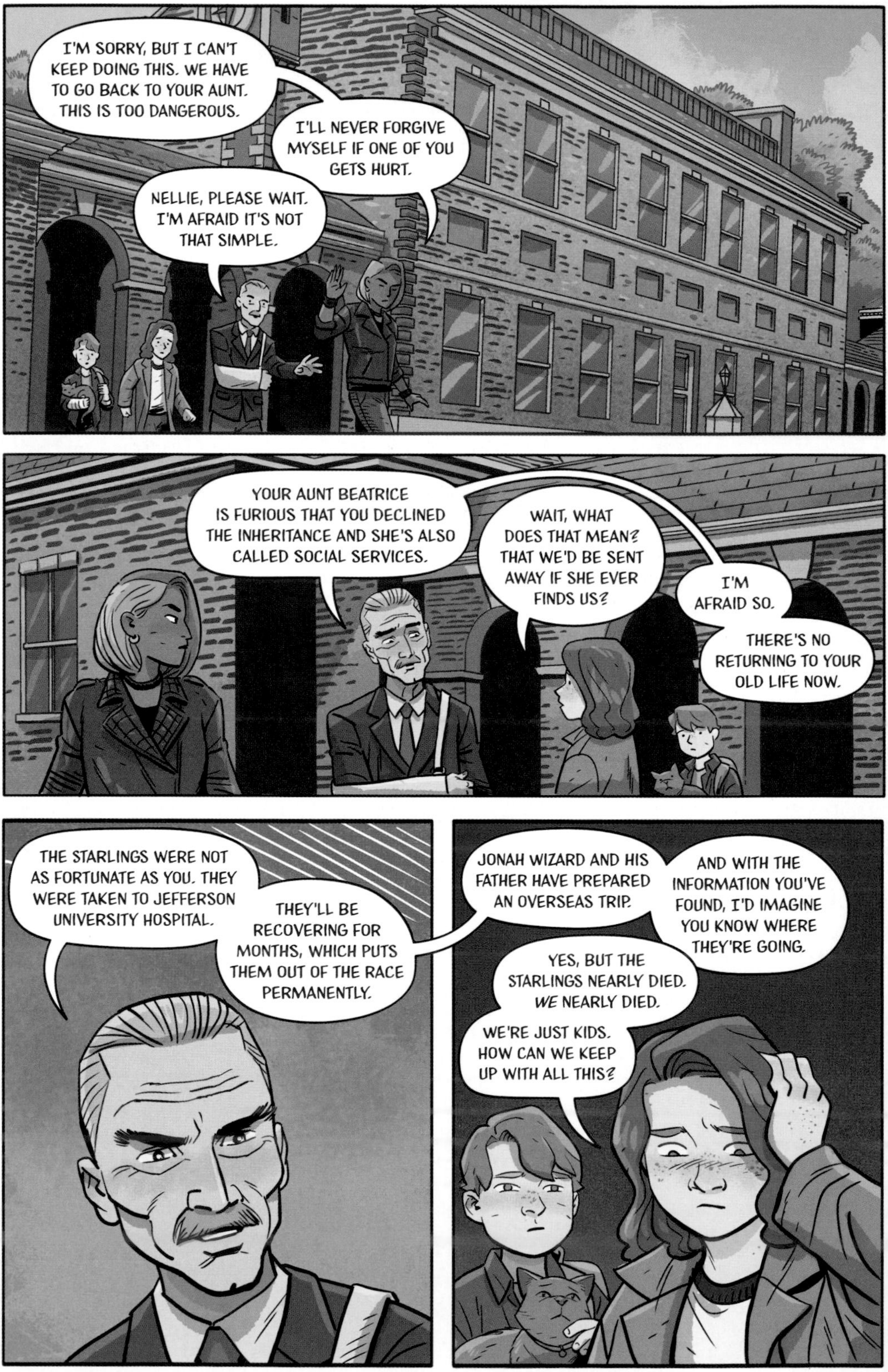
I'M SORRY, BUT I CAN'T KEEP DOING THIS. WE HAVE TO GO BACK TO YOUR AUNT. THIS IS TOO DANGEROUS.
I'LL NEVER FORGIVE MYSELF IF ONE OF YOU GETS HURT.
NELLIE, PLEASE WAIT. I'M AFRAID IT'S NOT THAT SIMPLE.
YOUR AUNT BEATRICE IS FURIOUS THAT YOU DECLINED THE INHERITANCE AND SHE'S ALSO CALLED SOCIAL SERVICES.
WAIT, WHAT DOES THAT MEAN? THAT WE'D BE SENT AWAY IF SHE EVER FINDS US?
I'M AFRAID SO.
THERE'S NO RETURNING TO YOUR OLD LIFE NOW.
THE STARLINGS WERE NOT AS FORTUNATE AS YOU. THEY WERE TAKEN TO JEFFERSON UNIVERSITY HOSPITAL.
THEY'LL BE RECOVERING FOR MONTHS, WHICH PUTS THEM OUT OF THE RACE PERMANENTLY.
JONAH WIZARD AND HIS FATHER HAVE PREPARED AN OVERSEAS TRIP.
AND WITH THE INFORMATION YOU'VE FOUND, I'D IMAGINE YOU KNOW WHERE THEY'RE GOING.
YES, BUT THE STARLINGS NEARLY DIED. *WE* NEARLY DIED.
WE'RE JUST KIDS. HOW CAN WE KEEP UP WITH ALL THIS?

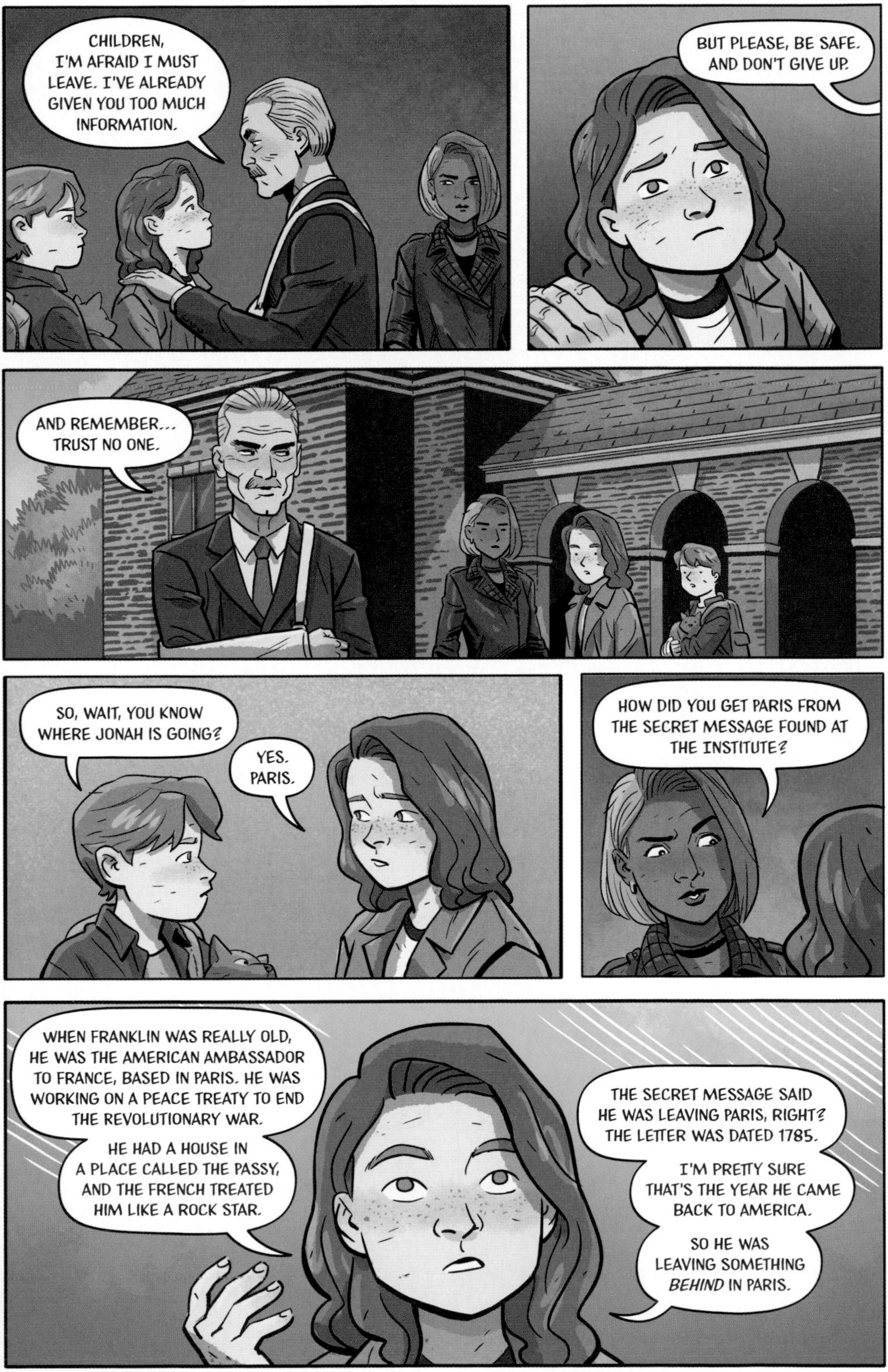
CHILDREN, I'M AFRAID I MUST LEAVE. I'VE ALREADY GIVEN YOU TOO MUCH INFORMATION.
BUT PLEASE, BE SAFE. AND DON'T GIVE UP.
AND REMEMBER... TRUST NO ONE.
SO, WAIT, YOU KNOW WHERE JONAH IS GOING?
YES. PARIS.
HOW DID YOU GET PARIS FROM THE SECRET MESSAGE FOUND AT THE INSTITUTE?
WHEN FRANKLIN WAS REALLY OLD, HE WAS THE AMERICAN AMBASSADOR TO FRANCE, BASED IN PARIS. HE WAS WORKING ON A PEACE TREATY TO END THE REVOLUTIONARY WAR.
HE HAD A HOUSE IN A PLACE CALLED THE PASSY, AND THE FRENCH TREATED HIM LIKE A ROCK STAR.
THE SECRET MESSAGE SAID HE WAS LEAVING PARIS, RIGHT? THE LETTER WAS DATED 1785.
I'M PRETTY SURE THAT'S THE YEAR HE CAME BACK TO AMERICA.
SO HE WAS LEAVING SOMETHING *BEHIND* IN PARIS.

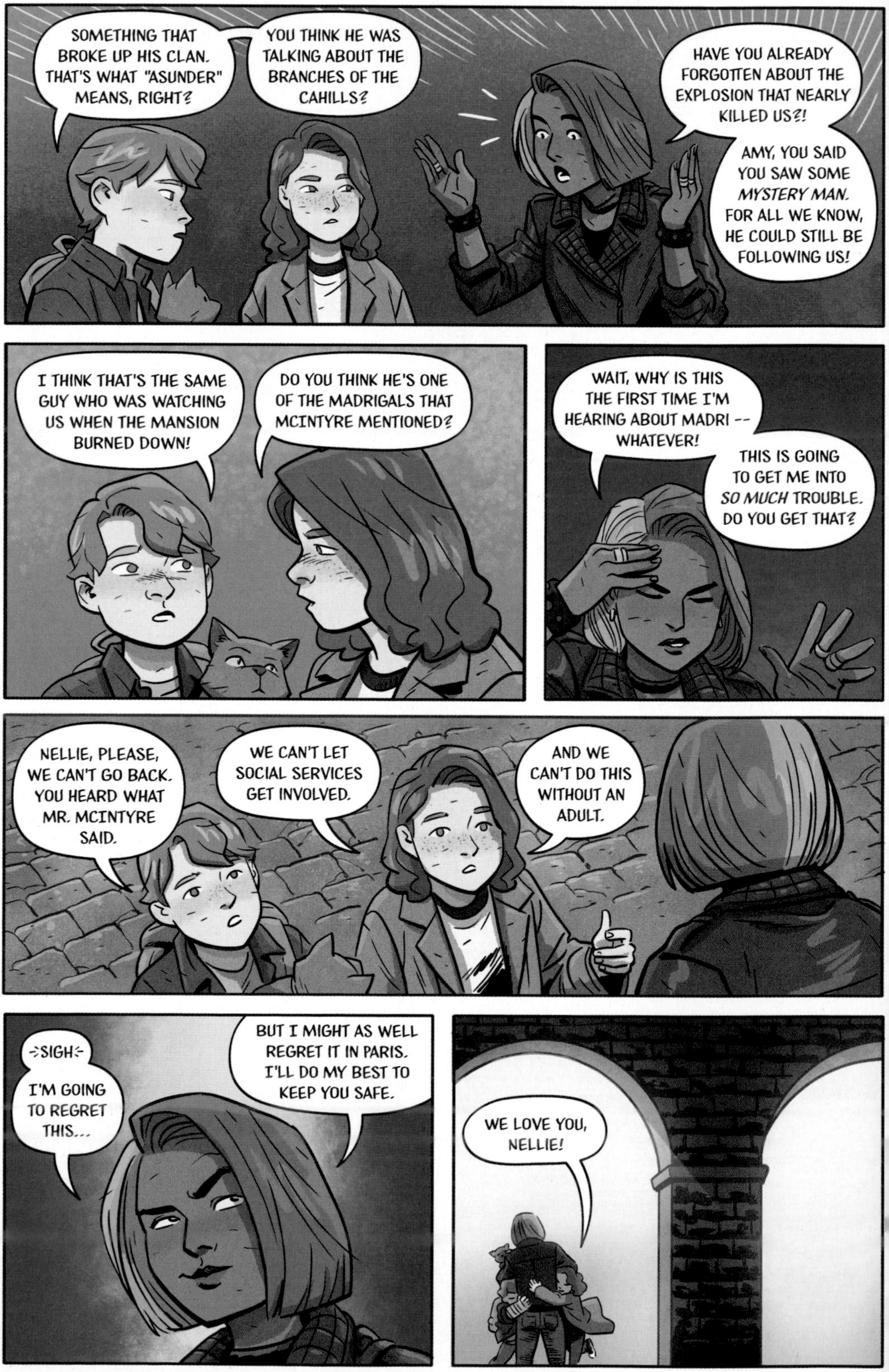
SOMETHING THAT BROKE UP HIS CLAN. THAT'S WHAT "ASUNDER" MEANS, RIGHT?
YOU THINK HE WAS TALKING ABOUT THE BRANCHES OF THE CAHILLS?
HAVE YOU ALREADY FORGOTTEN ABOUT THE EXPLOSION THAT NEARLY KILLED US?!
AMY, YOU SAID YOU SAW SOME *MYSTERY MAN.* FOR ALL WE KNOW, HE COULD STILL BE FOLLOWING US!
I THINK THAT'S THE SAME GUY WHO WAS WATCHING US WHEN THE MANSION BURNED DOWN!
DO YOU THINK HE'S ONE OF THE MADRIGALS THAT MCINTYRE MENTIONED?
WAIT, WHY IS THIS THE FIRST TIME I'M HEARING ABOUT MADRI -- WHATEVER!
THIS IS GOING TO GET ME INTO *SO MUCH* TROUBLE. DO YOU GET THAT?
NELLIE, PLEASE, WE CAN'T GO BACK. YOU HEARD WHAT MR. MCINTYRE SAID.
WE CAN'T LET SOCIAL SERVICES GET INVOLVED.
AND WE CAN'T DO THIS WITHOUT AN ADULT.
=SIGH=
I'M GOING TO REGRET THIS...
BUT I MIGHT AS WELL REGRET IT IN PARIS. I'LL DO MY BEST TO KEEP YOU SAFE.
WE LOVE YOU, NELLIE!

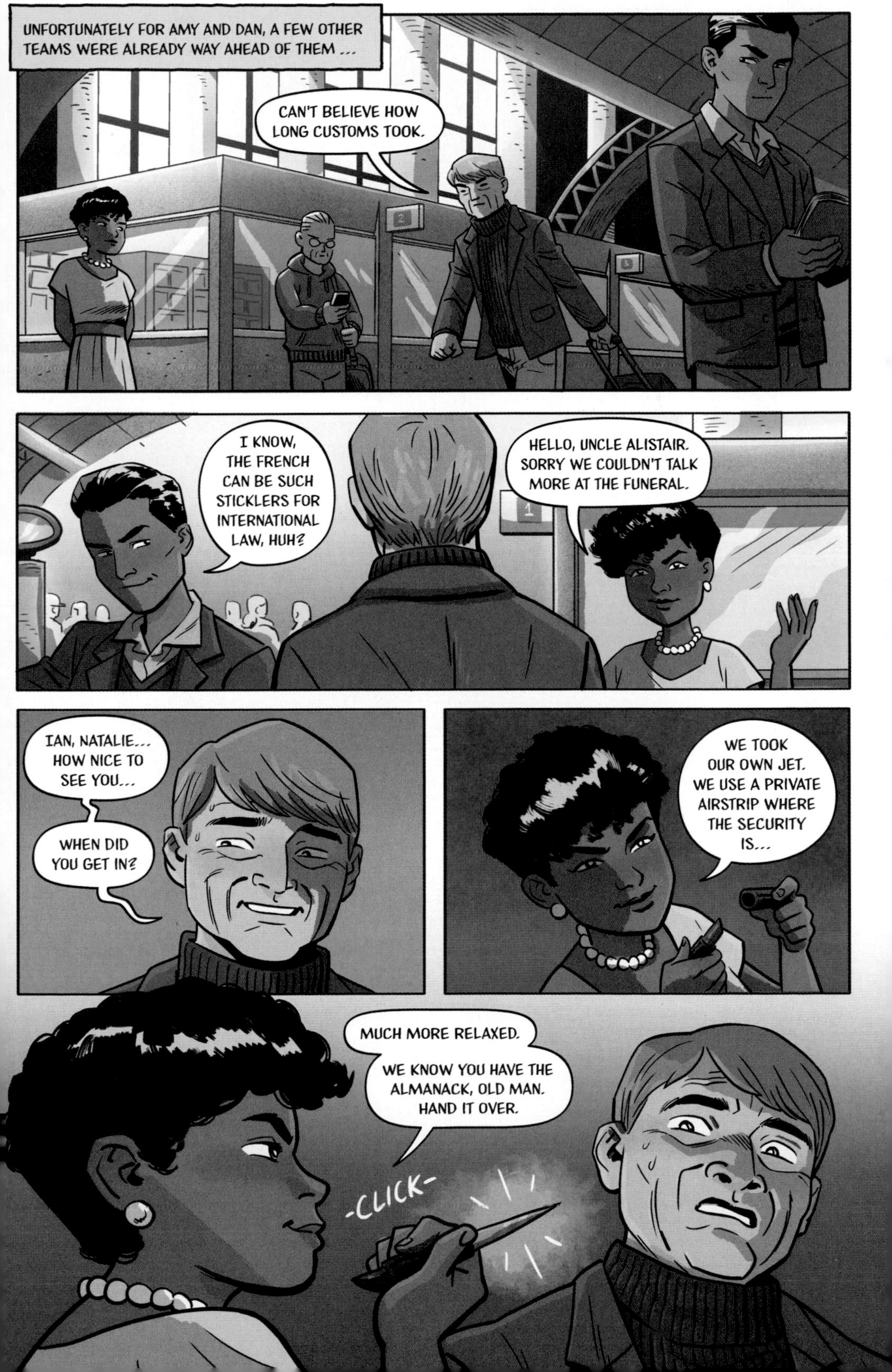
UNFORTUNATELY FOR AMY AND DAN, A FEW OTHER TEAMS WERE ALREADY WAY AHEAD OF THEM ...
CAN'T BELIEVE HOW LONG CUSTOMS TOOK.
I KNOW, THE FRENCH CAN BE SUCH STICKLERS FOR INTERNATIONAL LAW, HUH?
HELLO, UNCLE ALISTAIR. SORRY WE COULDN'T TALK MORE AT THE FUNERAL.
IAN, NATALIE... HOW NICE TO SEE YOU...
WHEN DID YOU GET IN?
WE TOOK OUR OWN JET. WE USE A PRIVATE AIRSTRIP WHERE THE SECURITY IS...
MUCH MORE RELAXED.
WE KNOW YOU HAVE THE ALMANACK, OLD MAN. HAND IT OVER.
-CLICK-

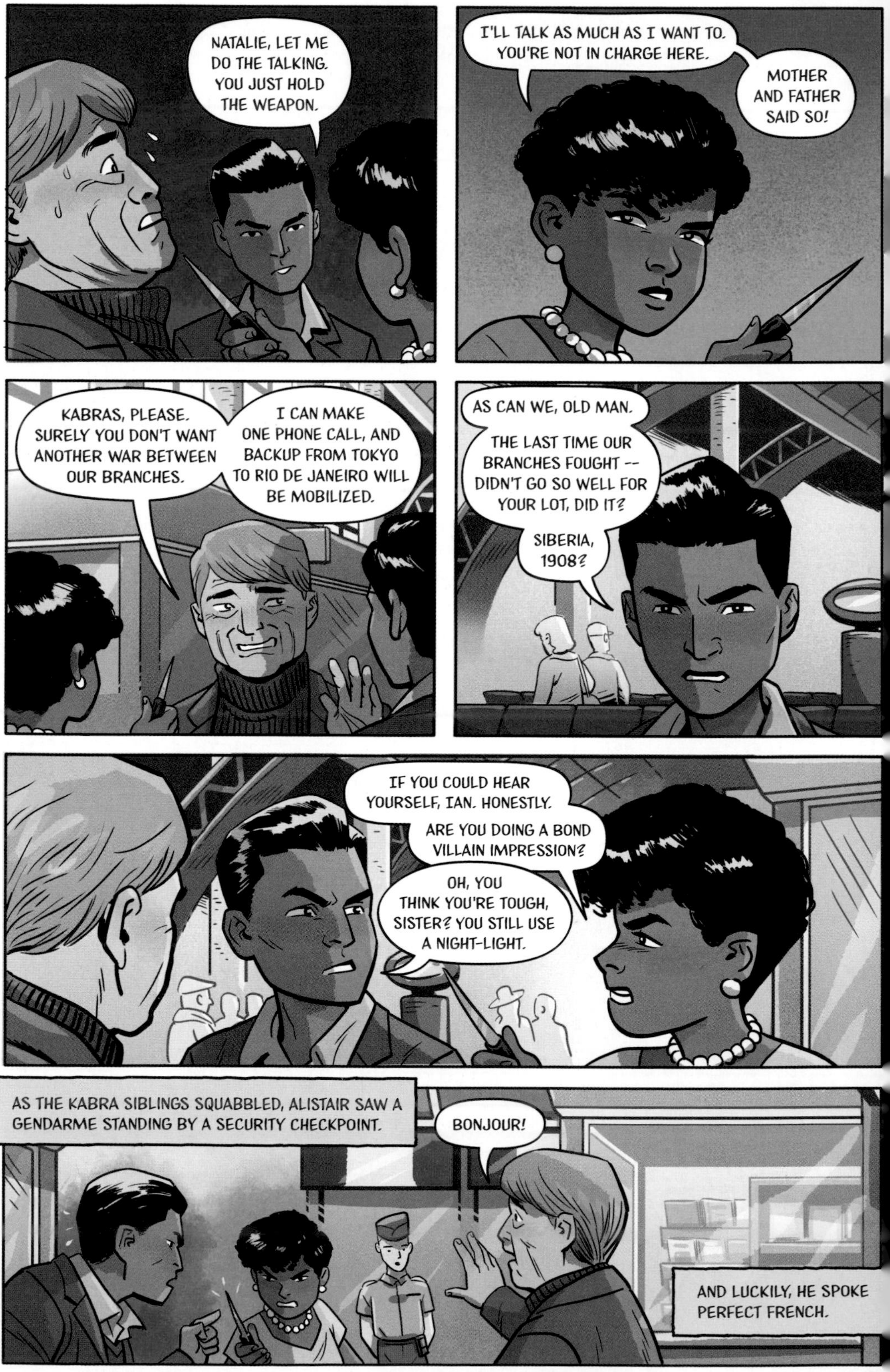
NATALIE, LET ME DO THE TALKING. YOU JUST HOLD THE WEAPON.
I'LL TALK AS MUCH AS I WANT TO. YOU'RE NOT IN CHARGE HERE.
MOTHER AND FATHER SAID SO!
KABRAS, PLEASE. SURELY YOU DON'T WANT ANOTHER WAR BETWEEN OUR BRANCHES.
I CAN MAKE ONE PHONE CALL, AND BACKUP FROM TOKYO TO RIO DE JANEIRO WILL BE MOBILIZED.
AS CAN WE, OLD MAN.
THE LAST TIME OUR BRANCHES FOUGHT -- DIDN'T GO SO WELL FOR YOUR LOT, DID IT?
SIBERIA, 1908?
IF YOU COULD HEAR YOURSELF, IAN. HONESTLY.
ARE YOU DOING A BOND VILLAIN IMPRESSION?
OH, YOU THINK YOU'RE TOUGH, SISTER? YOU STILL USE A NIGHT-LIGHT.
AS THE KABRA SIBLINGS SQUABBLED, ALISTAIR SAW A GENDARME STANDING BY A SECURITY CHECKPOINT.
BONJOUR!
AND LUCKILY, HE SPOKE PERFECT FRENCH.

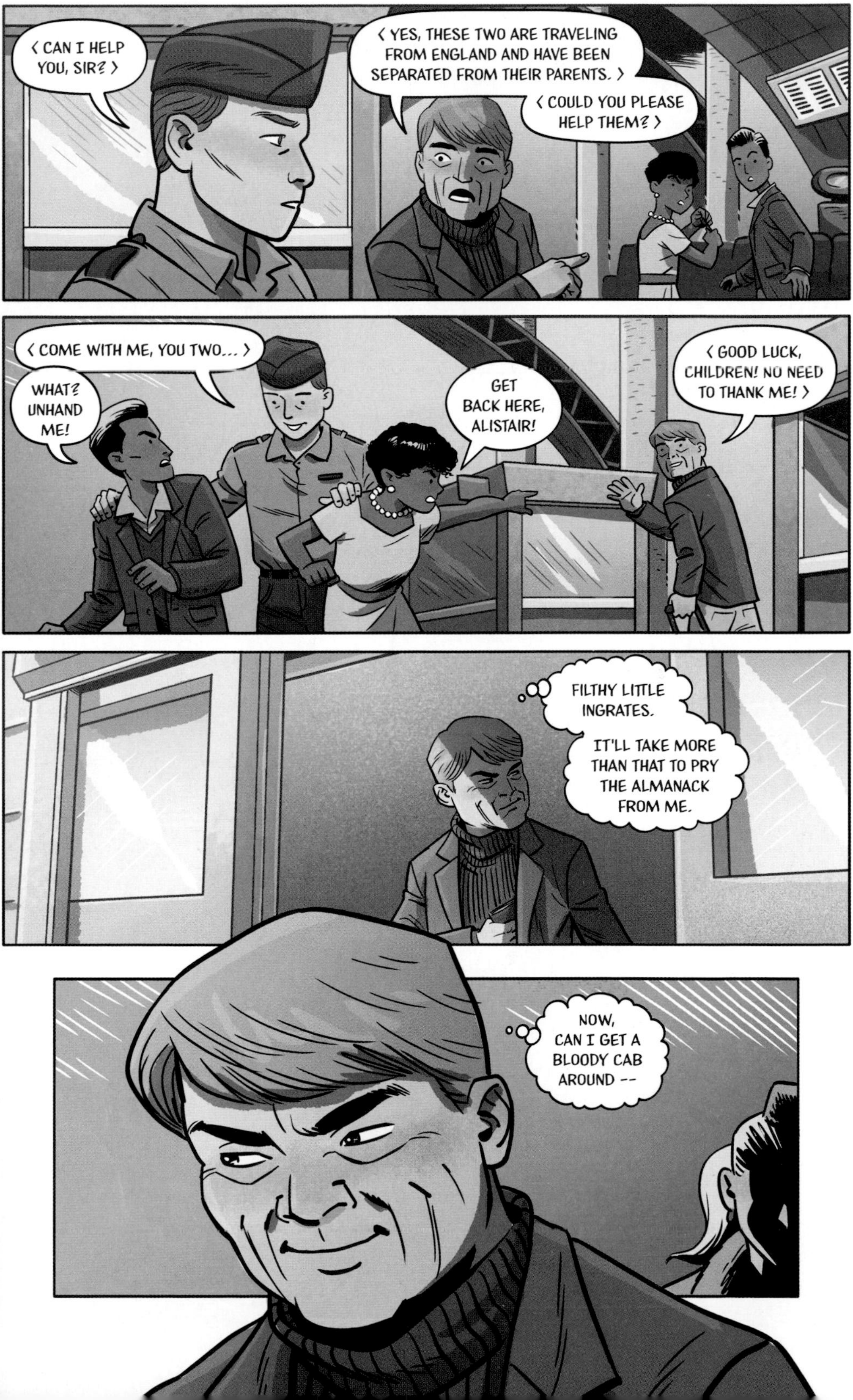
< CAN I HELP YOU, SIR? >
< YES, THESE TWO ARE TRAVELING FROM ENGLAND AND HAVE BEEN SEPARATED FROM THEIR PARENTS. >
< COULD YOU PLEASE HELP THEM? >
< COME WITH ME, YOU TWO... >
WHAT? UNHAND ME!
GET BACK HERE, ALISTAIR!
< GOOD LUCK, CHILDREN! NO NEED TO THANK ME! >
FILTHY LITTLE INGRATES.
IT'LL TAKE MORE THAN THAT TO PRY THE ALMANACK FROM ME.
NOW, CAN I GET A BLOODY CAB AROUND --

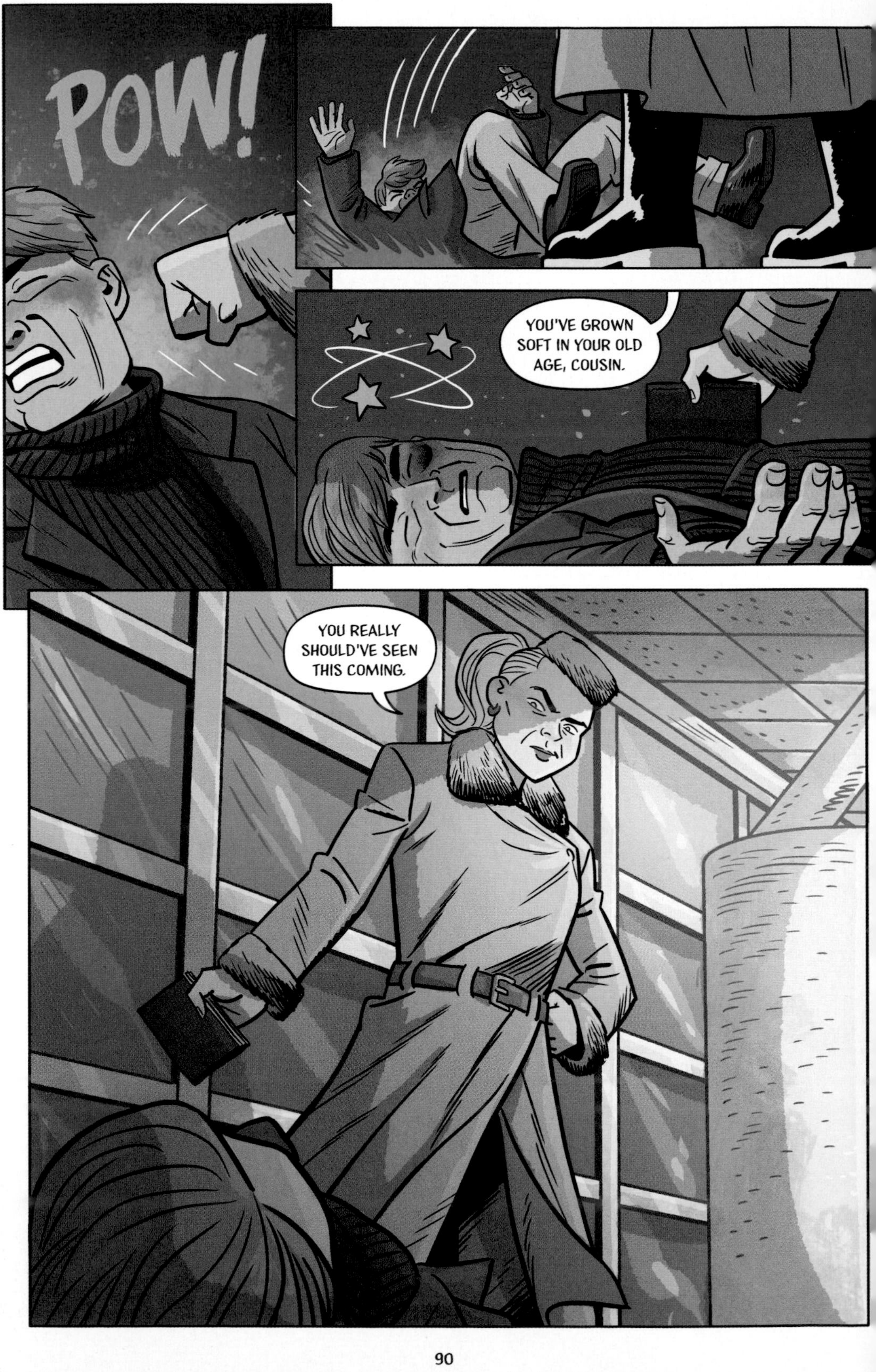
POW!
YOU'VE GROWN SOFT IN YOUR OLD AGE, COUSIN.
YOU REALLY SHOULD'VE SEEN THIS COMING.

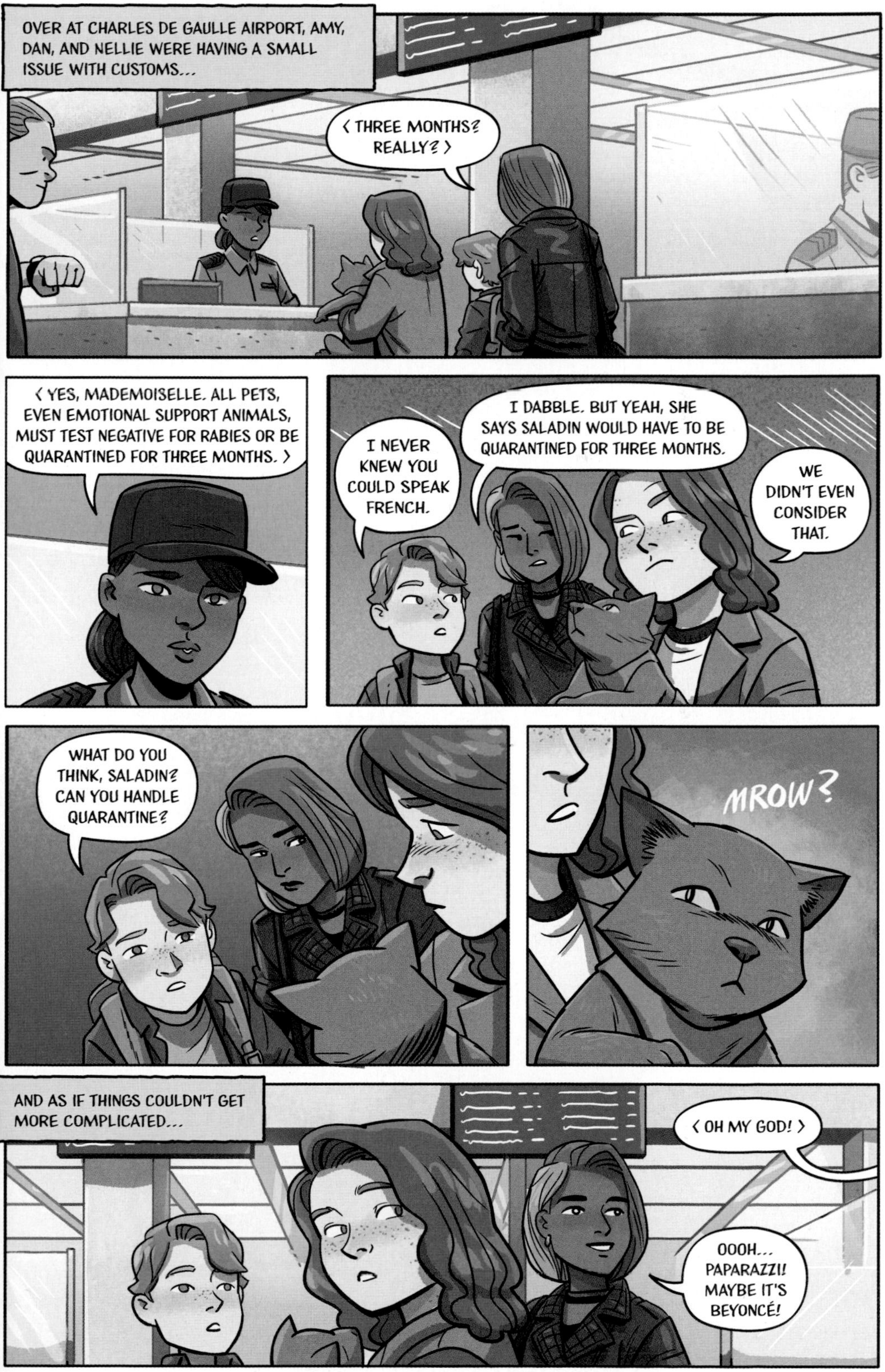
OVER AT CHARLES DE GAULLE AIRPORT, AMY, DAN, AND NELLIE WERE HAVING A SMALL ISSUE WITH CUSTOMS...
‹ THREE MONTHS? REALLY? ›
‹ YES, MADEMOISELLE. ALL PETS, EVEN EMOTIONAL SUPPORT ANIMALS, MUST TEST NEGATIVE FOR RABIES OR BE QUARANTINED FOR THREE MONTHS. ›
I NEVER KNEW YOU COULD SPEAK FRENCH.
I DABBLE. BUT YEAH, SHE SAYS SALADIN WOULD HAVE TO BE QUARANTINED FOR THREE MONTHS.
WE DIDN'T EVEN CONSIDER THAT.
WHAT DO YOU THINK, SALADIN? CAN YOU HANDLE QUARANTINE?
MROW?
AND AS IF THINGS COULDN'T GET MORE COMPLICATED...
‹ OH MY GOD! ›
OOOH... PAPARAZZI! MAYBE IT'S BEYONCÉ!

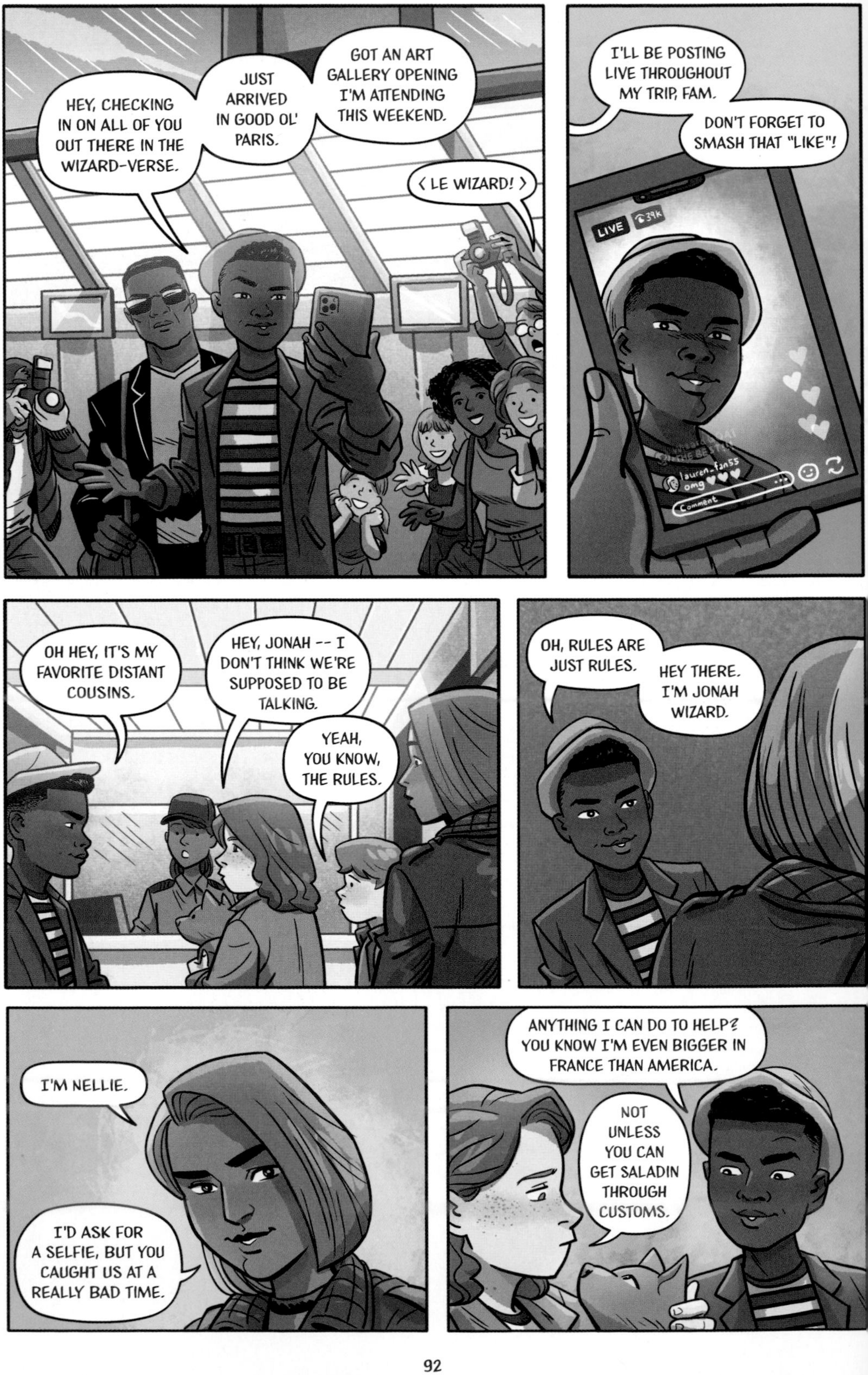
HEY, CHECKING IN ON ALL OF YOU OUT THERE IN THE WIZARD-VERSE.
JUST ARRIVED IN GOOD OL' PARIS.
GOT AN ART GALLERY OPENING I'M ATTENDING THIS WEEKEND.
⟨ LE WIZARD! ⟩
I'LL BE POSTING LIVE THROUGHOUT MY TRIP, FAM.
DON'T FORGET TO SMASH THAT "LIKE"!
LIVE
39K
lauren_fan55
omg ♥♥♥
Comment
OH HEY, IT'S MY FAVORITE DISTANT COUSINS.
HEY, JONAH -- I DON'T THINK WE'RE SUPPOSED TO BE TALKING.
YEAH, YOU KNOW, THE RULES.
OH, RULES ARE JUST RULES.
HEY THERE. I'M JONAH WIZARD.
I'M NELLIE.
I'D ASK FOR A SELFIE, BUT YOU CAUGHT US AT A REALLY BAD TIME.
ANYTHING I CAN DO TO HELP? YOU KNOW I'M EVEN BIGGER IN FRANCE THAN AMERICA.
NOT UNLESS YOU CAN GET SALADIN THROUGH CUSTOMS.

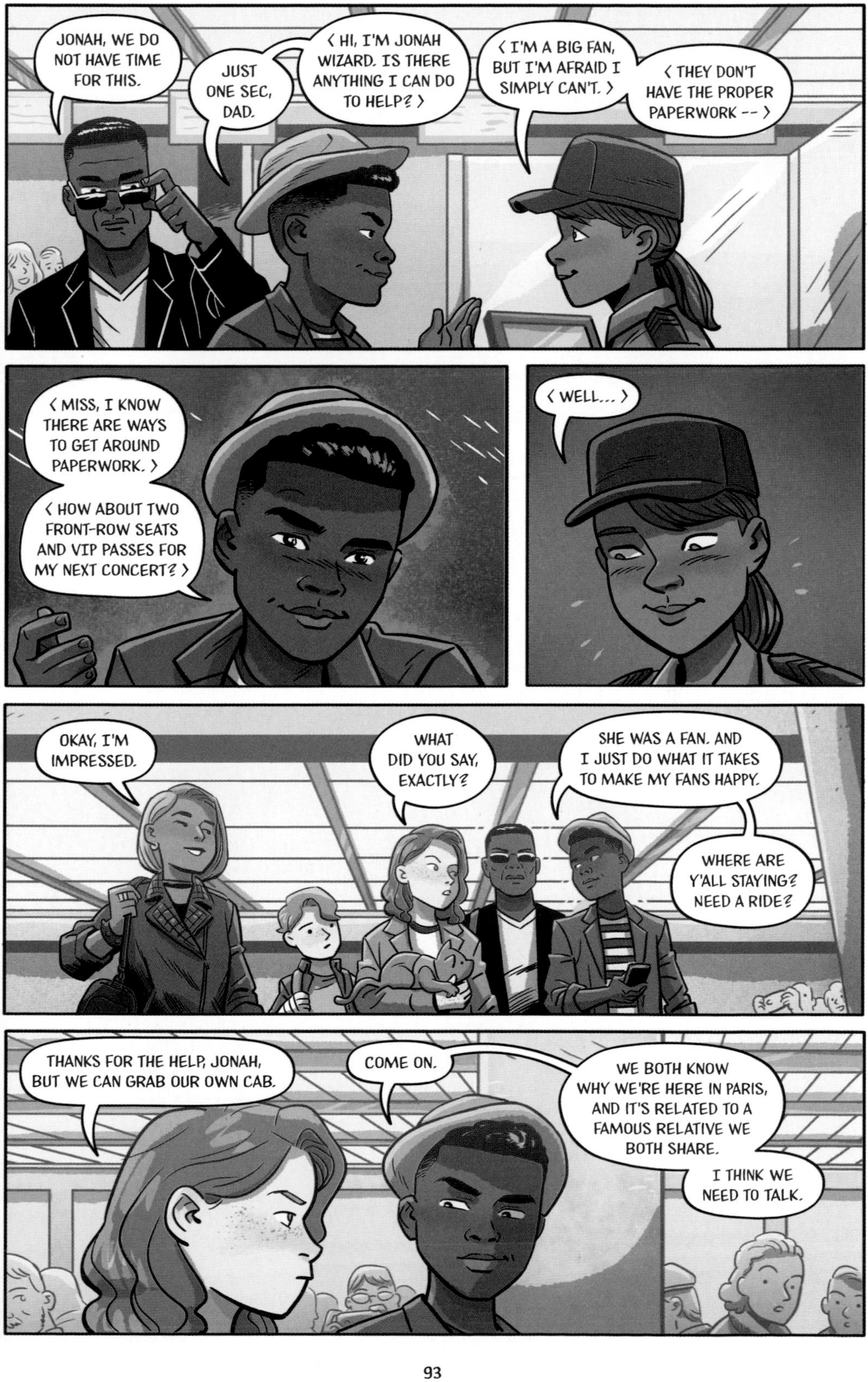
JONAH, WE DO NOT HAVE TIME FOR THIS.
JUST ONE SEC, DAD.
‹ HI, I'M JONAH WIZARD. IS THERE ANYTHING I CAN DO TO HELP? ›
‹ I'M A BIG FAN, BUT I'M AFRAID I SIMPLY CAN'T. ›
‹ THEY DON'T HAVE THE PROPER PAPERWORK -- ›
‹ MISS, I KNOW THERE ARE WAYS TO GET AROUND PAPERWORK. ›
‹ HOW ABOUT TWO FRONT-ROW SEATS AND VIP PASSES FOR MY NEXT CONCERT? ›
‹ WELL... ›
OKAY, I'M IMPRESSED.
WHAT DID YOU SAY, EXACTLY?
SHE WAS A FAN. AND I JUST DO WHAT IT TAKES TO MAKE MY FANS HAPPY.
WHERE ARE Y'ALL STAYING? NEED A RIDE?
THANKS FOR THE HELP, JONAH, BUT WE CAN GRAB OUR OWN CAB.
COME ON.
WE BOTH KNOW WHY WE'RE HERE IN PARIS, AND IT'S RELATED TO A FAMOUS RELATIVE WE BOTH SHARE.
I THINK WE NEED TO TALK.

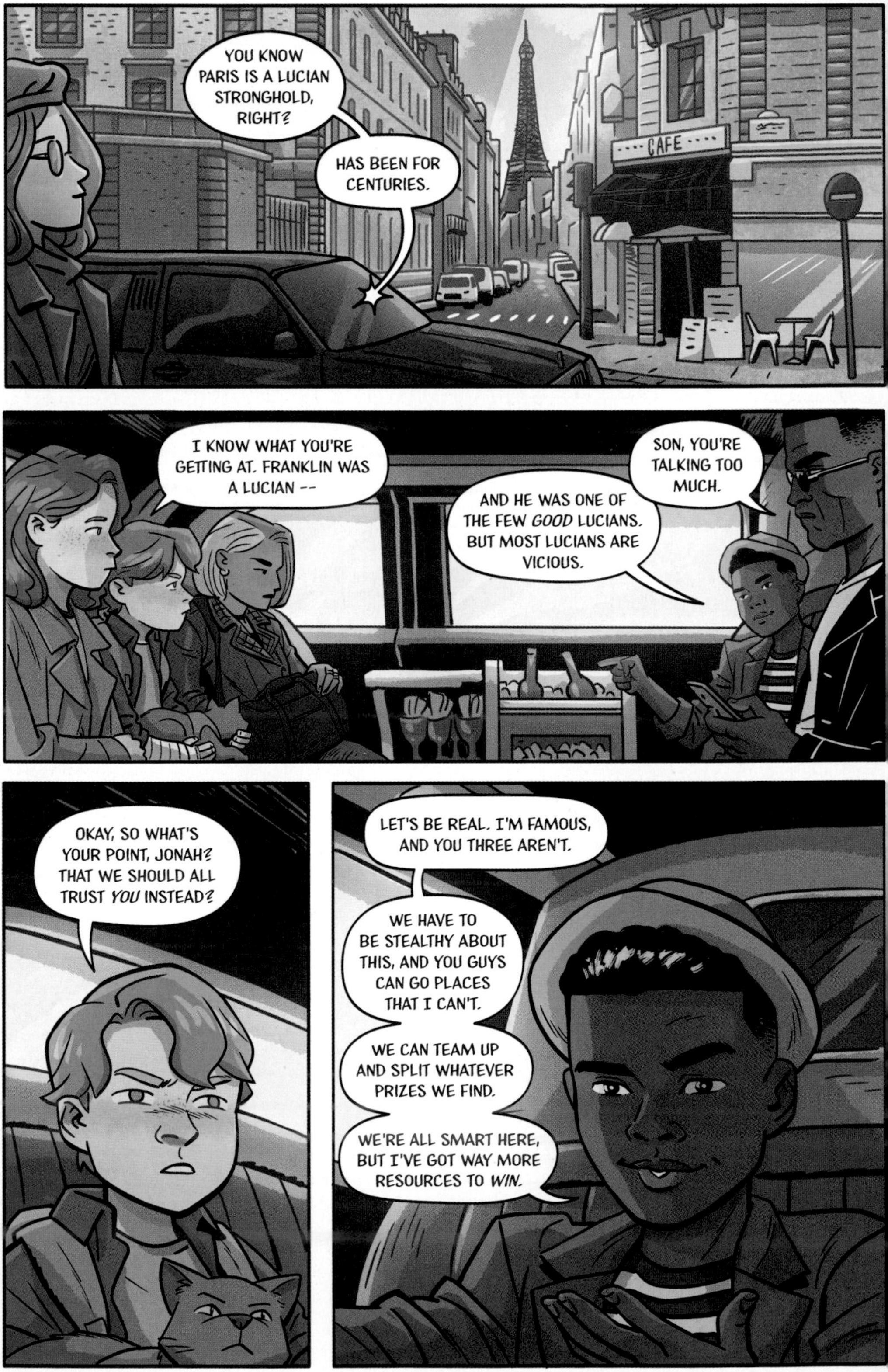
YOU KNOW PARIS IS A LUCIAN STRONGHOLD, RIGHT?
HAS BEEN FOR CENTURIES.
CAFE
I KNOW WHAT YOU'RE GETTING AT. FRANKLIN WAS A LUCIAN --
AND HE WAS ONE OF THE FEW *GOOD* LUCIANS. BUT MOST LUCIANS ARE VICIOUS.
SON, YOU'RE TALKING TOO MUCH.
OKAY, SO WHAT'S YOUR POINT, JONAH? THAT WE SHOULD ALL TRUST *YOU* INSTEAD?
LET'S BE REAL. I'M FAMOUS, AND YOU THREE AREN'T.
WE HAVE TO BE STEALTHY ABOUT THIS, AND YOU GUYS CAN GO PLACES THAT I CAN'T.
WE CAN TEAM UP AND SPLIT WHATEVER PRIZES WE FIND.
WE'RE ALL SMART HERE, BUT I'VE GOT WAY MORE RESOURCES TO *WIN*.

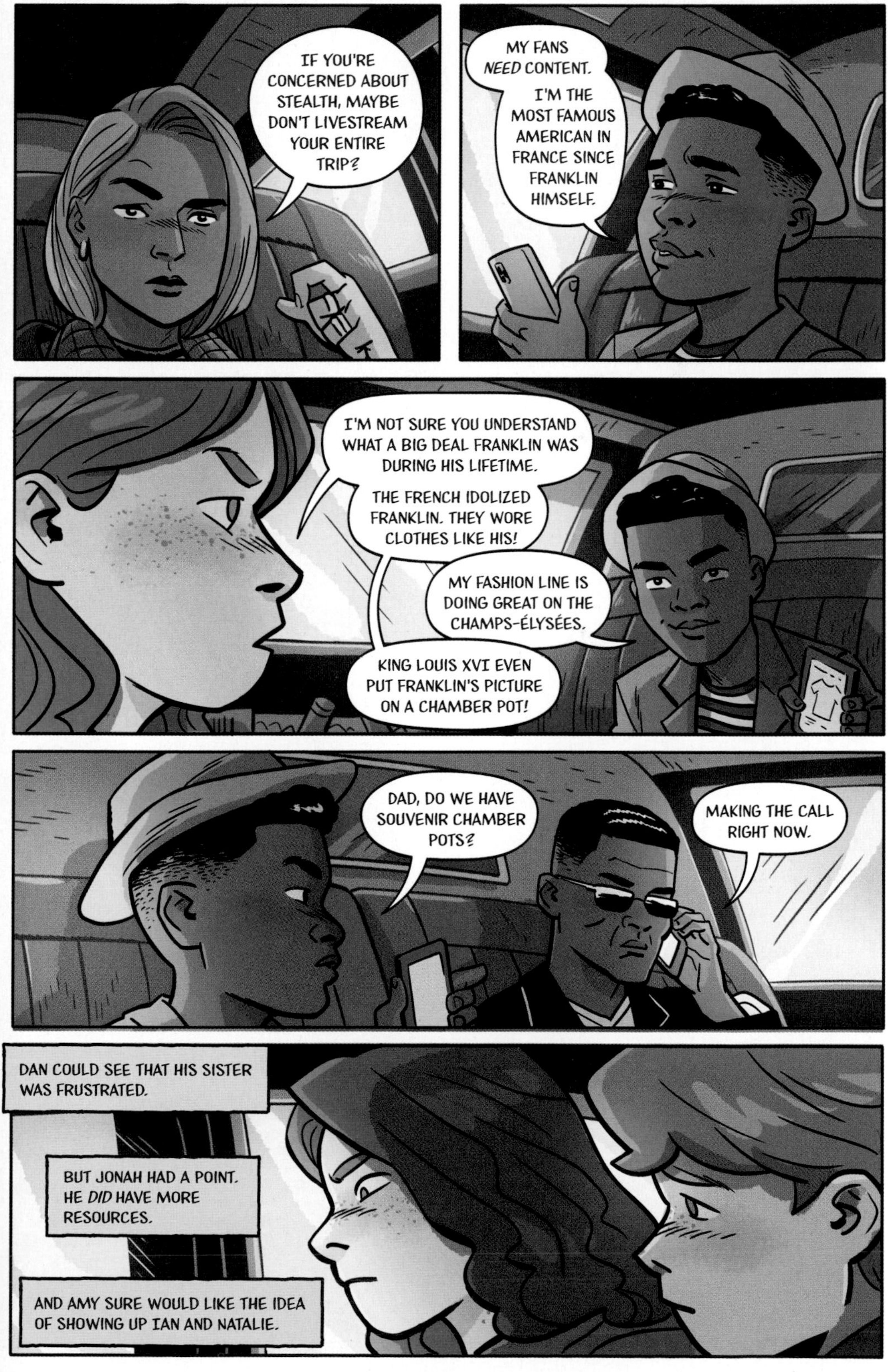
IF YOU'RE CONCERNED ABOUT STEALTH, MAYBE DON'T LIVESTREAM YOUR ENTIRE TRIP?
MY FANS *NEED* CONTENT.
I'M THE MOST FAMOUS AMERICAN IN FRANCE SINCE FRANKLIN HIMSELF.
I'M NOT SURE YOU UNDERSTAND WHAT A BIG DEAL FRANKLIN WAS DURING HIS LIFETIME.
THE FRENCH IDOLIZED FRANKLIN. THEY WORE CLOTHES LIKE HIS!
MY FASHION LINE IS DOING GREAT ON THE CHAMPS-ÉLYSÉES.
KING LOUIS XVI EVEN PUT FRANKLIN'S PICTURE ON A CHAMBER POT!
DAD, DO WE HAVE SOUVENIR CHAMBER POTS?
MAKING THE CALL RIGHT NOW.
DAN COULD SEE THAT HIS SISTER WAS FRUSTRATED.
BUT JONAH HAD A POINT. HE *DID* HAVE MORE RESOURCES.
AND AMY SURE WOULD LIKE THE IDEA OF SHOWING UP IAN AND NATALIE.

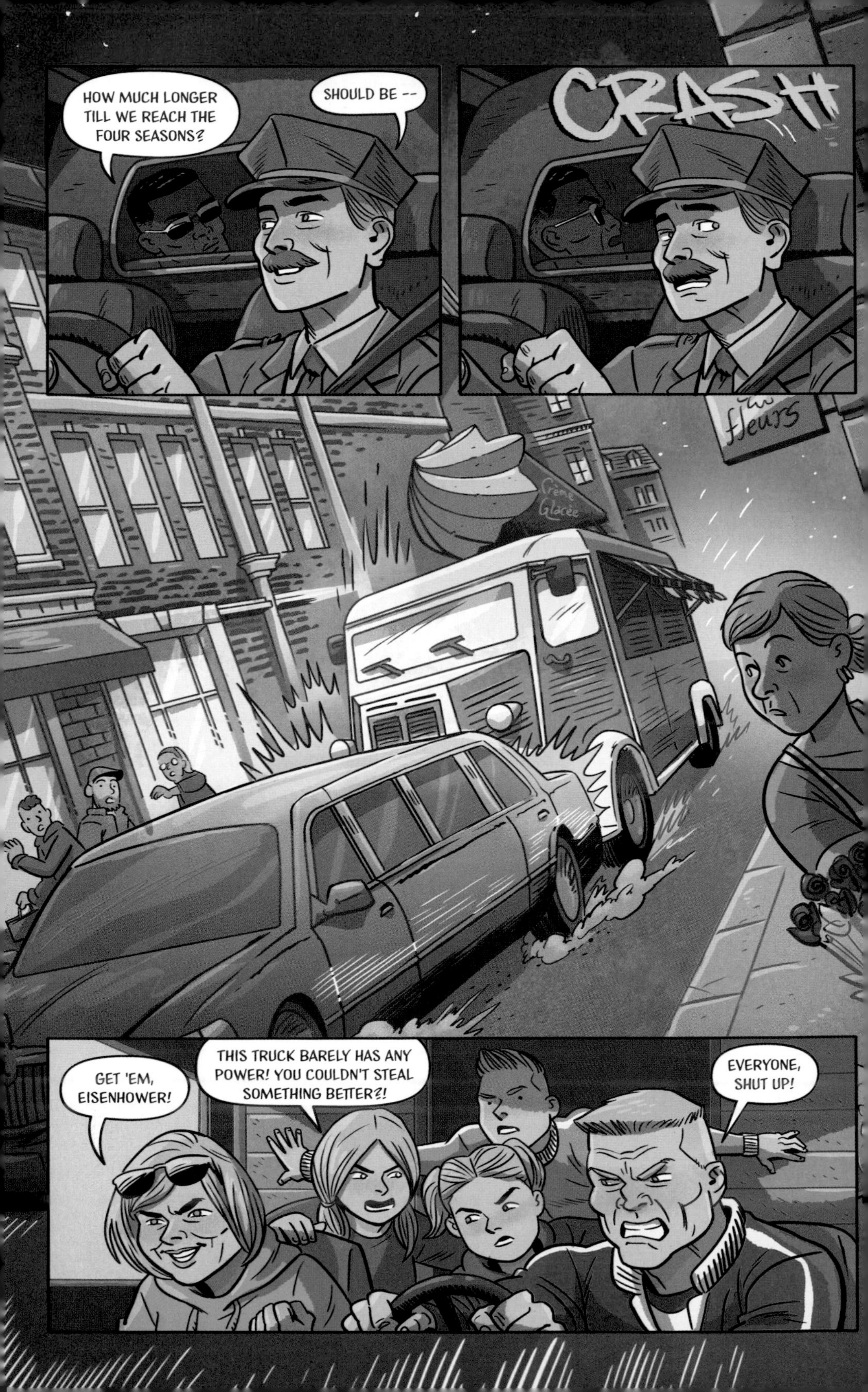

HOW MUCH LONGER TILL WE REACH THE FOUR SEASONS?
SHOULD BE --
CRASH
fleurs
Crème Glacée
GET 'EM, EISENHOWER!
THIS TRUCK BARELY HAS ANY POWER! YOU COULDN'T STEAL SOMETHING BETTER?!
EVERYONE, SHUT UP!

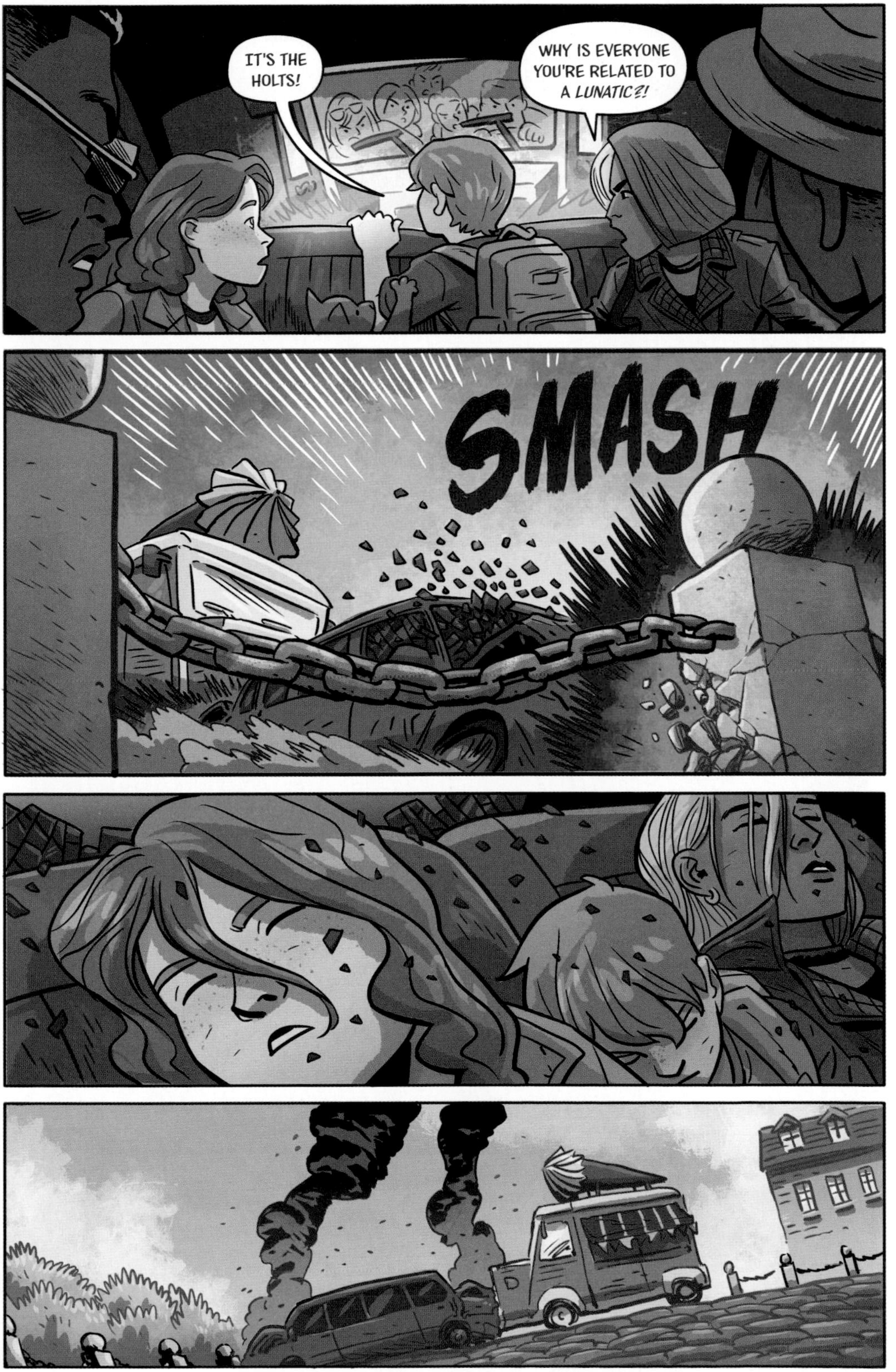
IT'S THE HOLTS!
WHY IS EVERYONE YOU'RE RELATED TO A *LUNATIC*?!
SMASH

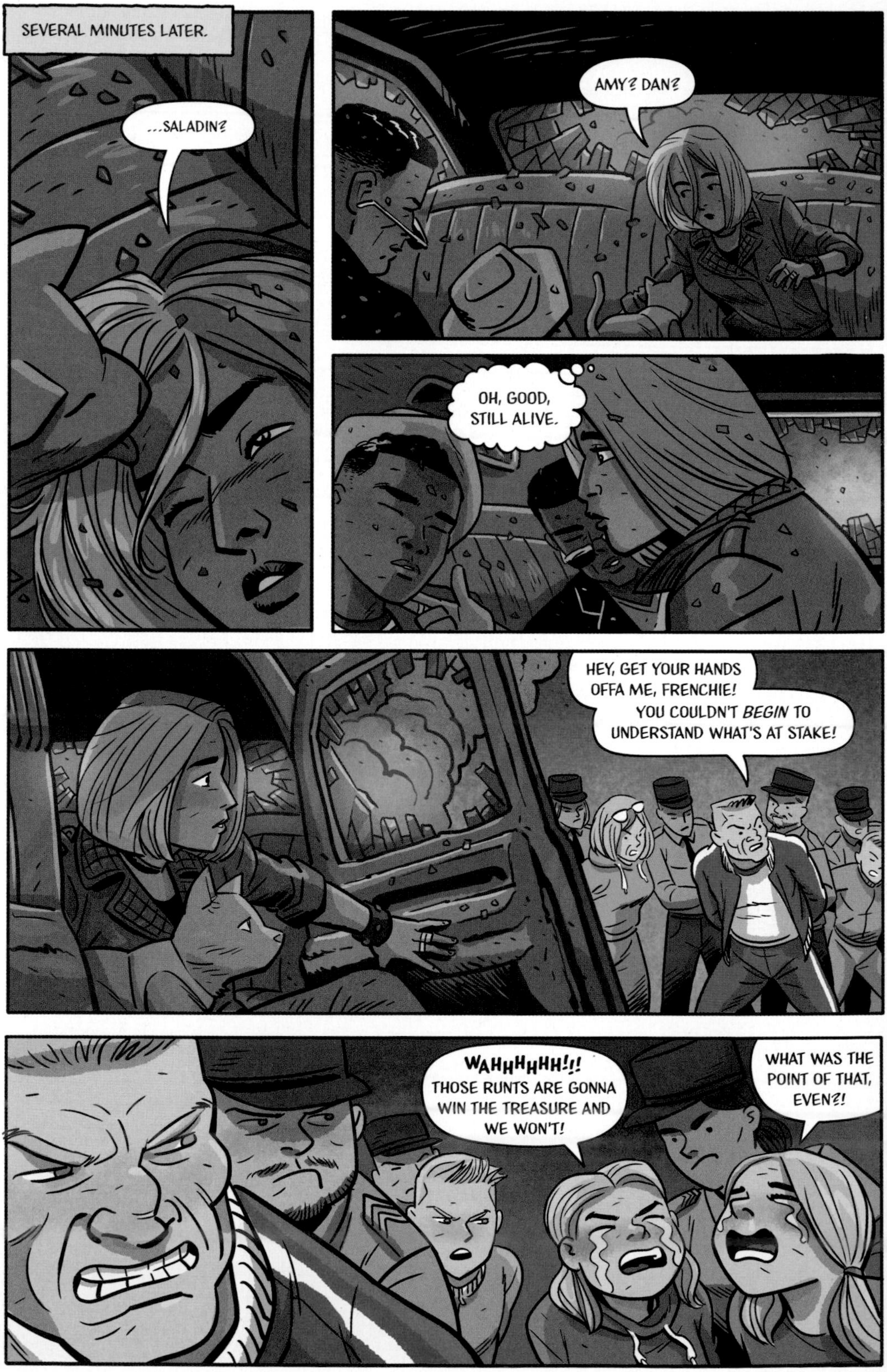
SEVERAL MINUTES LATER.
...SALADIN?
AMY? DAN?
OH, GOOD, STILL ALIVE.
HEY, GET YOUR HANDS OFFA ME, FRENCHIE! YOU COULDN'T *BEGIN* TO UNDERSTAND WHAT'S AT STAKE!
WAHHHHHH!!! THOSE RUNTS ARE GONNA WIN THE TREASURE AND WE WON'T!
WHAT WAS THE POINT OF THAT, EVEN?!

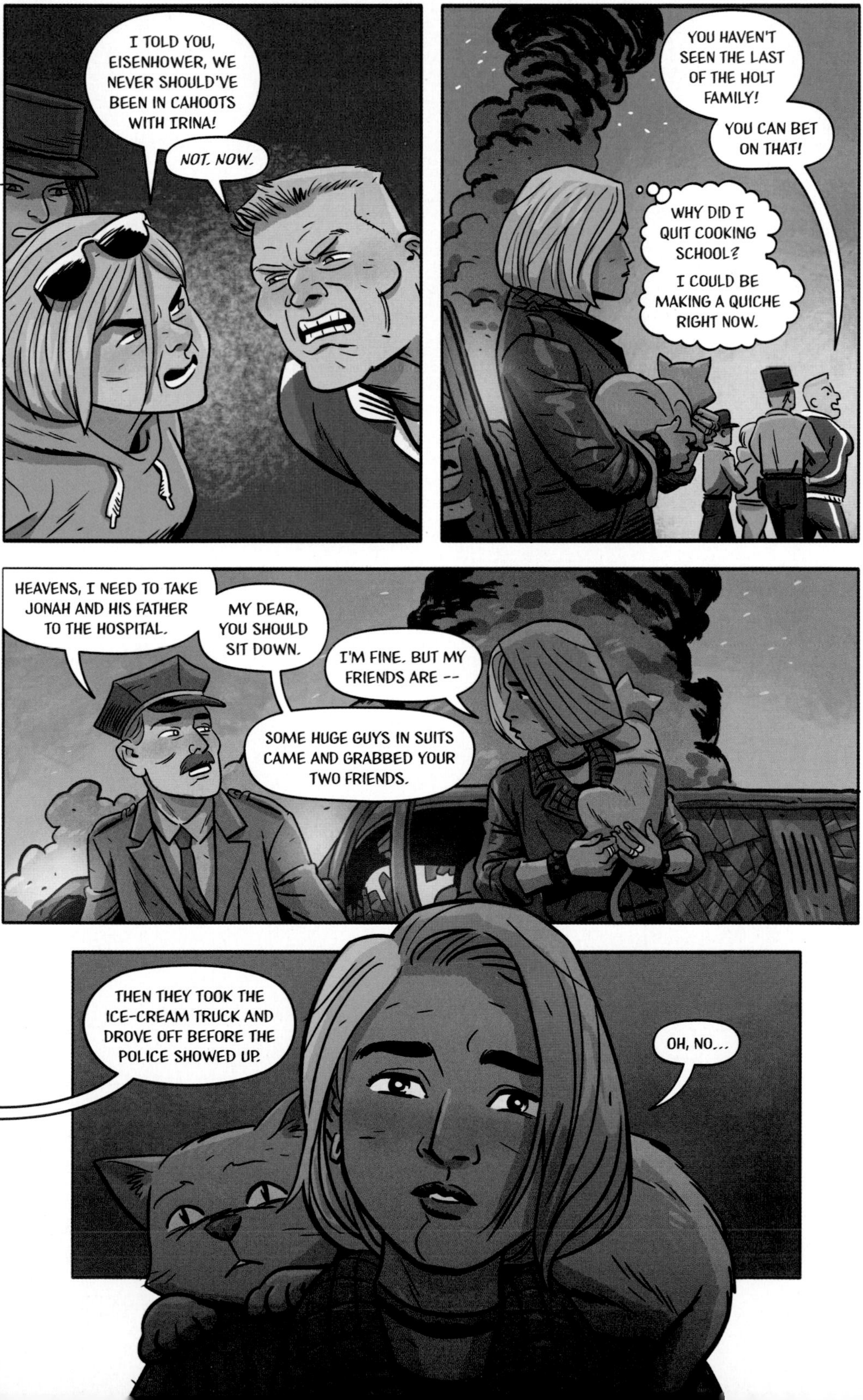
I TOLD YOU, EISENHOWER, WE NEVER SHOULD'VE BEEN IN CAHOOTS WITH IRINA!
NOT. NOW.
YOU HAVEN'T SEEN THE LAST OF THE HOLT FAMILY!
YOU CAN BET ON THAT!
WHY DID I QUIT COOKING SCHOOL?
I COULD BE MAKING A QUICHE RIGHT NOW.
HEAVENS, I NEED TO TAKE JONAH AND HIS FATHER TO THE HOSPITAL.
MY DEAR, YOU SHOULD SIT DOWN.
I'M FINE. BUT MY FRIENDS ARE --
SOME HUGE GUYS IN SUITS CAME AND GRABBED YOUR TWO FRIENDS.
THEN THEY TOOK THE ICE-CREAM TRUCK AND DROVE OFF BEFORE THE POLICE SHOWED UP.
OH, NO...

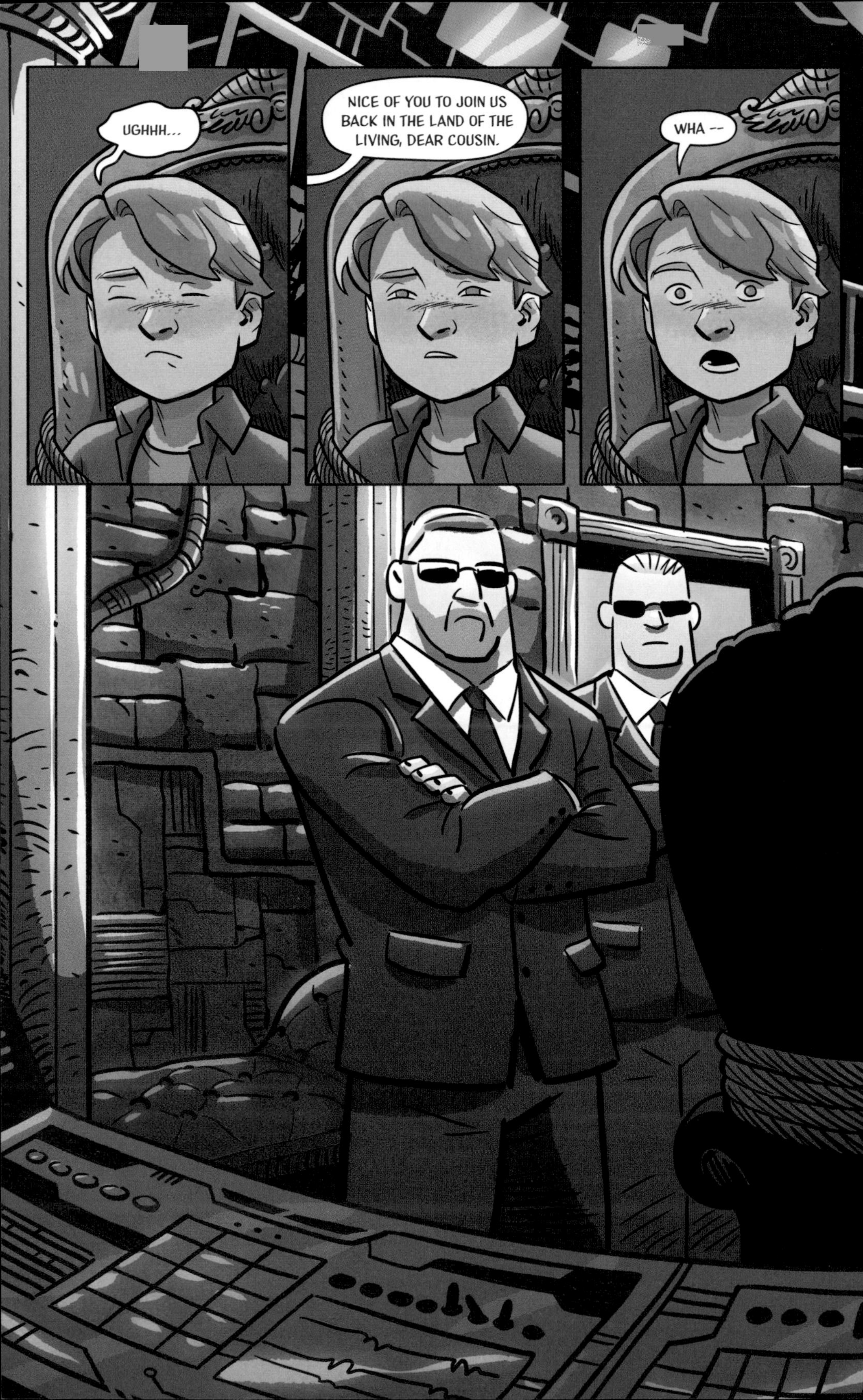
UGHHH...
NICE OF YOU TO JOIN US BACK IN THE LAND OF THE LIVING, DEAR COUSIN.
WHA --

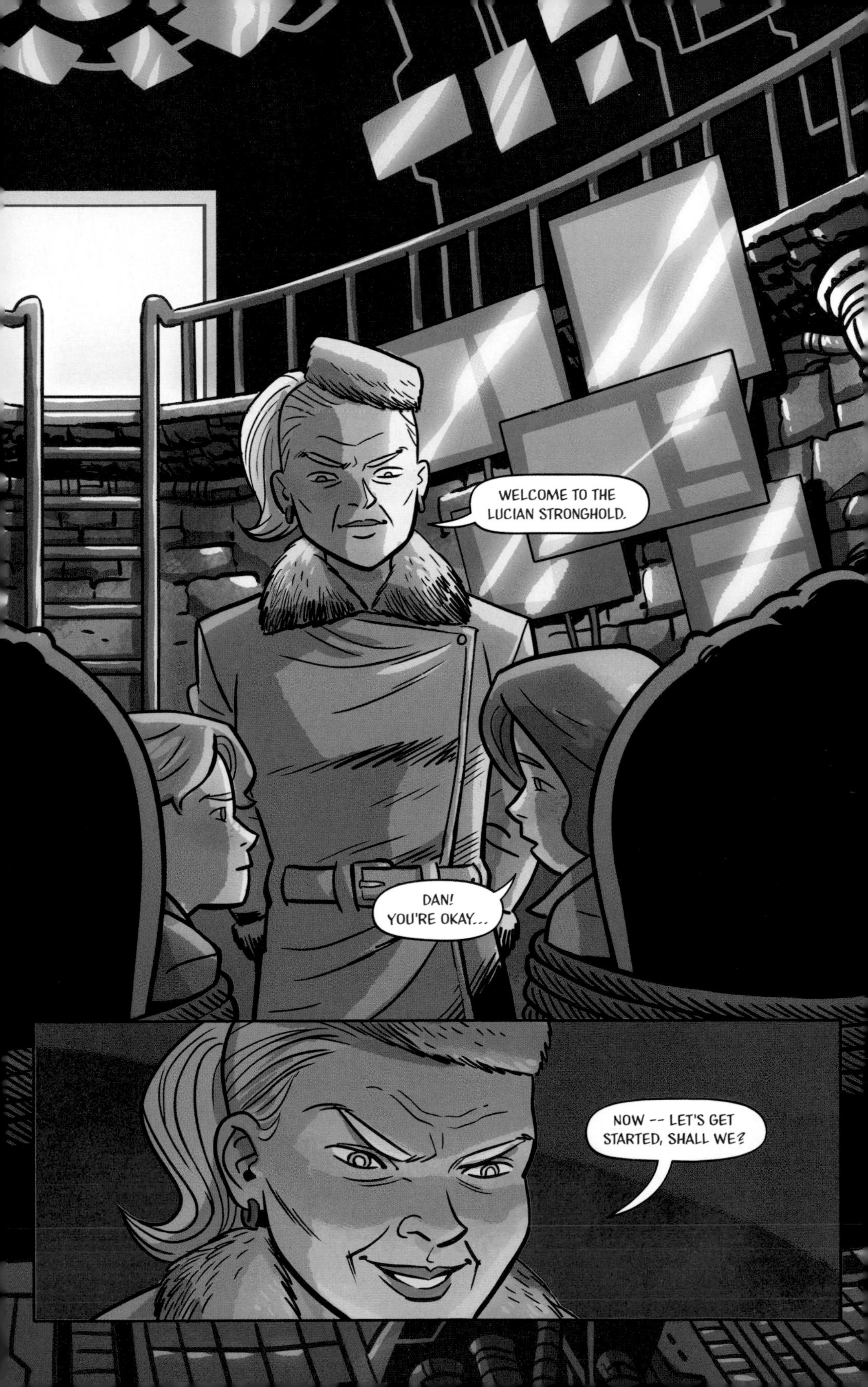
WELCOME TO THE LUCIAN STRONGHOLD.
DAN! YOU'RE OKAY...
NOW -- LET'S GET STARTED, SHALL WE?

SIX

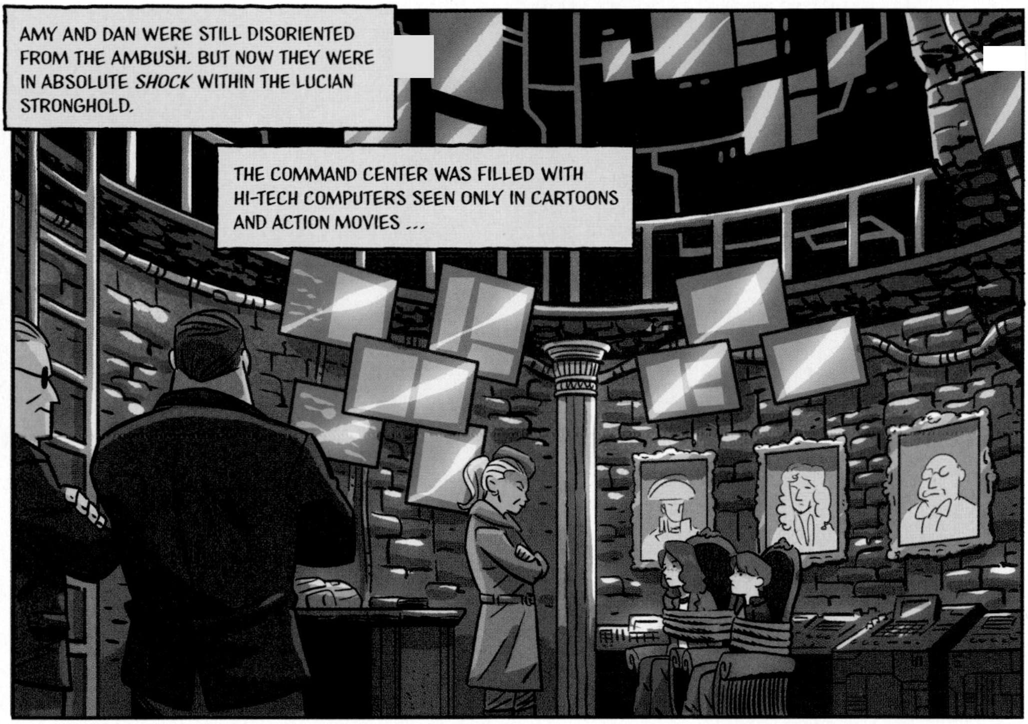
AMY AND DAN WERE STILL DISORIENTED FROM THE AMBUSH. BUT NOW THEY WERE IN ABSOLUTE *SHOCK* WITHIN THE LUCIAN STRONGHOLD.
THE COMMAND CENTER WAS FILLED WITH HI-TECH COMPUTERS SEEN ONLY IN CARTOONS AND ACTION MOVIES ...

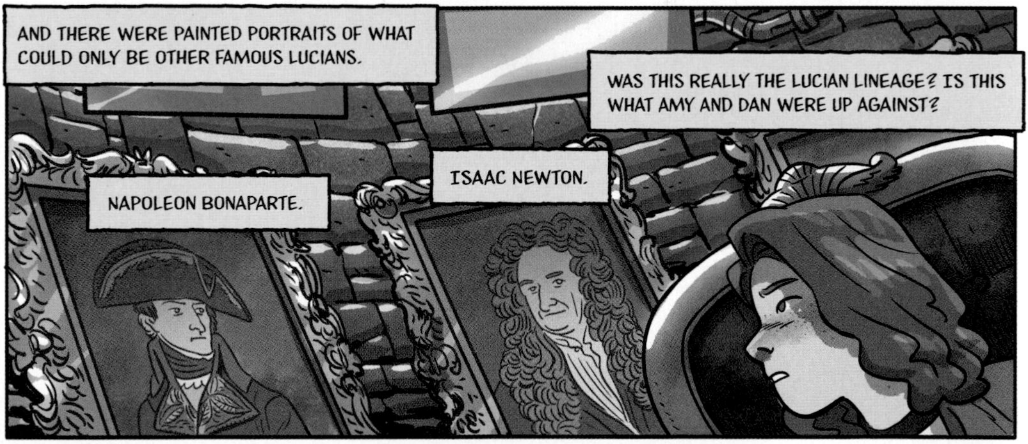
AND THERE WERE PAINTED PORTRAITS OF WHAT COULD ONLY BE OTHER FAMOUS LUCIANS.
NAPOLEON BONAPARTE.
ISAAC NEWTON.
WAS THIS REALLY THE LUCIAN LINEAGE? IS THIS WHAT AMY AND DAN WERE UP AGAINST?

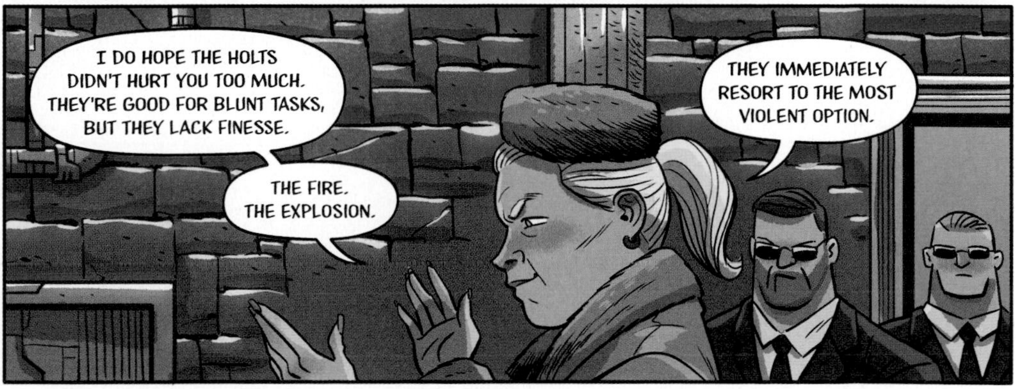
I DO HOPE THE HOLTS DIDN'T HURT YOU TOO MUCH. THEY'RE GOOD FOR BLUNT TASKS, BUT THEY LACK FINESSE.
THE FIRE. THE EXPLOSION.
THEY IMMEDIATELY RESORT TO THE MOST VIOLENT OPTION.

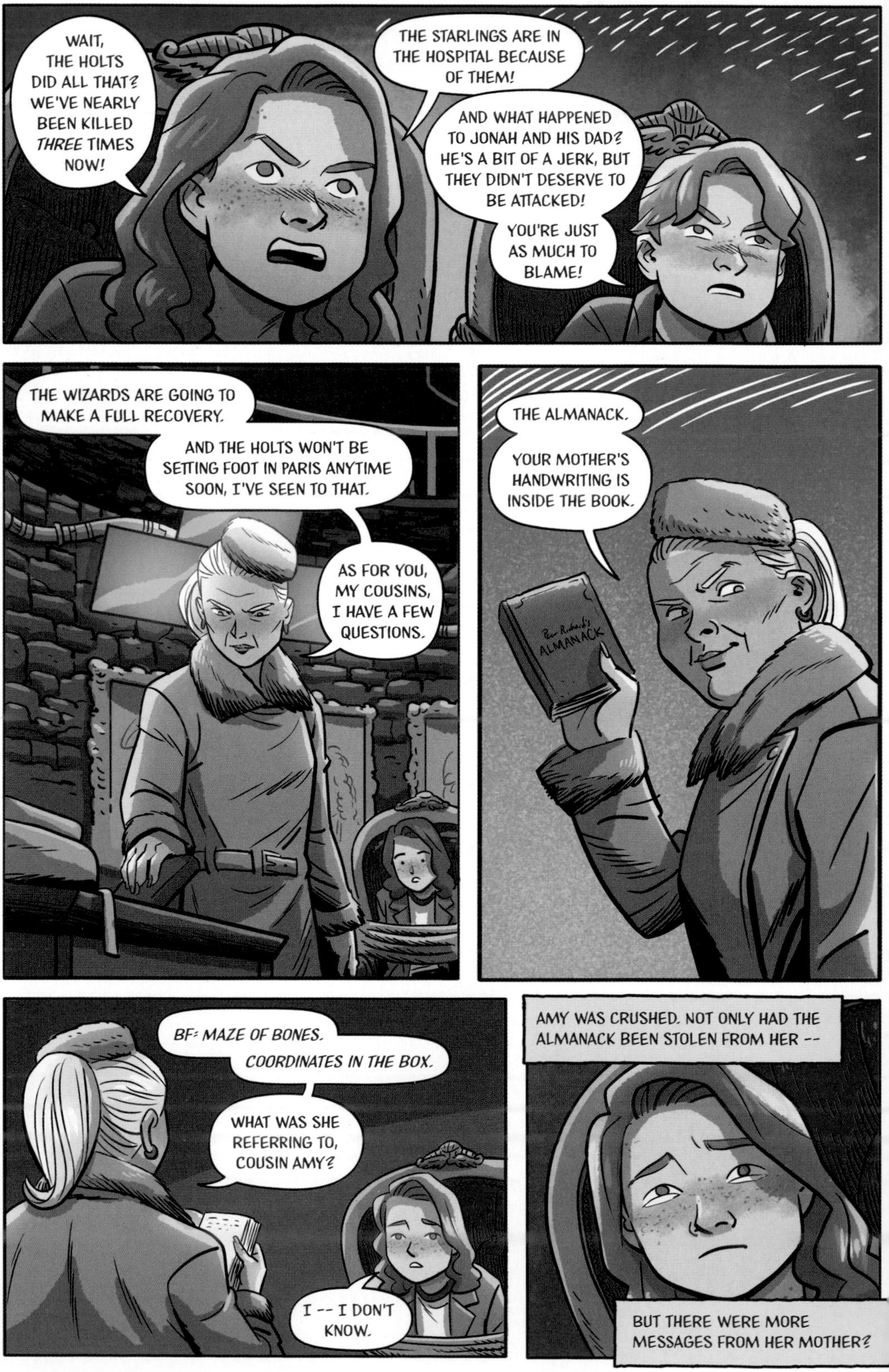
WAIT, THE HOLTS DID ALL THAT? WE'VE NEARLY BEEN KILLED *THREE* TIMES NOW!
THE STARLINGS ARE IN THE HOSPITAL BECAUSE OF THEM!
AND WHAT HAPPENED TO JONAH AND HIS DAD? HE'S A BIT OF A JERK, BUT THEY DIDN'T DESERVE TO BE ATTACKED!
YOU'RE JUST AS MUCH TO BLAME!
THE WIZARDS ARE GOING TO MAKE A FULL RECOVERY.
AND THE HOLTS WON'T BE SETTING FOOT IN PARIS ANYTIME SOON, I'VE SEEN TO THAT.
AS FOR YOU, MY COUSINS, I HAVE A FEW QUESTIONS.
THE ALMANACK.
YOUR MOTHER'S HANDWRITING IS INSIDE THE BOOK.
ALMANACK
BF: MAZE OF BONES.
COORDINATES IN THE BOX.
WHAT WAS SHE REFERRING TO, COUSIN AMY?
I -- I DON'T KNOW.
AMY WAS CRUSHED. NOT ONLY HAD THE ALMANACK BEEN STOLEN FROM HER --
BUT THERE WERE MORE MESSAGES FROM HER MOTHER?

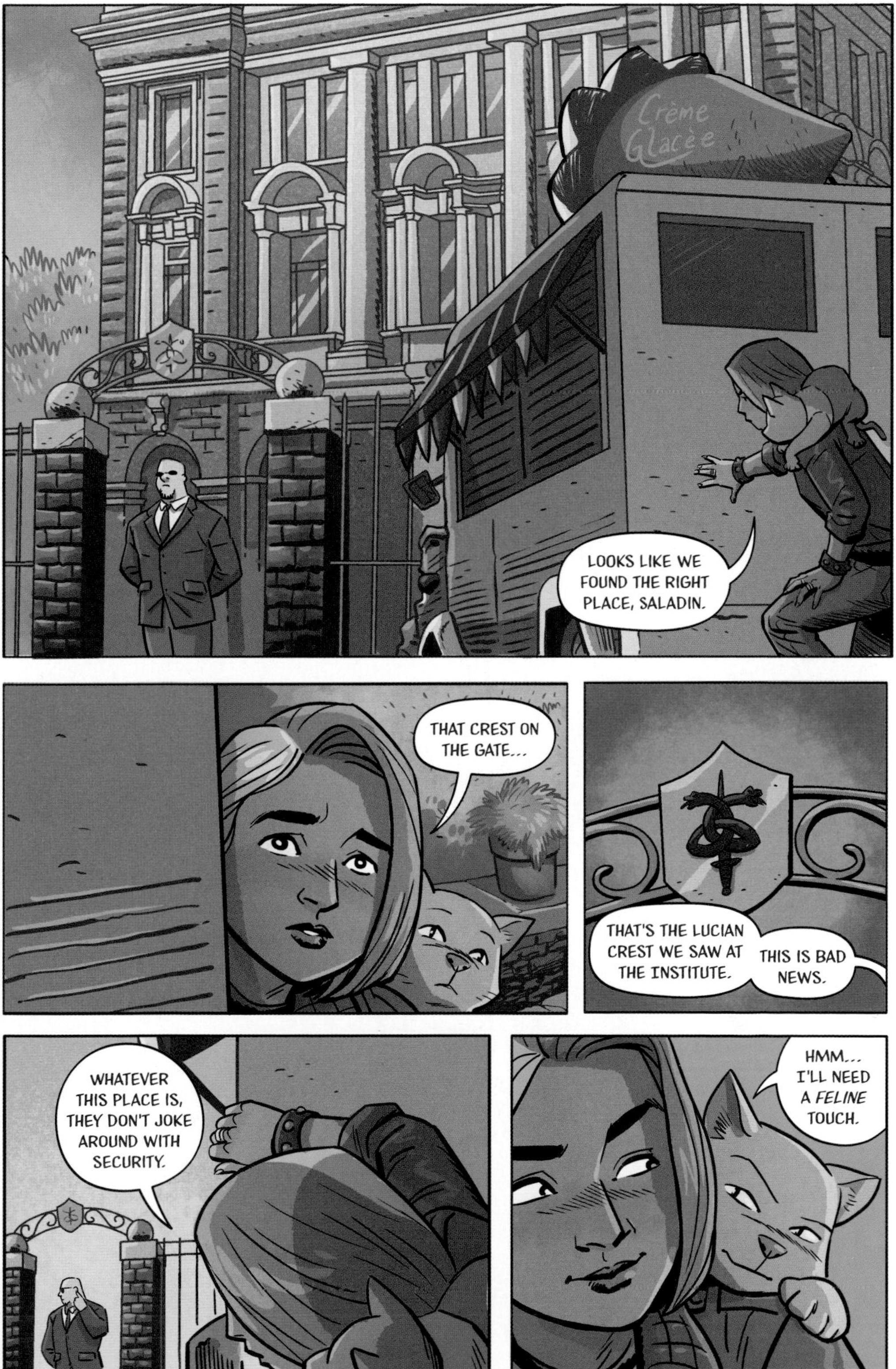
Crème Glacèe
LOOKS LIKE WE FOUND THE RIGHT PLACE, SALADIN.
THAT CREST ON THE GATE...
THAT'S THE LUCIAN CREST WE SAW AT THE INSTITUTE.
THIS IS BAD NEWS.
WHATEVER THIS PLACE IS, THEY DON'T JOKE AROUND WITH SECURITY.
HMM... I'LL NEED A *FELINE* TOUCH.

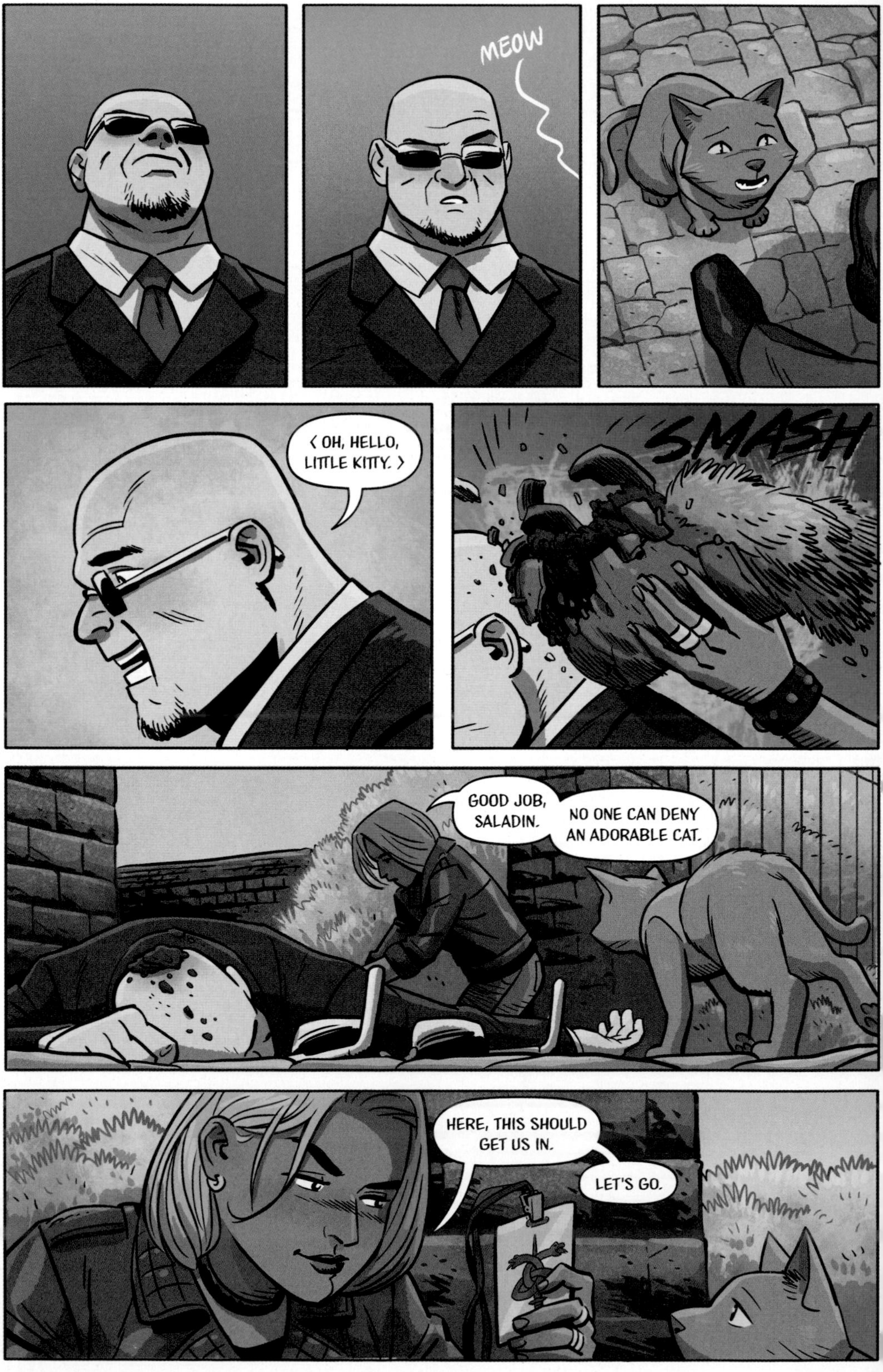
MEOW
< OH, HELLO, LITTLE KITTY. >
SMASH
GOOD JOB, SALADIN.
NO ONE CAN DENY AN ADORABLE CAT.
HERE, THIS SHOULD GET US IN.
LET'S GO.

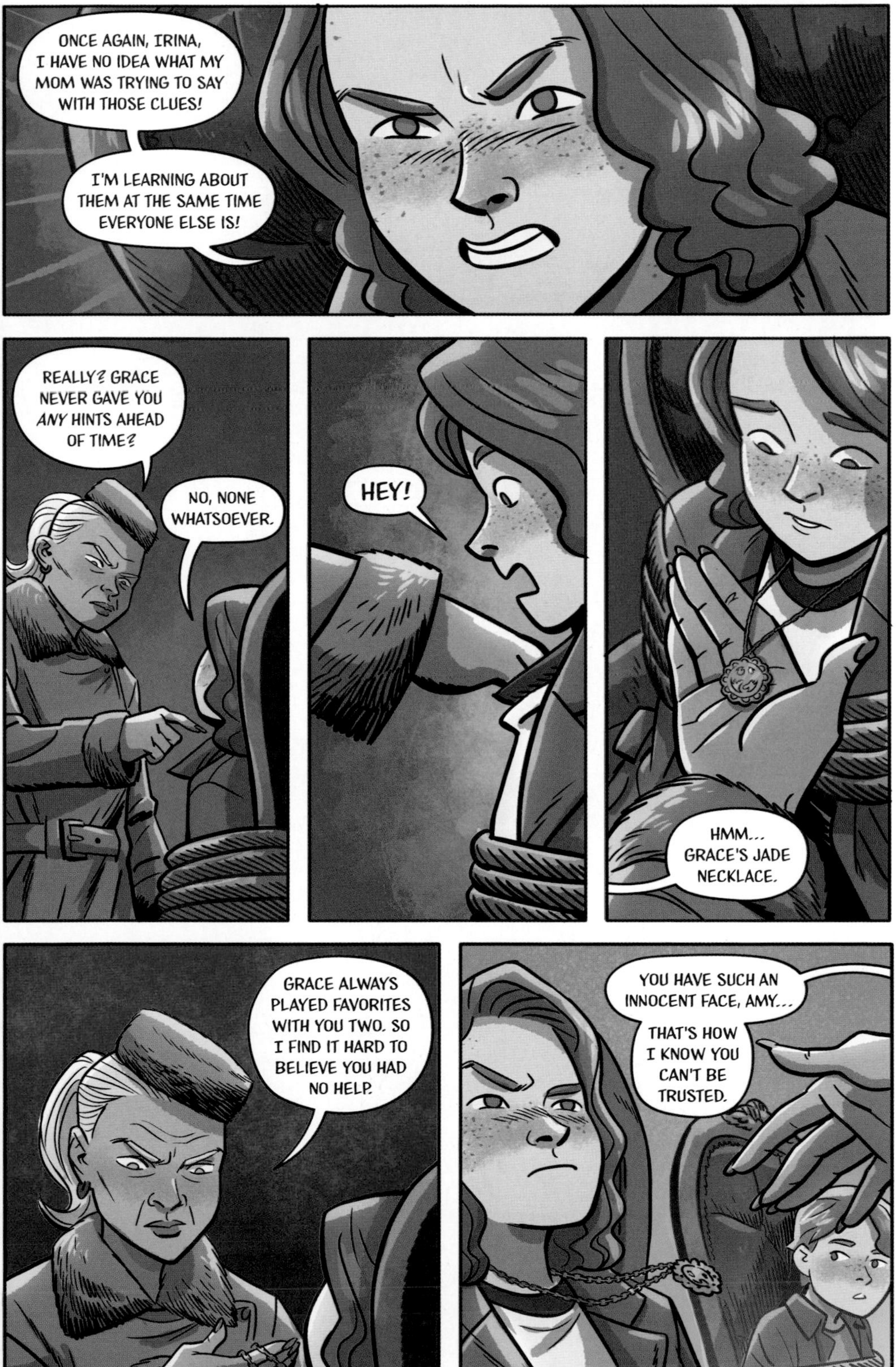
ONCE AGAIN, IRINA, I HAVE NO IDEA WHAT MY MOM WAS TRYING TO SAY WITH THOSE CLUES!
I'M LEARNING ABOUT THEM AT THE SAME TIME EVERYONE ELSE IS!
REALLY? GRACE NEVER GAVE YOU *ANY* HINTS AHEAD OF TIME?
NO, NONE WHATSOEVER.
HEY!
HMM... GRACE'S JADE NECKLACE.
GRACE ALWAYS PLAYED FAVORITES WITH YOU TWO. SO I FIND IT HARD TO BELIEVE YOU HAD NO HELP.
YOU HAVE SUCH AN INNOCENT FACE, AMY...
THAT'S HOW I KNOW YOU CAN'T BE TRUSTED.

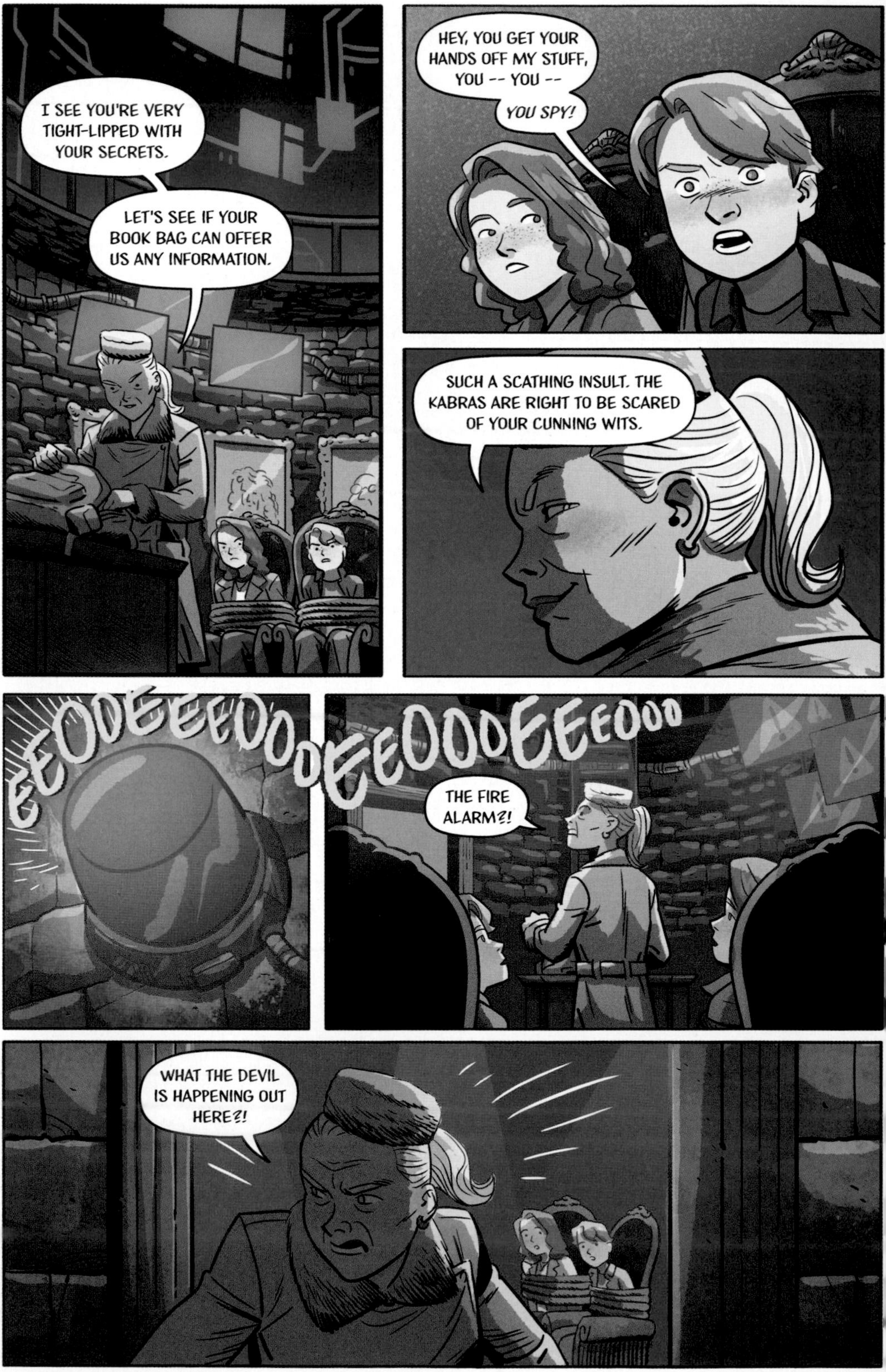
I SEE YOU'RE VERY TIGHT-LIPPED WITH YOUR SECRETS.
LET'S SEE IF YOUR BOOK BAG CAN OFFER US ANY INFORMATION.
HEY, YOU GET YOUR HANDS OFF MY STUFF, YOU -- YOU --
YOU SPY!
SUCH A SCATHING INSULT. THE KABRAS ARE RIGHT TO BE SCARED OF YOUR CUNNING WITS.
EEOOEEEOOOOEEOOOEEEOOO
THE FIRE ALARM?!
WHAT THE DEVIL IS HAPPENING OUT HERE?!

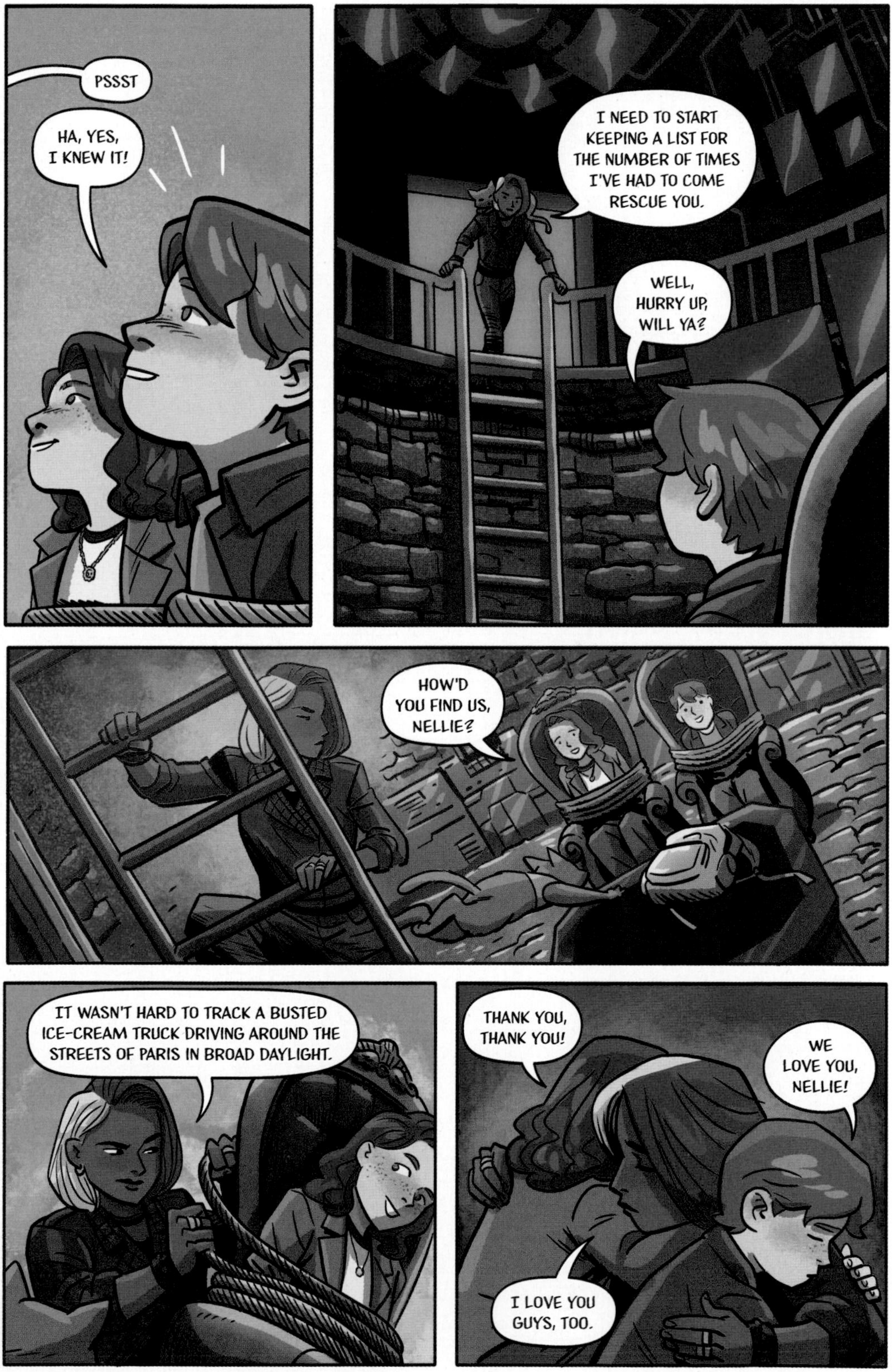
PSSST
HA, YES, I KNEW IT!
I NEED TO START KEEPING A LIST FOR THE NUMBER OF TIMES I'VE HAD TO COME RESCUE YOU.
WELL, HURRY UP, WILL YA?
HOW'D YOU FIND US, NELLIE?
IT WASN'T HARD TO TRACK A BUSTED ICE-CREAM TRUCK DRIVING AROUND THE STREETS OF PARIS IN BROAD DAYLIGHT.
THANK YOU, THANK YOU!
WE LOVE YOU, NELLIE!
I LOVE YOU GUYS, TOO.

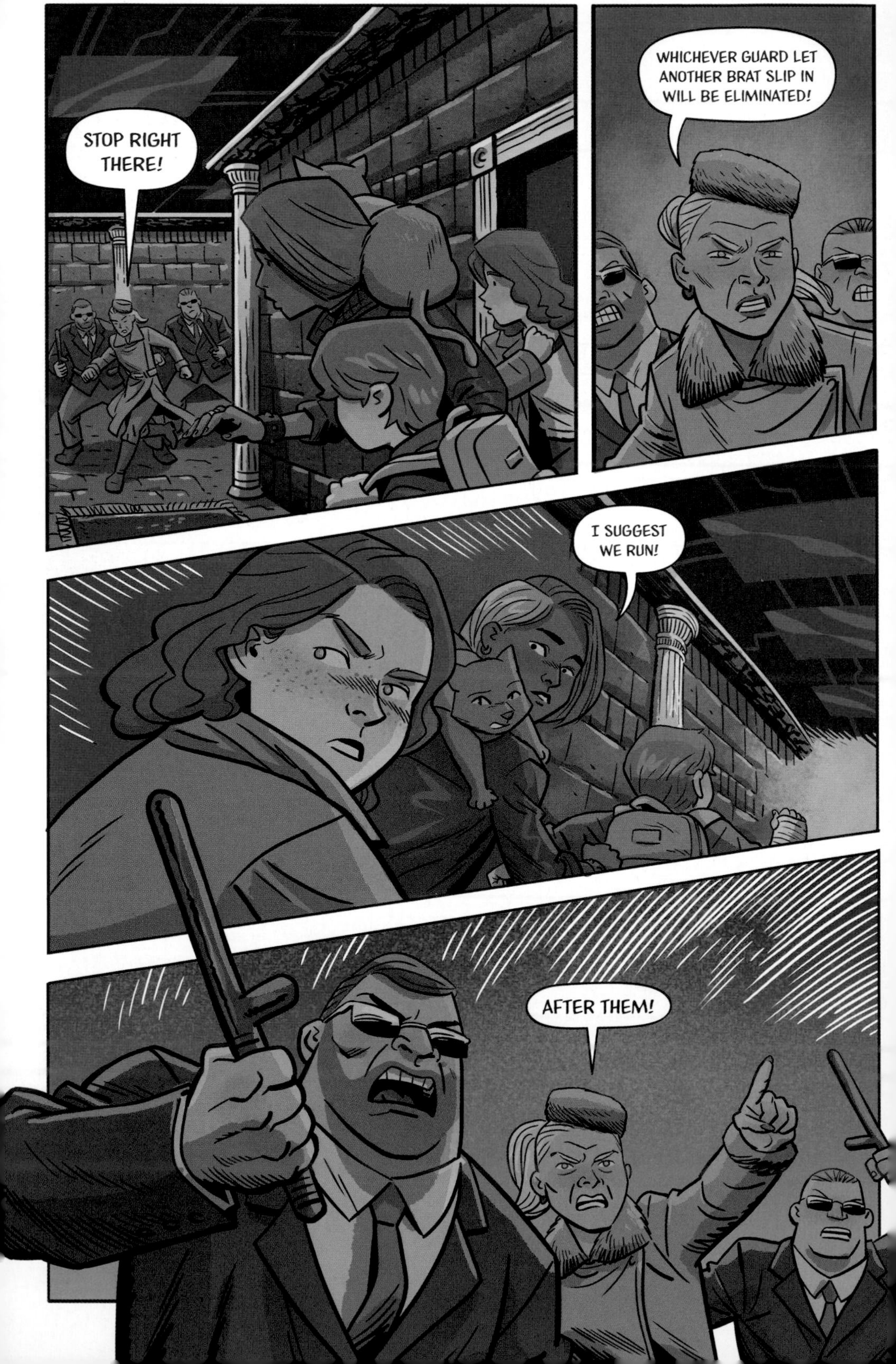
STOP RIGHT THERE!
WHICHEVER GUARD LET ANOTHER BRAT SLIP IN WILL BE ELIMINATED!
I SUGGEST WE RUN!
AFTER THEM!

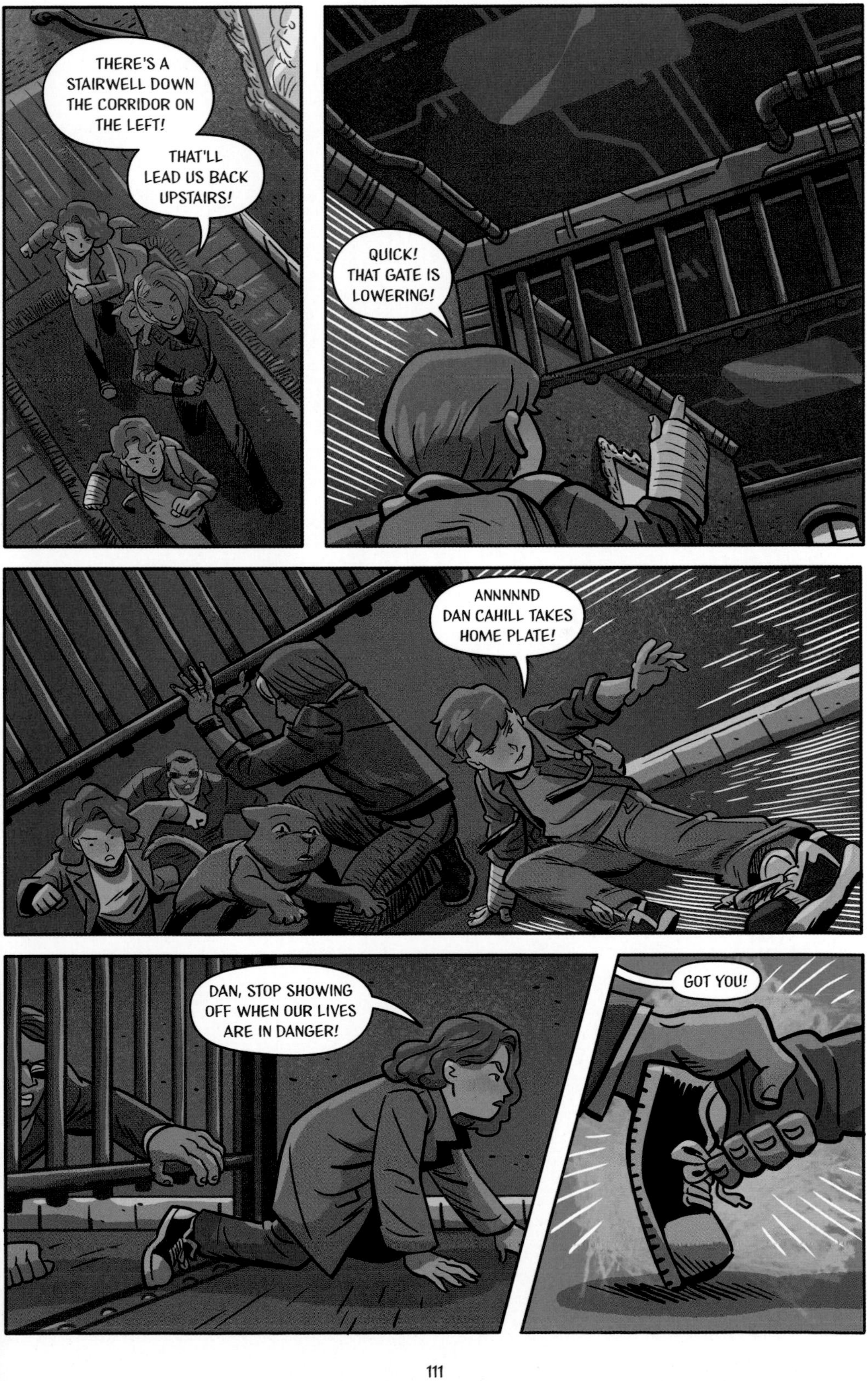
THERE'S A STAIRWELL DOWN THE CORRIDOR ON THE LEFT!
THAT'LL LEAD US BACK UPSTAIRS!
QUICK! THAT GATE IS LOWERING!
ANNNNND DAN CAHILL TAKES HOME PLATE!
DAN, STOP SHOWING OFF WHEN OUR LIVES ARE IN DANGER!
GOT YOU!

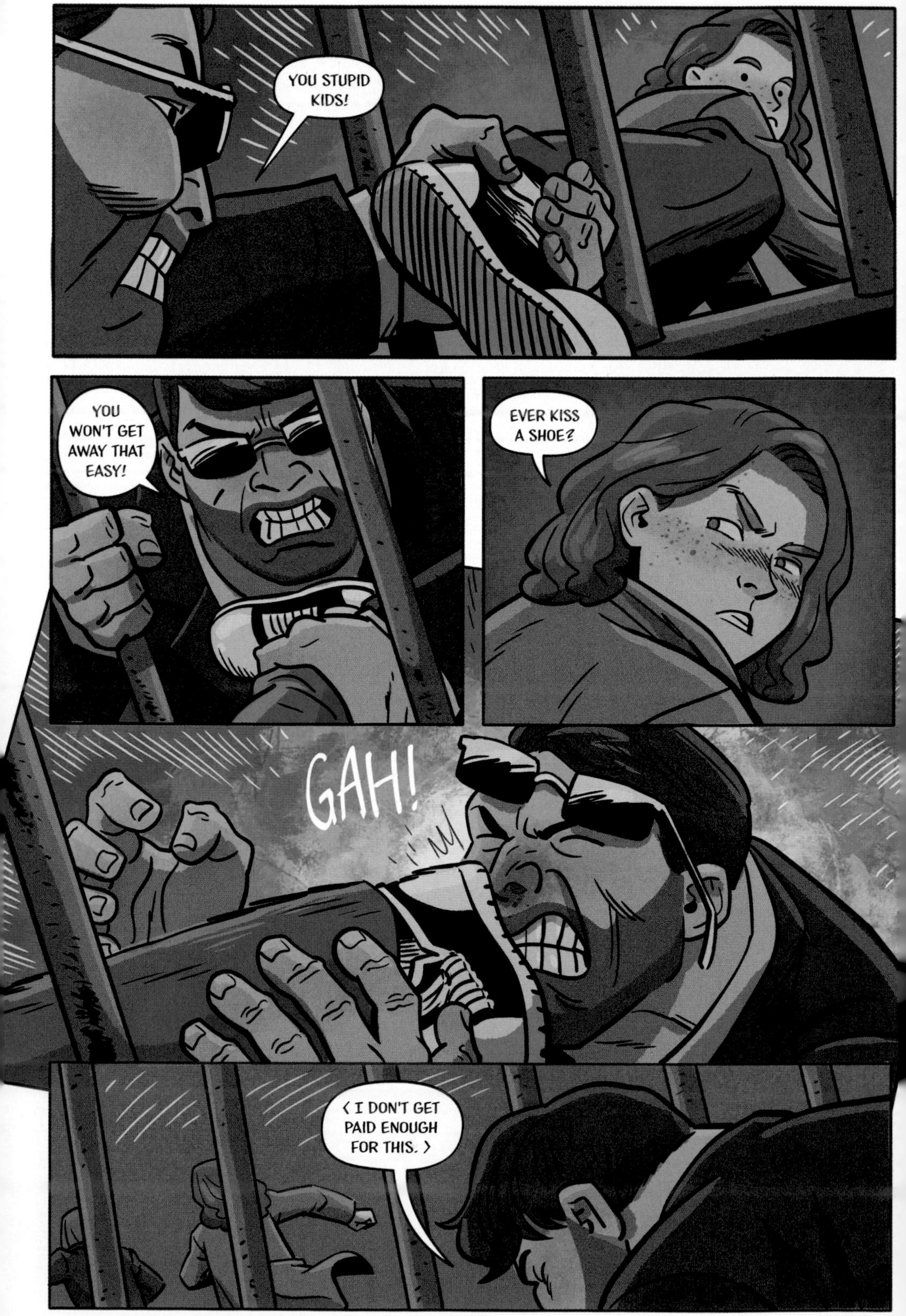

YOU STUPID KIDS!
YOU WON'T GET AWAY THAT EASY!
EVER KISS A SHOE?
GAH!
< I DON'T GET PAID ENOUGH FOR THIS. >

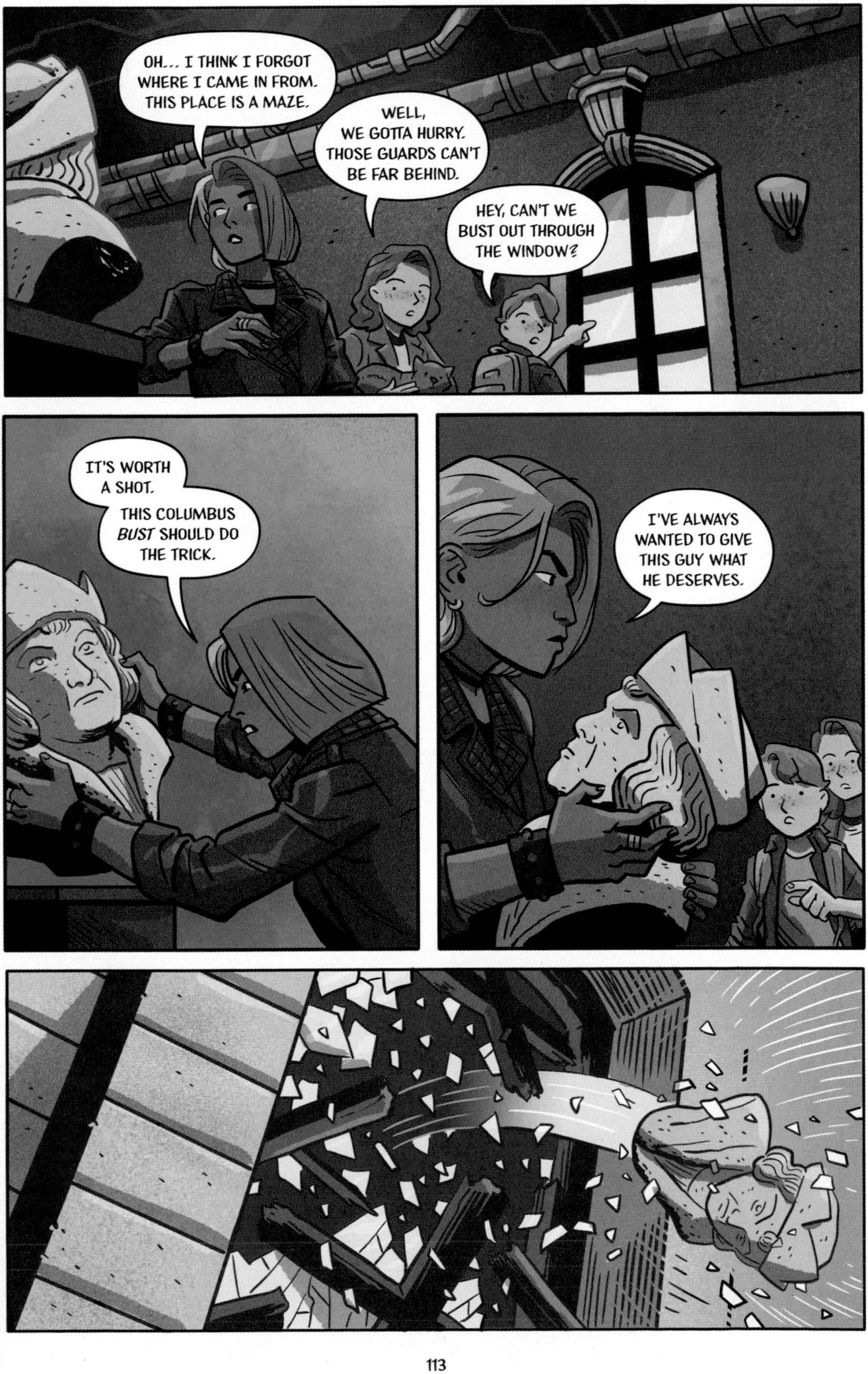
OH... I THINK I FORGOT WHERE I CAME IN FROM. THIS PLACE IS A MAZE.
WELL, WE GOTTA HURRY. THOSE GUARDS CAN'T BE FAR BEHIND.
HEY, CAN'T WE BUST OUT THROUGH THE WINDOW?
IT'S WORTH A SHOT.
THIS COLUMBUS *BUST* SHOULD DO THE TRICK.
I'VE ALWAYS WANTED TO GIVE THIS GUY WHAT HE DESERVES.

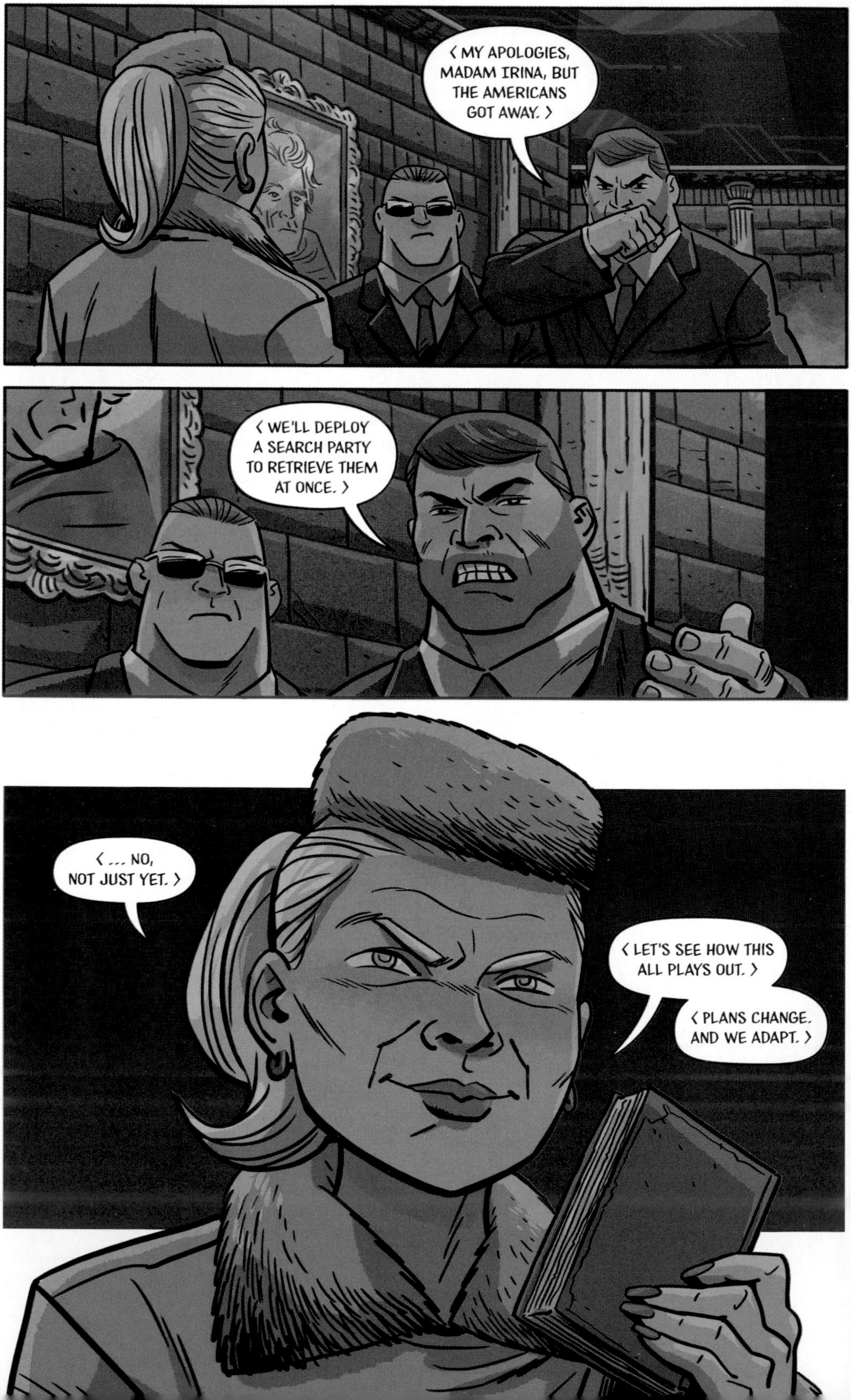
< MY APOLOGIES, MADAM IRINA, BUT THE AMERICANS GOT AWAY. >
< WE'LL DEPLOY A SEARCH PARTY TO RETRIEVE THEM AT ONCE. >
< ... NO, NOT JUST YET. >
< LET'S SEE HOW THIS ALL PLAYS OUT. >
< PLANS CHANGE. AND WE ADAPT. >

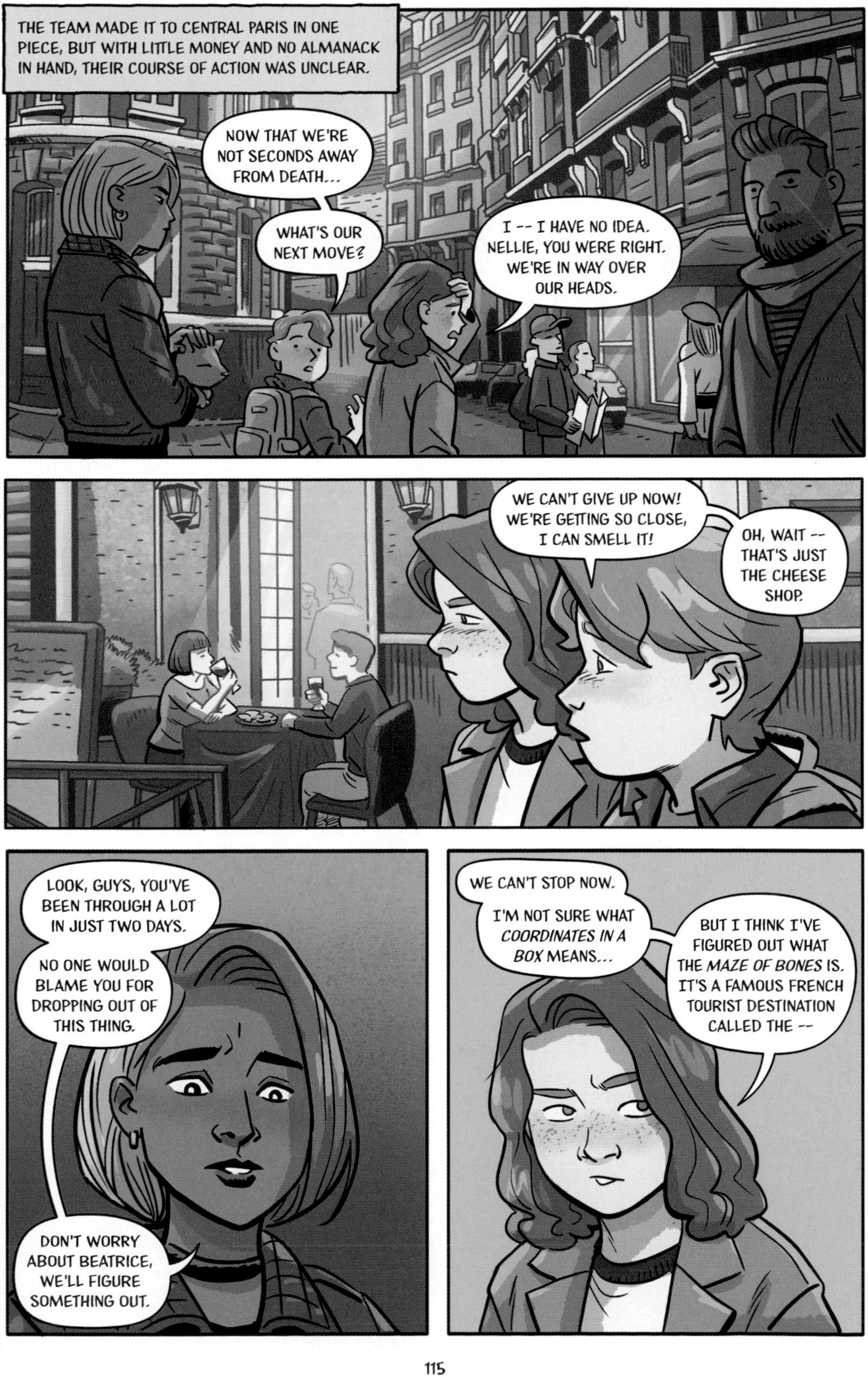
THE TEAM MADE IT TO CENTRAL PARIS IN ONE PIECE, BUT WITH LITTLE MONEY AND NO ALMANACK IN HAND, THEIR COURSE OF ACTION WAS UNCLEAR.
NOW THAT WE'RE NOT SECONDS AWAY FROM DEATH...
WHAT'S OUR NEXT MOVE?
I -- I HAVE NO IDEA. NELLIE, YOU WERE RIGHT. WE'RE IN WAY OVER OUR HEADS.
WE CAN'T GIVE UP NOW! WE'RE GETTING SO CLOSE, I CAN SMELL IT!
OH, WAIT -- THAT'S JUST THE CHEESE SHOP.
LOOK, GUYS, YOU'VE BEEN THROUGH A LOT IN JUST TWO DAYS.
NO ONE WOULD BLAME YOU FOR DROPPING OUT OF THIS THING.
DON'T WORRY ABOUT BEATRICE, WE'LL FIGURE SOMETHING OUT.
WE CAN'T STOP NOW.
I'M NOT SURE WHAT *COORDINATES IN A BOX* MEANS...
BUT I THINK I'VE FIGURED OUT WHAT THE *MAZE OF BONES* IS. IT'S A FAMOUS FRENCH TOURIST DESTINATION CALLED THE --

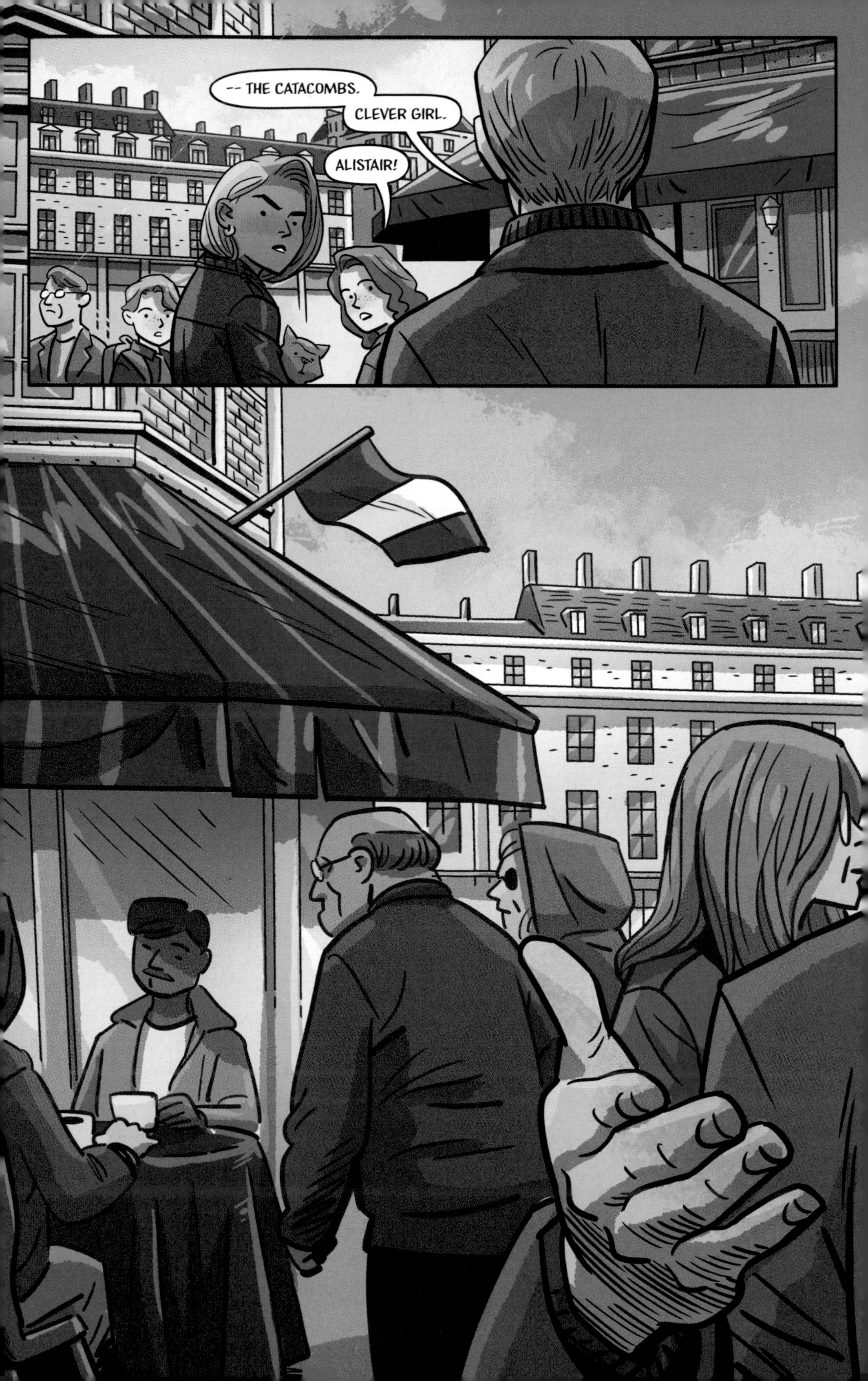
-- THE CATACOMBS.
CLEVER GIRL.
ALISTAIR!

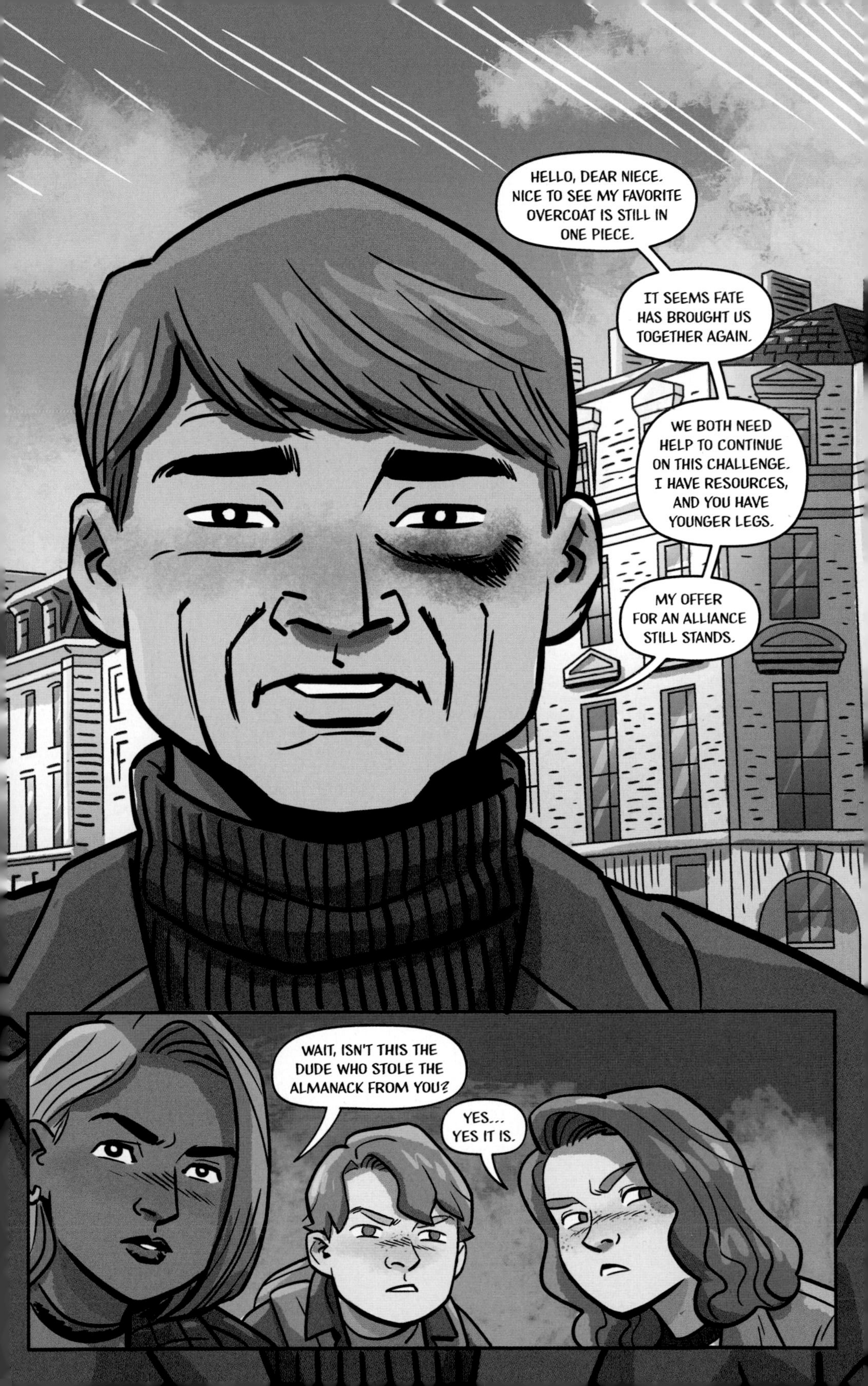
HELLO, DEAR NIECE. NICE TO SEE MY FAVORITE OVERCOAT IS STILL IN ONE PIECE.
IT SEEMS FATE HAS BROUGHT US TOGETHER AGAIN.
WE BOTH NEED HELP TO CONTINUE ON THIS CHALLENGE. I HAVE RESOURCES, AND YOU HAVE YOUNGER LEGS.
MY OFFER FOR AN ALLIANCE STILL STANDS.
WAIT, ISN'T THIS THE DUDE WHO STOLE THE ALMANACK FROM YOU?
YES... YES IT IS.

SEVEN

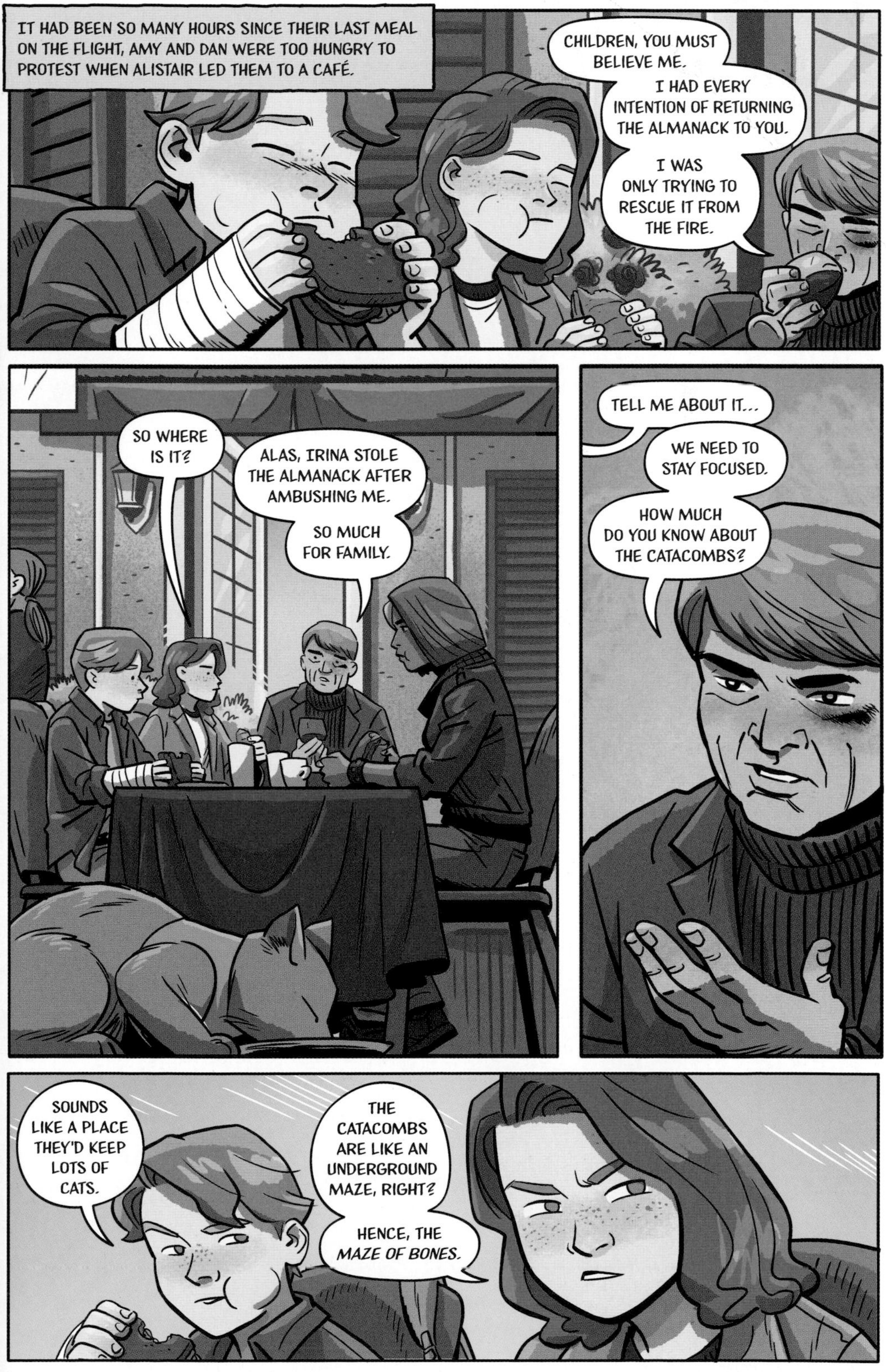

IT HAD BEEN SO MANY HOURS SINCE THEIR LAST MEAL ON THE FLIGHT, AMY AND DAN WERE TOO HUNGRY TO PROTEST WHEN ALISTAIR LED THEM TO A CAFÉ.
CHILDREN, YOU MUST BELIEVE ME.
I HAD EVERY INTENTION OF RETURNING THE ALMANACK TO YOU.
I WAS ONLY TRYING TO RESCUE IT FROM THE FIRE.
SO WHERE IS IT?
ALAS, IRINA STOLE THE ALMANACK AFTER AMBUSHING ME.
SO MUCH FOR FAMILY.
TELL ME ABOUT IT...
WE NEED TO STAY FOCUSED.
HOW MUCH DO YOU KNOW ABOUT THE CATACOMBS?
SOUNDS LIKE A PLACE THEY'D KEEP LOTS OF CATS.
THE CATACOMBS ARE LIKE AN UNDERGROUND MAZE, RIGHT?
HENCE, THE *MAZE OF BONES*.

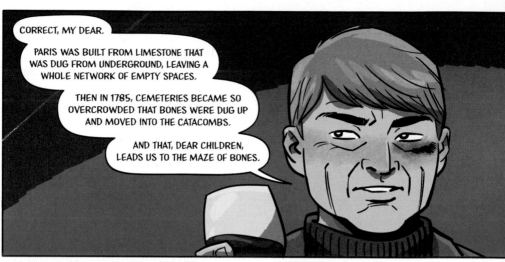

CORRECT, MY DEAR.

PARIS WAS BUILT FROM LIMESTONE THAT WAS DUG FROM UNDERGROUND, LEAVING A WHOLE NETWORK OF EMPTY SPACES.

THEN IN 1785, CEMETERIES BECAME SO OVERCROWDED THAT BONES WERE DUG UP AND MOVED INTO THE CATACOMBS.

AND THAT, DEAR CHILDREN, LEADS US TO THE MAZE OF BONES.

1785? THAT'S THE LAST YEAR FRANKLIN WAS IN PARIS.

WAIT, IF YOU HAD THE BOOK STOLEN FROM YOU, HOW'D YOU PIECE ALL THIS TOGETHER?

MAYBE HE HID SOMETHING DOWN THERE FOR US TO FIND?

THERE WAS ALWAYS MORE THAN ONE PATH TO THE NEXT CLUE.

THIS PAINTING. SEE ANYTHING INTERESTING?

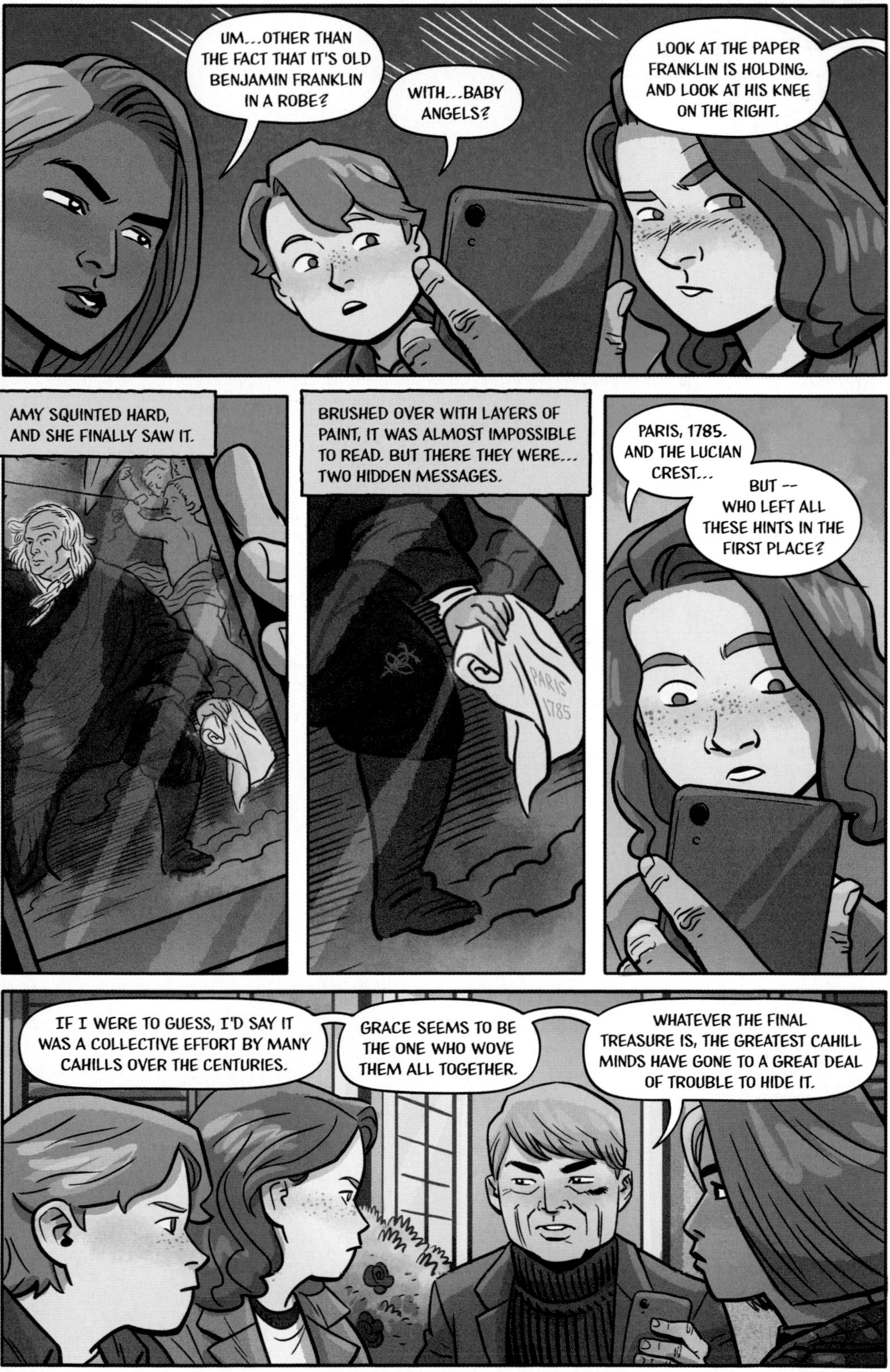
UM...OTHER THAN THE FACT THAT IT'S OLD BENJAMIN FRANKLIN IN A ROBE?
WITH...BABY ANGELS?
LOOK AT THE PAPER FRANKLIN IS HOLDING. AND LOOK AT HIS KNEE ON THE RIGHT.
AMY SQUINTED HARD, AND SHE FINALLY SAW IT.
BRUSHED OVER WITH LAYERS OF PAINT, IT WAS ALMOST IMPOSSIBLE TO READ. BUT THERE THEY WERE... TWO HIDDEN MESSAGES.
PARIS 1785
PARIS, 1785. AND THE LUCIAN CREST...
BUT -- WHO LEFT ALL THESE HINTS IN THE FIRST PLACE?
IF I WERE TO GUESS, I'D SAY IT WAS A COLLECTIVE EFFORT BY MANY CAHILLS OVER THE CENTURIES.
GRACE SEEMS TO BE THE ONE WHO WOVE THEM ALL TOGETHER.
WHATEVER THE FINAL TREASURE IS, THE GREATEST CAHILL MINDS HAVE GONE TO A GREAT DEAL OF TROUBLE TO HIDE IT.

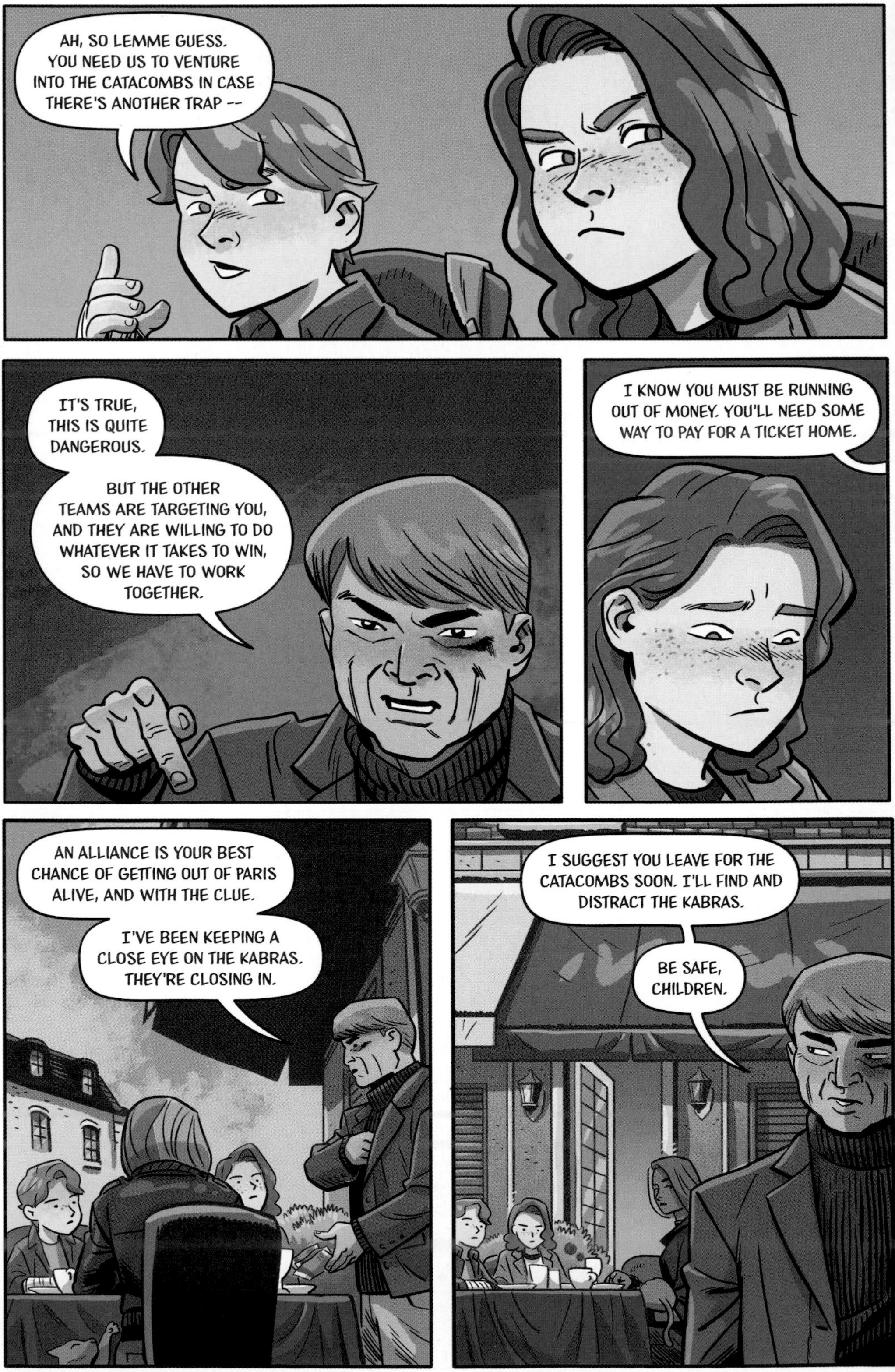
AH, SO LEMME GUESS. YOU NEED US TO VENTURE INTO THE CATACOMBS IN CASE THERE'S ANOTHER TRAP --
IT'S TRUE, THIS IS QUITE DANGEROUS.
BUT THE OTHER TEAMS ARE TARGETING YOU, AND THEY ARE WILLING TO DO WHATEVER IT TAKES TO WIN, SO WE HAVE TO WORK TOGETHER.
I KNOW YOU MUST BE RUNNING OUT OF MONEY. YOU'LL NEED SOME WAY TO PAY FOR A TICKET HOME.
AN ALLIANCE IS YOUR BEST CHANCE OF GETTING OUT OF PARIS ALIVE, AND WITH THE CLUE.
I'VE BEEN KEEPING A CLOSE EYE ON THE KABRAS. THEY'RE CLOSING IN.
I SUGGEST YOU LEAVE FOR THE CATACOMBS SOON. I'LL FIND AND DISTRACT THE KABRAS.
BE SAFE, CHILDREN.

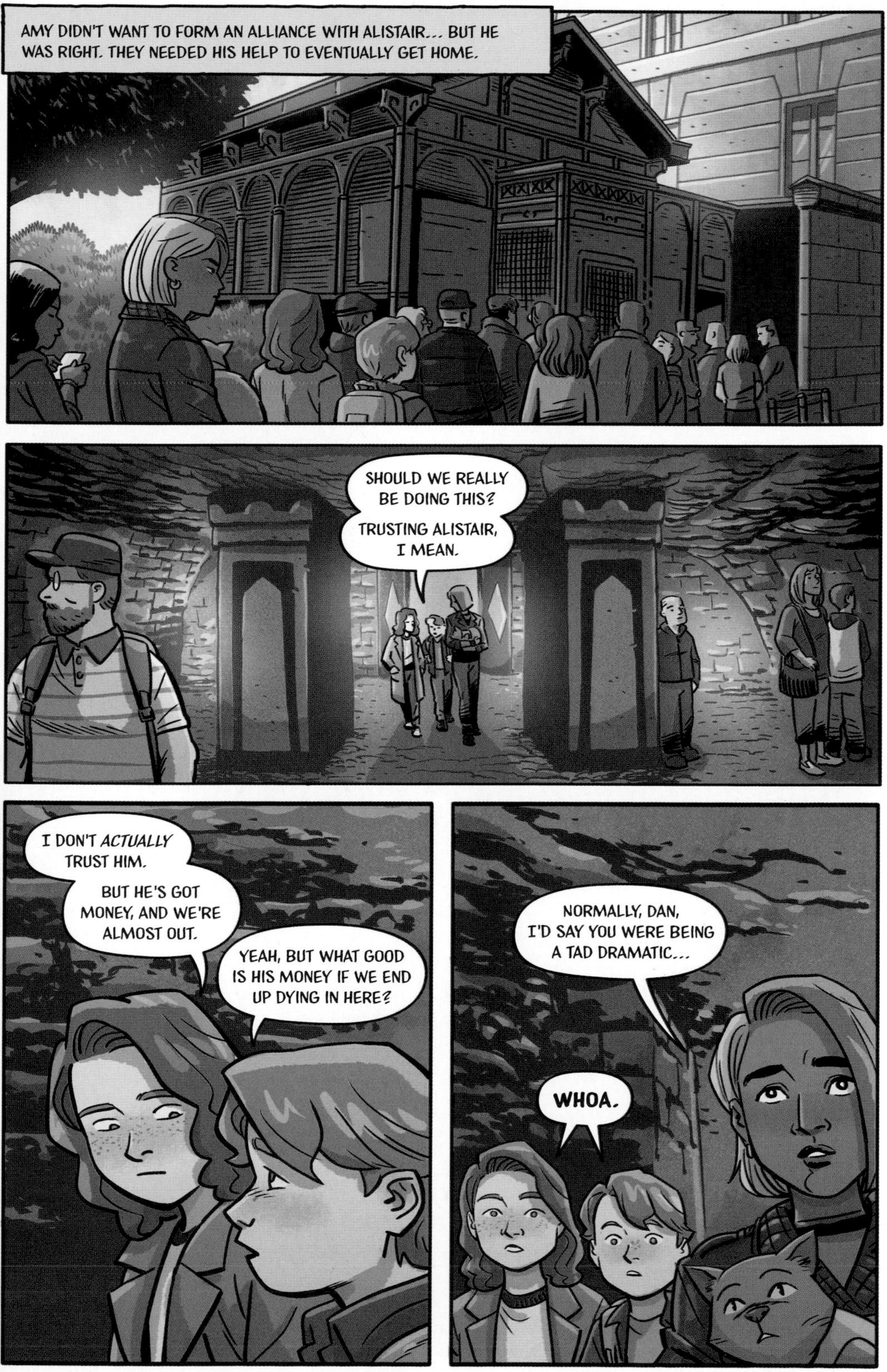
AMY DIDN'T WANT TO FORM AN ALLIANCE WITH ALISTAIR... BUT HE WAS RIGHT. THEY NEEDED HIS HELP TO EVENTUALLY GET HOME.
SHOULD WE REALLY BE DOING THIS?
TRUSTING ALISTAIR, I MEAN.
I DON'T *ACTUALLY* TRUST HIM.
BUT HE'S GOT MONEY, AND WE'RE ALMOST OUT.
YEAH, BUT WHAT GOOD IS HIS MONEY IF WE END UP DYING IN HERE?
NORMALLY, DAN, I'D SAY YOU WERE BEING A TAD DRAMATIC...
WHOA.

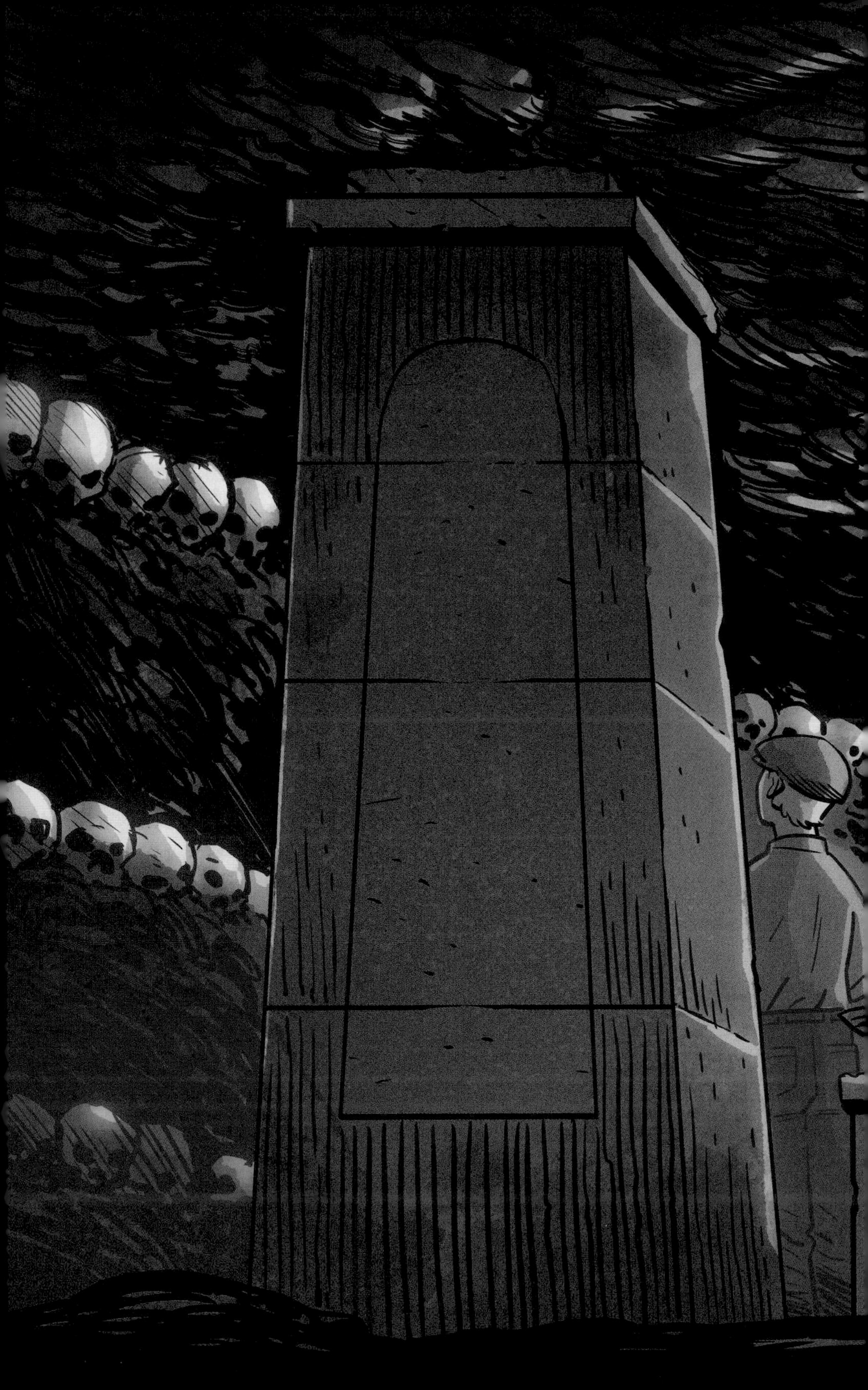

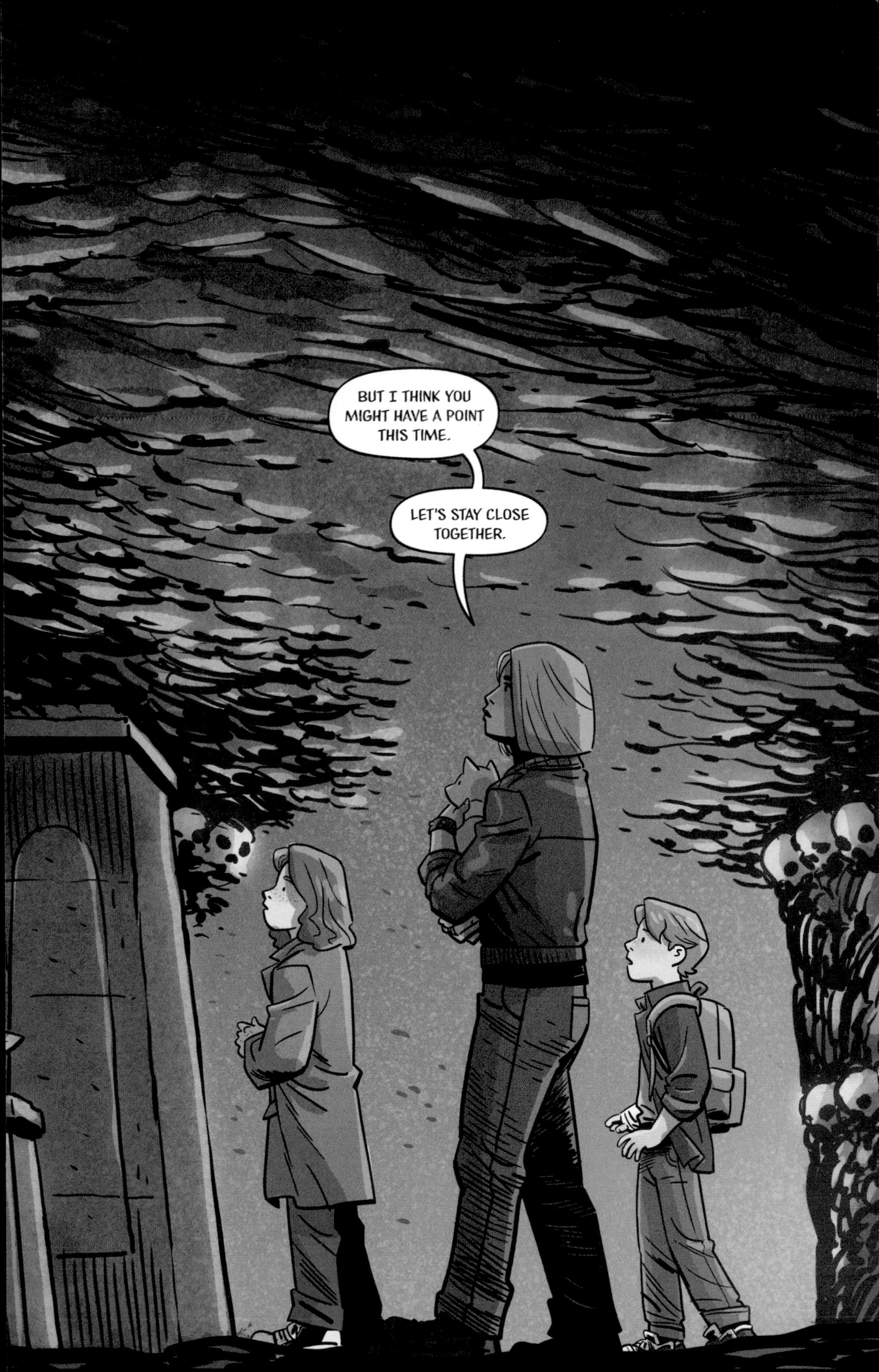
BUT I THINK YOU MIGHT HAVE A POINT THIS TIME.
LET'S STAY CLOSE TOGETHER.

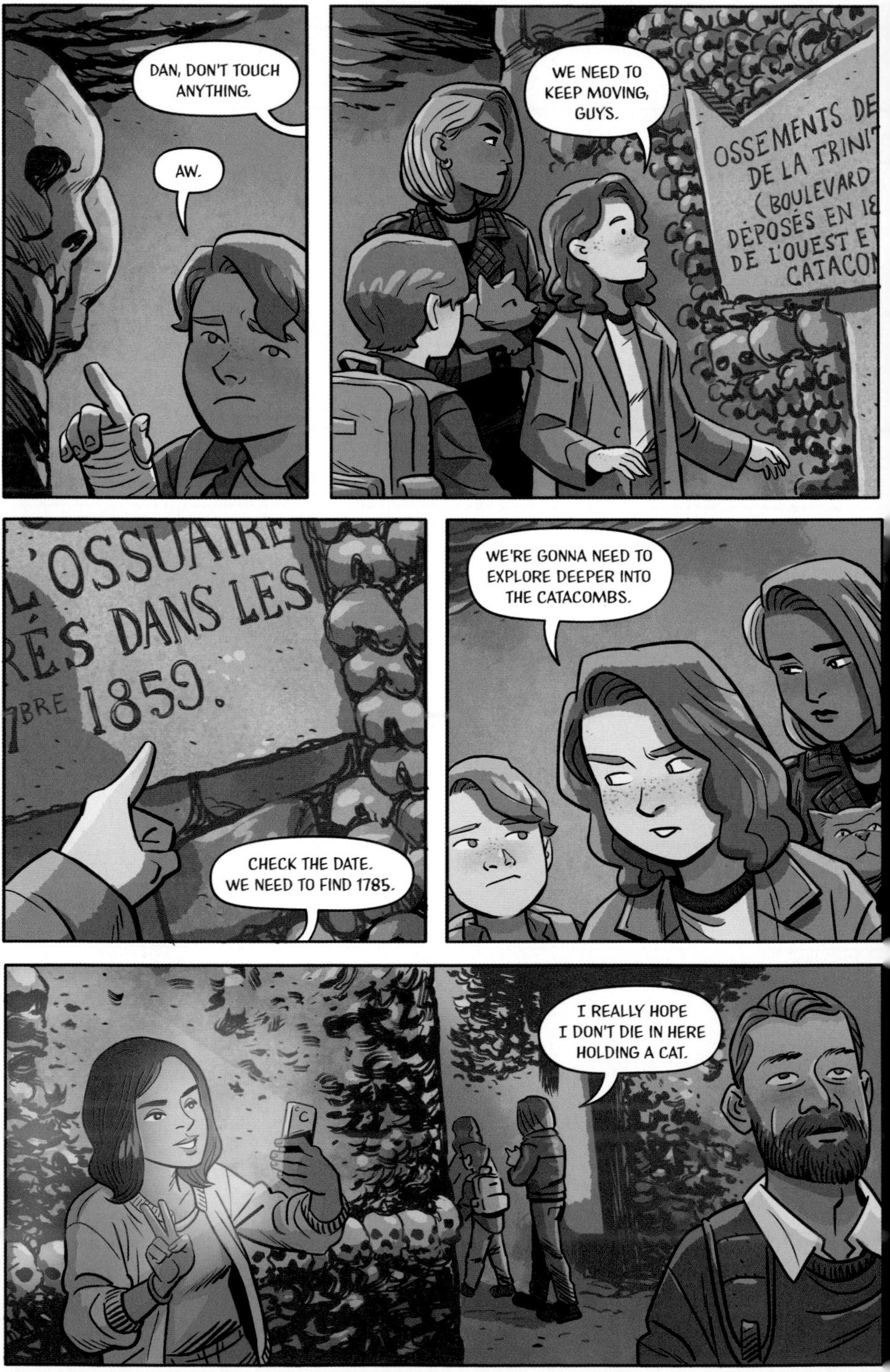
DAN, DON'T TOUCH ANYTHING.
AW.
WE NEED TO KEEP MOVING, GUYS.
OSSEMENTS DE
DE LA TRINIT
(BOULEVARD
DÉPOSÉS EN 18
DE L'OUEST ET
CATACOM
L'OSSUAIRE
RÉS DANS LES
7BRE 1859.
CHECK THE DATE. WE NEED TO FIND 1785.
WE'RE GONNA NEED TO EXPLORE DEEPER INTO THE CATACOMBS.
I REALLY HOPE I DON'T DIE IN HERE HOLDING A CAT.

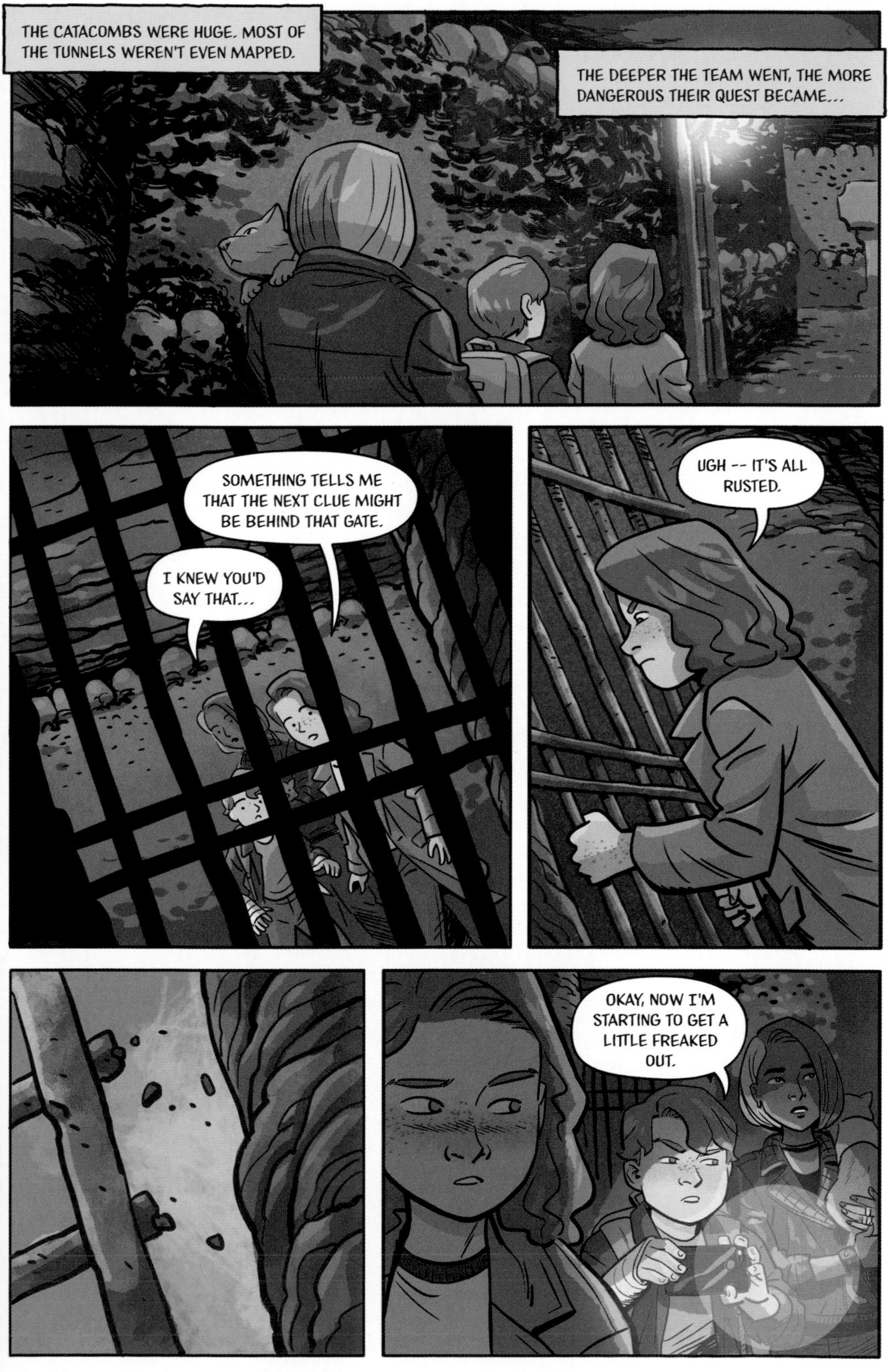
THE CATACOMBS WERE HUGE. MOST OF THE TUNNELS WEREN'T EVEN MAPPED.
THE DEEPER THE TEAM WENT, THE MORE DANGEROUS THEIR QUEST BECAME...
SOMETHING TELLS ME THAT THE NEXT CLUE MIGHT BE BEHIND THAT GATE.
I KNEW YOU'D SAY THAT...
UGH -- IT'S ALL RUSTED.
OKAY, NOW I'M STARTING TO GET A LITTLE FREAKED OUT.

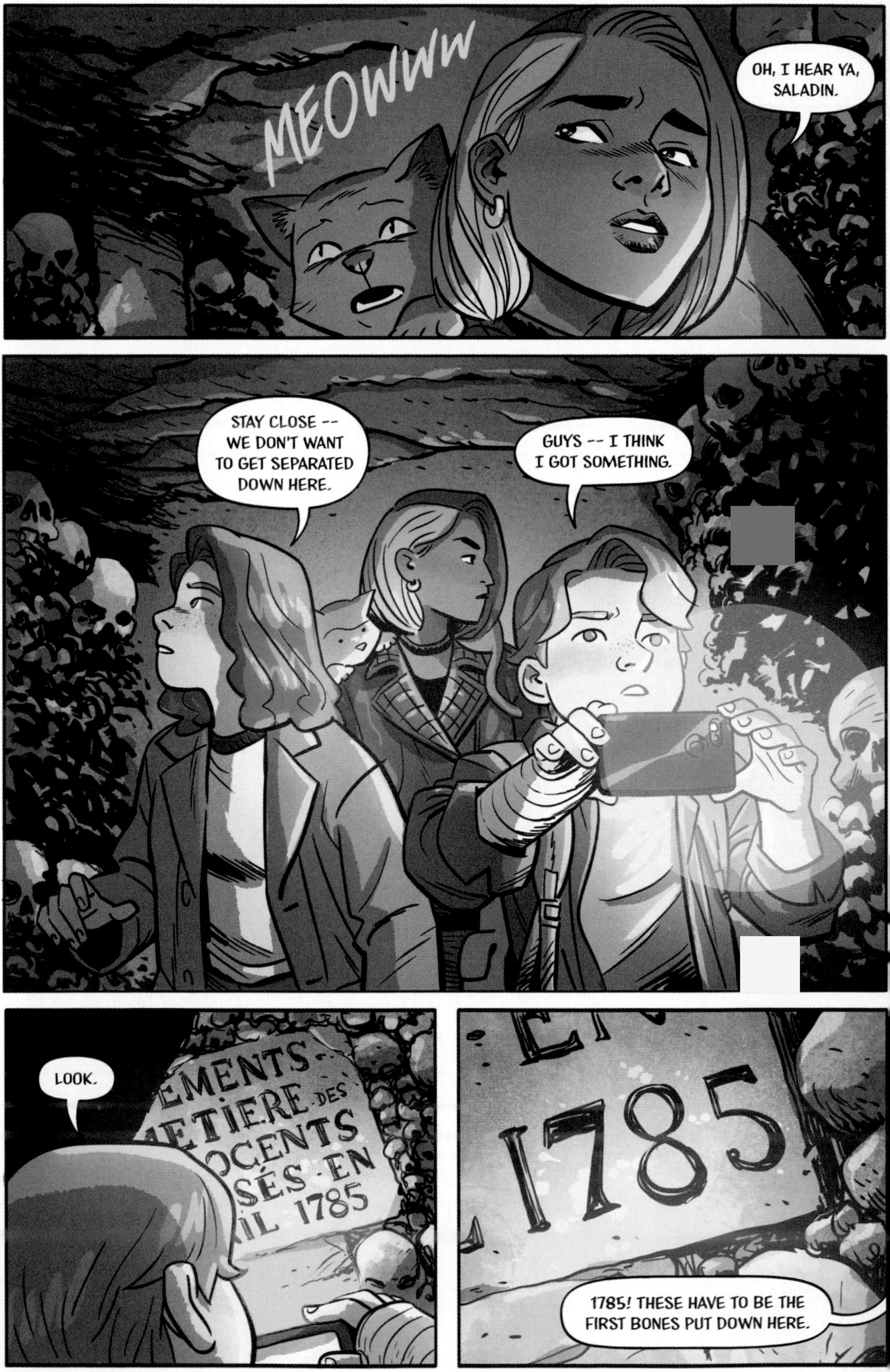
MEOWWW
OH, I HEAR YA, SALADIN.
STAY CLOSE -- WE DON'T WANT TO GET SEPARATED DOWN HERE.
GUYS -- I THINK I GOT SOMETHING.
LOOK.
1785
1785! THESE HAVE TO BE THE FIRST BONES PUT DOWN HERE.

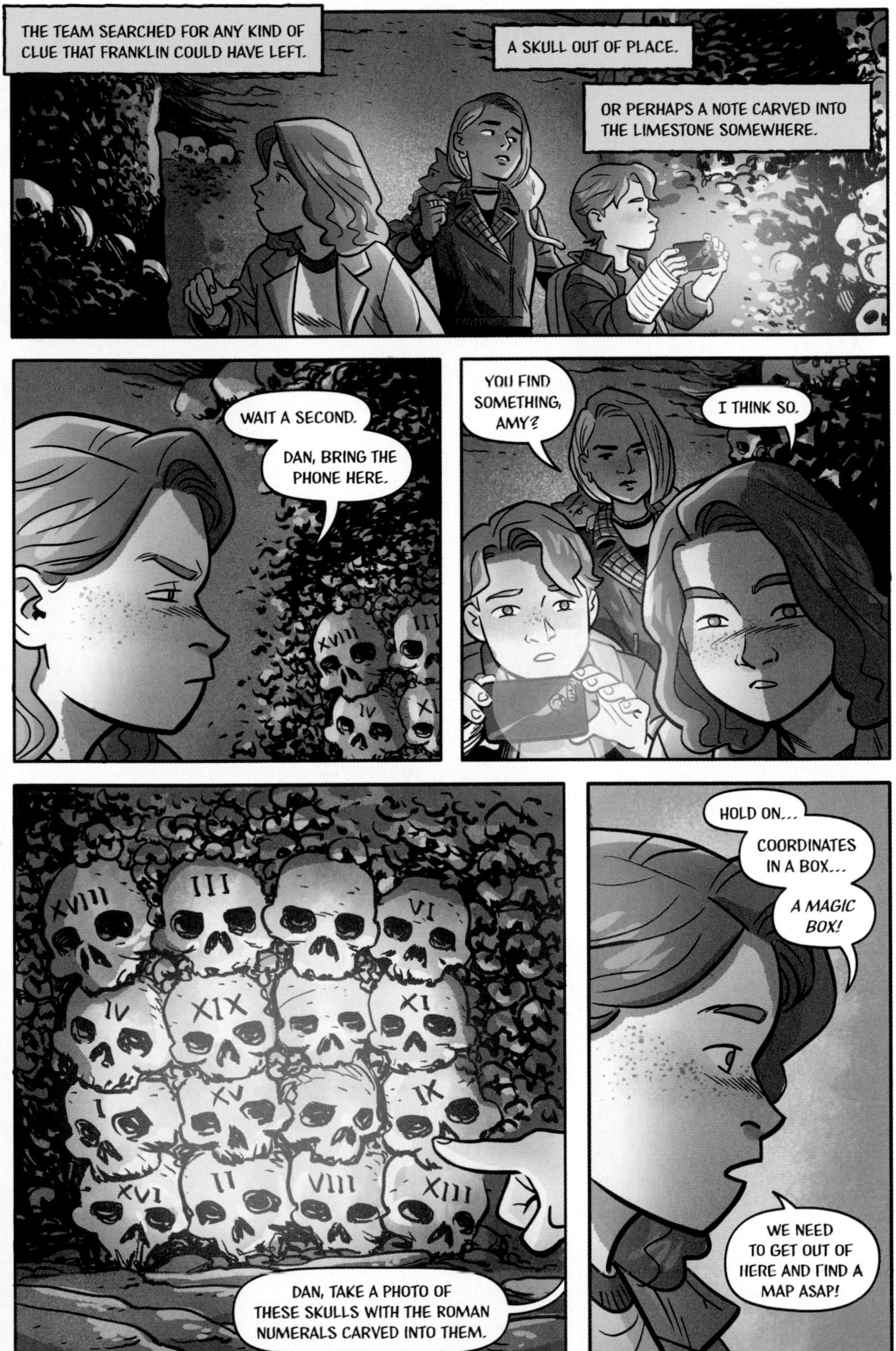
THE TEAM SEARCHED FOR ANY KIND OF CLUE THAT FRANKLIN COULD HAVE LEFT.
A SKULL OUT OF PLACE.
OR PERHAPS A NOTE CARVED INTO THE LIMESTONE SOMEWHERE.
WAIT A SECOND.
DAN, BRING THE PHONE HERE.
YOU FIND SOMETHING, AMY?
I THINK SO.
DAN, TAKE A PHOTO OF THESE SKULLS WITH THE ROMAN NUMERALS CARVED INTO THEM.
HOLD ON...
COORDINATES IN A BOX...
A MAGIC BOX!
WE NEED TO GET OUT OF HERE AND FIND A MAP ASAP!

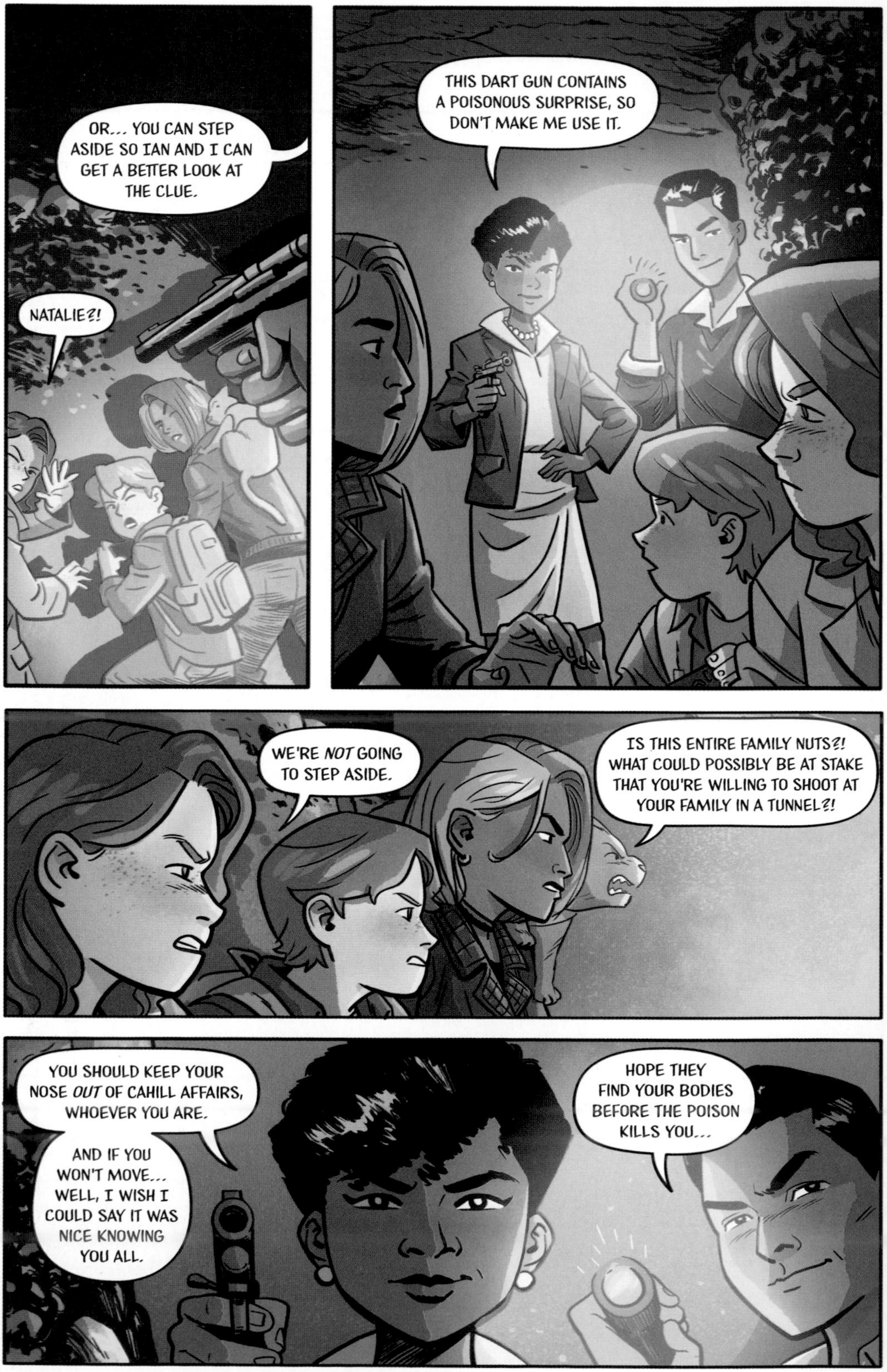
OR... YOU CAN STEP ASIDE SO IAN AND I CAN GET A BETTER LOOK AT THE CLUE.
NATALIE?!
THIS DART GUN CONTAINS A POISONOUS SURPRISE, SO DON'T MAKE ME USE IT.
WE'RE *NOT* GOING TO STEP ASIDE.
IS THIS ENTIRE FAMILY NUTS?! WHAT COULD POSSIBLY BE AT STAKE THAT YOU'RE WILLING TO SHOOT AT YOUR FAMILY IN A TUNNEL?!
YOU SHOULD KEEP YOUR NOSE *OUT* OF CAHILL AFFAIRS, WHOEVER YOU ARE.
AND IF YOU WON'T MOVE... WELL, I WISH I COULD SAY IT WAS NICE KNOWING YOU ALL.
HOPE THEY FIND YOUR BODIES BEFORE THE POISON KILLS YOU...

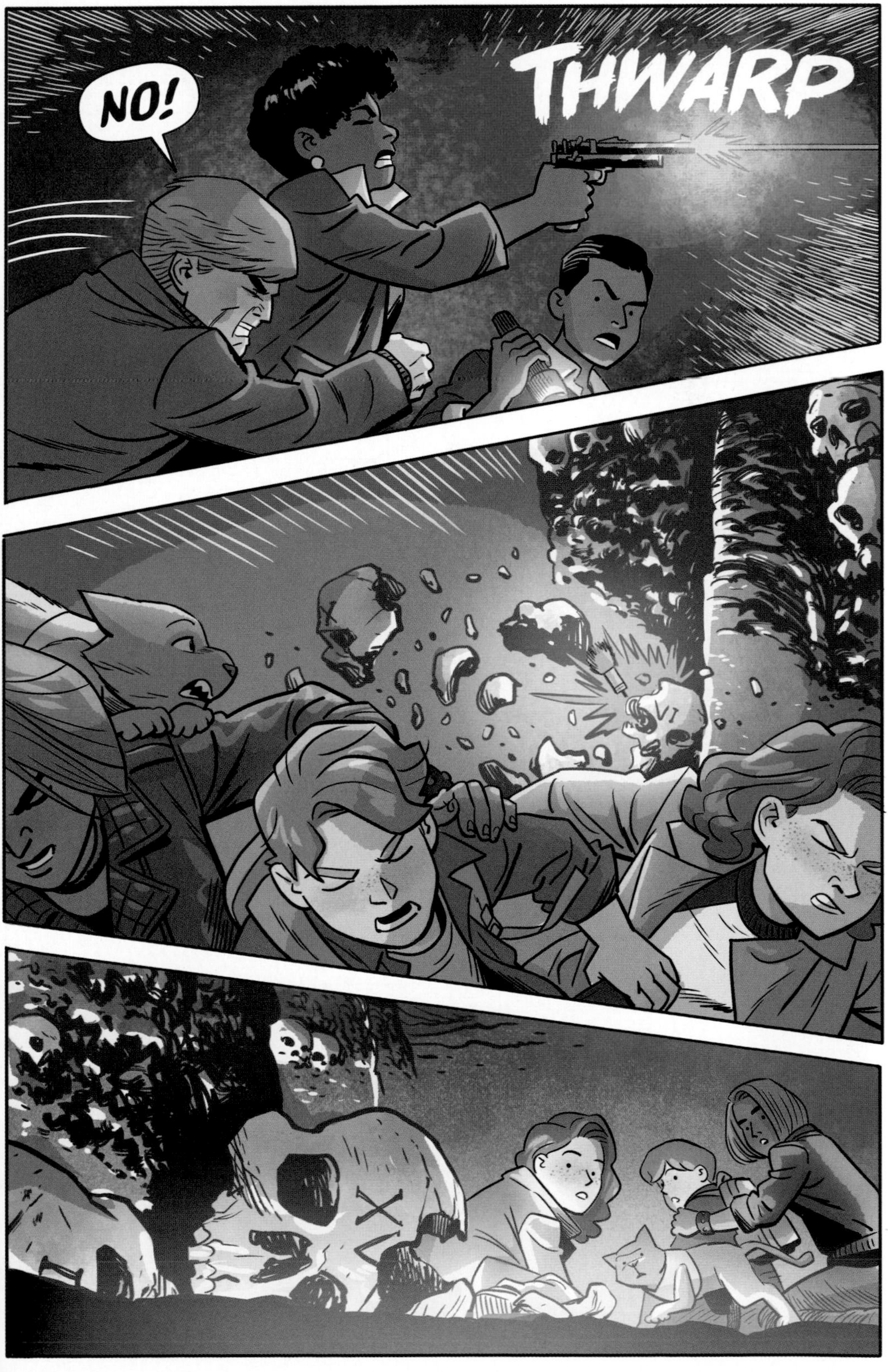
NO!
THWARP

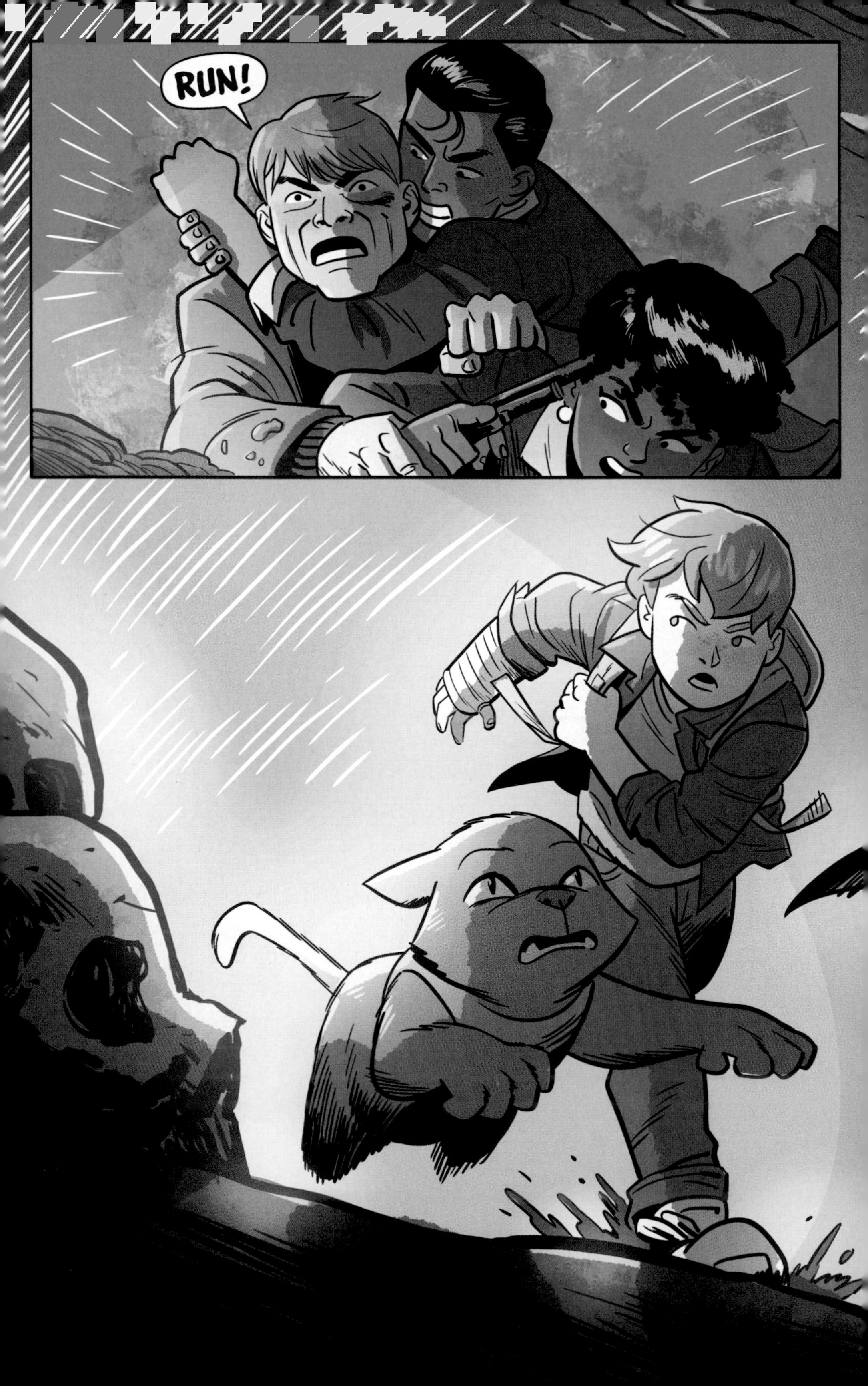
RUN!

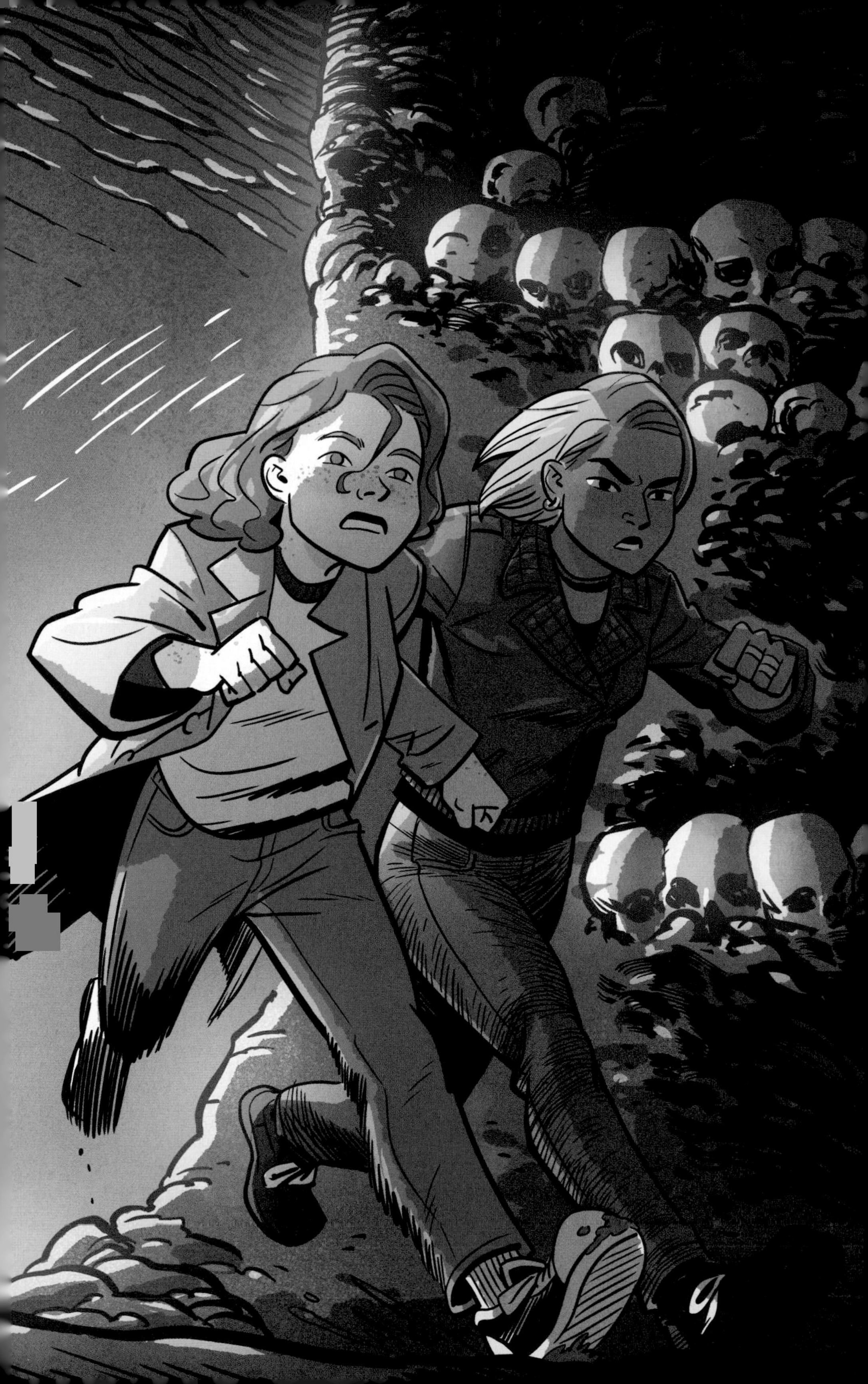

EIGHT

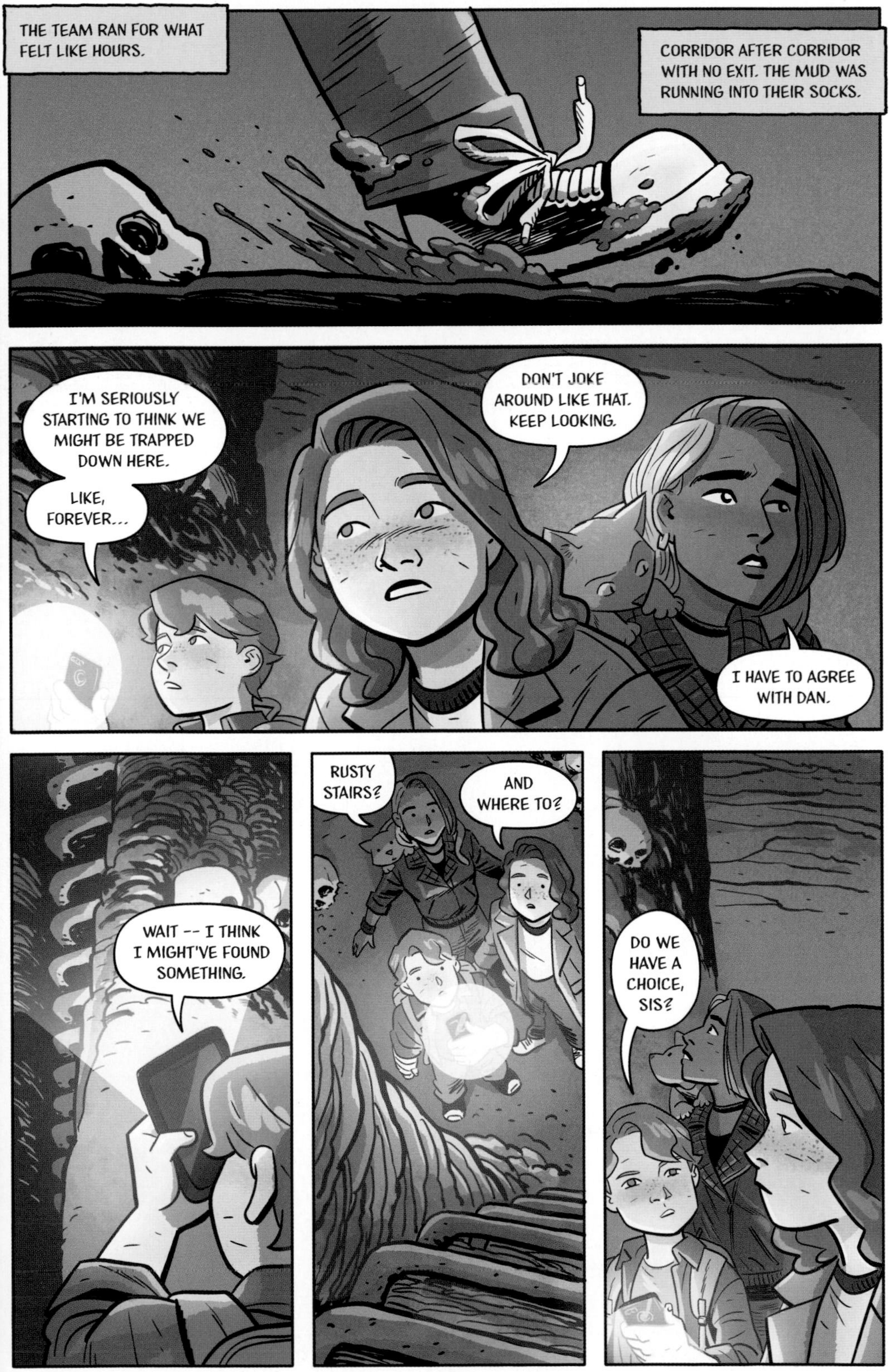
THE TEAM RAN FOR WHAT FELT LIKE HOURS.
CORRIDOR AFTER CORRIDOR WITH NO EXIT. THE MUD WAS RUNNING INTO THEIR SOCKS.
I'M SERIOUSLY STARTING TO THINK WE MIGHT BE TRAPPED DOWN HERE.
LIKE, FOREVER...
DON'T JOKE AROUND LIKE THAT. KEEP LOOKING.
I HAVE TO AGREE WITH DAN.
WAIT -- I THINK I MIGHT'VE FOUND SOMETHING.
RUSTY STAIRS?
AND WHERE TO?
DO WE HAVE A CHOICE, SIS?

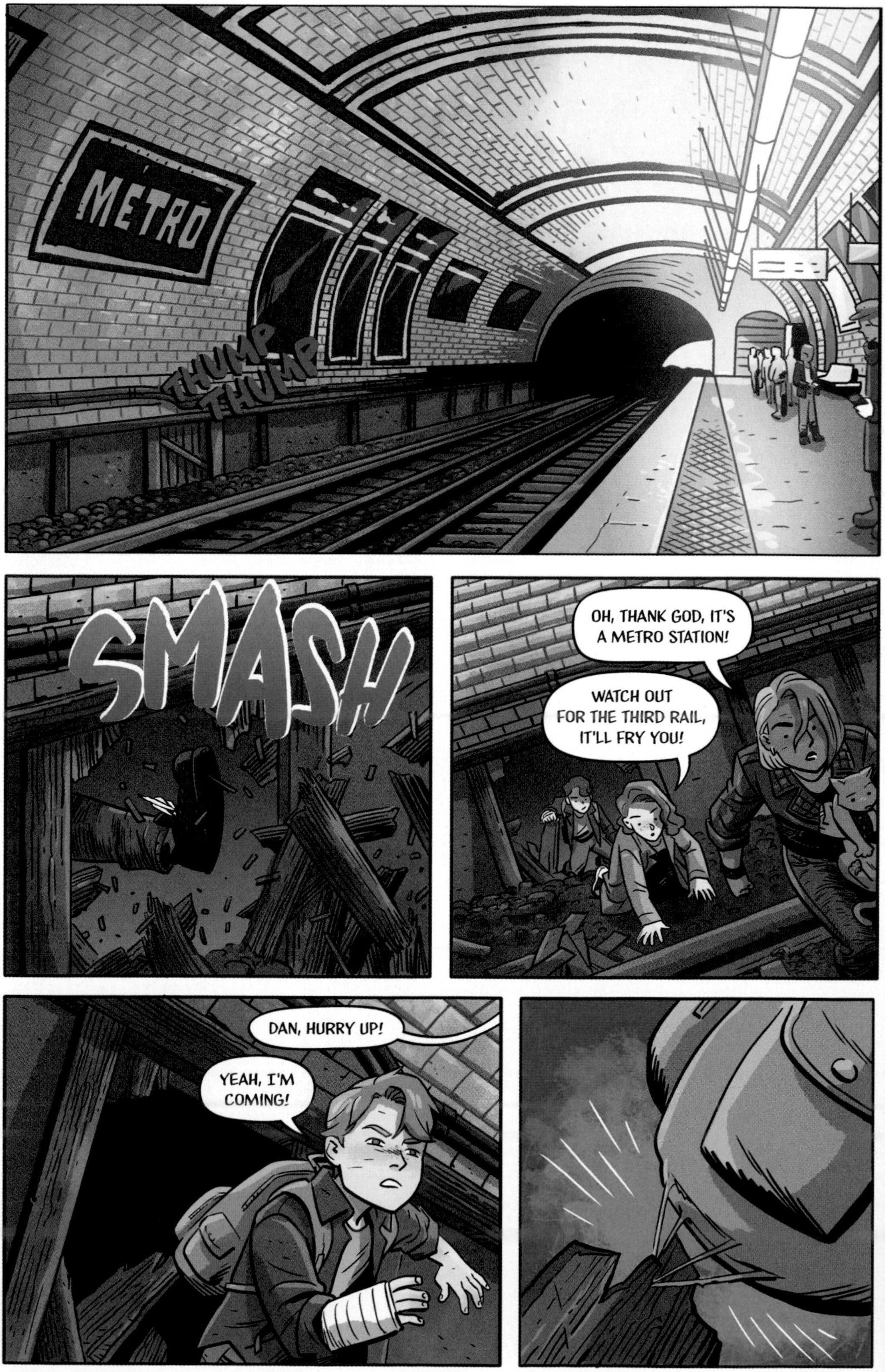
METRO
THUMP THUMP
SMASH
OH, THANK GOD, IT'S A METRO STATION!
WATCH OUT FOR THE THIRD RAIL, IT'LL FRY YOU!
DAN, HURRY UP!
YEAH, I'M COMING!

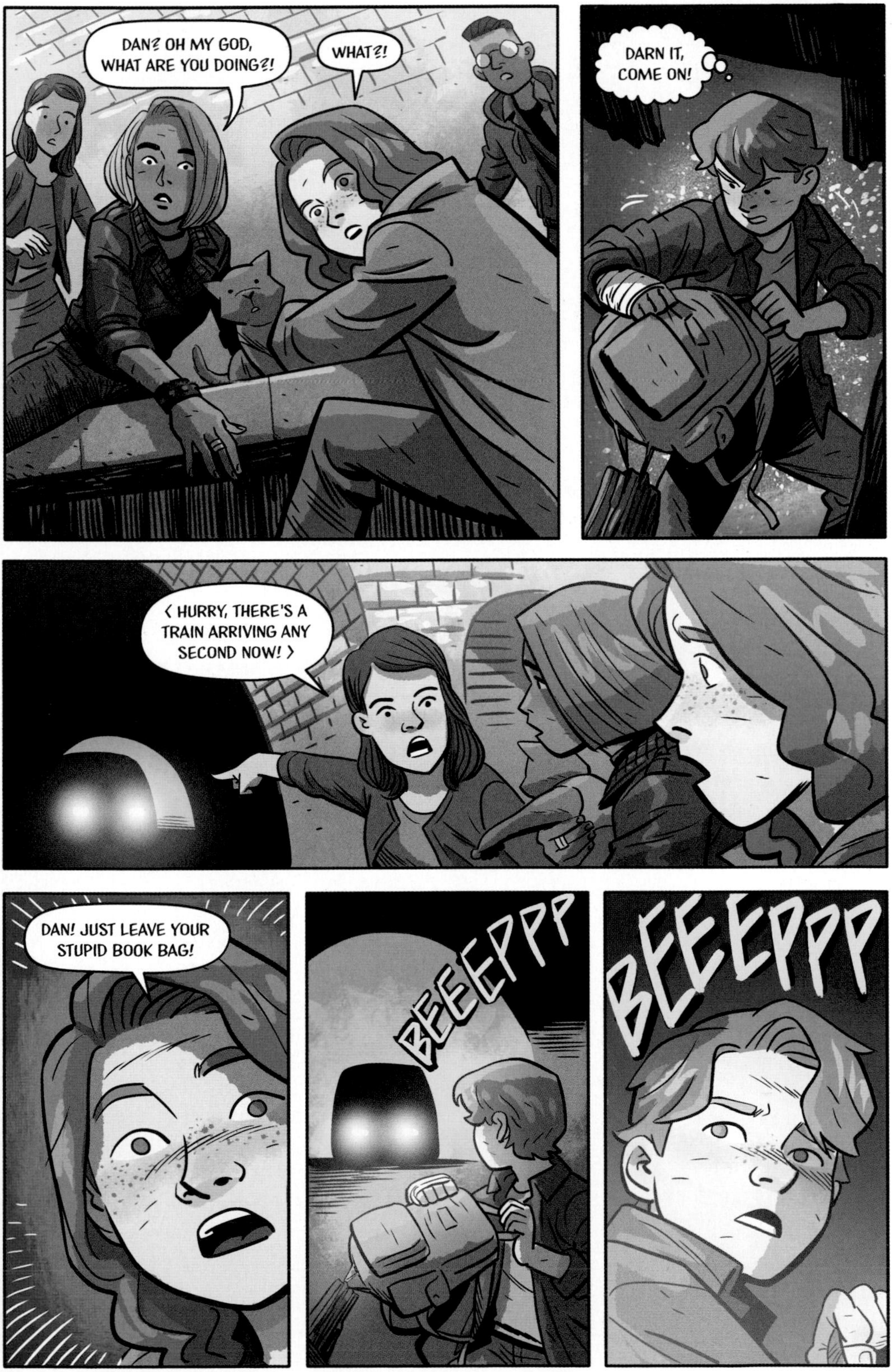
DAN? OH MY GOD, WHAT ARE YOU DOING?!
WHAT?!
DARN IT, COME ON!
< HURRY, THERE'S A TRAIN ARRIVING ANY SECOND NOW! >
DAN! JUST LEAVE YOUR STUPID BOOK BAG!
BEEEPPP
BEEEPPP

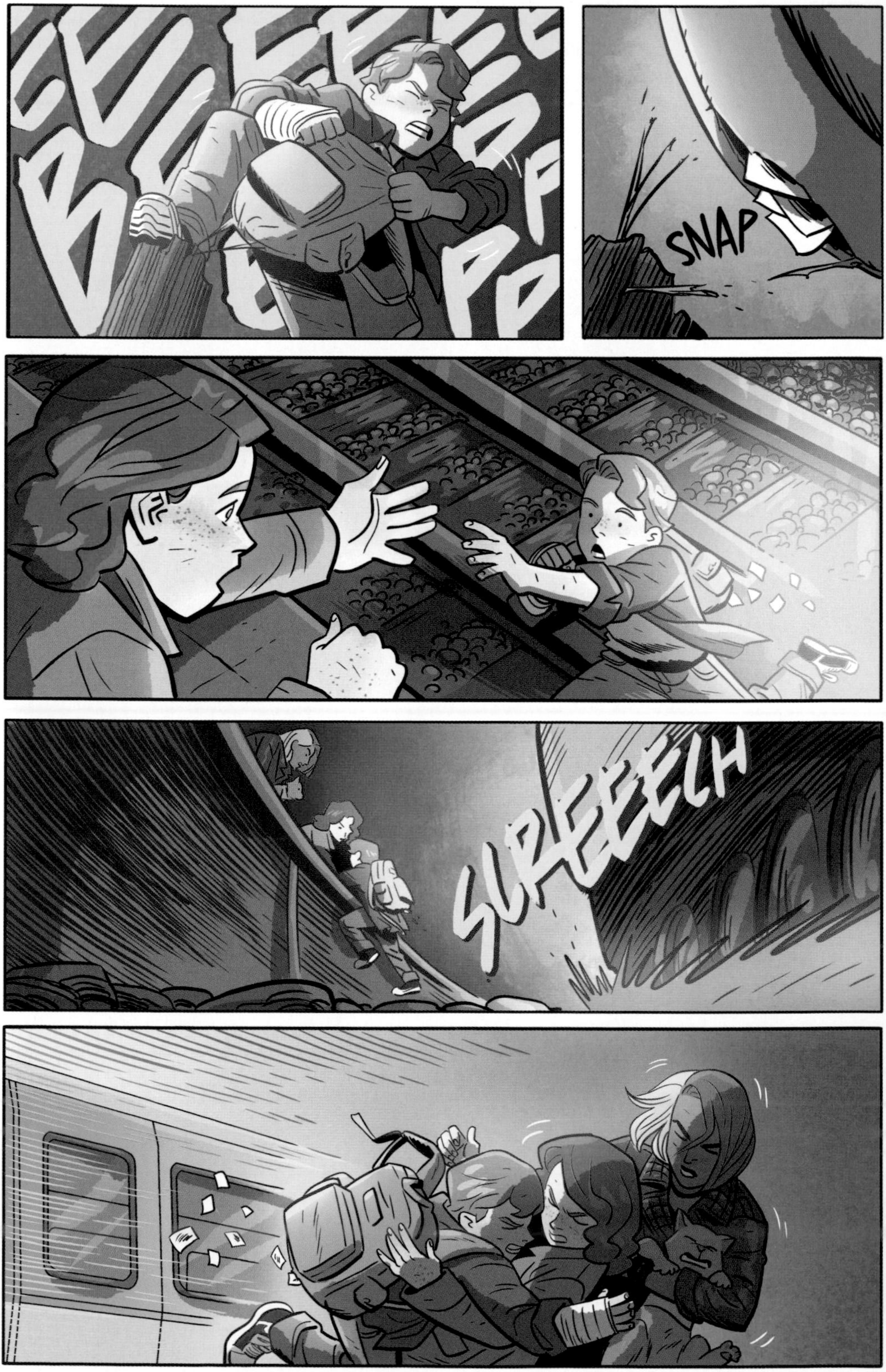
SNAP
SCREEECH

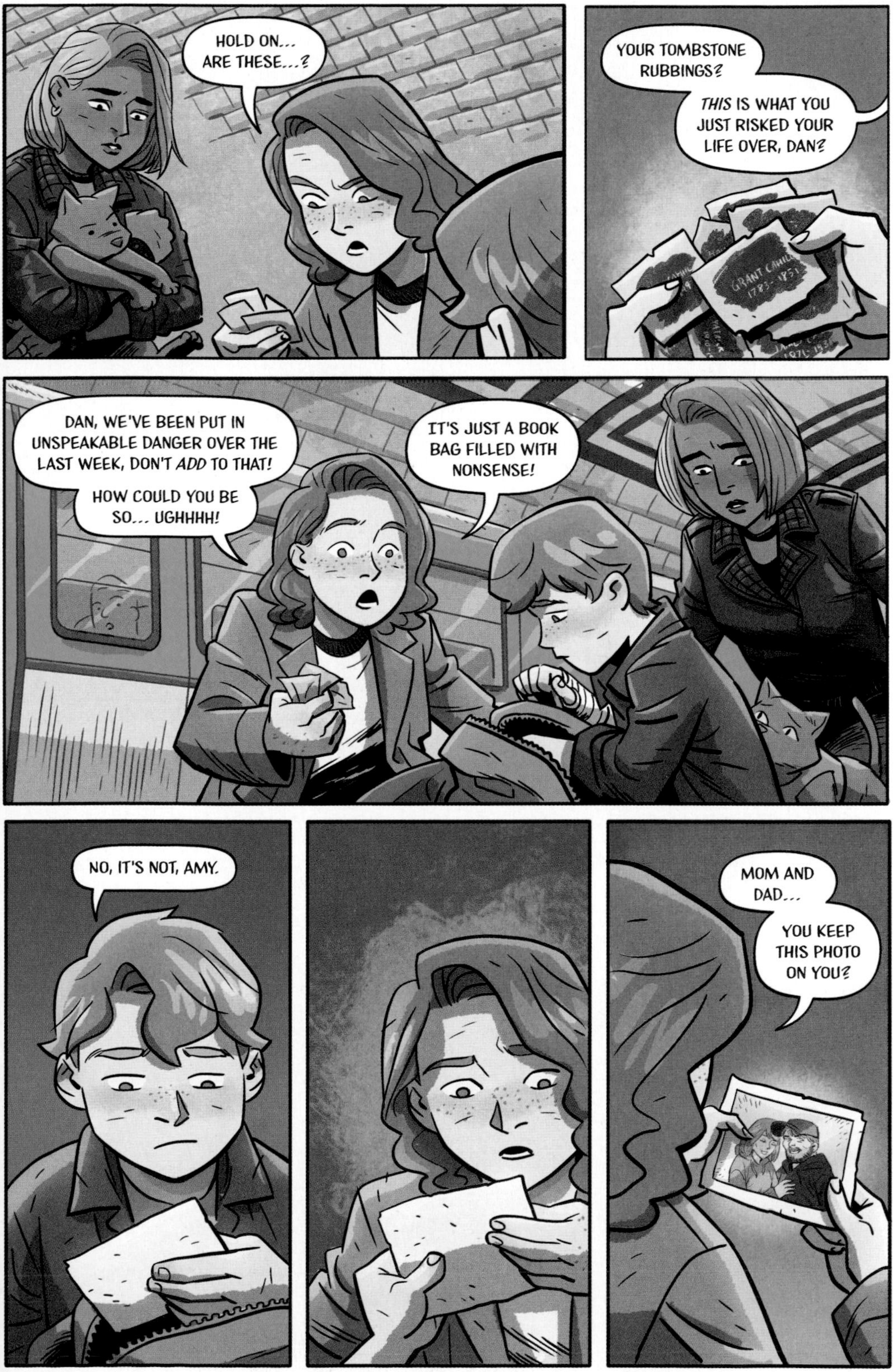
HOLD ON... ARE THESE...?
YOUR TOMBSTONE RUBBINGS?
THIS IS WHAT YOU JUST RISKED YOUR LIFE OVER, DAN?
GRANT CAHILL 1783-1851
DAN, WE'VE BEEN PUT IN UNSPEAKABLE DANGER OVER THE LAST WEEK, DON'T ADD TO THAT!
HOW COULD YOU BE SO... UGHHHH!
IT'S JUST A BOOK BAG FILLED WITH NONSENSE!
NO, IT'S NOT, AMY.
MOM AND DAD...
YOU KEEP THIS PHOTO ON YOU?

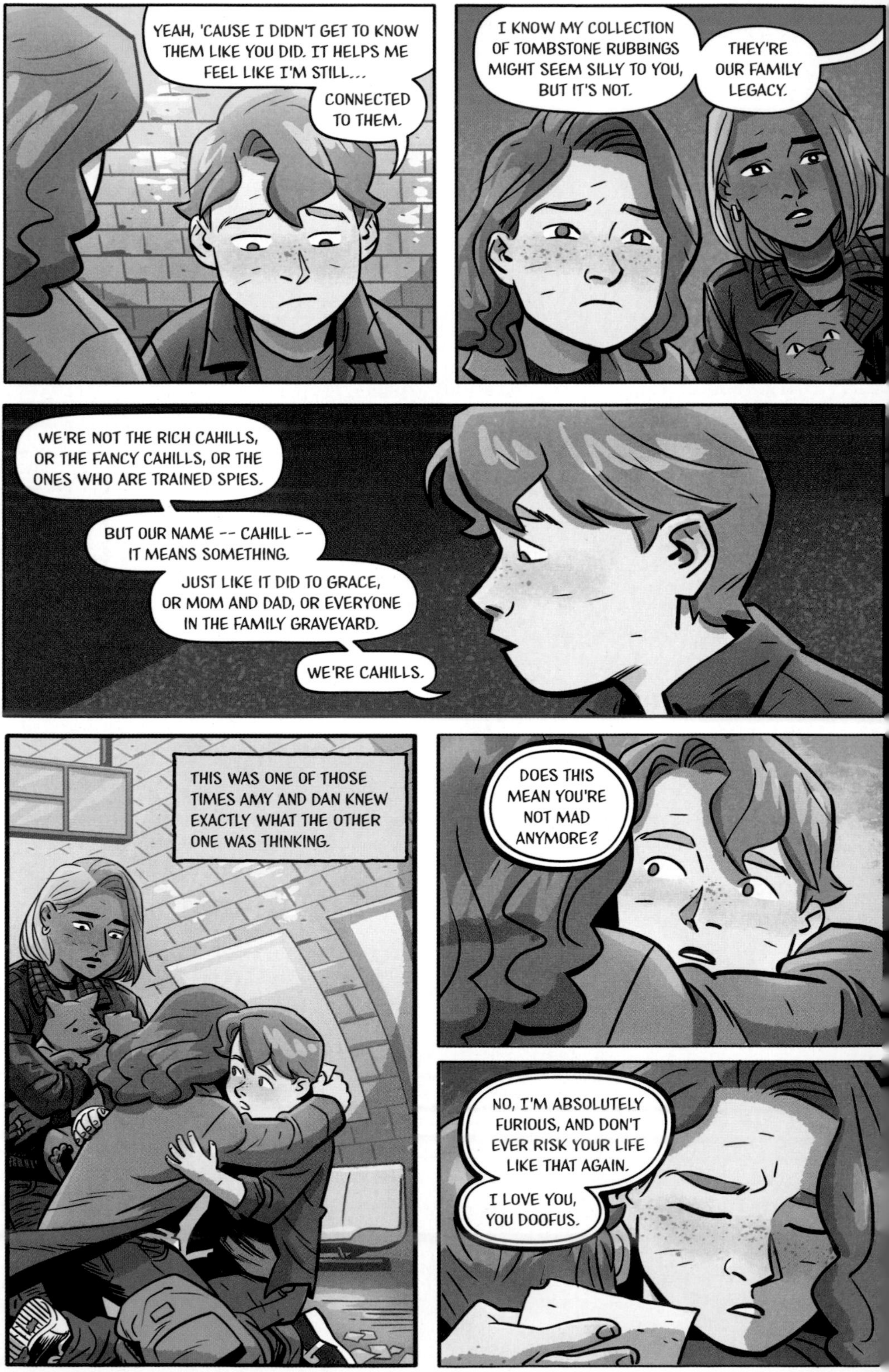
YEAH, 'CAUSE I DIDN'T GET TO KNOW THEM LIKE YOU DID. IT HELPS ME FEEL LIKE I'M STILL...
CONNECTED TO THEM.
I KNOW MY COLLECTION OF TOMBSTONE RUBBINGS MIGHT SEEM SILLY TO YOU, BUT IT'S NOT.
THEY'RE OUR FAMILY LEGACY.
WE'RE NOT THE RICH CAHILLS, OR THE FANCY CAHILLS, OR THE ONES WHO ARE TRAINED SPIES.
BUT OUR NAME -- CAHILL -- IT MEANS SOMETHING.
JUST LIKE IT DID TO GRACE, OR MOM AND DAD, OR EVERYONE IN THE FAMILY GRAVEYARD.
WE'RE CAHILLS.
THIS WAS ONE OF THOSE TIMES AMY AND DAN KNEW EXACTLY WHAT THE OTHER ONE WAS THINKING.
DOES THIS MEAN YOU'RE NOT MAD ANYMORE?
NO, I'M ABSOLUTELY FURIOUS, AND DON'T EVER RISK YOUR LIFE LIKE THAT AGAIN.
I LOVE YOU, YOU DOOFUS.

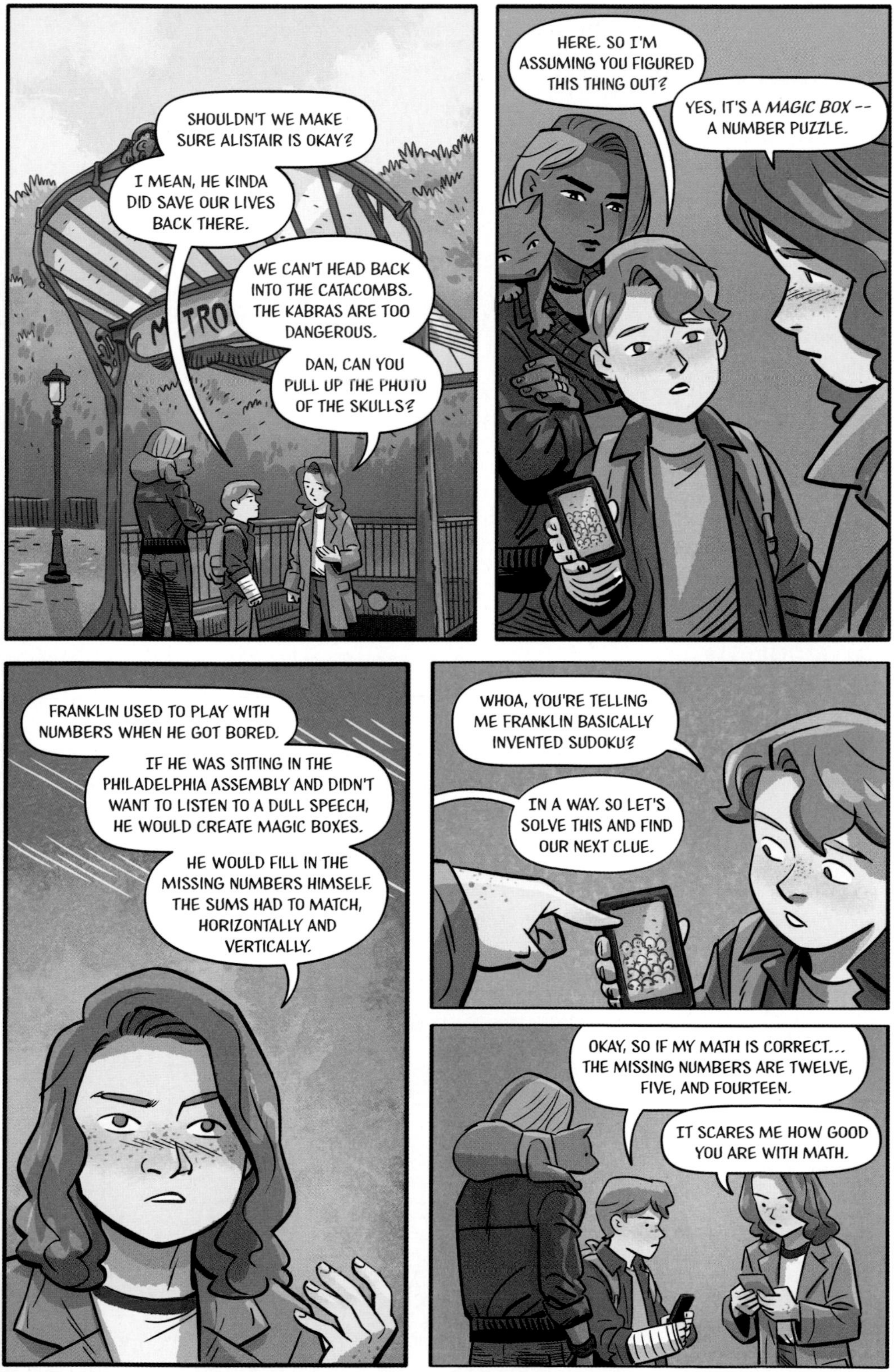
SHOULDN'T WE MAKE SURE ALISTAIR IS OKAY?
I MEAN, HE KINDA DID SAVE OUR LIVES BACK THERE.
WE CAN'T HEAD BACK INTO THE CATACOMBS. THE KABRAS ARE TOO DANGEROUS.
DAN, CAN YOU PULL UP THE PHOTO OF THE SKULLS?
METRO
HERE. SO I'M ASSUMING YOU FIGURED THIS THING OUT?
YES, IT'S A *MAGIC BOX* -- A NUMBER PUZZLE.
FRANKLIN USED TO PLAY WITH NUMBERS WHEN HE GOT BORED.
IF HE WAS SITTING IN THE PHILADELPHIA ASSEMBLY AND DIDN'T WANT TO LISTEN TO A DULL SPEECH, HE WOULD CREATE MAGIC BOXES.
HE WOULD FILL IN THE MISSING NUMBERS HIMSELF. THE SUMS HAD TO MATCH, HORIZONTALLY AND VERTICALLY.
WHOA, YOU'RE TELLING ME FRANKLIN BASICALLY INVENTED SUDOKU?
IN A WAY. SO LET'S SOLVE THIS AND FIND OUR NEXT CLUE.
OKAY, SO IF MY MATH IS CORRECT... THE MISSING NUMBERS ARE TWELVE, FIVE, AND FOURTEEN.
IT SCARES ME HOW GOOD YOU ARE WITH MATH.

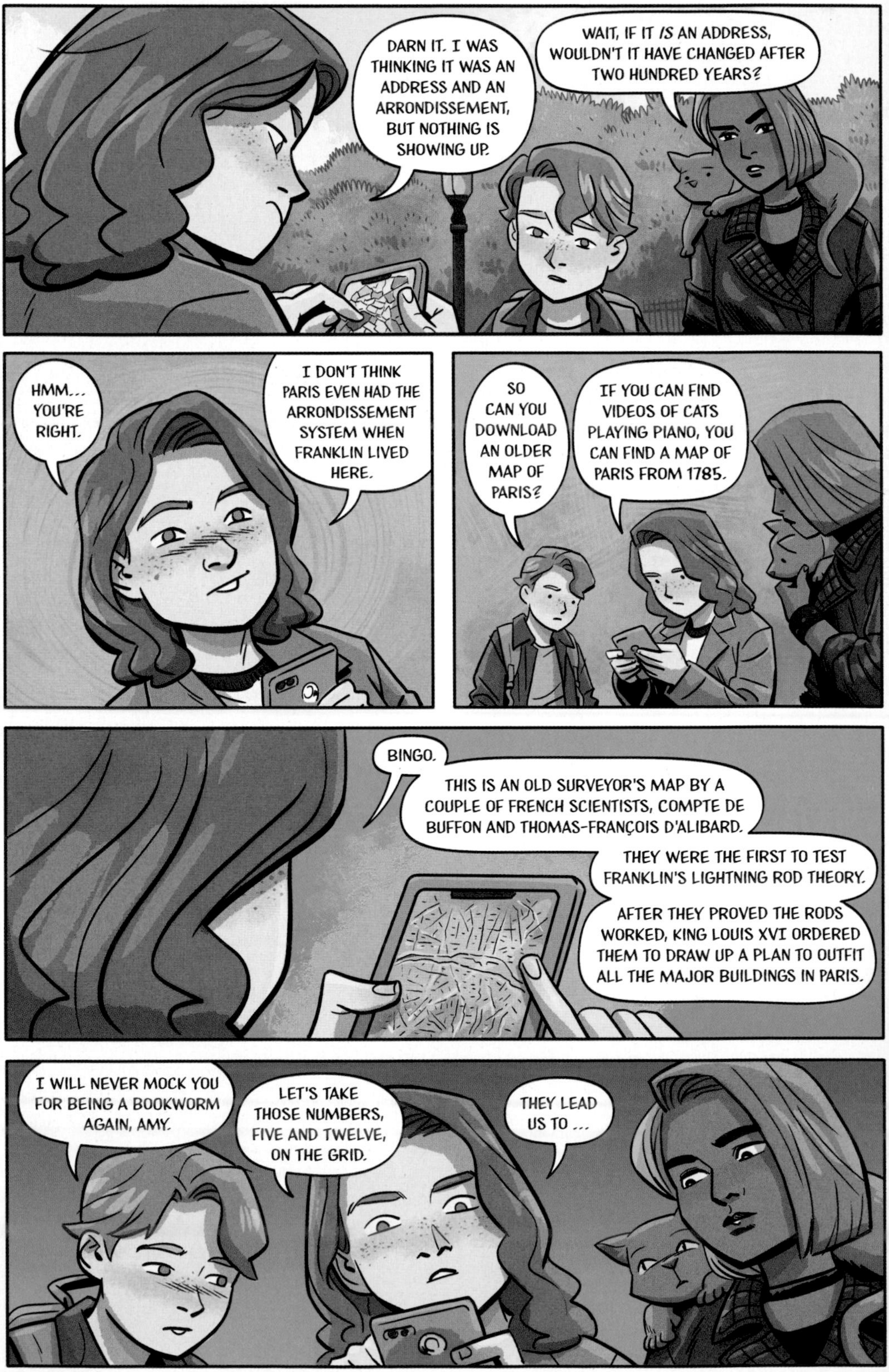
DARN IT. I WAS THINKING IT WAS AN ADDRESS AND AN ARRONDISSEMENT, BUT NOTHING IS SHOWING UP.
WAIT, IF IT *IS* AN ADDRESS, WOULDN'T IT HAVE CHANGED AFTER TWO HUNDRED YEARS?
HMM... YOU'RE RIGHT.
I DON'T THINK PARIS EVEN HAD THE ARRONDISSEMENT SYSTEM WHEN FRANKLIN LIVED HERE.
SO CAN YOU DOWNLOAD AN OLDER MAP OF PARIS?
IF YOU CAN FIND VIDEOS OF CATS PLAYING PIANO, YOU CAN FIND A MAP OF PARIS FROM 1785.
BINGO.
THIS IS AN OLD SURVEYOR'S MAP BY A COUPLE OF FRENCH SCIENTISTS, COMPTE DE BUFFON AND THOMAS-FRANÇOIS D'ALIBARD.
THEY WERE THE FIRST TO TEST FRANKLIN'S LIGHTNING ROD THEORY.
AFTER THEY PROVED THE RODS WORKED, KING LOUIS XVI ORDERED THEM TO DRAW UP A PLAN TO OUTFIT ALL THE MAJOR BUILDINGS IN PARIS.
I WILL NEVER MOCK YOU FOR BEING A BOOKWORM AGAIN, AMY.
LET'S TAKE THOSE NUMBERS, FIVE AND TWELVE, ON THE GRID.
THEY LEAD US TO ...

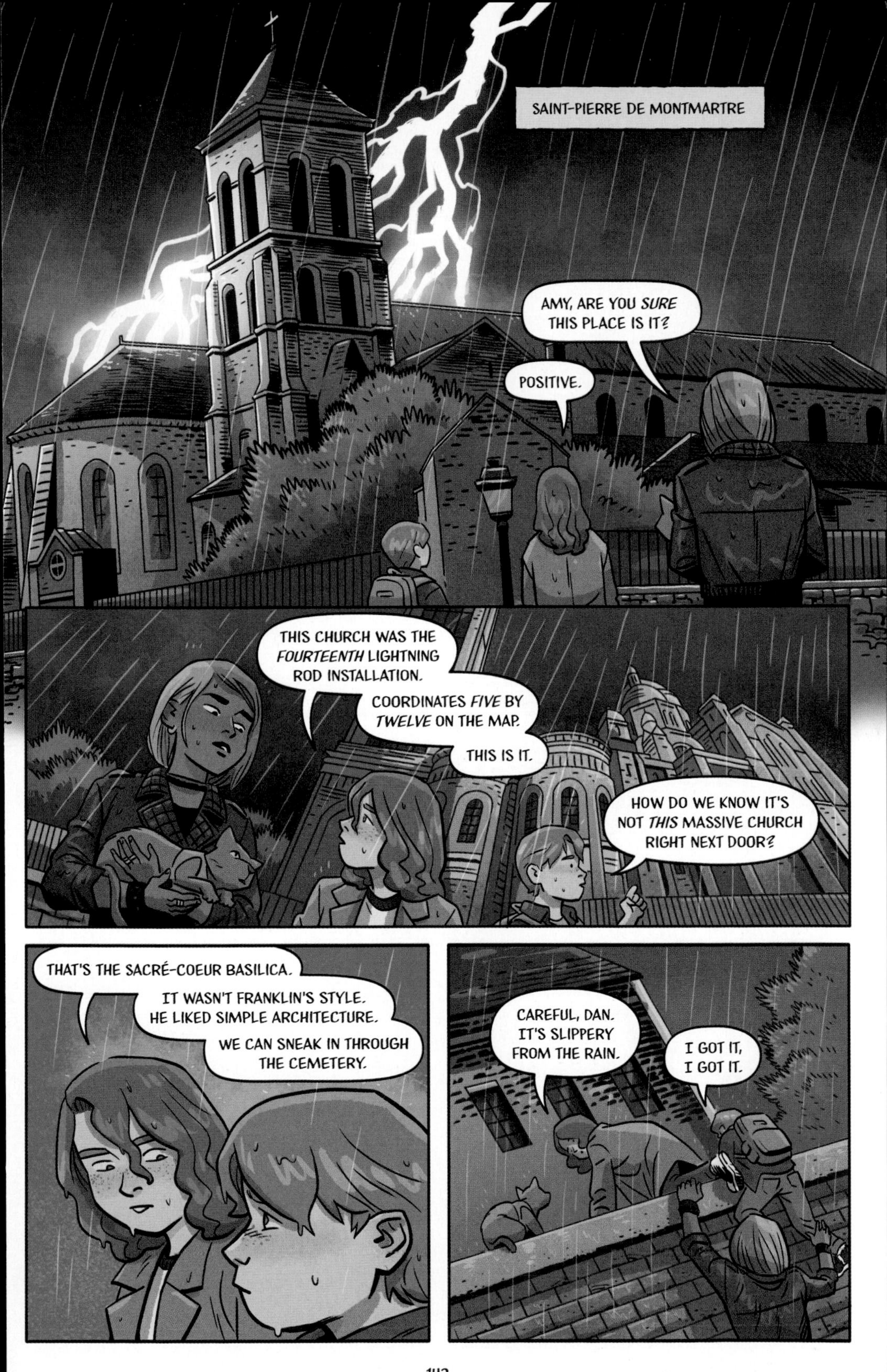
SAINT-PIERRE DE MONTMARTRE
AMY, ARE YOU *SURE* THIS PLACE IS IT?
POSITIVE.
THIS CHURCH WAS THE *FOURTEENTH* LIGHTNING ROD INSTALLATION.
COORDINATES *FIVE* BY *TWELVE* ON THE MAP.
THIS IS IT.
HOW DO WE KNOW IT'S NOT *THIS* MASSIVE CHURCH RIGHT NEXT DOOR?
THAT'S THE SACRÉ-COEUR BASILICA.
IT WASN'T FRANKLIN'S STYLE. HE LIKED SIMPLE ARCHITECTURE.
WE CAN SNEAK IN THROUGH THE CEMETERY.
CAREFUL, DAN. IT'S SLIPPERY FROM THE RAIN.
I GOT IT, I GOT IT.

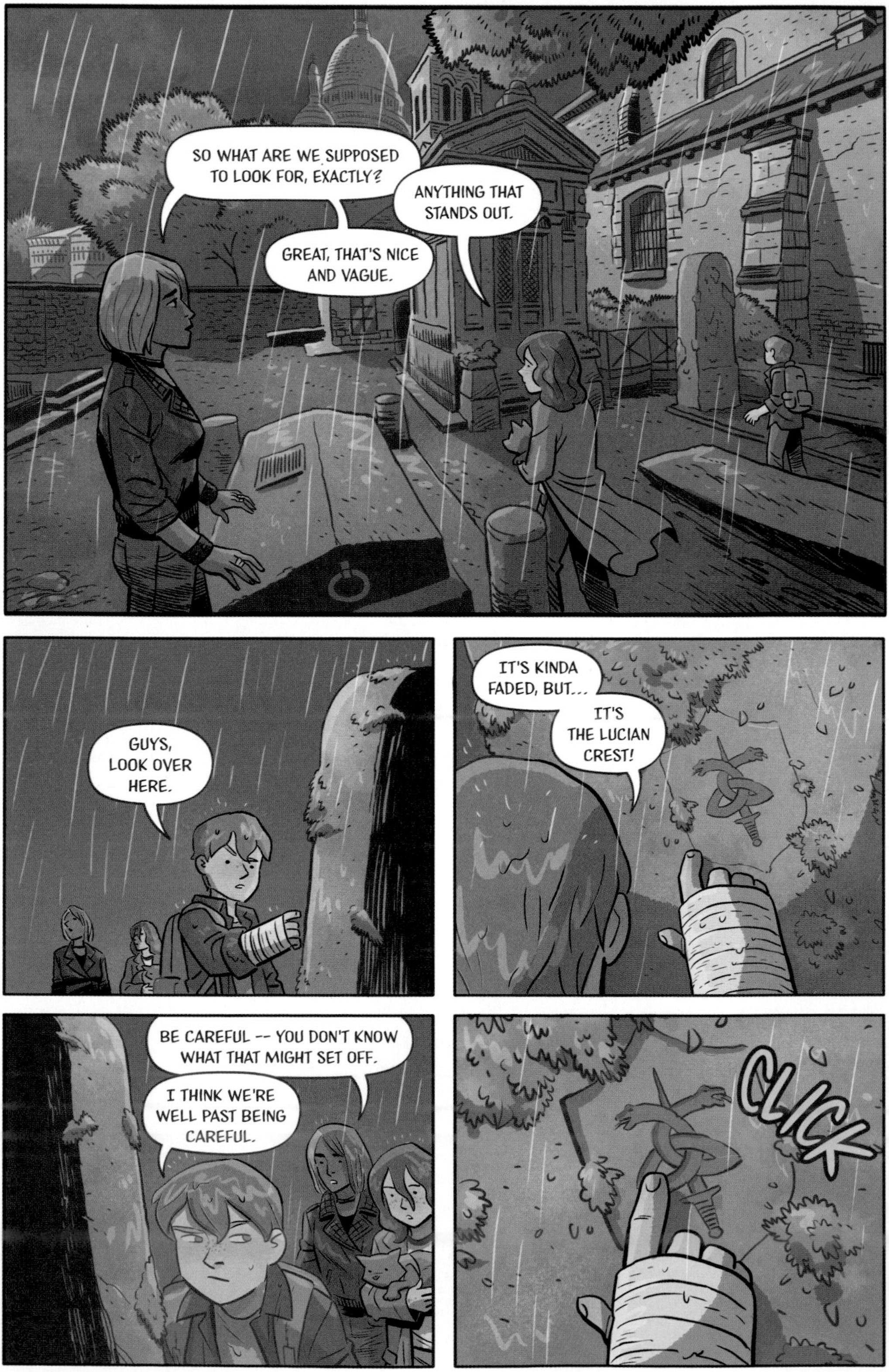
SO WHAT ARE WE SUPPOSED TO LOOK FOR, EXACTLY?
ANYTHING THAT STANDS OUT.
GREAT, THAT'S NICE AND VAGUE.
GUYS, LOOK OVER HERE.
IT'S KINDA FADED, BUT...
IT'S THE LUCIAN CREST!
BE CAREFUL -- YOU DON'T KNOW WHAT THAT MIGHT SET OFF.
I THINK WE'RE WELL PAST BEING CAREFUL.
CLICK

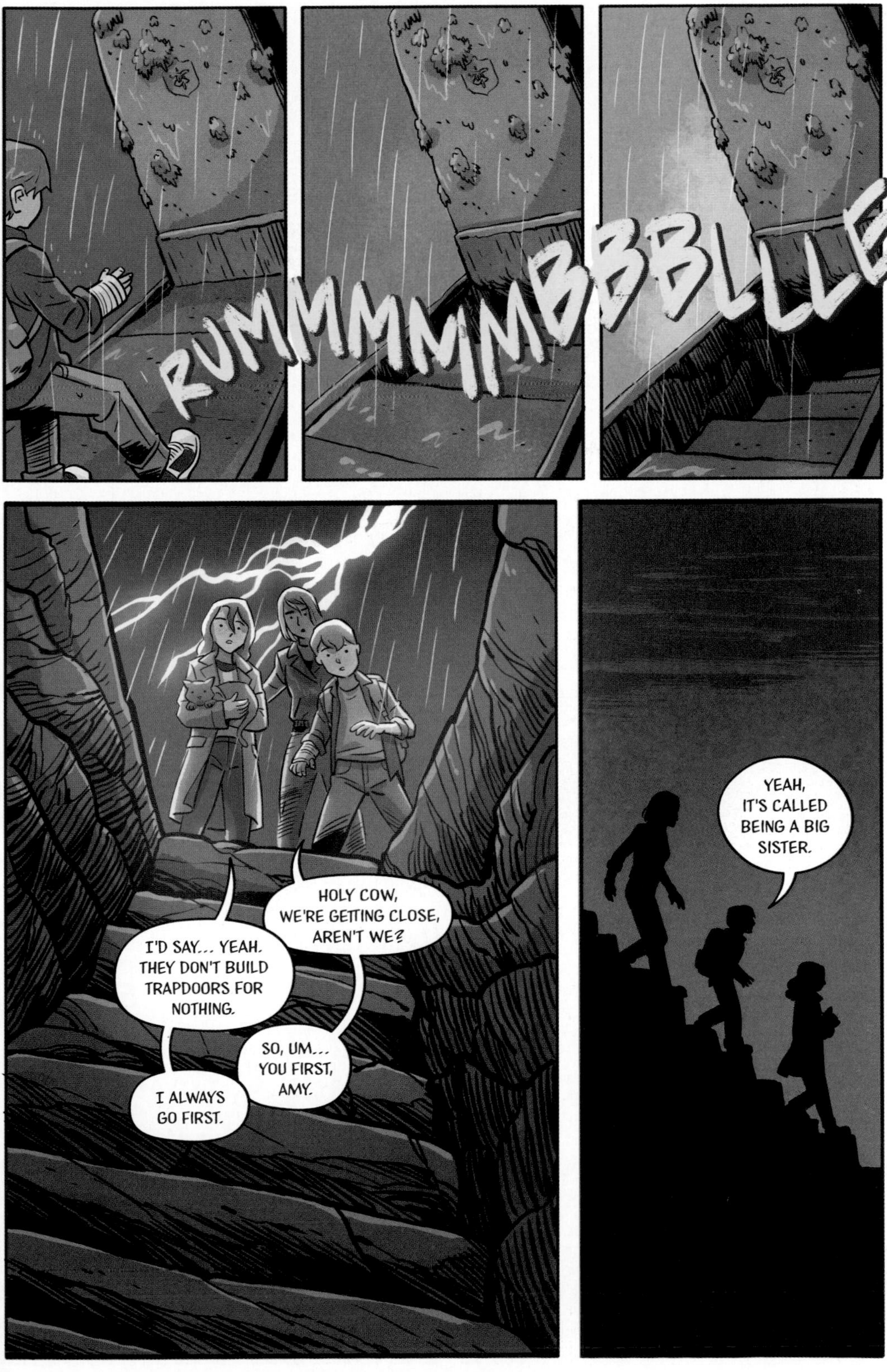
RUMMMMMBBBLLLE
HOLY COW, WE'RE GETTING CLOSE, AREN'T WE?
I'D SAY... YEAH. THEY DON'T BUILD TRAPDOORS FOR NOTHING.
SO, UM... YOU FIRST, AMY.
I ALWAYS GO FIRST.
YEAH, IT'S CALLED BEING A BIG SISTER.

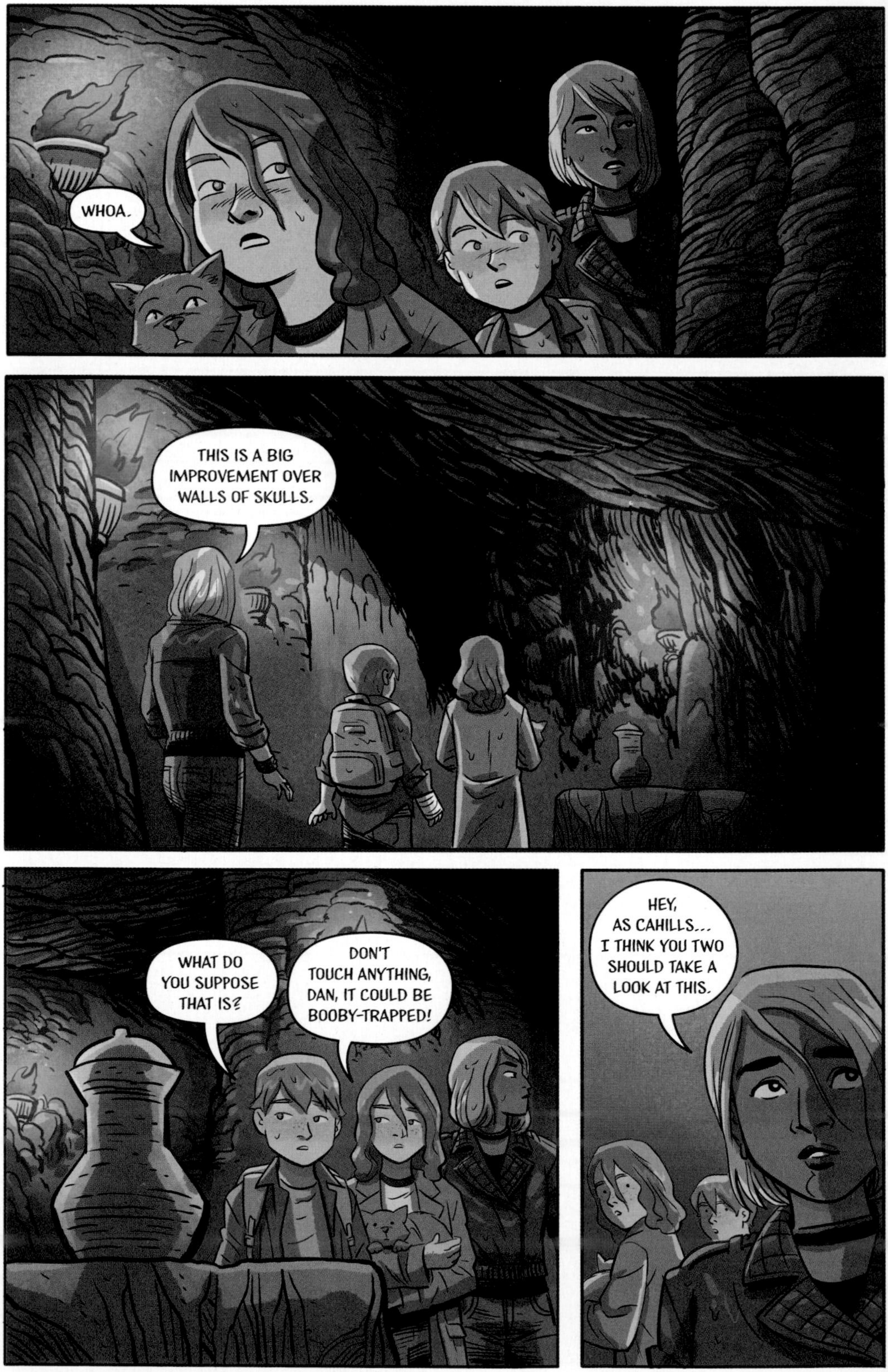
WHOA.
THIS IS A BIG IMPROVEMENT OVER WALLS OF SKULLS.
WHAT DO YOU SUPPOSE THAT IS?
DON'T TOUCH ANYTHING, DAN, IT COULD BE BOOBY-TRAPPED!
HEY, AS CAHILLS... I THINK YOU TWO SHOULD TAKE A LOOK AT THIS.

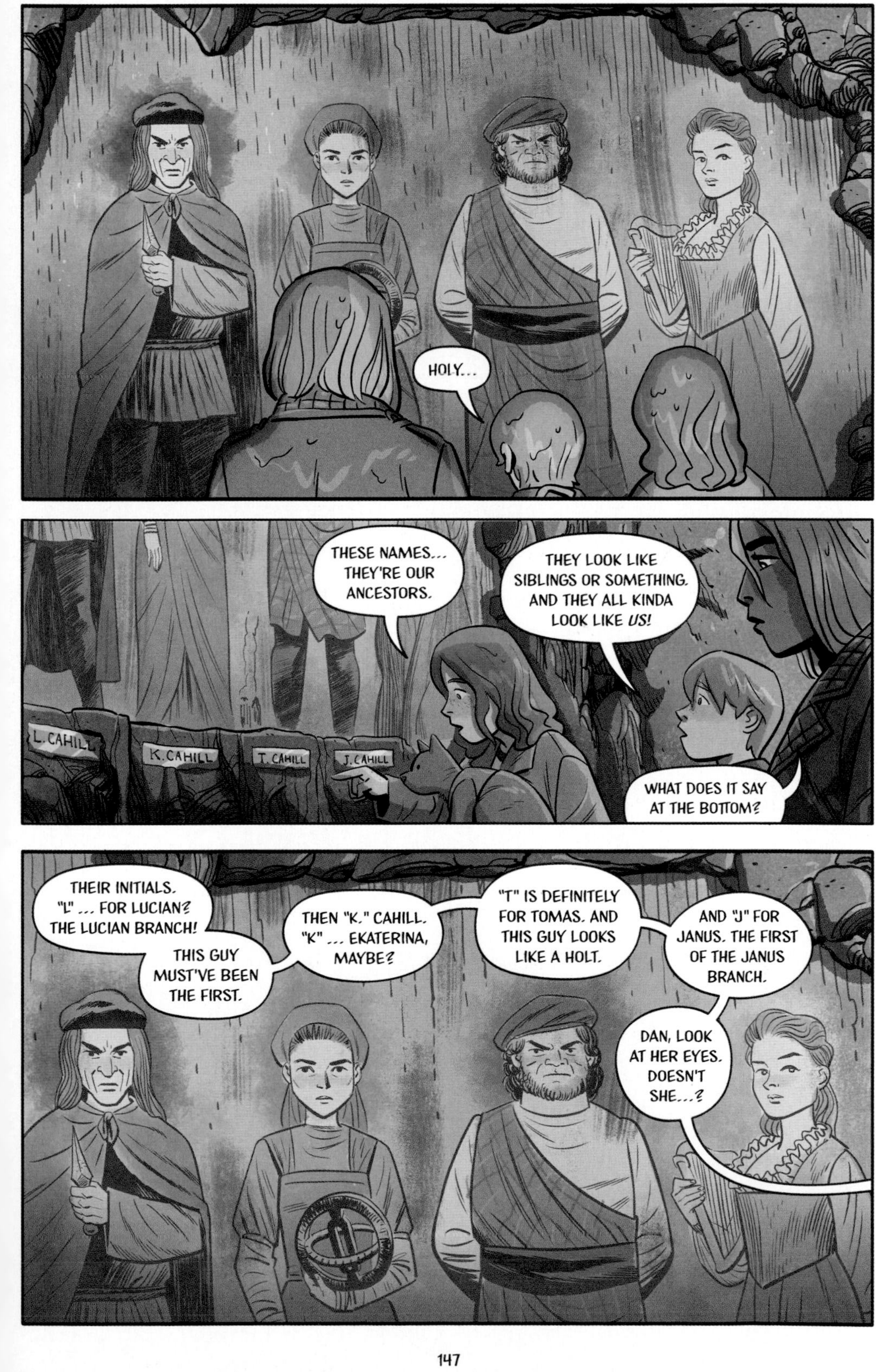

HOLY...
THESE NAMES... THEY'RE OUR ANCESTORS.
THEY LOOK LIKE SIBLINGS OR SOMETHING. AND THEY ALL KINDA LOOK LIKE *US!*
L. CAHILL
K. CAHILL
T. CAHILL
J. CAHILL
WHAT DOES IT SAY AT THE BOTTOM?
THEIR INITIALS. "L" ... FOR LUCIAN? THE LUCIAN BRANCH!
THIS GUY MUST'VE BEEN THE FIRST.
THEN "K." CAHILL. "K" ... EKATERINA, MAYBE?
"T" IS DEFINITELY FOR TOMAS. AND THIS GUY LOOKS LIKE A HOLT.
AND "J" FOR JANUS. THE FIRST OF THE JANUS BRANCH.
DAN, LOOK AT HER EYES. DOESN'T SHE...?

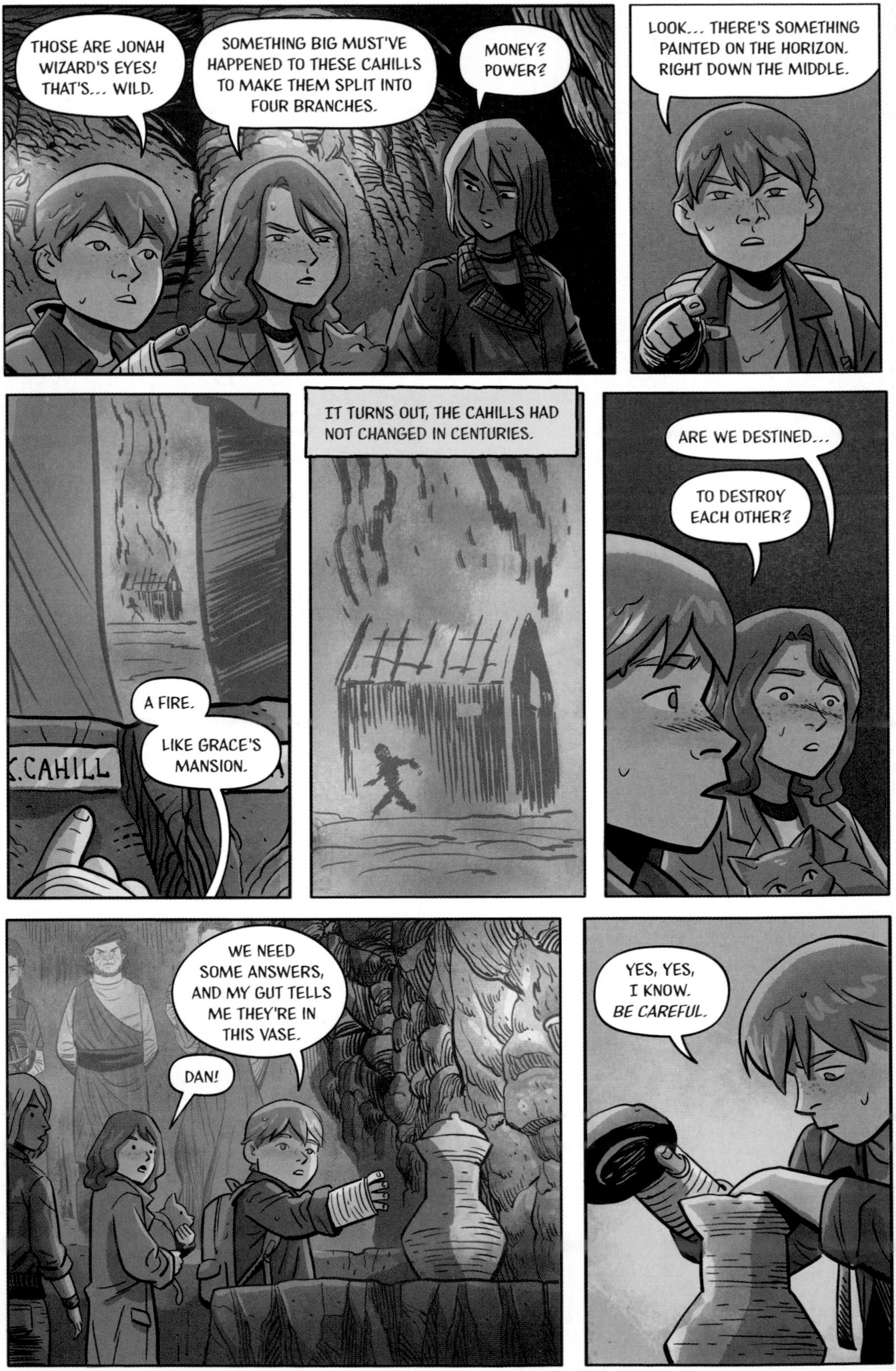
THOSE ARE JONAH WIZARD'S EYES! THAT'S... WILD.
SOMETHING BIG MUST'VE HAPPENED TO THESE CAHILLS TO MAKE THEM SPLIT INTO FOUR BRANCHES.
MONEY? POWER?
LOOK... THERE'S SOMETHING PAINTED ON THE HORIZON. RIGHT DOWN THE MIDDLE.
.CAHILL
A FIRE.
LIKE GRACE'S MANSION.
IT TURNS OUT, THE CAHILLS HAD NOT CHANGED IN CENTURIES.
ARE WE DESTINED...
TO DESTROY EACH OTHER?
WE NEED SOME ANSWERS, AND MY GUT TELLS ME THEY'RE IN THIS VASE.
DAN!
YES, YES, I KNOW. *BE CAREFUL.*

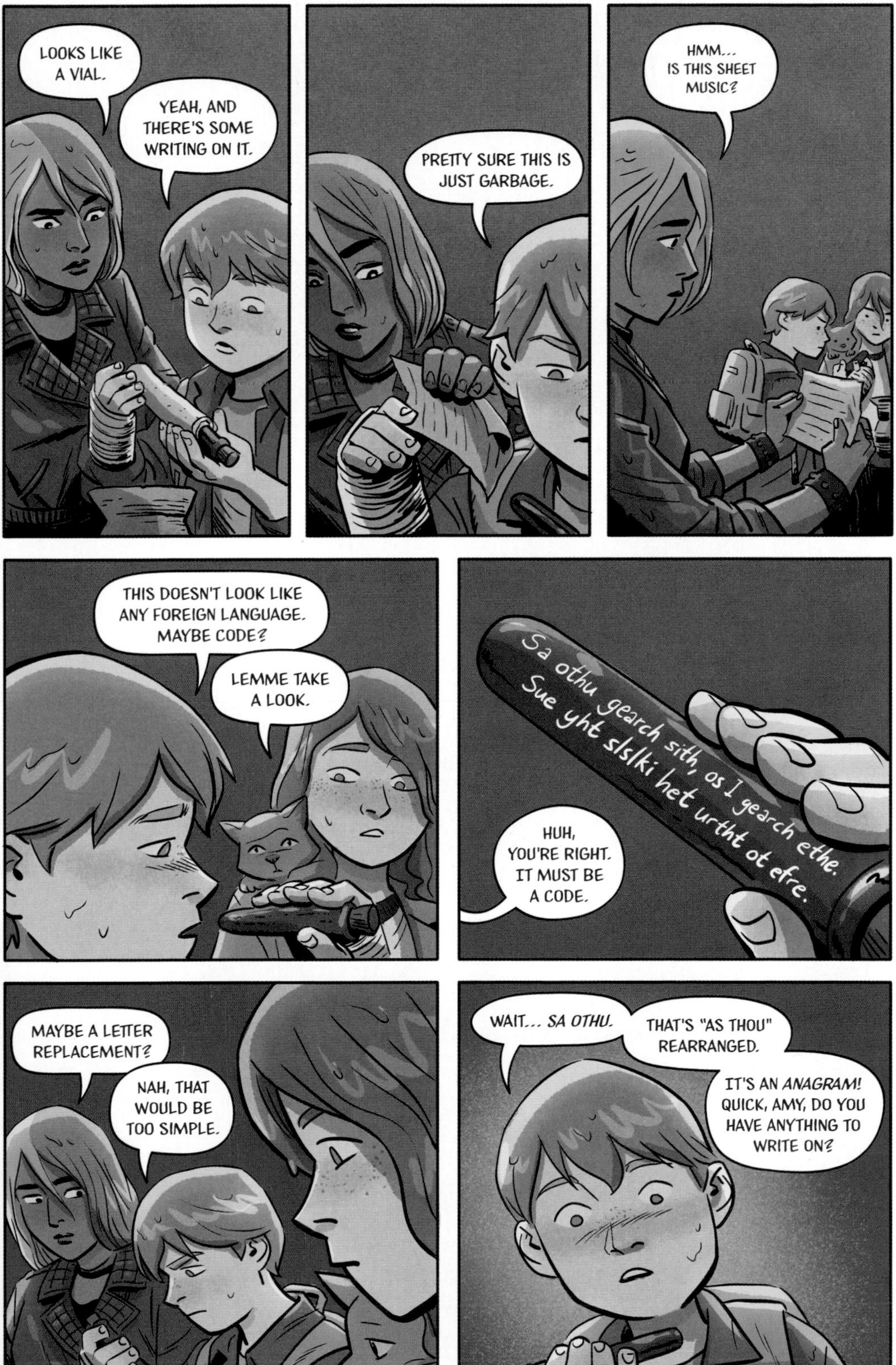
LOOKS LIKE A VIAL.
YEAH, AND THERE'S SOME WRITING ON IT.
PRETTY SURE THIS IS JUST GARBAGE.
HMM... IS THIS SHEET MUSIC?
THIS DOESN'T LOOK LIKE ANY FOREIGN LANGUAGE. MAYBE CODE?
LEMME TAKE A LOOK.
Sa othu gearch sith, os I gearch ethe.
Sue yht slslki het urtht ot efre.
HUH, YOU'RE RIGHT. IT MUST BE A CODE.
MAYBE A LETTER REPLACEMENT?
NAH, THAT WOULD BE TOO SIMPLE.
WAIT... *SA OTHU.*
THAT'S "AS THOU" REARRANGED.
IT'S AN *ANAGRAM!* QUICK, AMY, DO YOU HAVE ANYTHING TO WRITE ON?

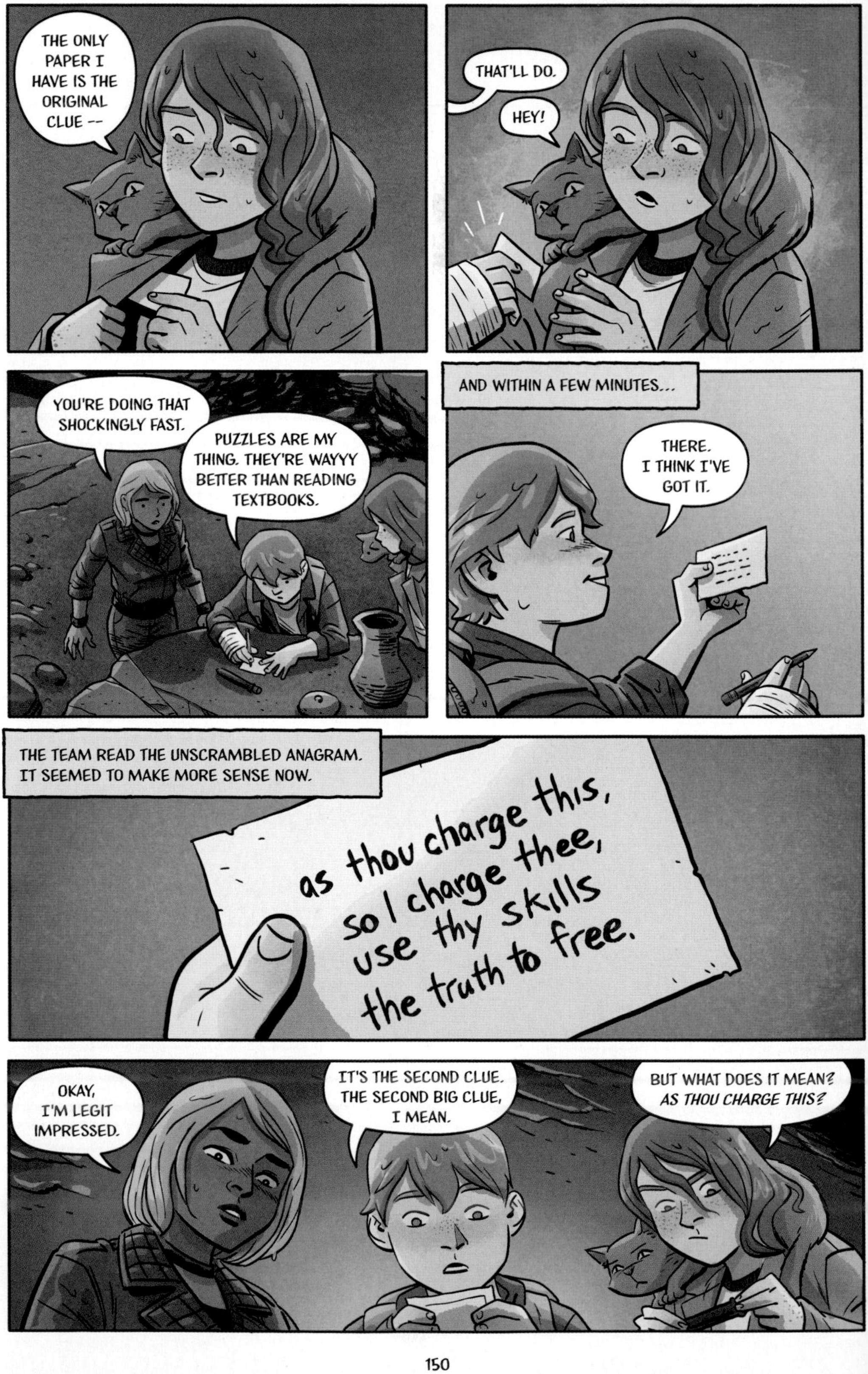
THE ONLY PAPER I HAVE IS THE ORIGINAL CLUE --
THAT'LL DO.
HEY!
YOU'RE DOING THAT SHOCKINGLY FAST.
PUZZLES ARE MY THING. THEY'RE WAYYY BETTER THAN READING TEXTBOOKS.
AND WITHIN A FEW MINUTES...
THERE. I THINK I'VE GOT IT.
THE TEAM READ THE UNSCRAMBLED ANAGRAM. IT SEEMED TO MAKE MORE SENSE NOW.
as thou charge this,
so I charge thee,
use thy skills
the truth to free.
OKAY, I'M LEGIT IMPRESSED.
IT'S THE SECOND CLUE. THE SECOND BIG CLUE, I MEAN.
BUT WHAT DOES IT MEAN? *AS THOU CHARGE THIS?*

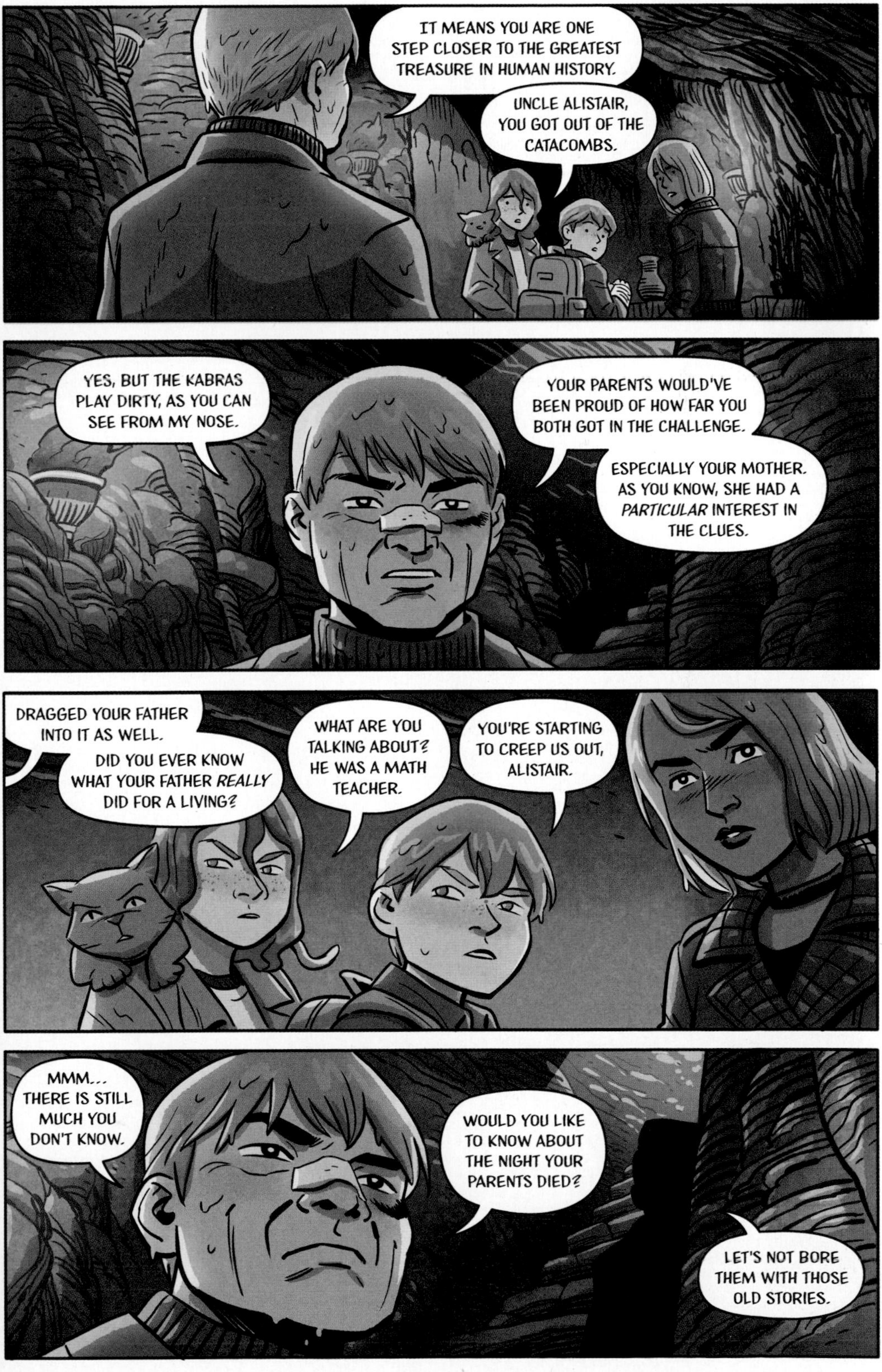
IT MEANS YOU ARE ONE STEP CLOSER TO THE GREATEST TREASURE IN HUMAN HISTORY.
UNCLE ALISTAIR, YOU GOT OUT OF THE CATACOMBS.
YES, BUT THE KABRAS PLAY DIRTY, AS YOU CAN SEE FROM MY NOSE.
YOUR PARENTS WOULD'VE BEEN PROUD OF HOW FAR YOU BOTH GOT IN THE CHALLENGE.
ESPECIALLY YOUR MOTHER. AS YOU KNOW, SHE HAD A *PARTICULAR* INTEREST IN THE CLUES.
DRAGGED YOUR FATHER INTO IT AS WELL.
DID YOU EVER KNOW WHAT YOUR FATHER *REALLY* DID FOR A LIVING?
WHAT ARE YOU TALKING ABOUT? HE WAS A MATH TEACHER.
YOU'RE STARTING TO CREEP US OUT, ALISTAIR.
MMM... THERE IS STILL MUCH YOU DON'T KNOW.
WOULD YOU LIKE TO KNOW ABOUT THE NIGHT YOUR PARENTS DIED?
LET'S NOT BORE THEM WITH THOSE OLD STORIES.

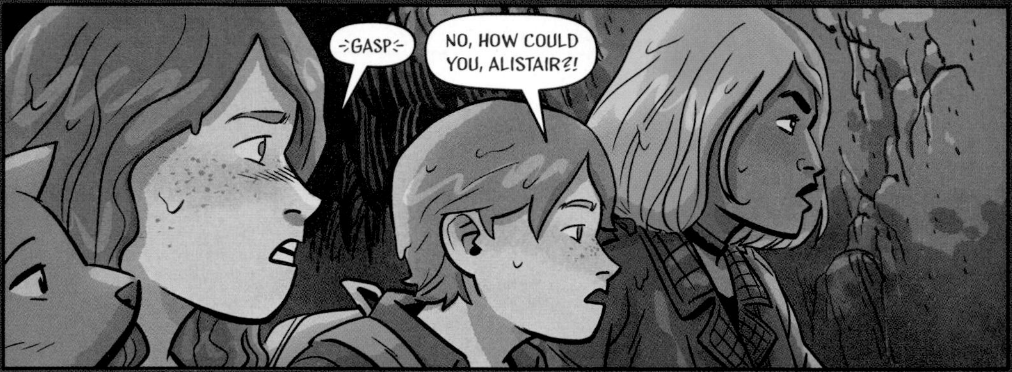
GASP
NO, HOW COULD YOU, ALISTAIR?!

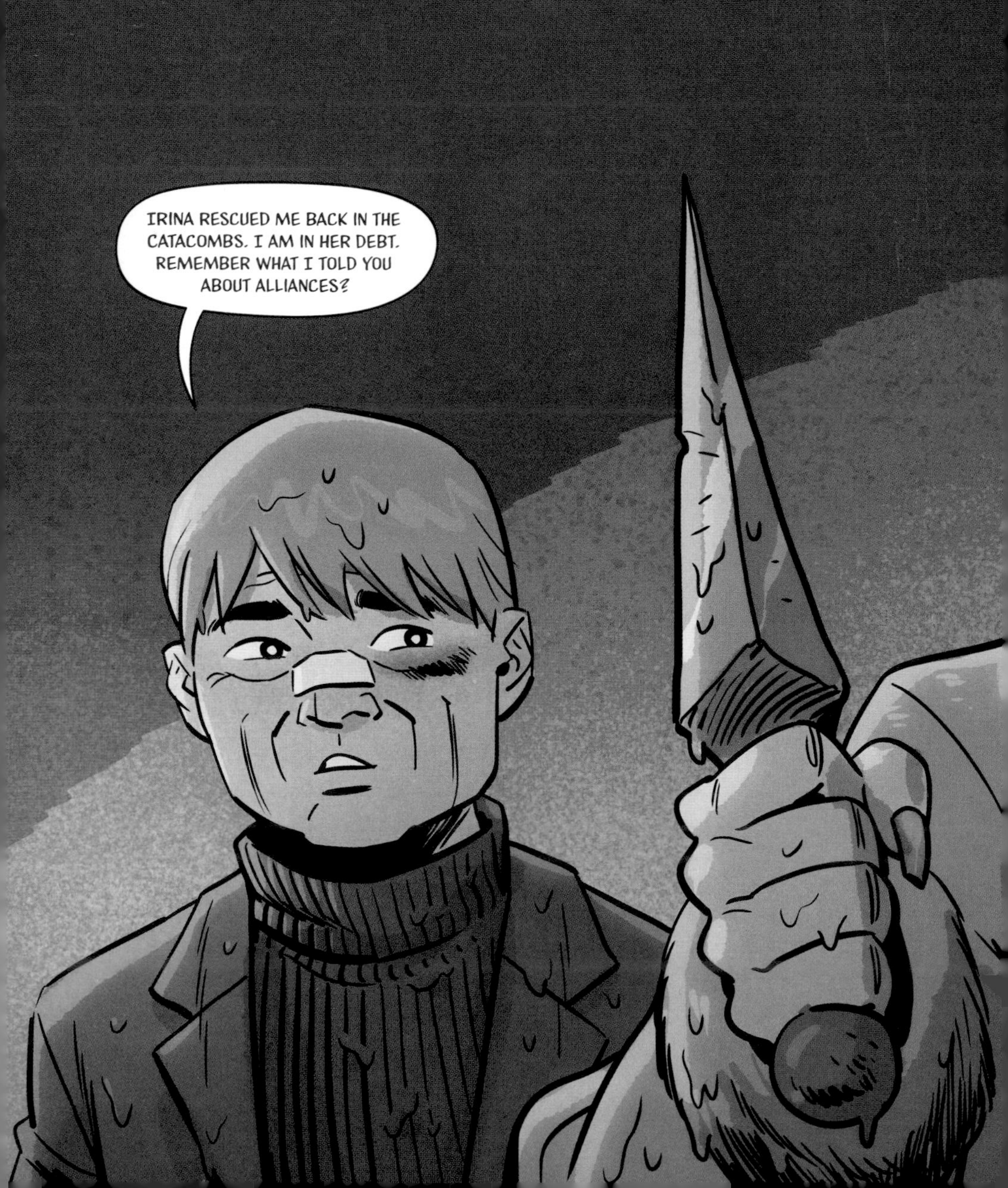
IRINA RESCUED ME BACK IN THE CATACOMBS. I AM IN HER DEBT. REMEMBER WHAT I TOLD YOU ABOUT ALLIANCES?

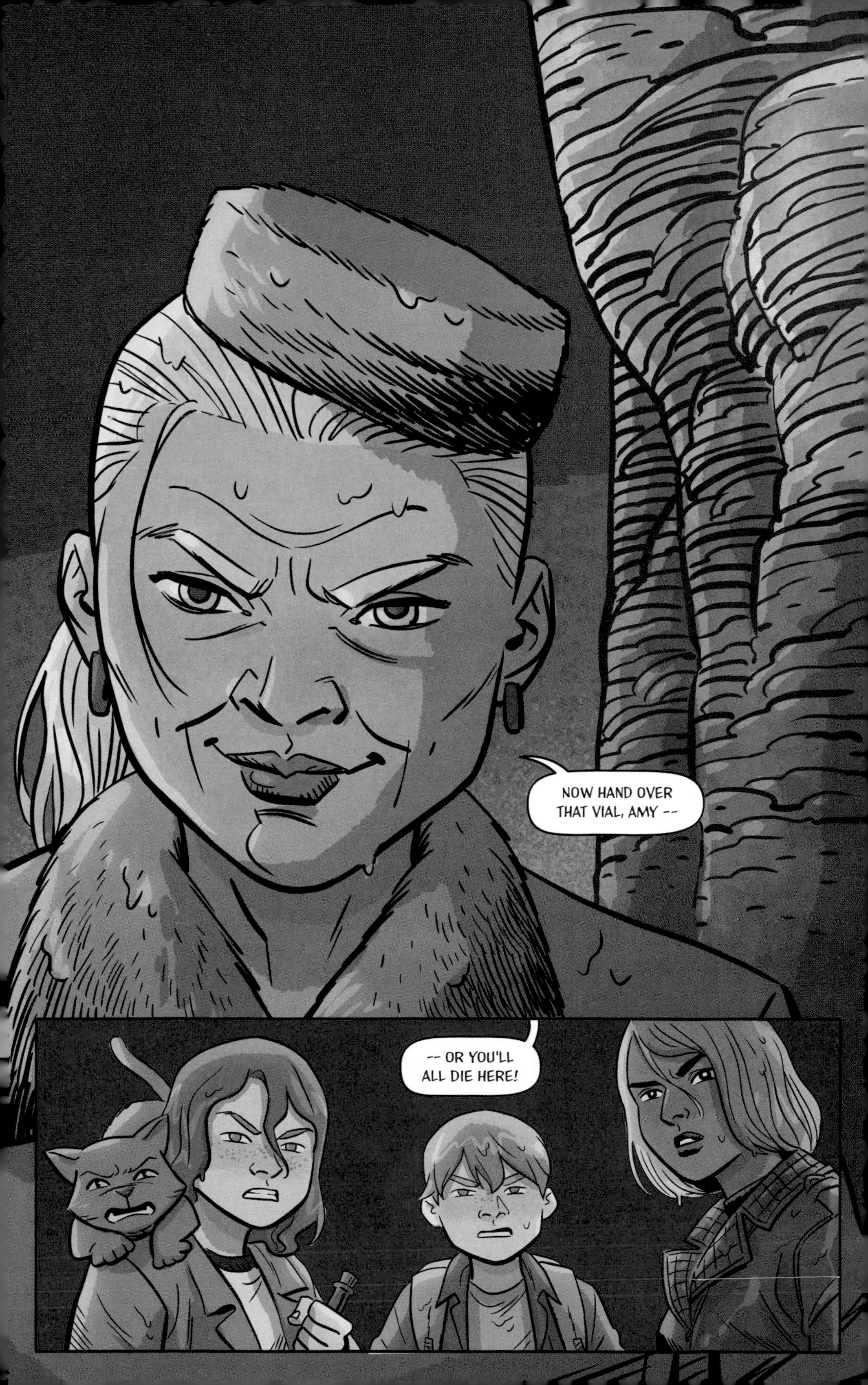
NOW HAND OVER THAT VIAL, AMY --
-- OR YOU'LL ALL DIE HERE!

NINE

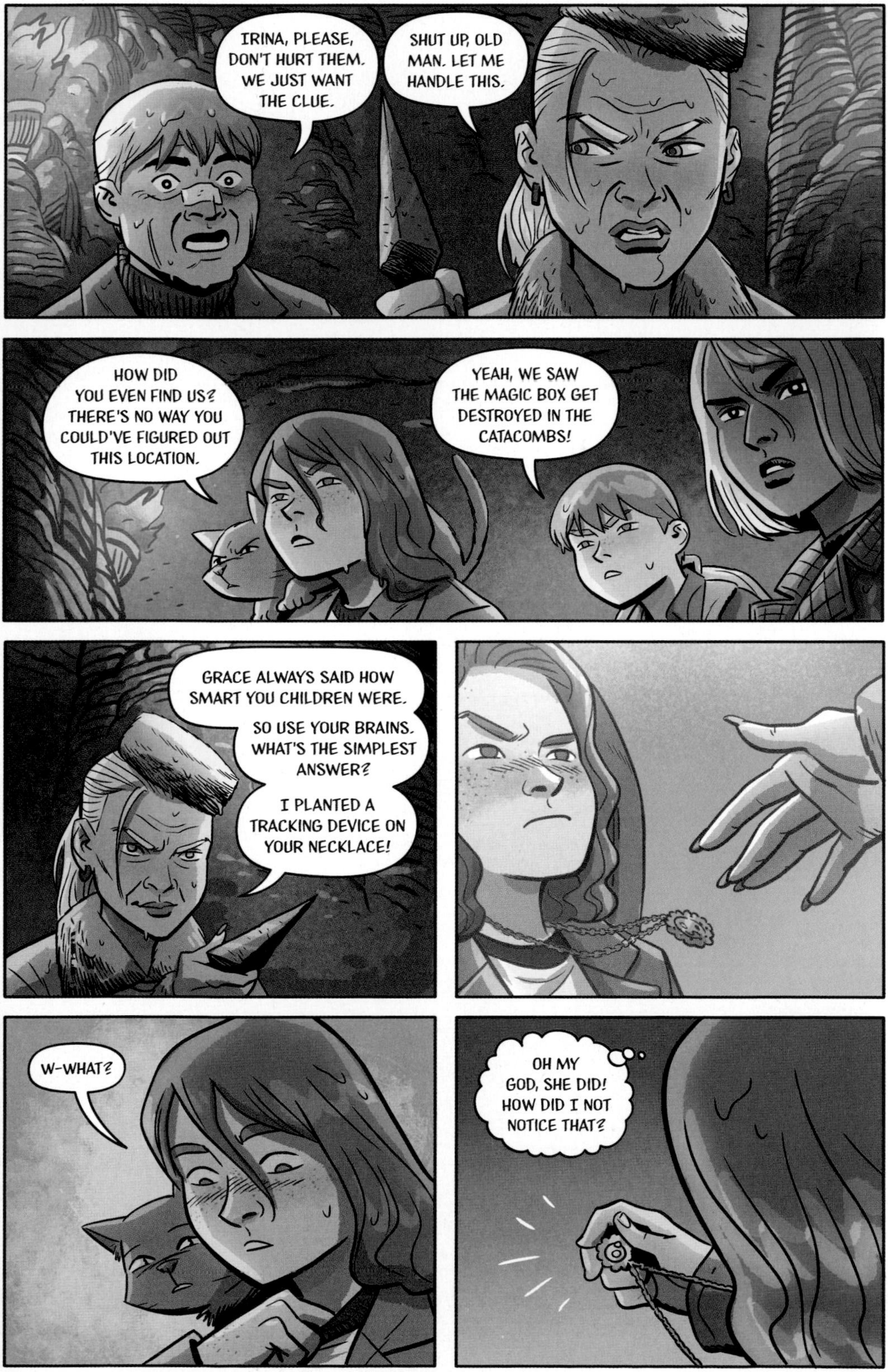
IRINA, PLEASE, DON'T HURT THEM. WE JUST WANT THE CLUE.
SHUT UP, OLD MAN. LET ME HANDLE THIS.
HOW DID YOU EVEN FIND US? THERE'S NO WAY YOU COULD'VE FIGURED OUT THIS LOCATION.
YEAH, WE SAW THE MAGIC BOX GET DESTROYED IN THE CATACOMBS!
GRACE ALWAYS SAID HOW SMART YOU CHILDREN WERE.
SO USE YOUR BRAINS. WHAT'S THE SIMPLEST ANSWER?
I PLANTED A TRACKING DEVICE ON YOUR NECKLACE!
W-WHAT?
OH MY GOD, SHE DID! HOW DID I NOT NOTICE THAT?

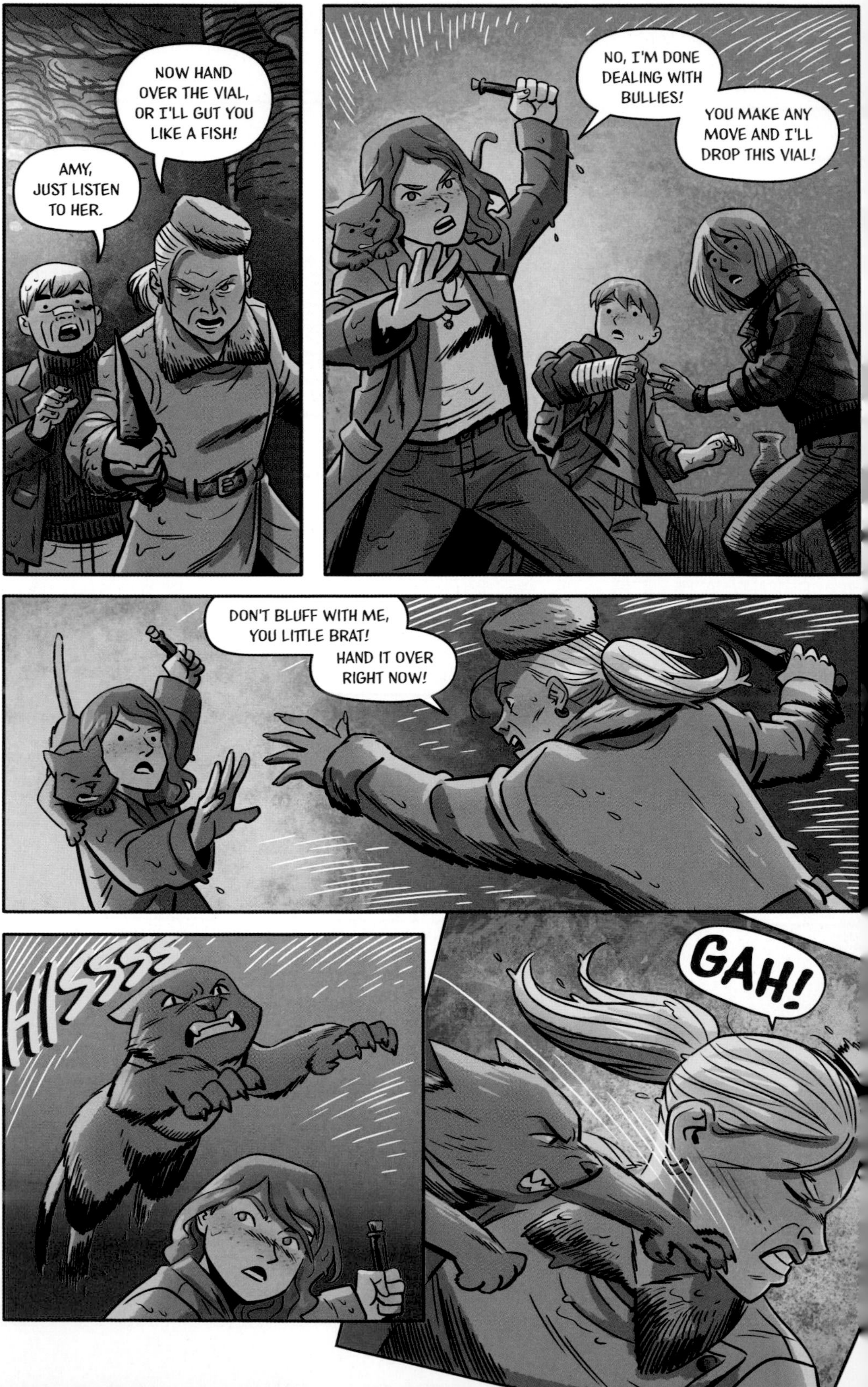
NOW HAND OVER THE VIAL, OR I'LL GUT YOU LIKE A FISH!
AMY, JUST LISTEN TO HER.
NO, I'M DONE DEALING WITH BULLIES!
YOU MAKE ANY MOVE AND I'LL DROP THIS VIAL!
DON'T BLUFF WITH ME, YOU LITTLE BRAT!
HAND IT OVER RIGHT NOW!
HISSSS
GAH!

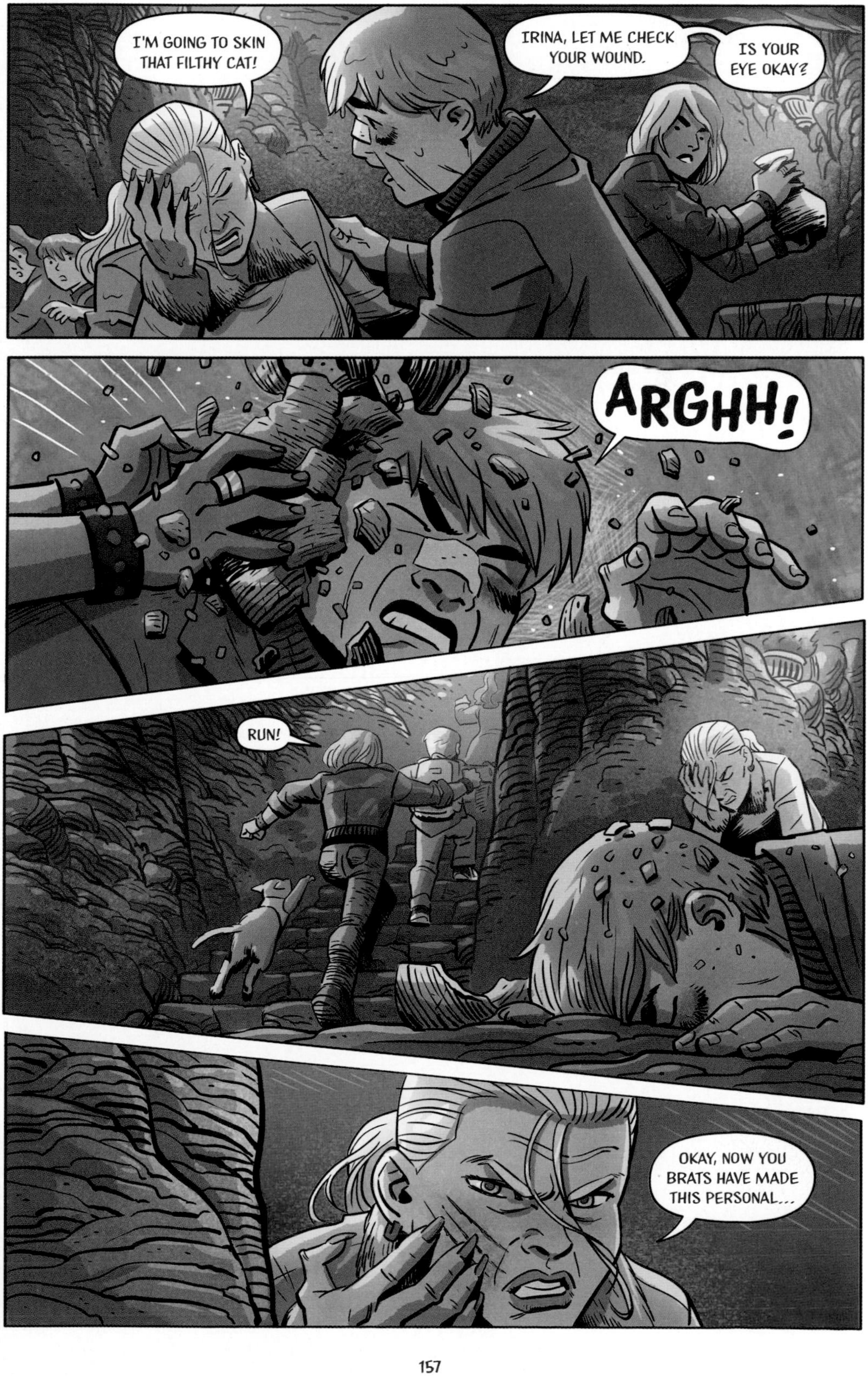
I'M GOING TO SKIN THAT FILTHY CAT!
IRINA, LET ME CHECK YOUR WOUND.
IS YOUR EYE OKAY?
ARGHH!
RUN!
OKAY, NOW YOU BRATS HAVE MADE THIS PERSONAL...

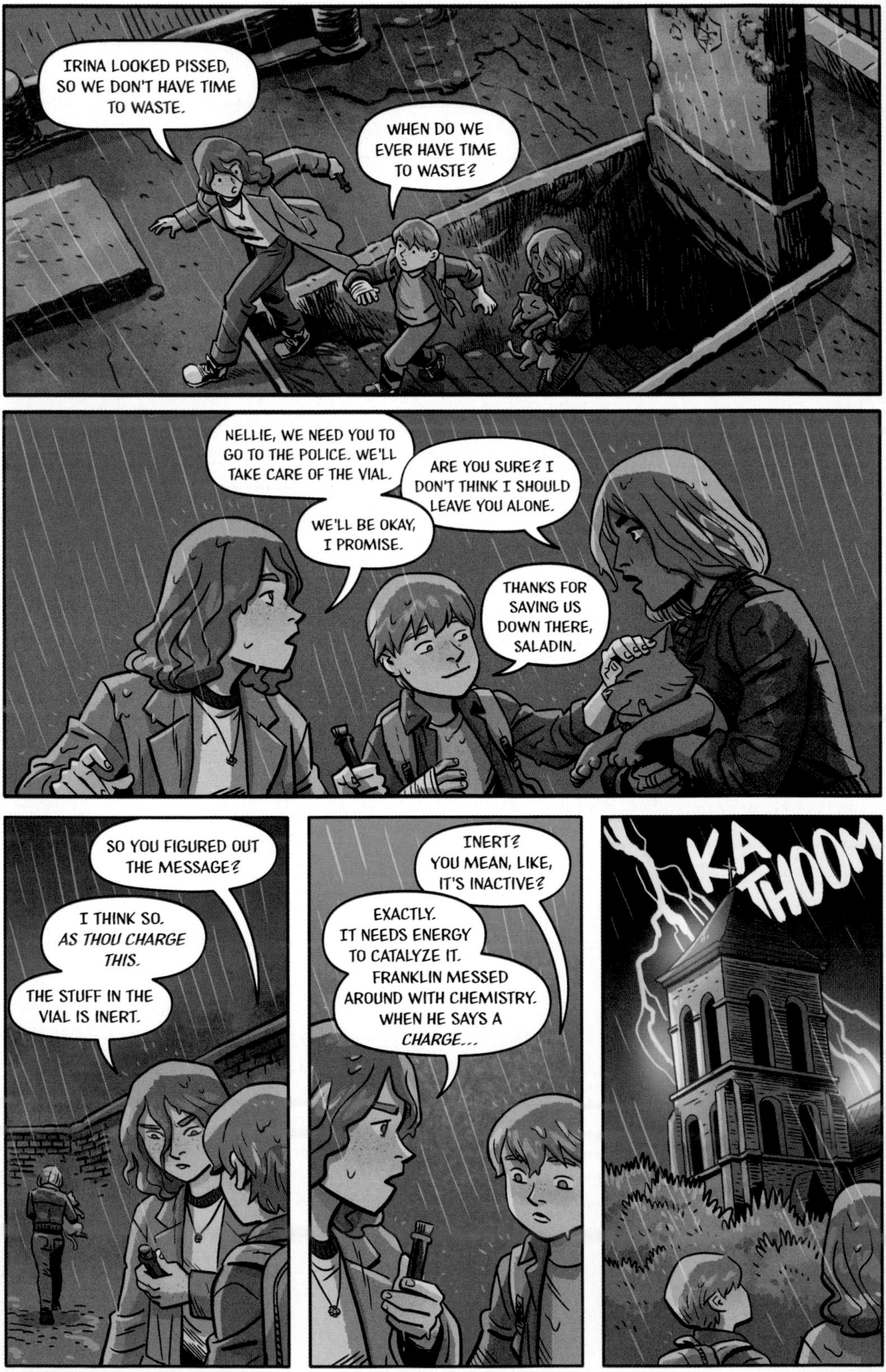
IRINA LOOKED PISSED, SO WE DON'T HAVE TIME TO WASTE.
WHEN DO WE EVER HAVE TIME TO WASTE?
NELLIE, WE NEED YOU TO GO TO THE POLICE. WE'LL TAKE CARE OF THE VIAL.
ARE YOU SURE? I DON'T THINK I SHOULD LEAVE YOU ALONE.
WE'LL BE OKAY, I PROMISE.
THANKS FOR SAVING US DOWN THERE, SALADIN.
SO YOU FIGURED OUT THE MESSAGE?
I THINK SO. *AS THOU CHARGE THIS.*
THE STUFF IN THE VIAL IS INERT.
INERT? YOU MEAN, LIKE, IT'S INACTIVE?
EXACTLY. IT NEEDS ENERGY TO CATALYZE IT. FRANKLIN MESSED AROUND WITH CHEMISTRY. WHEN HE SAYS A *CHARGE...*
KA THOOM

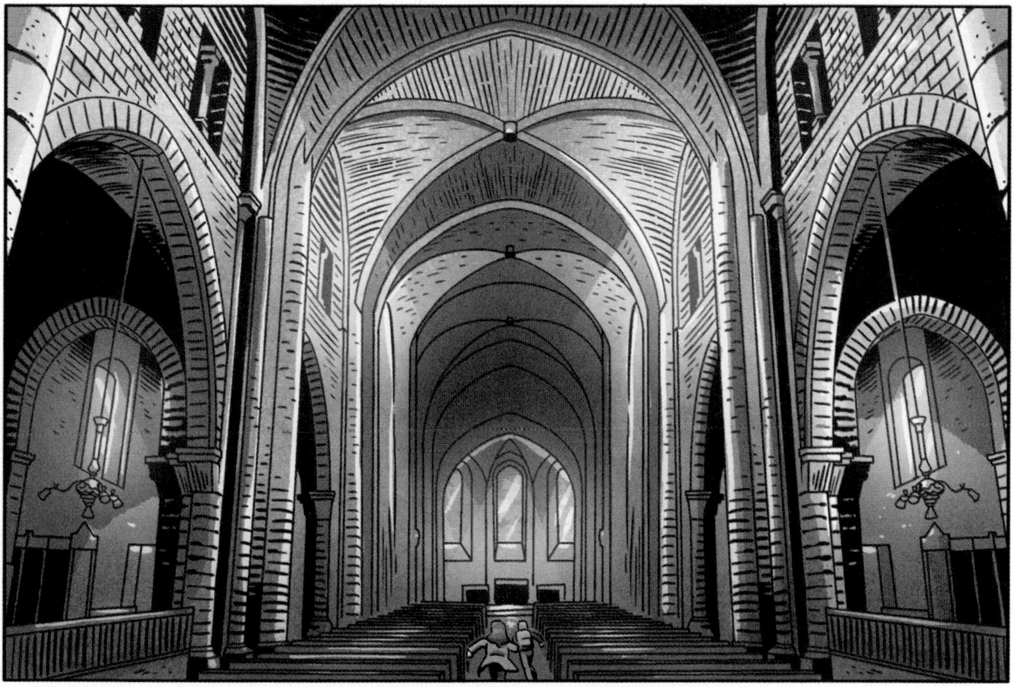

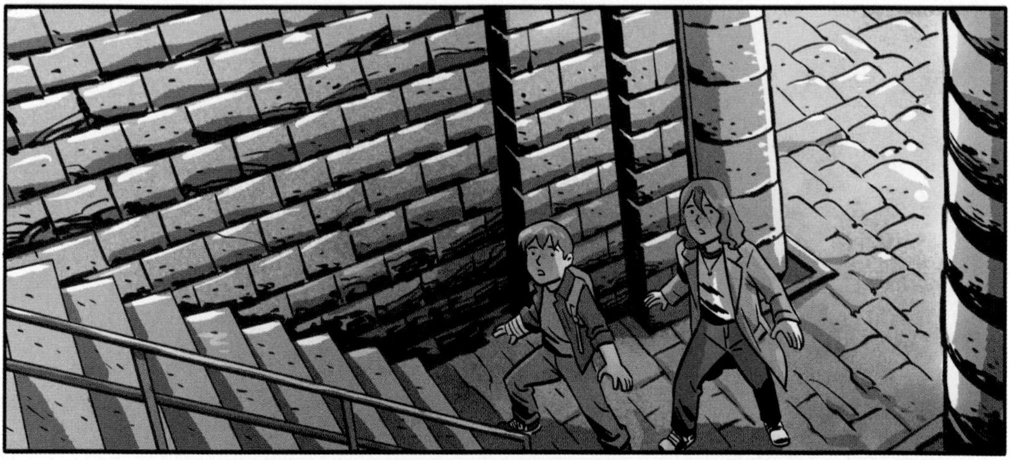

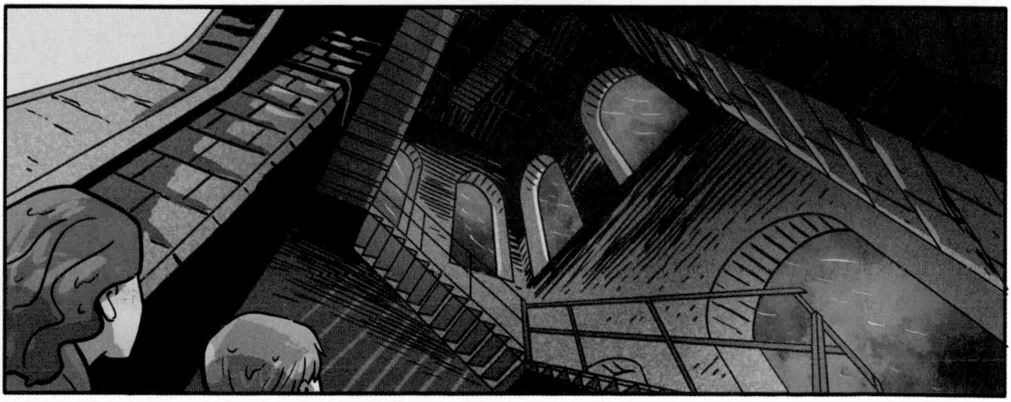

I AM NEVER SKIPPING GYM CLASS EVER AGAIN.
YEAH, BUT LOOK, WE MADE IT.
WOW, THAT'S... BIG.
SO HOW DO WE CHARGE THE VIAL WITHOUT BEING FRIED TO A CRISP?

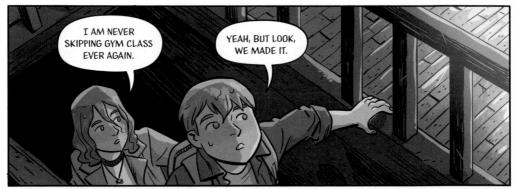

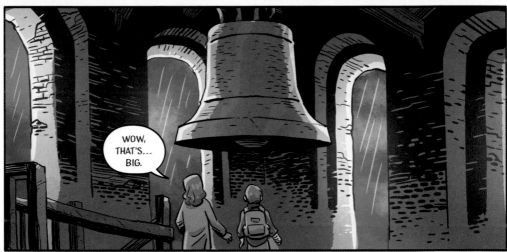

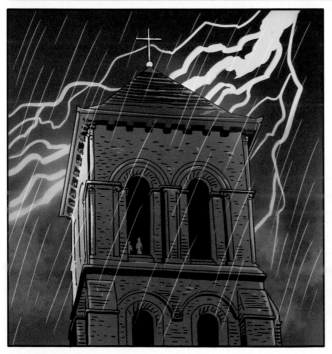

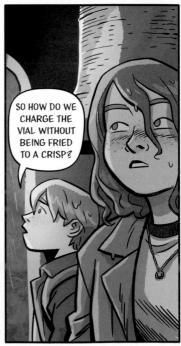

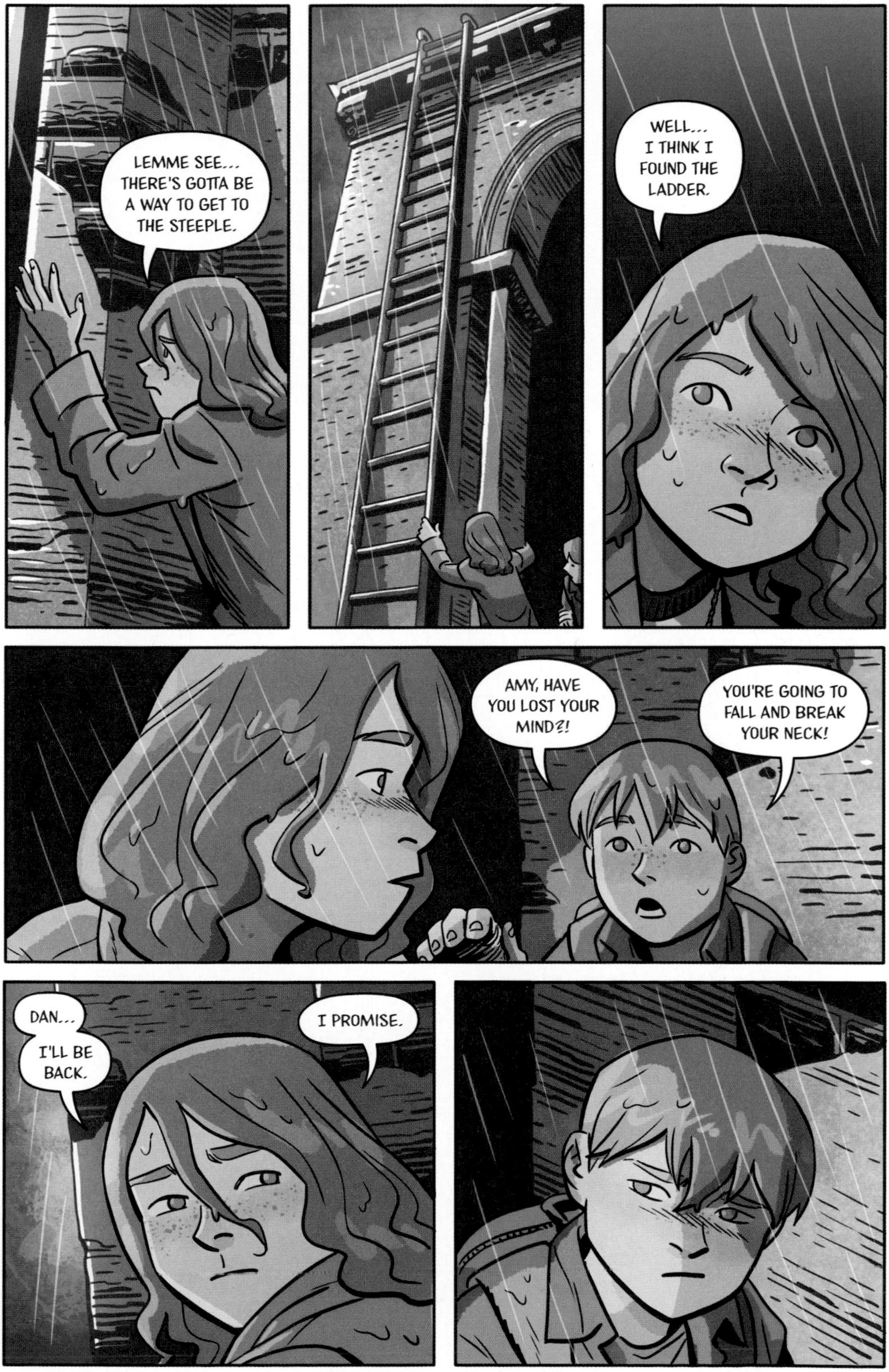
LEMME SEE... THERE'S GOTTA BE A WAY TO GET TO THE STEEPLE.
WELL... I THINK I FOUND THE LADDER.
AMY, HAVE YOU LOST YOUR MIND?!
YOU'RE GOING TO FALL AND BREAK YOUR NECK!
DAN...
I'LL BE BACK.
I PROMISE.

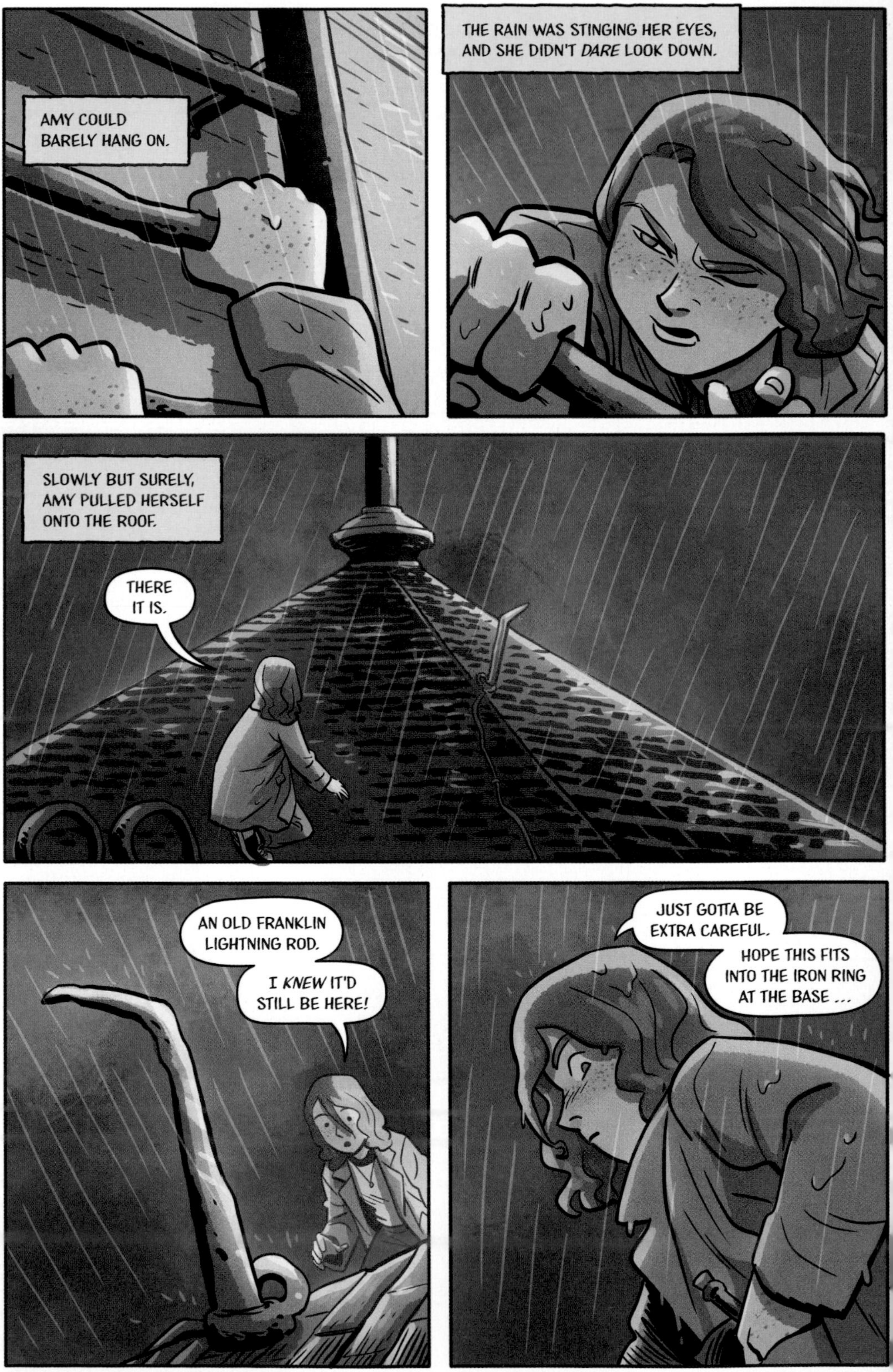
AMY COULD BARELY HANG ON.
THE RAIN WAS STINGING HER EYES, AND SHE DIDN'T *DARE* LOOK DOWN.
SLOWLY BUT SURELY, AMY PULLED HERSELF ONTO THE ROOF.
THERE IT IS.
AN OLD FRANKLIN LIGHTNING ROD.
I *KNEW* IT'D STILL BE HERE!
JUST GOTTA BE EXTRA CAREFUL.
HOPE THIS FITS INTO THE IRON RING AT THE BASE ...

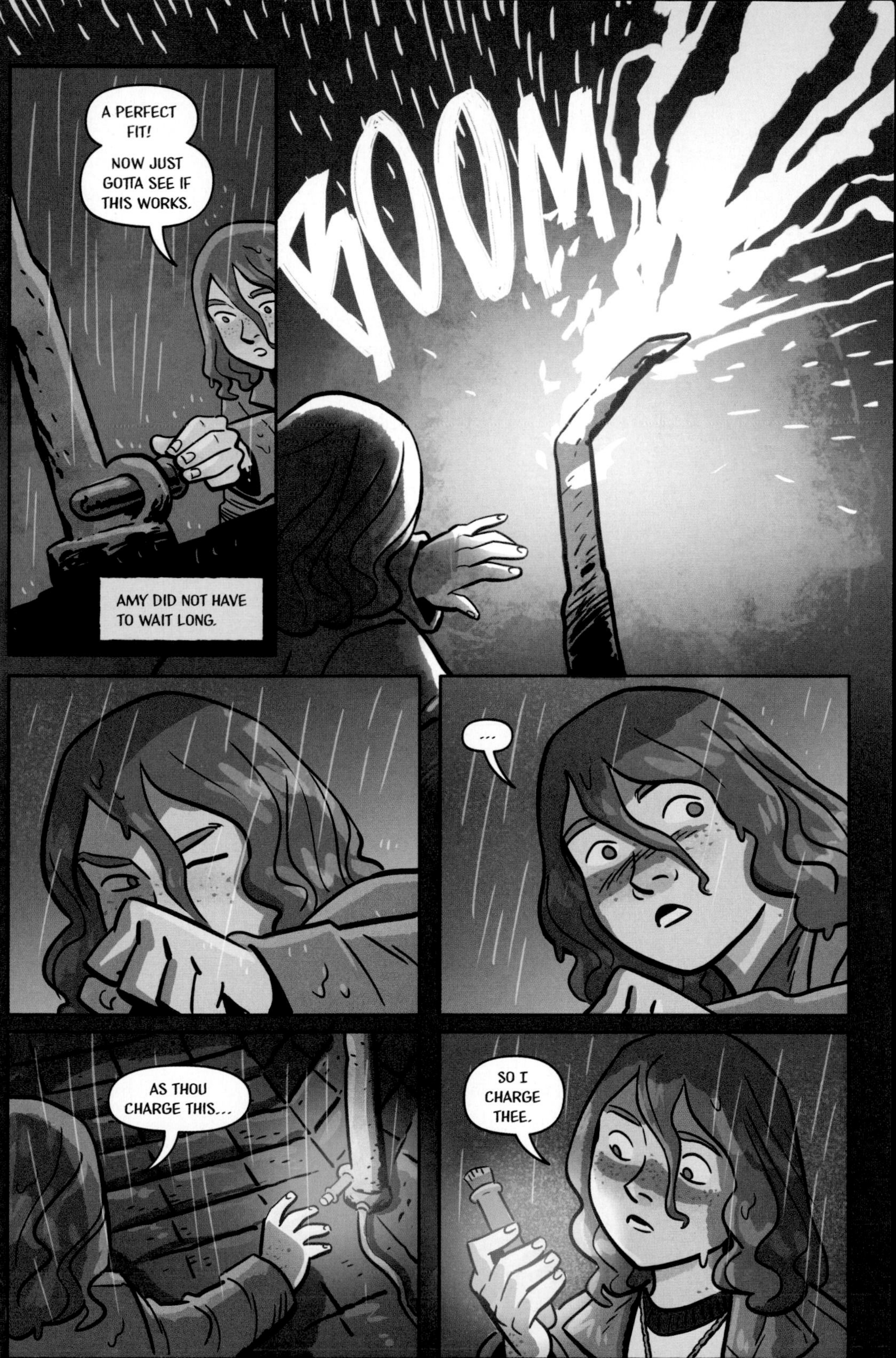
A PERFECT FIT!
NOW JUST GOTTA SEE IF THIS WORKS.
BOOM!
AMY DID NOT HAVE TO WAIT LONG.
...
AS THOU CHARGE THIS...
SO I CHARGE THEE.

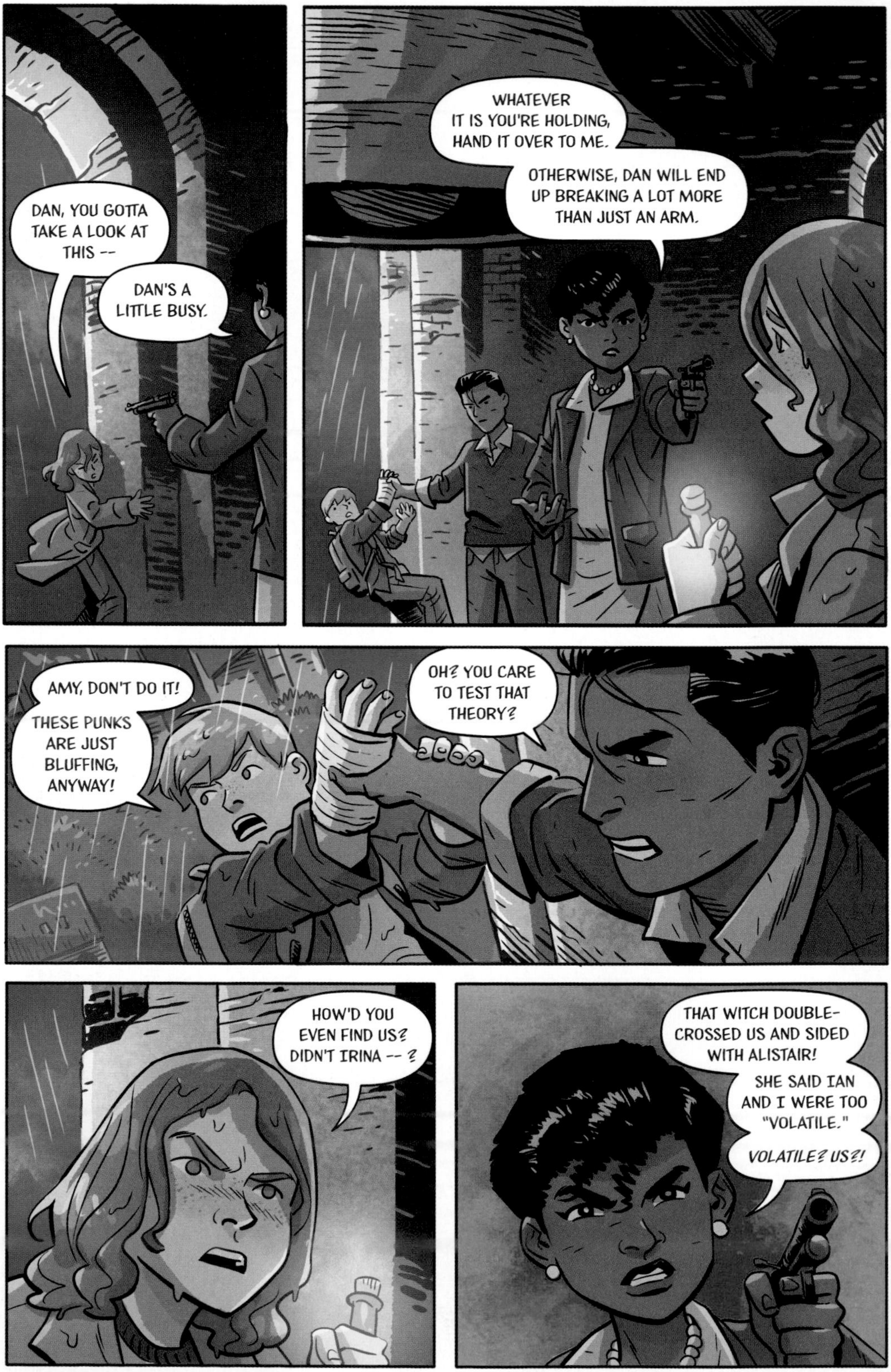
DAN, YOU GOTTA TAKE A LOOK AT THIS --
DAN'S A LITTLE BUSY.
WHATEVER IT IS YOU'RE HOLDING, HAND IT OVER TO ME.
OTHERWISE, DAN WILL END UP BREAKING A LOT MORE THAN JUST AN ARM.
AMY, DON'T DO IT!
THESE PUNKS ARE JUST BLUFFING, ANYWAY!
OH? YOU CARE TO TEST THAT THEORY?
HOW'D YOU EVEN FIND US? DIDN'T IRINA -- ?
THAT WITCH DOUBLE-CROSSED US AND SIDED WITH ALISTAIR!
SHE SAID IAN AND I WERE TOO "VOLATILE."
VOLATILE? US?!

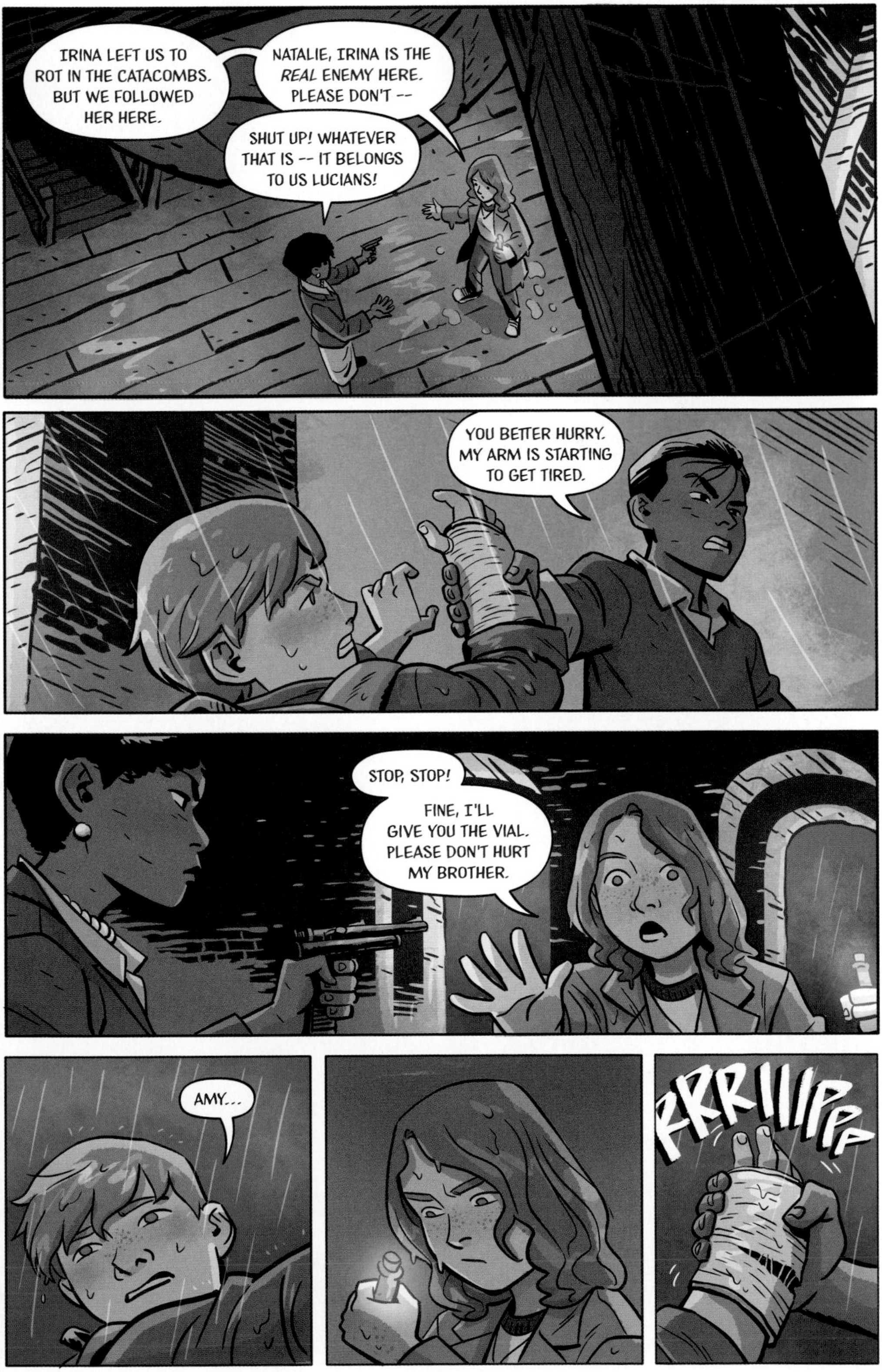
IRINA LEFT US TO ROT IN THE CATACOMBS. BUT WE FOLLOWED HER HERE.
NATALIE, IRINA IS THE *REAL* ENEMY HERE. PLEASE DON'T --
SHUT UP! WHATEVER THAT IS -- IT BELONGS TO US LUCIANS!
YOU BETTER HURRY. MY ARM IS STARTING TO GET TIRED.
STOP, STOP!
FINE, I'LL GIVE YOU THE VIAL. PLEASE DON'T HURT MY BROTHER.
AMY...
RRRIIIPPP

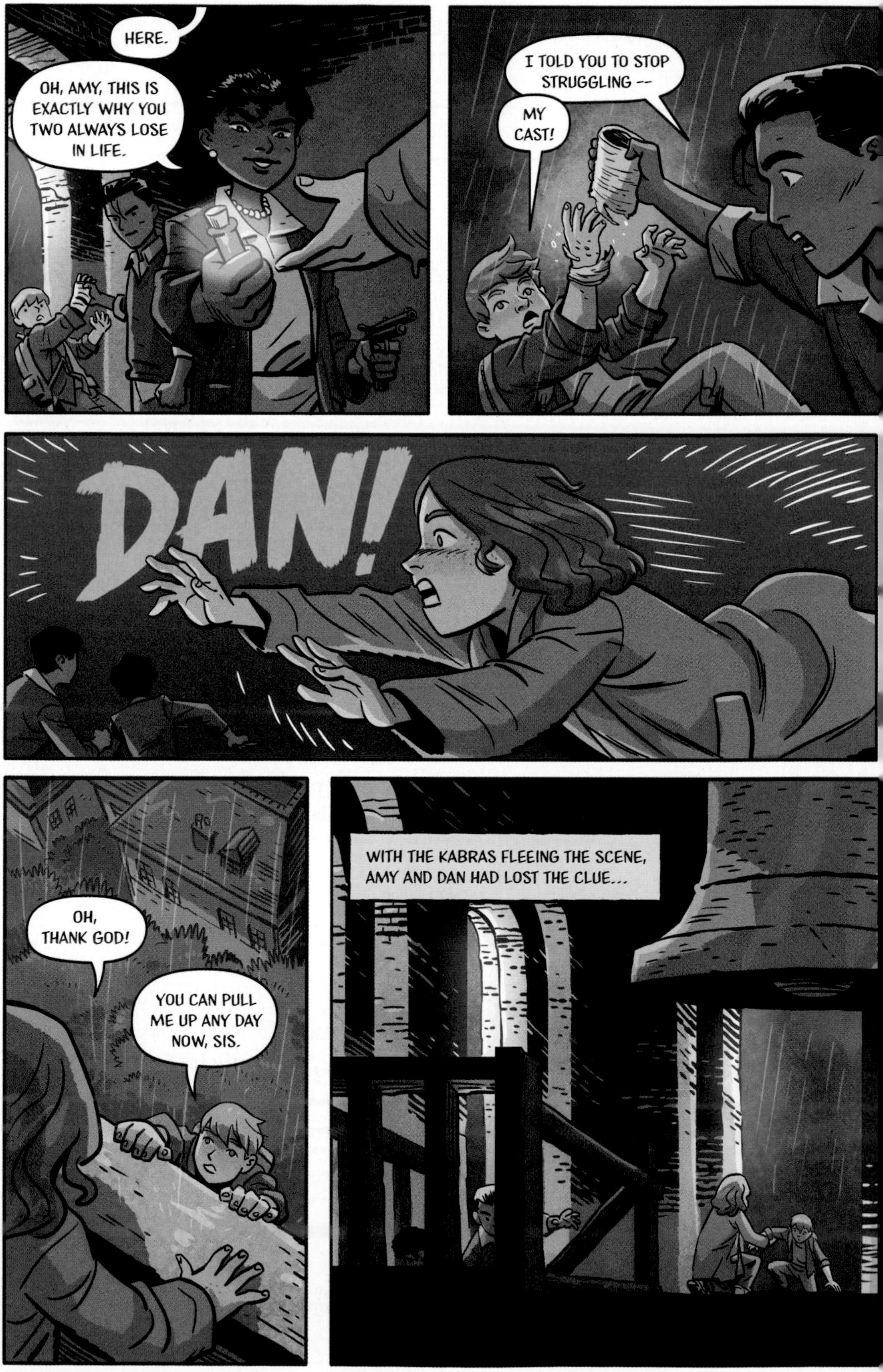
HERE.
OH, AMY, THIS IS EXACTLY WHY YOU TWO ALWAYS LOSE IN LIFE.
I TOLD YOU TO STOP STRUGGLING --
MY CAST!
DAN!
WITH THE KABRAS FLEEING THE SCENE, AMY AND DAN HAD LOST THE CLUE...
OH, THANK GOD!
YOU CAN PULL ME UP ANY DAY NOW, SIS.

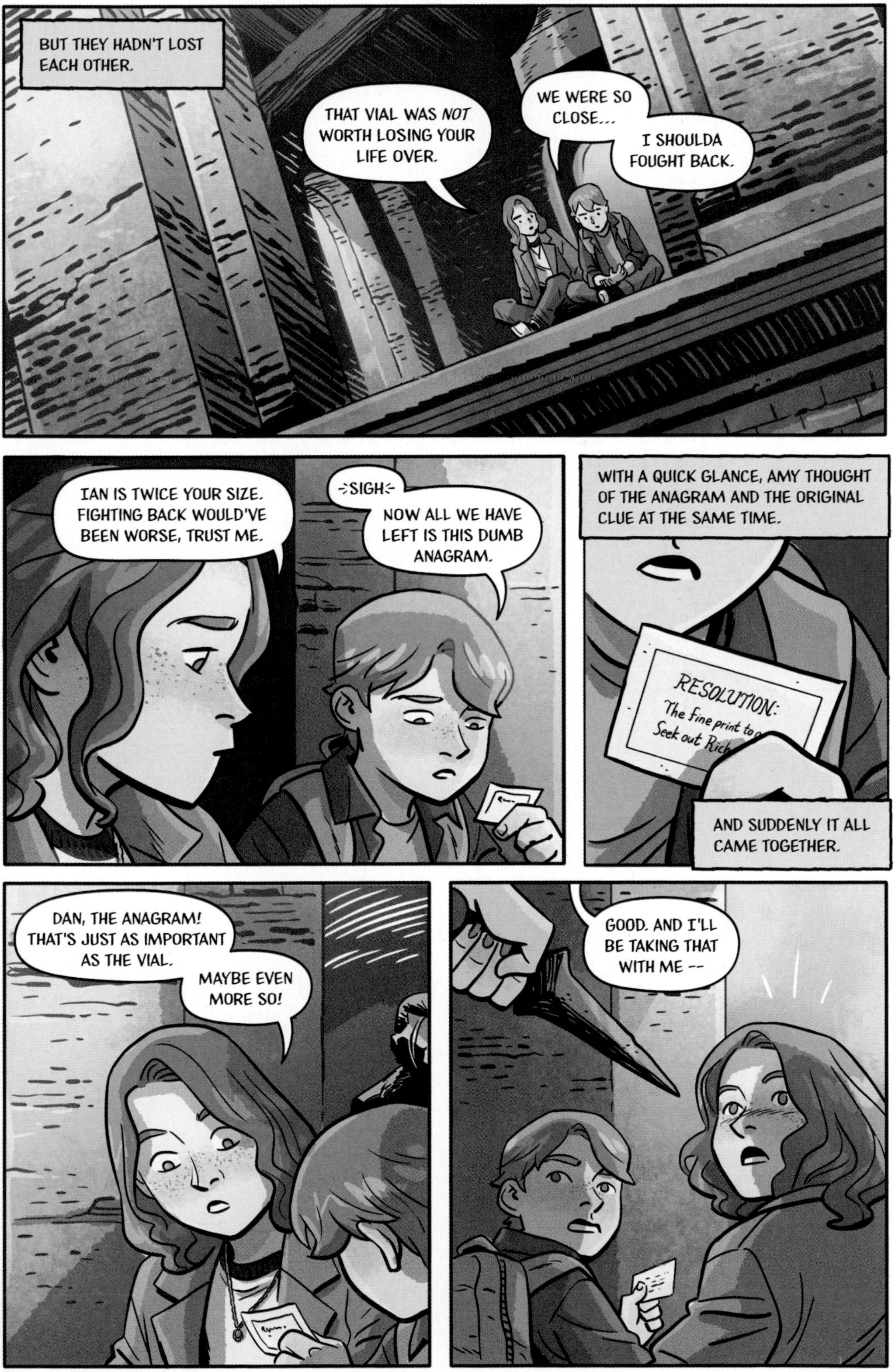
BUT THEY HADN'T LOST EACH OTHER.
THAT VIAL WAS *NOT* WORTH LOSING YOUR LIFE OVER.
WE WERE SO CLOSE...
I SHOULDA FOUGHT BACK.
IAN IS TWICE YOUR SIZE. FIGHTING BACK WOULD'VE BEEN WORSE, TRUST ME.
-SIGH-
NOW ALL WE HAVE LEFT IS THIS DUMB ANAGRAM.
WITH A QUICK GLANCE, AMY THOUGHT OF THE ANAGRAM AND THE ORIGINAL CLUE AT THE SAME TIME.
RESOLUTION:
The fine print to
Seek out Rich
AND SUDDENLY IT ALL CAME TOGETHER.
DAN, THE ANAGRAM! THAT'S JUST AS IMPORTANT AS THE VIAL.
MAYBE EVEN MORE SO!
GOOD. AND I'LL BE TAKING THAT WITH ME --

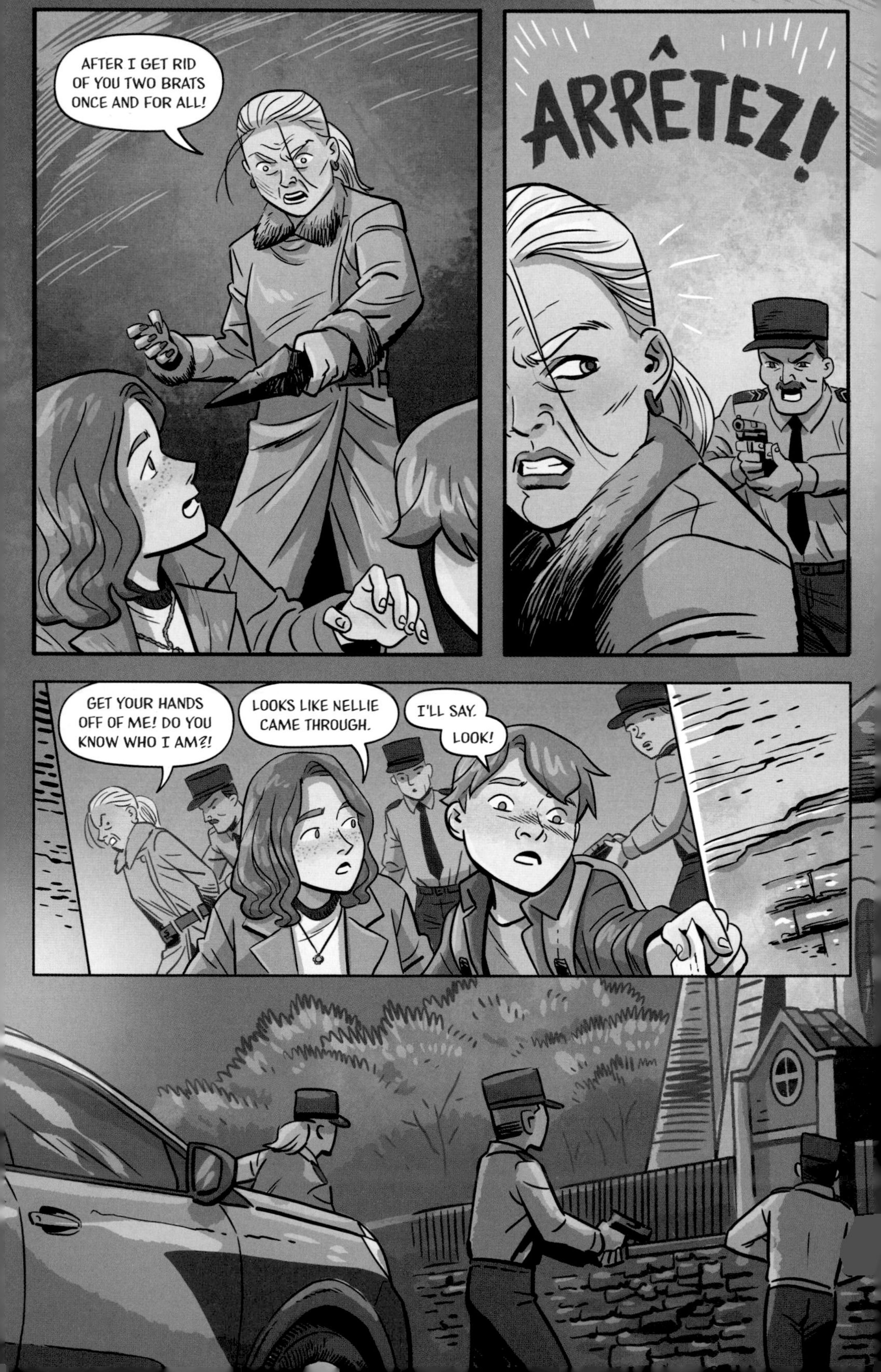

AFTER I GET RID OF YOU TWO BRATS ONCE AND FOR ALL!
ARRÊTEZ!
GET YOUR HANDS OFF OF ME! DO YOU KNOW WHO I AM?!
LOOKS LIKE NELLIE CAME THROUGH.
I'LL SAY.
LOOK!

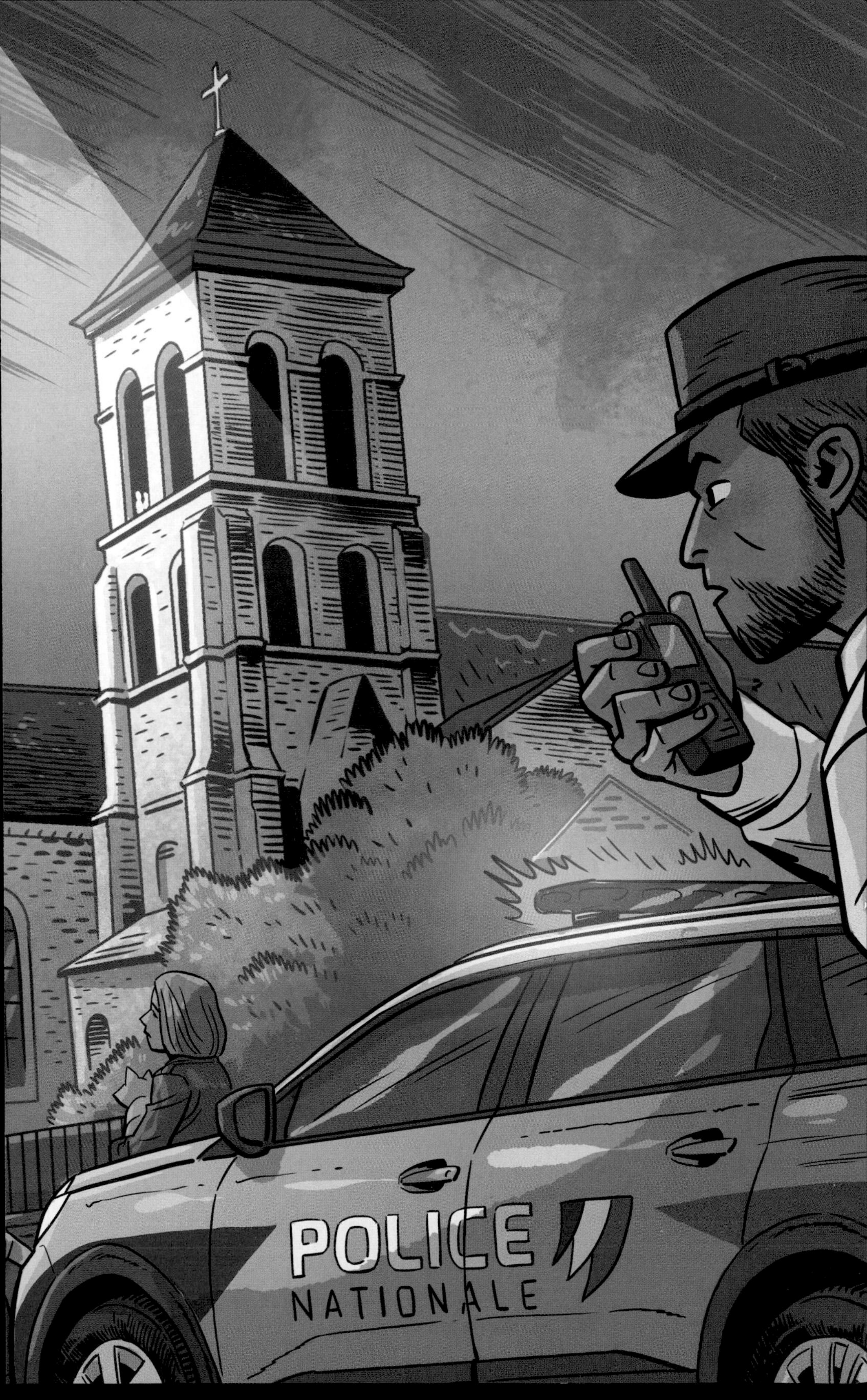
POLICE
NATIONALE

TEN

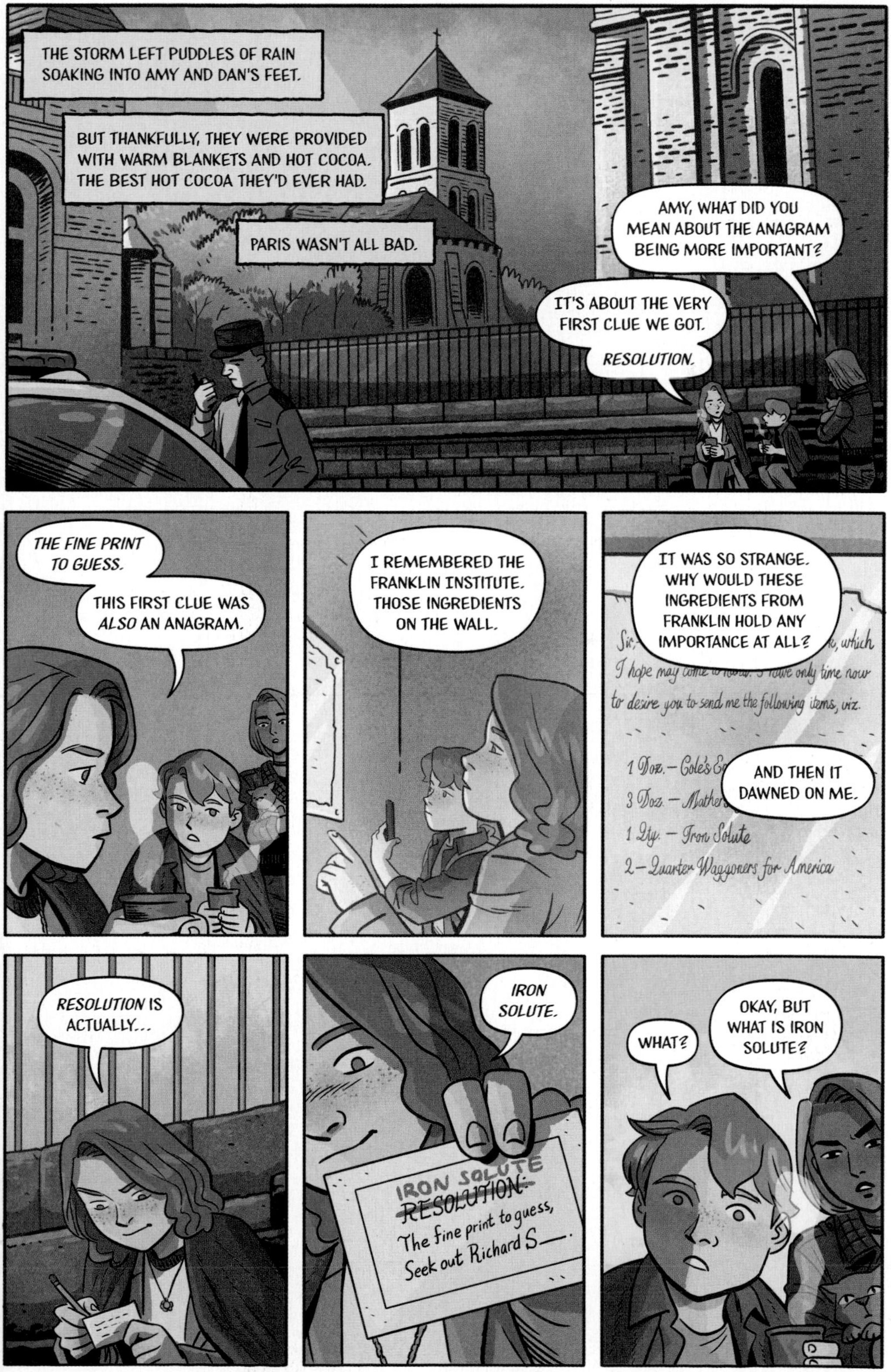
THE STORM LEFT PUDDLES OF RAIN SOAKING INTO AMY AND DAN'S FEET.
BUT THANKFULLY, THEY WERE PROVIDED WITH WARM BLANKETS AND HOT COCOA. THE BEST HOT COCOA THEY'D EVER HAD.
PARIS WASN'T ALL BAD.
AMY, WHAT DID YOU MEAN ABOUT THE ANAGRAM BEING MORE IMPORTANT?
IT'S ABOUT THE VERY FIRST CLUE WE GOT.
RESOLUTION.
THE FINE PRINT TO GUESS.
THIS FIRST CLUE WAS *ALSO* AN ANAGRAM.
I REMEMBERED THE FRANKLIN INSTITUTE. THOSE INGREDIENTS ON THE WALL.
IT WAS SO STRANGE. WHY WOULD THESE INGREDIENTS FROM FRANKLIN HOLD ANY IMPORTANCE AT ALL?
I hope may come to hand. I have only time now to desire you to send me the following items, viz.
1 Doz. — Cole's
3 Doz. — Mathers
1 Qty. — Iron Solute
2 — Quarter Waggoners for America
AND THEN IT DAWNED ON ME.
RESOLUTION IS ACTUALLY...
IRON SOLUTE.
IRON SOLUTE
RESOLUTION:
The fine print to guess,
Seek out Richard S___.
WHAT?
OKAY, BUT WHAT IS IRON SOLUTE?

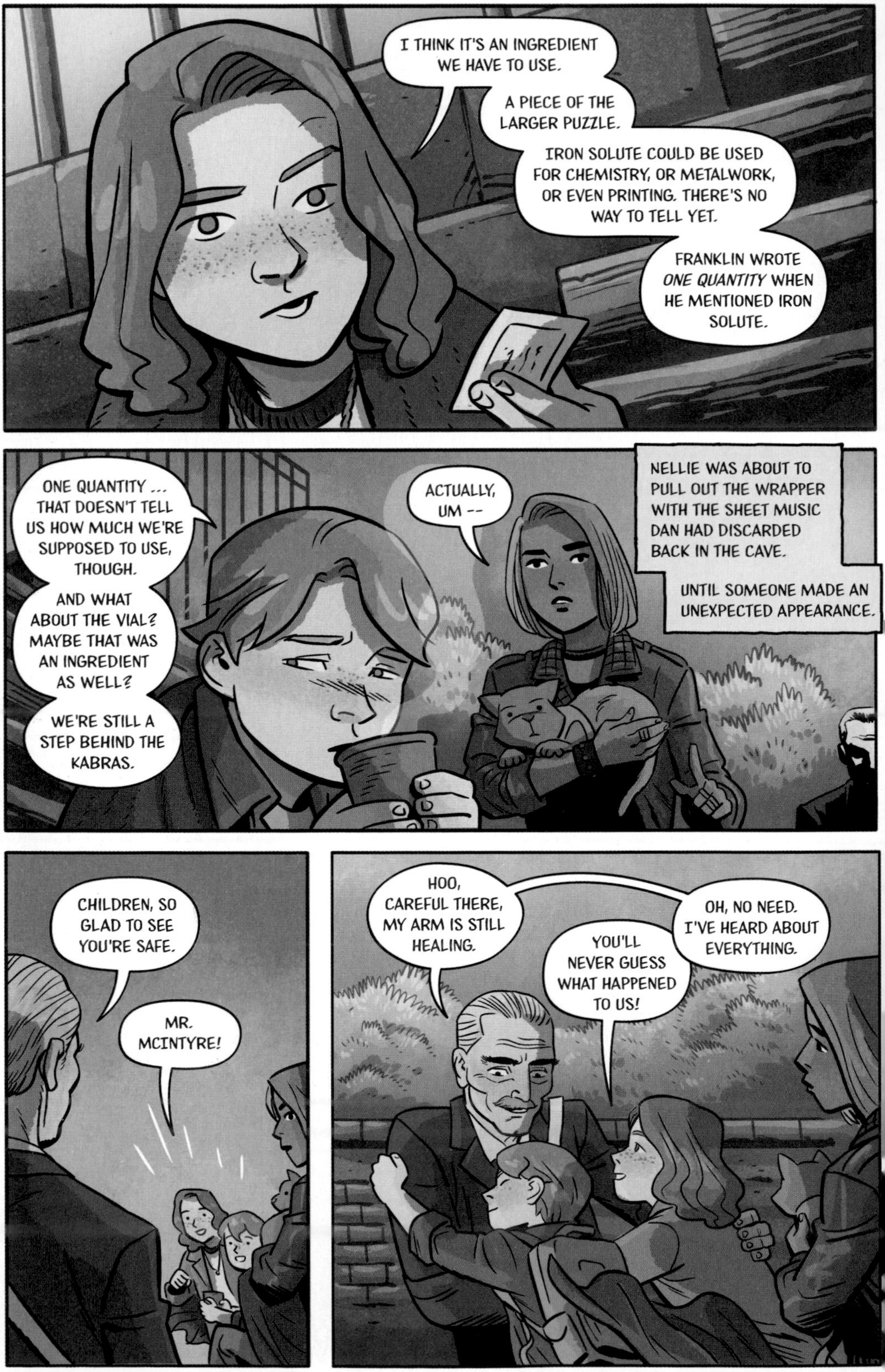
I THINK IT'S AN INGREDIENT WE HAVE TO USE.
A PIECE OF THE LARGER PUZZLE.
IRON SOLUTE COULD BE USED FOR CHEMISTRY, OR METALWORK, OR EVEN PRINTING. THERE'S NO WAY TO TELL YET.
FRANKLIN WROTE *ONE QUANTITY* WHEN HE MENTIONED IRON SOLUTE.
ONE QUANTITY ... THAT DOESN'T TELL US HOW MUCH WE'RE SUPPOSED TO USE, THOUGH.
AND WHAT ABOUT THE VIAL? MAYBE THAT WAS AN INGREDIENT AS WELL?
WE'RE STILL A STEP BEHIND THE KABRAS.
ACTUALLY, UM --
NELLIE WAS ABOUT TO PULL OUT THE WRAPPER WITH THE SHEET MUSIC DAN HAD DISCARDED BACK IN THE CAVE.
UNTIL SOMEONE MADE AN UNEXPECTED APPEARANCE.
CHILDREN, SO GLAD TO SEE YOU'RE SAFE.
MR. MCINTYRE!
HOO, CAREFUL THERE, MY ARM IS STILL HEALING.
YOU'LL NEVER GUESS WHAT HAPPENED TO US!
OH, NO NEED. I'VE HEARD ABOUT EVERYTHING.

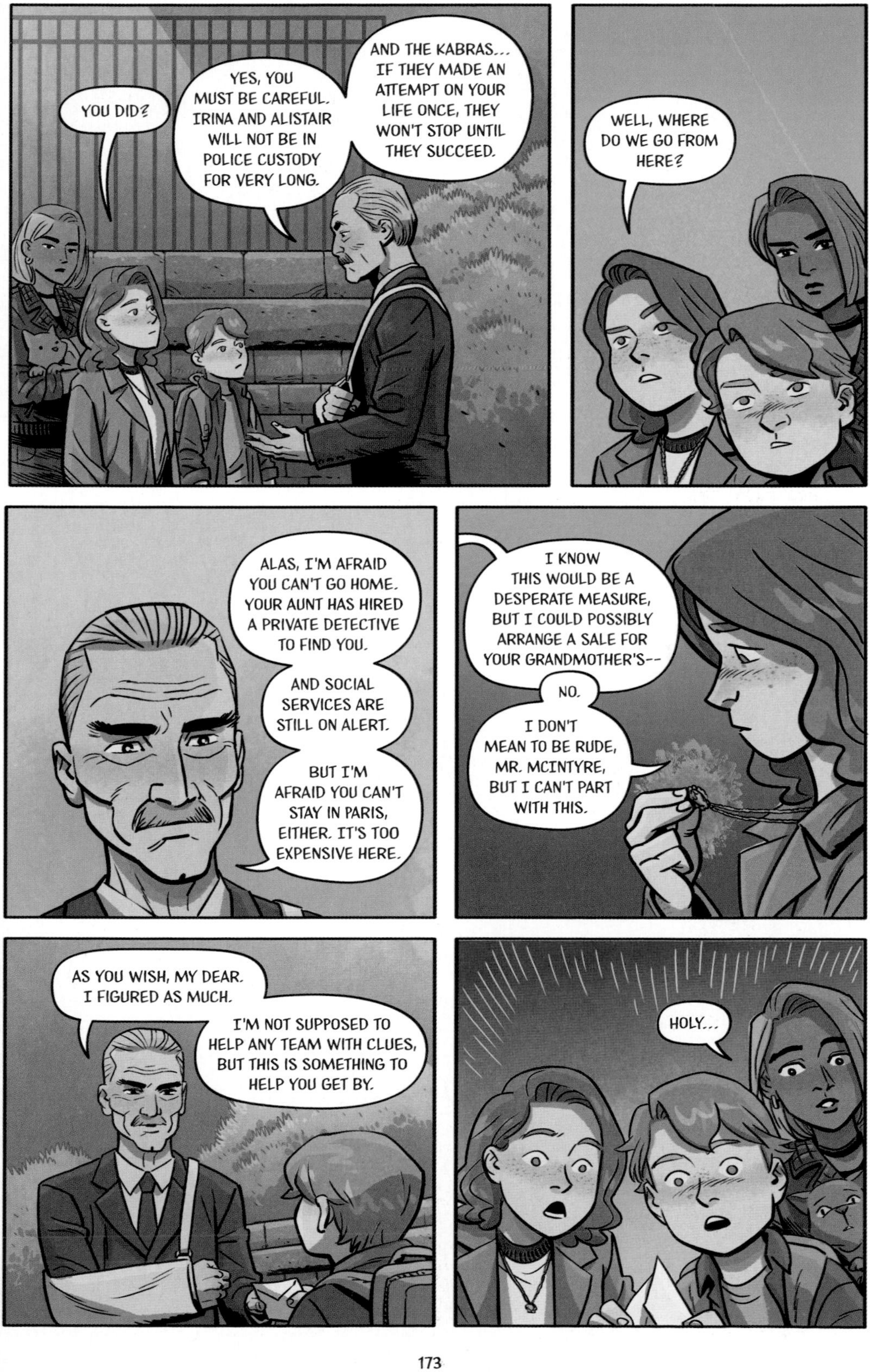
YOU DID?
YES, YOU MUST BE CAREFUL. IRINA AND ALISTAIR WILL NOT BE IN POLICE CUSTODY FOR VERY LONG.
AND THE KABRAS... IF THEY MADE AN ATTEMPT ON YOUR LIFE ONCE, THEY WON'T STOP UNTIL THEY SUCCEED.
WELL, WHERE DO WE GO FROM HERE?
ALAS, I'M AFRAID YOU CAN'T GO HOME. YOUR AUNT HAS HIRED A PRIVATE DETECTIVE TO FIND YOU.
AND SOCIAL SERVICES ARE STILL ON ALERT.
BUT I'M AFRAID YOU CAN'T STAY IN PARIS, EITHER. IT'S TOO EXPENSIVE HERE.
I KNOW THIS WOULD BE A DESPERATE MEASURE, BUT I COULD POSSIBLY ARRANGE A SALE FOR YOUR GRANDMOTHER'S--
NO.
I DON'T MEAN TO BE RUDE, MR. MCINTYRE, BUT I CAN'T PART WITH THIS.
AS YOU WISH, MY DEAR. I FIGURED AS MUCH.
I'M NOT SUPPOSED TO HELP ANY TEAM WITH CLUES, BUT THIS IS SOMETHING TO HELP YOU GET BY.
HOLY...

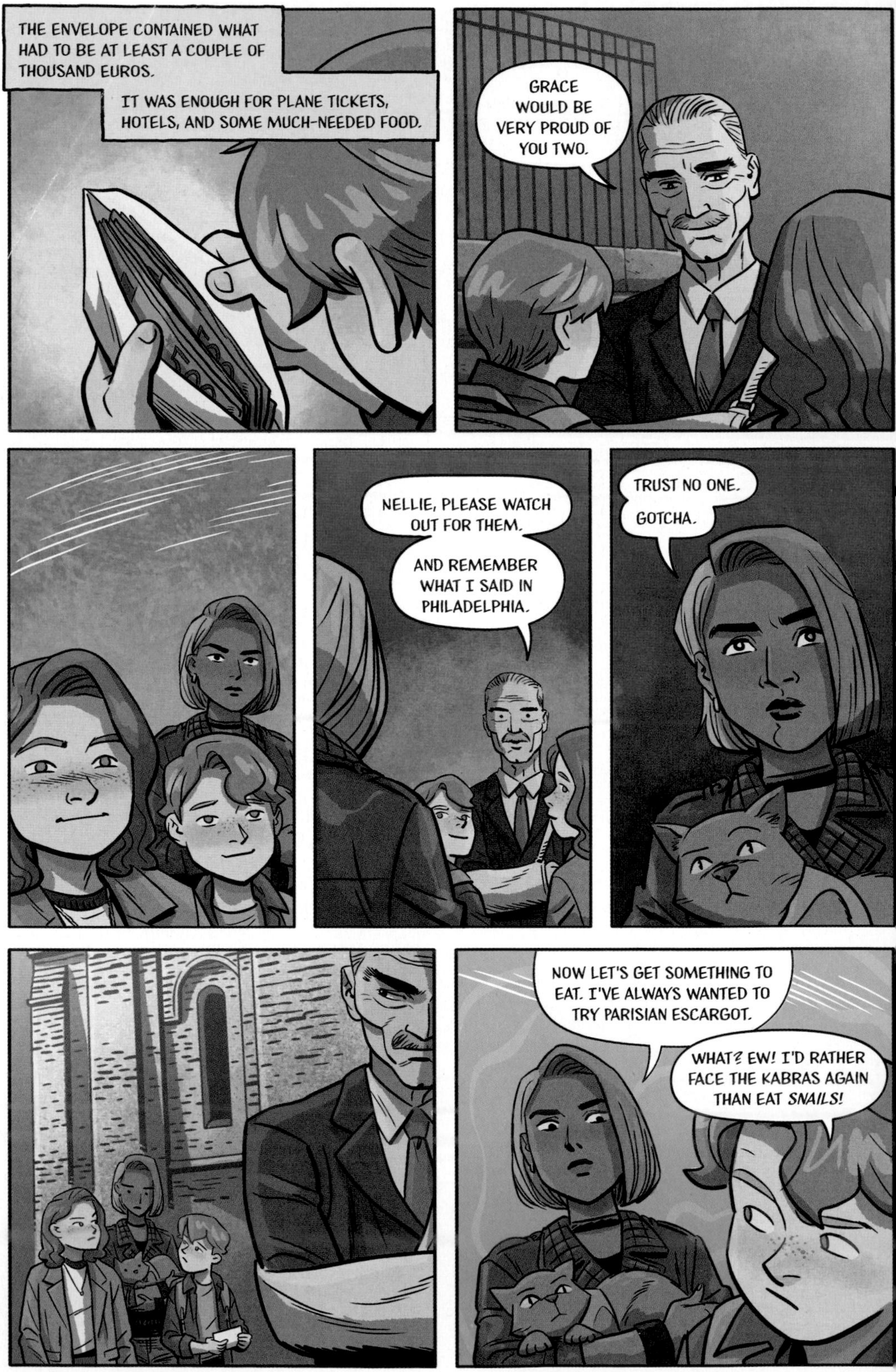
THE ENVELOPE CONTAINED WHAT HAD TO BE AT LEAST A COUPLE OF THOUSAND EUROS.
IT WAS ENOUGH FOR PLANE TICKETS, HOTELS, AND SOME MUCH-NEEDED FOOD.
GRACE WOULD BE VERY PROUD OF YOU TWO.
NELLIE, PLEASE WATCH OUT FOR THEM.
AND REMEMBER WHAT I SAID IN PHILADELPHIA.
TRUST NO ONE.
GOTCHA.
NOW LET'S GET SOMETHING TO EAT. I'VE ALWAYS WANTED TO TRY PARISIAN ESCARGOT.
WHAT? EW! I'D RATHER FACE THE KABRAS AGAIN THAN EAT *SNAILS!*

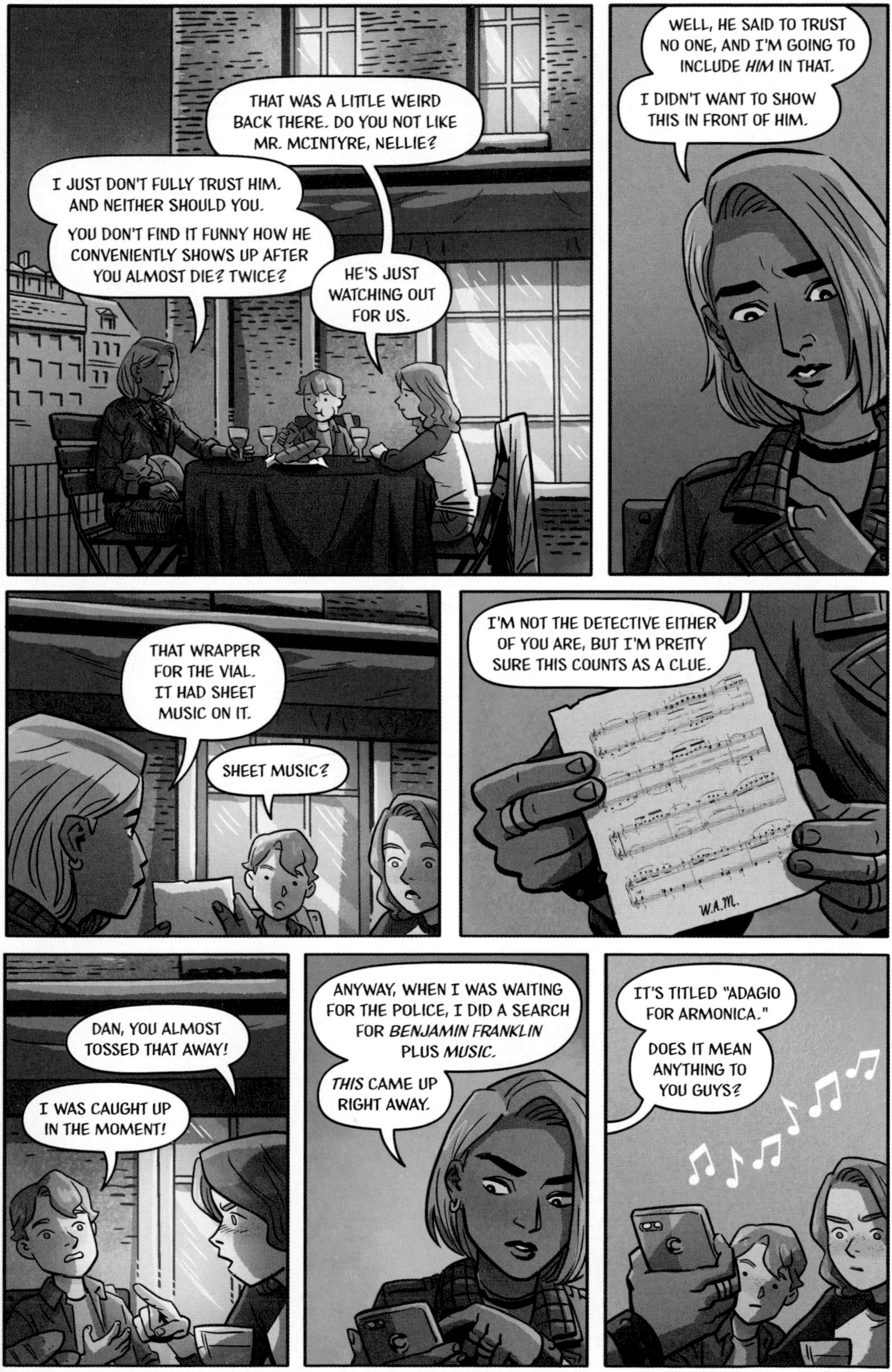
THAT WAS A LITTLE WEIRD BACK THERE. DO YOU NOT LIKE MR. MCINTYRE, NELLIE?
I JUST DON'T FULLY TRUST HIM. AND NEITHER SHOULD YOU.
YOU DON'T FIND IT FUNNY HOW HE CONVENIENTLY SHOWS UP AFTER YOU ALMOST DIE? TWICE?
HE'S JUST WATCHING OUT FOR US.
WELL, HE SAID TO TRUST NO ONE, AND I'M GOING TO INCLUDE *HIM* IN THAT.
I DIDN'T WANT TO SHOW THIS IN FRONT OF HIM.
THAT WRAPPER FOR THE VIAL. IT HAD SHEET MUSIC ON IT.
SHEET MUSIC?
I'M NOT THE DETECTIVE EITHER OF YOU ARE, BUT I'M PRETTY SURE THIS COUNTS AS A CLUE.
W.A.M.
DAN, YOU ALMOST TOSSED THAT AWAY!
I WAS CAUGHT UP IN THE MOMENT!
ANYWAY, WHEN I WAS WAITING FOR THE POLICE, I DID A SEARCH FOR *BENJAMIN FRANKLIN* PLUS *MUSIC*.
THIS CAME UP RIGHT AWAY.
IT'S TITLED "ADAGIO FOR ARMONICA."
DOES IT MEAN ANYTHING TO YOU GUYS?

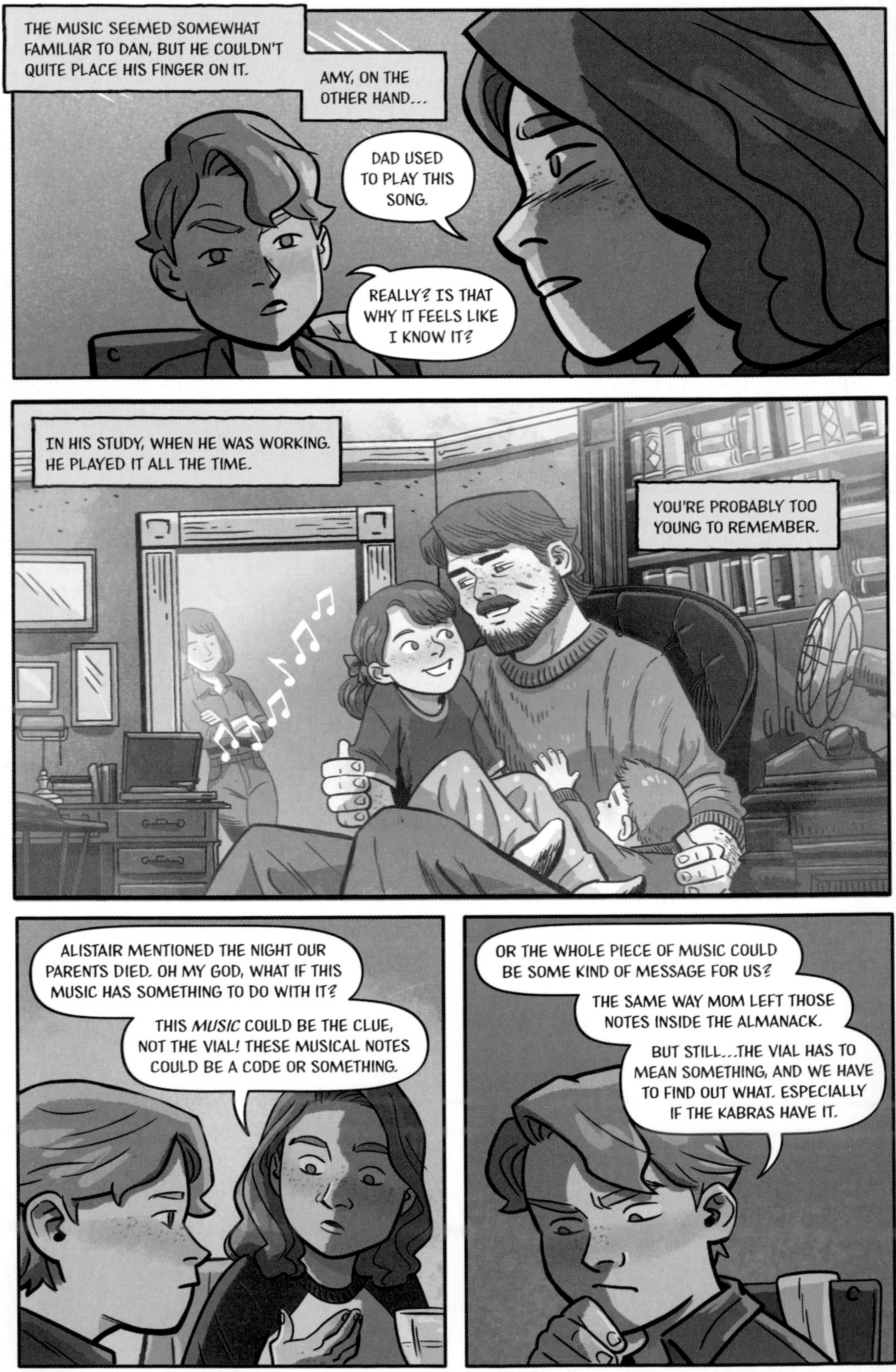
THE MUSIC SEEMED SOMEWHAT FAMILIAR TO DAN, BUT HE COULDN'T QUITE PLACE HIS FINGER ON IT.
AMY, ON THE OTHER HAND...
DAD USED TO PLAY THIS SONG.
REALLY? IS THAT WHY IT FEELS LIKE I KNOW IT?
IN HIS STUDY, WHEN HE WAS WORKING. HE PLAYED IT ALL THE TIME.
YOU'RE PROBABLY TOO YOUNG TO REMEMBER.
ALISTAIR MENTIONED THE NIGHT OUR PARENTS DIED. OH MY GOD, WHAT IF THIS MUSIC HAS SOMETHING TO DO WITH IT?
THIS *MUSIC* COULD BE THE CLUE, NOT THE VIAL! THESE MUSICAL NOTES COULD BE A CODE OR SOMETHING.
OR THE WHOLE PIECE OF MUSIC COULD BE SOME KIND OF MESSAGE FOR US?
THE SAME WAY MOM LEFT THOSE NOTES INSIDE THE ALMANACK.
BUT STILL...THE VIAL HAS TO MEAN SOMETHING, AND WE HAVE TO FIND OUT WHAT. ESPECIALLY IF THE KABRAS HAVE IT.

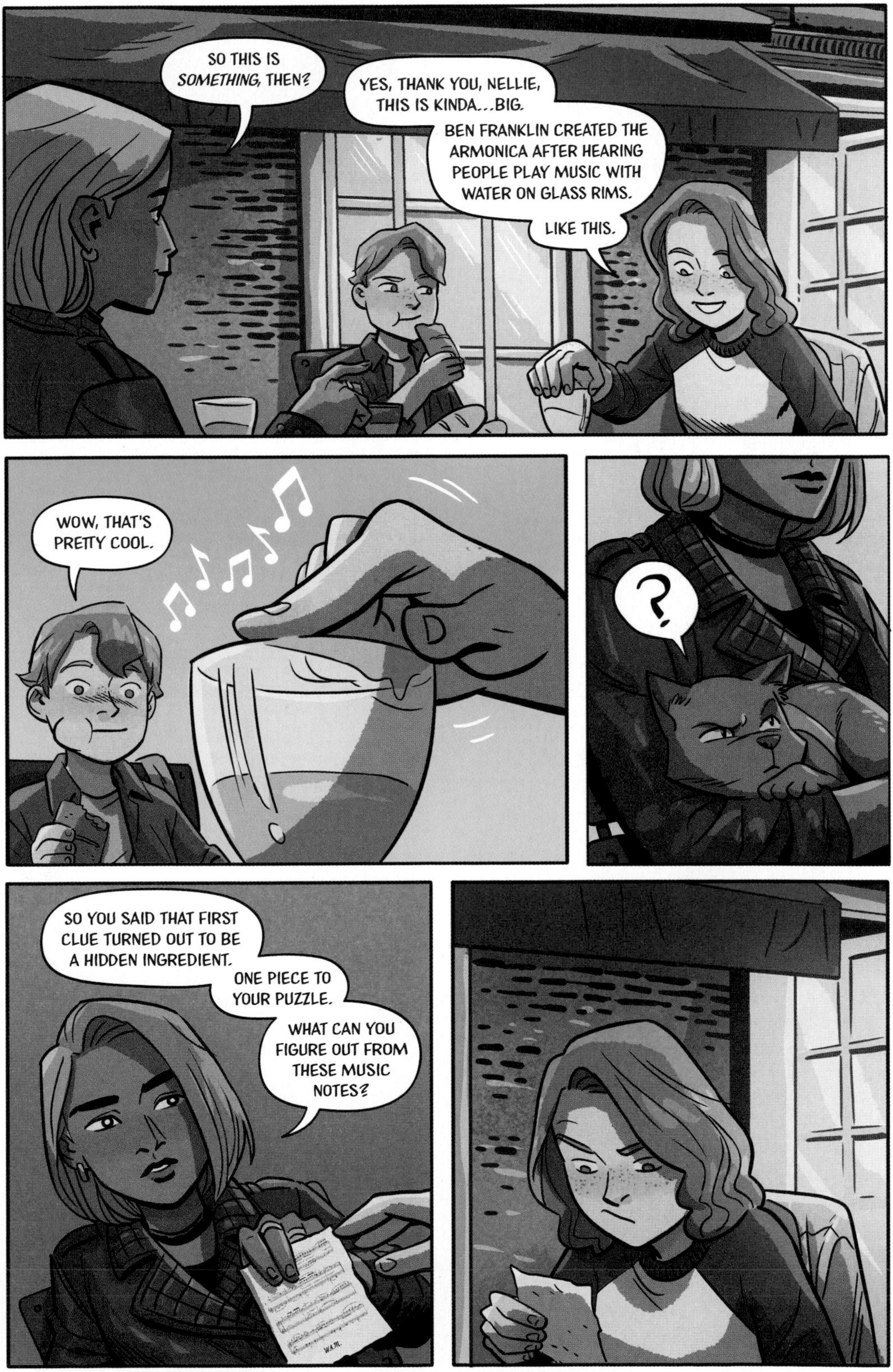
SO THIS IS *SOMETHING*, THEN?
YES, THANK YOU, NELLIE, THIS IS KINDA...BIG.
BEN FRANKLIN CREATED THE ARMONICA AFTER HEARING PEOPLE PLAY MUSIC WITH WATER ON GLASS RIMS.
LIKE THIS.
WOW, THAT'S PRETTY COOL.
?
SO YOU SAID THAT FIRST CLUE TURNED OUT TO BE A HIDDEN INGREDIENT.
ONE PIECE TO YOUR PUZZLE.
WHAT CAN YOU FIGURE OUT FROM THESE MUSIC NOTES?

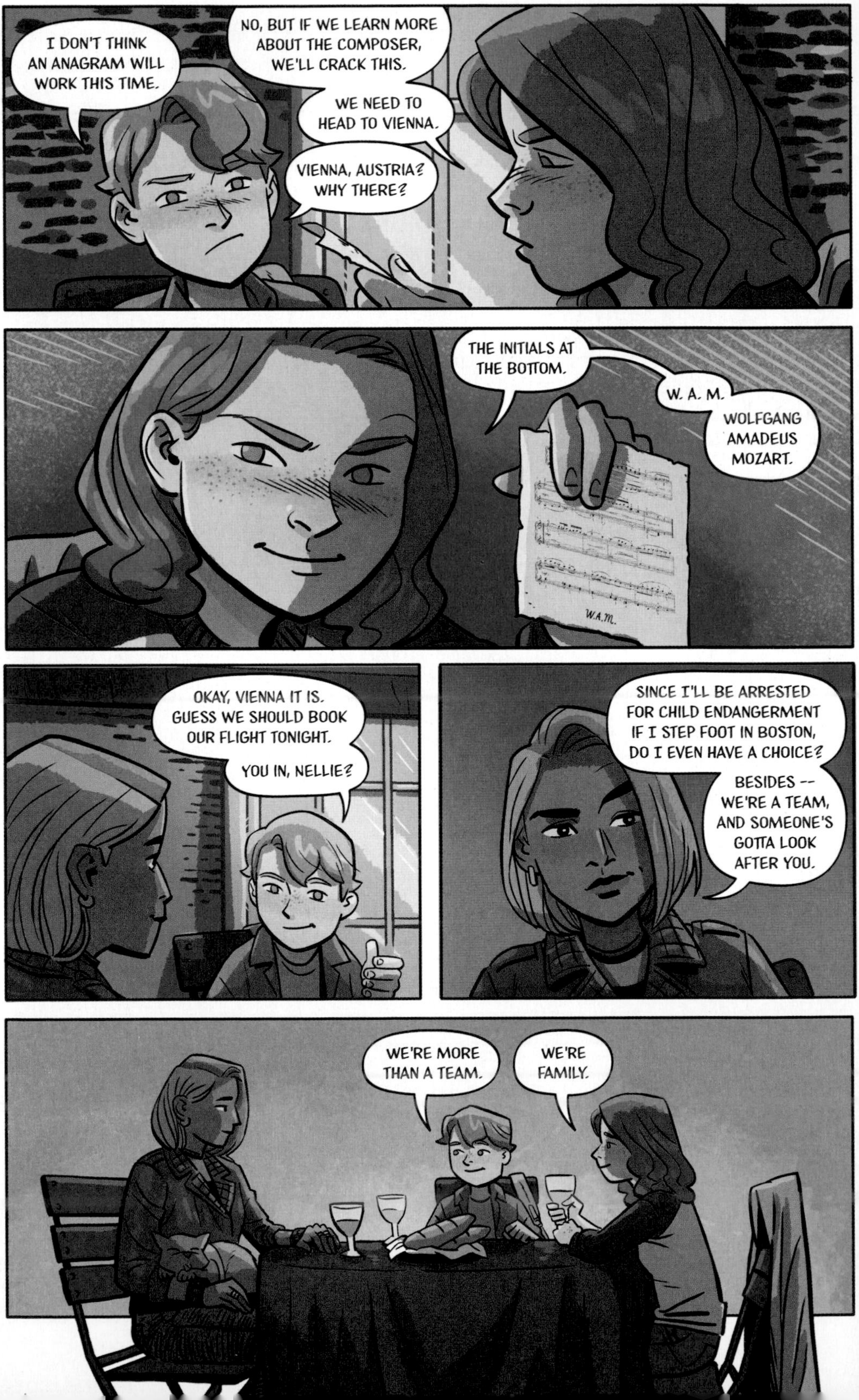
I DON'T THINK AN ANAGRAM WILL WORK THIS TIME.
NO, BUT IF WE LEARN MORE ABOUT THE COMPOSER, WE'LL CRACK THIS.
WE NEED TO HEAD TO VIENNA.
VIENNA, AUSTRIA? WHY THERE?
THE INITIALS AT THE BOTTOM.
W. A. M.
WOLFGANG AMADEUS MOZART.
W.A.M.
OKAY, VIENNA IT IS. GUESS WE SHOULD BOOK OUR FLIGHT TONIGHT.
YOU IN, NELLIE?
SINCE I'LL BE ARRESTED FOR CHILD ENDANGERMENT IF I STEP FOOT IN BOSTON, DO I EVEN HAVE A CHOICE?
BESIDES -- WE'RE A TEAM, AND SOMEONE'S GOTTA LOOK AFTER YOU.
WE'RE MORE THAN A TEAM.
WE'RE FAMILY.

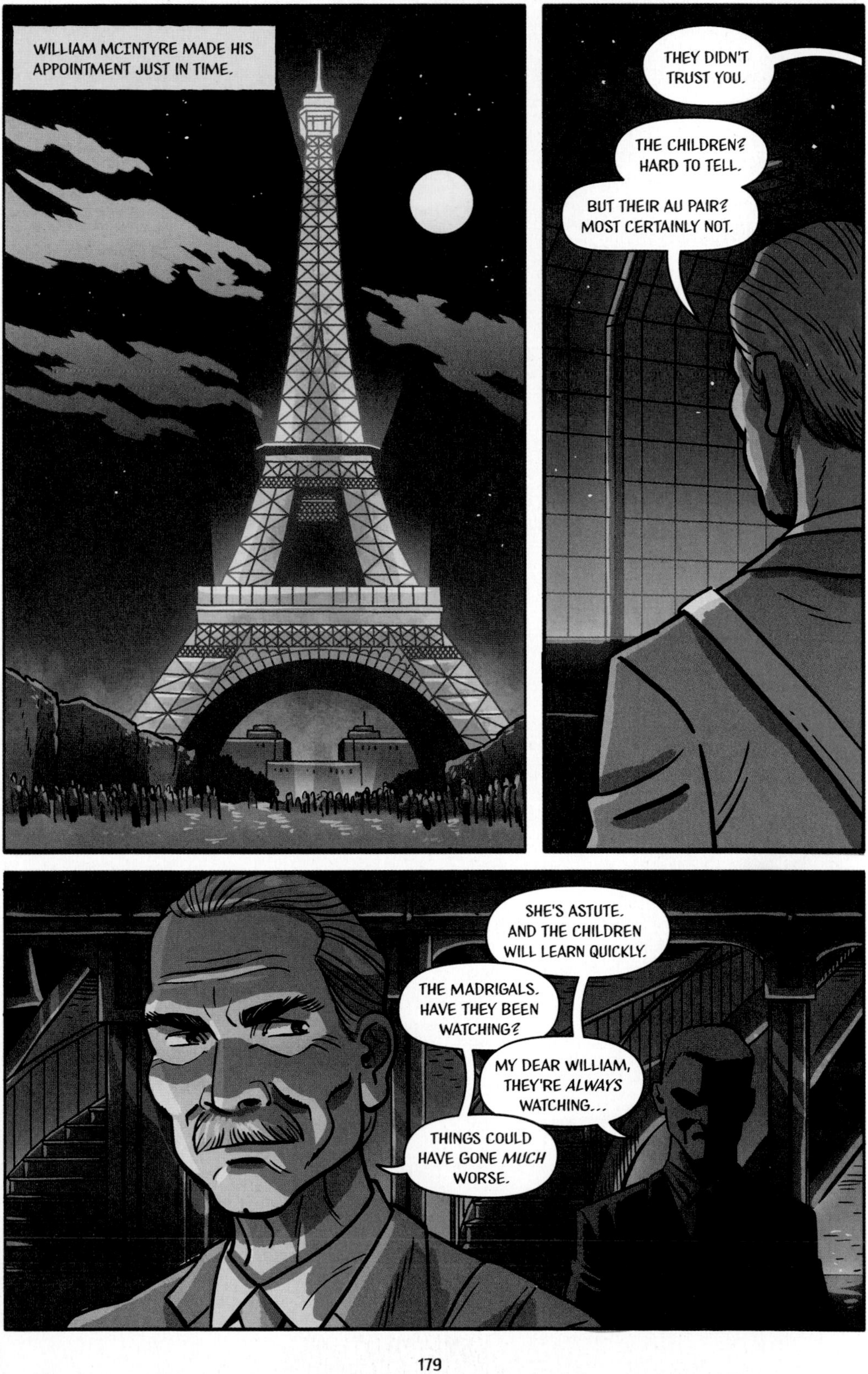
WILLIAM MCINTYRE MADE HIS APPOINTMENT JUST IN TIME.
THEY DIDN'T TRUST YOU.
THE CHILDREN? HARD TO TELL.
BUT THEIR AU PAIR? MOST CERTAINLY NOT.
SHE'S ASTUTE. AND THE CHILDREN WILL LEARN QUICKLY.
THE MADRIGALS. HAVE THEY BEEN WATCHING?
MY DEAR WILLIAM, THEY'RE *ALWAYS* WATCHING...
THINGS COULD HAVE GONE *MUCH* WORSE.

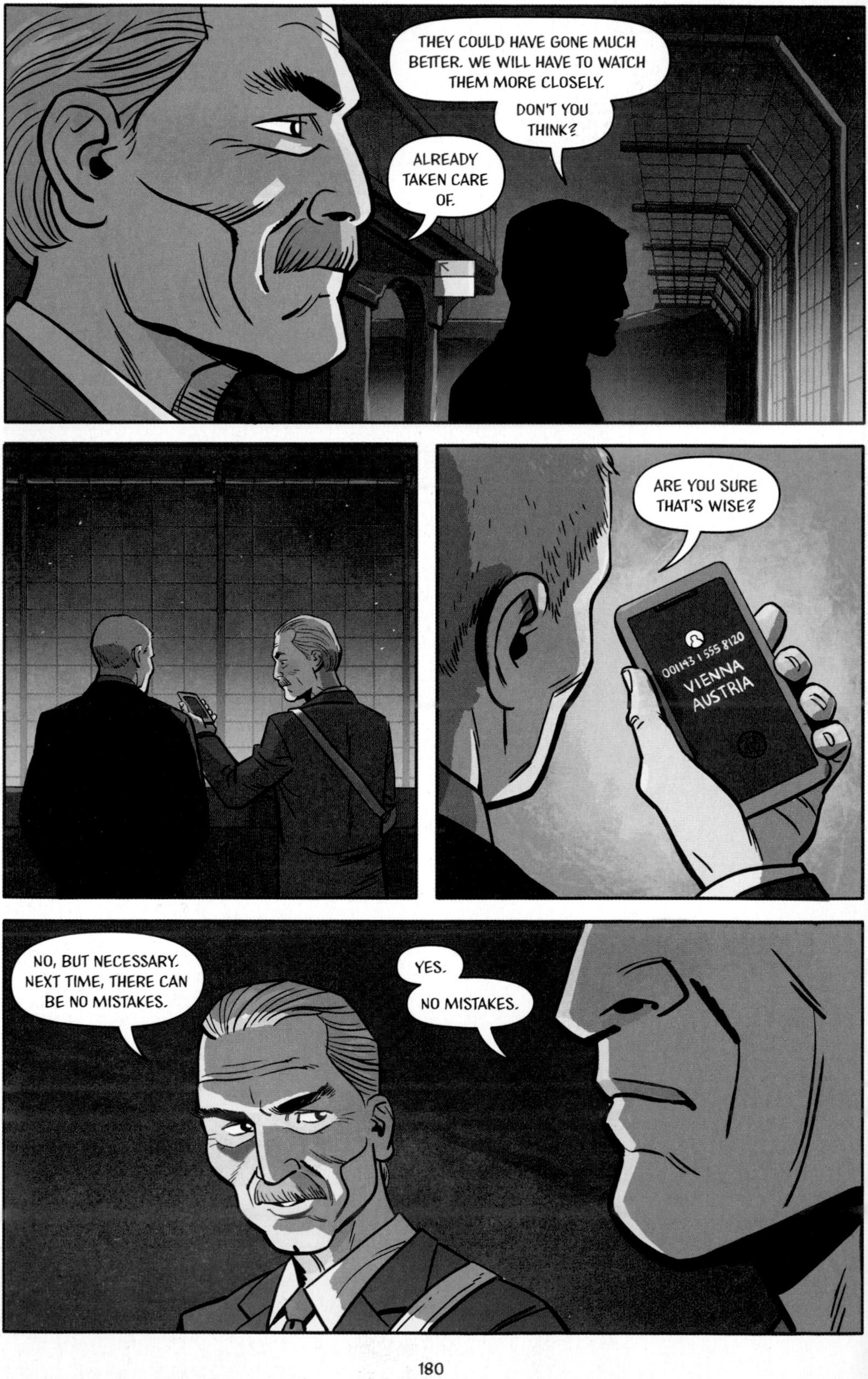
THEY COULD HAVE GONE MUCH BETTER. WE WILL HAVE TO WATCH THEM MORE CLOSELY.
DON'T YOU THINK?
ALREADY TAKEN CARE OF.
ARE YOU SURE THAT'S WISE?
001143 1 555 8120
VIENNA AUSTRIA
NO, BUT NECESSARY. NEXT TIME, THERE CAN BE NO MISTAKES.
YES.
NO MISTAKES.

THE ADVENTURE CONTINUES!

THE 39 CLUES

CAHILLS vs. VESPERS

CAHILLS vs. VESPERS
BOOK ONE
THE MEDUSA PLOT
THE 39 CLUES
GORDON KORMAN
READ THE BOOKS. COLLECT THE CARDS. PLAY THE GAME.

CAHILLS vs. VESPERS
BOOK TWO
A KING'S RANSOM
THE 39 CLUES
JUDE WATSON
READ THE BOOKS. PLAY THE GAME. STOP THE VESPERS.

CAHILLS vs. VESPERS
BOOK THREE
THE DEAD OF NIGHT
THE 39 CLUES
PETER LERANGIS
READ THE BOOKS. COLLECT THE CARDS. PLAY THE GAME.

CAHILLS vs. VESPERS
BOOK FOUR
SHATTERPROOF
THE 39 CLUES
ROLAND SMITH
READ THE BOOKS. COLLECT THE CARDS. PLAY THE GAME.

CAHILLS vs. VESPERS
BOOK FIVE
TRUST NO ONE
THE 39 CLUES
LINDA SUE PARK
READ THE BOOKS. COLLECT THE CARDS. PLAY THE GAME.

CAHILLS vs. VESPERS
BOOK SIX
DAY OF DOOM
THE 39 CLUES
DAVID BALDACCI
READ THE BOOKS. COLLECT THE CARDS. PLAY THE GAME.

START YOUR OWN CLUE HUNT ONLINE—
YOUR DESTINY IS WAITING!

WWW.THE39CLUES.COM

THE CLUES ARE OUT THERE, AND IT'S UP TO *YOU* TO FIND THEM.

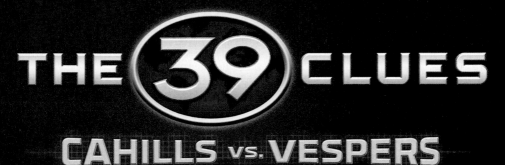

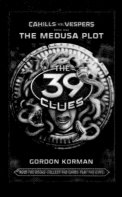

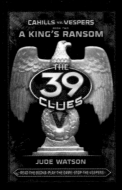

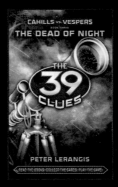

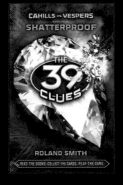

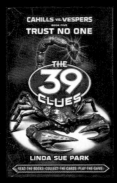

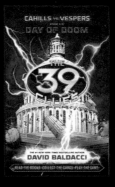

TOP SECRET

Memo

To: The Cahill Family

If you are reading this, it means you are a long-lost member of the Cahill family—the most powerful family in the world. The source of the family's power has been lost and can only be recovered by assembling 39 Clues that are scattered around the globe.

Rumor has it that Amy and Dan Cahill have the best shot finding all 39 Clues. But they haven't met their greatest competition yet . . . YOU!

START YOUR CLUE HUNT

1. Go to www.the39clues.com and sign up for Home Base.

2. Visit the 39 Clues zone on the hub.

3. Discover what branch of the Cahill family you belong to.

4. Explore the Cahill world and track down Clues.

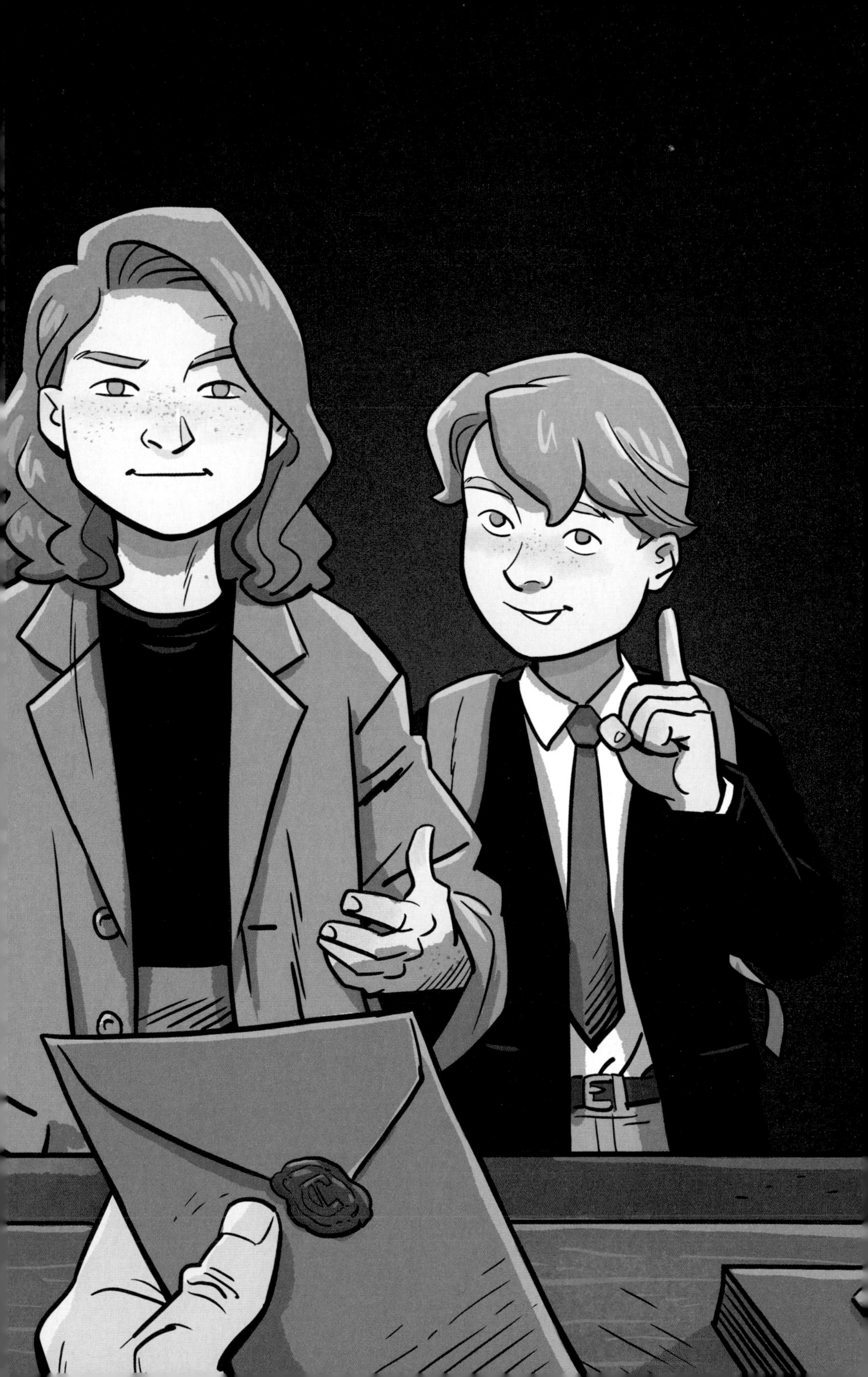

RICK RIORDAN is the #1 *New York Times* bestselling author of over twenty novels for young readers, including the Percy Jackson series, the *Kane Chronicles*, *The Maze of Bones*, the Magnus Chase series and the *Trials of Apollo*.

ETHAN YOUNG is an Asian-American cartoonist from NYC. He's worked on many graphic novels including *The Dragon Path*, *NANJING: The Burning City*, and *Space Bear*. He is currently a character designer for Marvel Studios.

Thank you to my agent, Seth Fishman, my background assistant, Carson Thorn, colorist George Williams, and letterer Sara Linsley.